BIRTH

'It's midnight, Tuesday April 19th, 2022, I'm Noa, and the phones are already ringing, so let's take the first call.'

'I killed and ate my neighbour's dog with a bottle of nice Chianti. I also touch kids and plan to blow up a school. Come get me, if you dare.'

The caller started to list his address, but Noa hit the kill switch to terminate the call.

'He forgot the fava beans,' she told her audience. 'That call allows a nice segue into my introduction. I am Noa Vickerman and this is *Confessions*, midnight until 1am, every night here only on Divine Radio. For one hour, ring me and admit anything. Jealousy, cheating, lies, even crimes. I can't promise you absolution, but I'll listen. I can't guarantee legal immunity, but I'll listen. I can't even promise good advice, but I'll listen. Confess to me and maybe you'll find peace. Or a good night's sleep. Or just a laugh.'

After a radio jingle, Noa said, 'Welcome all. Now, my caveat. You all just heard me cut a call. I will never ask for your name or address, but if you give those things, it will be deemed consent to inform the police. No such information, though, will be aired live. That's my promise here.'

She had cleverly worded her pledge. The dog-eater's call had been cut from live broadcast, but not terminated. Instead, it had been routed to another phone. The switch had been seamless; only if the caller was listening to the radio show would he know he no longer had the ears of thousands, only an old man who was recording everything. Joke or not, Dog Man had threatened to attack children and the police needed to know. Confidentiality was one thing. Moral duty was another.

'Now, down to business,' Noa continued. 'The lines are buzzing. Myriad heavy hearts wish to unburden.' She hit a button to patch through a waiting call. 'Hello, friend. What's bugging you at this late hour?'

'*My mum's a stripper,*' a young, screechy female voice said. '*I stabbed her car tyres so she can't go to work. Did it three days running and now she thinks some punter is jealous and trying to stop her and stalking her...*'

———

'*So what should I do? Kiss him? Or just admit it to him?*'

'In my opinion,' Noa said, 'end the relationship. Staying with your boyfriend in order to be around his hot dad will make things worse in the long run. But that's just my opinion.'

The call continued for a few more minutes. Afterwards, it was 12.50am and Noa decided to take just one more call, and drag it out for ten minutes if necessary. Three callers were on hold and two got an automated message with instructions to try again next time. She made the final guest live with the touch of a button.

'Hello, friend. What's bugging you at this late hour?'

Six calls over the last fifty minutes. Three foul-mouthed

CAPTIVES

JANE HEAFIELD

www.bloodhoundbooks.com

Print ISBN: 978-1-5040-8549-6

ALSO BY JANE HEAFIELD

THE YORKSHIRE MURDER THRILLERS

Dead Cold (Book 1)

Cold Blood (Book 2)

Cold Heart (Book 3)

———

Don't Believe Her

———

Her Dark Past

———

Obsessed

pranksters who got cut off quickly. One man who wanted to know if his wife had ever called the show to admit cheating. A lady who'd been stealing from her grandson's house because he'd never repaid her for sweets and toys given when he was a kid. And the last, a teenager who'd started dating and had even become engaged to a former schoolfriend just so she could hang around his father. All told, a night that was par for the course, and Noa didn't expect anything memorable from the show's final guest.

Even Larry Faulds, the bald, ageing station's producer, was close to nodding off in his wheelchair in the doorway to his office. They both sat bolt upright when a male voice said, *'I've got a prisoner. I've had her about a year and a half.'*

'I'm sorry, repeat that, please.'

She'd heard perfectly fine, but needed a moment to compose herself. By the time the caller had repeated himself, word-for-word, all eight switchboard lights were on: callers eager to talk about this very admission.

'What else would you like to tell us?' Noa said.

'You mean like who she is?' His words were perfectly formed and slow, like high-end speech synthesis. She got the impression he was trying to hide an accent. *'Perhaps her name? Where I kidnapped her from? My name, even? A postcode?'*

'I'm not trying to trick you. You called my show. I'm here to listen. Usually, those who call here have heavy hearts.'

A pause. *'I do, too. But I don't know if I want to do this. I found this show while surfing the net, so thought I'd call. I didn't plan it. I can tell you I don't plan to hurt her. I want to give her up. I don't know how to. You can help.'*

'I hope so. Is the young girl okay? Hurt, or ill?'

'She's not a young girl. She's a woman. She's fine. I have her somewhere safe. I feed and look after her.'

She'd called the captive a young girl in the hope that the caller would correct her – or not. Now she knew a little more.

'Can I ask why you took her?'

'You've been doing this for a while. I bet the police are tracing this call. I'm on the move with a burner phone, so that won't help. If they trace me to location A, I'll be long gone by the time they get there. Still, no risks. I need to think a bit. I'll call your show back tomorrow night. This is just the start. This is the birth of something big.'

She began to protest, but the line went dead.

She looked round at Larry. The seventy-year-old shrugged. 'Bullshit. Another damn prankster.'

'Probably,' Noa said.

CHAPTER ONE

'For all your local news and gossip, head over to UbyU dot com and on social media. Goodnight.'

After her regular sign-off, Noa hit a button to play music for the final seconds of the show. She sat back in her chair. Larry rolled his wheelchair to her side. 'Prankster or not,' he said, 'we'll get a big headache from this.'

She looked at the switchboard, where all eight lines were still ringing. 'For sure. Tomorrow night it will be people moaning that I didn't ask enough questions. And people calling about their own missing wives and sisters and stuff.'

'And the police, they'll be on your case before long.'

Noa stood up and grabbed her bag, and shifted the chair from the desk so Larry could roll up to the computer. The final show of the night, *Bizarre Tales*, was hosted by him.

Noa said, 'I know. Been there, done that, bought the T-shirt. We'll see if he calls back tomorrow.'

'Doubt it. Probably bullshit.'

'Maybe. I'll see you tomorrow.'

And she would. Larry owned not just the radio station, but also the whole building floor. He had installed a bedroom, bathroom and kitchen and called it home; given that he slept here, had food delivered, and was present for every show, every day, Noa knew he hadn't been outside in at least a few months. He was present for every show from 6am until 2am.

She left. The station occupied the top floor of a three-storey building, with offices in the middle and a department store on the ground. Noa used to like to run up and down the stairs, but ten days ago that had changed and now she always took the lift. While it lowered her, she called her solicitor.

When she stepped out into the foyer, one of her bodyguards was waiting for her. He was about her age of thirty and very flirty, although she'd told him on day one that while she didn't mind playful banter, she was uninterested in him romantically. Since then he'd concentrated on his job, which was to stay close but not noticeably so, make sure she got safely to her car, follow the vehicle to her home, and watch her house until his relief came in the morning.

'I don't need you overnight,' she said as they walked. 'I have guests coming. Take the night off with pay.'

He nodded, watched her get into her car, and jogged to his own. While she drove home, her phone rang. The screen said BOKAYO.

'I hear we've got some nice frozen mash and sausages in,' he said.

She groaned. 'I swear half my listeners are you guys. Should I head down there, or is this more about pissing me off?'

'The latter. As always.'

'When can I expect them? The usual time?'

'The night shift can be boring. I'll see you tomorrow, when it's done. Enjoy the mash.'

'Piss off,' she said with a laugh, and hung up.

―――――

Home was almost four miles north-east of Hammersmith, site of the radio station. Formerly composed of stables and coach houses for Grosvenor Square mansions, Adam's Row was a luxury residential area in Mayfair where Noa's father, now deceased three years, had managed to buy a four-bedroomed property for half the advertised price. Today it was worth ten million pounds.

He had died very rich. His will had bequeathed Noa exactly one million pounds to live on. She also got the house, but wasn't permitted to sell it until her fortieth birthday. Locked in a private bank account was another hefty sum of cash that would be released to her when she turned fifty. How much she wasn't sure and, since that day was two decades away, barely thought about.

With no father around, the house had felt empty and Noa had rented out one of the bedrooms. That hadn't solved the problem because her tenant was a movie producer with a jet-set lifestyle. He spent half the year shooting music videos and TV films in America, but was quite happy to pay the rent of £1,400 every week. She hadn't seen him for a month and he wasn't due home for a long time yet.

She parked in the garage, between her Fiat 500 and the producer's Bentley, and entered the empty house. As the shutter rolled down, her bodyguard drove away.

After a quick bite to eat, she headed up to her bedroom. It was next to a room she'd kitted out as a home studio, but had yet to call upon: Larry was old and lonely and liked the company, so refused to let any of his presenters work from home.

It was closing on 2am. Fully dressed, she lay down and read a book. The house was too silent without the TV on, but she needed silence in order to hear the arrival of her imminent guests. She was unable to concentrate, however, her mind too consumed by what was to come.

At just past 3am, she heard cars arrive outside and went to her opened window. Two vehicles and four police officers for some reason. She waited until they were about to knock at her door and called down: 'Hey, I'll be out in a second.'

That surprised them even more than a late-night arrest mission in a place like Mayfair. She gave a smile and a thumbs up. Puzzled, one officer returned it. If he thought his target didn't seem fazed, he was right. Noa was thinking way past a night in the cells, to tomorrow's confessions show. She hoped for another call from the man who'd said he'd abducted a woman. She prayed it wasn't, as Larry had said, complete bullshit.

———

The two officers sent to interview her were, like last time, fresh-faced newbies. But of course. She was no terrorist or serial killer and would face no charges. These arrests were nought but reminders that the police weren't fans of her show.

They waited until 9am to come for her, although she'd only slept for two of the five hours she was locked in a cell. She was offered breakfast – not mash and sausage – but Noa declined in order to speed things along. Ten minutes later, by which time her solicitor had arrived, she was in an interview room, where they started with general questions they already knew the answers to, and she gave responses identical to ones already on tape in a file box somewhere. The male spoke first. He was handsome except for an old, white scar that ran across his left jawline.

Why had she chosen to host a radio show that invited people to admit crimes?

'It's not about crimes, it's about sins. Seven days a week, call numbers between five and as many as fifteen each show, which makes a minimum of thirty-five confessions every week. Most laughable. Many outright lies designed to shock. At most a couple will be genuine ones of the sort you guys are interested in.'

How long had she been doing this?

'Since the new year, so four months now. I hit the big 3-0 on Christmas Day. Some say that's latter adulthood. It felt like it, so I fancied a change in life. No more jollying about. And in those four months, you've only come to me on four occasions. Four times only that someone has admitted something criminal worthy enough for you to hound me with these silly arrests.'

Why had she chosen to deal with people's confessions?

'Just an idea I had and ran with. I like to help people. You know about my charity work. I often hold raffles. I've paid for fêtes and festivals. I helped pay for the renovation to a youth club not half a mile from this station, which I'm sure gives you lot extra peace in the evenings. I give hard cash away. I also work two days a week at a charity shop, which is where I should be right now. But I'm not there, am I?'

They understood. Charity work, good and proper. Well done. But the confession show hardly fit into that genre. After all, she hadn't taken a job at the radio station: she had contacted the owner/producer and asked for airtime. Unlike his other presenters, she wasn't on the payroll, wasn't paid a penny. It seemed off.

'I'm not trained in communications or media or journalism. There was no way I could walk into such a job. That's why I don't have a drivetime slot. That's the peak time, late-afternoon, when the station draws three hundred thousand listeners. My slot is the zombie hour and gets less than five thousand tuning in.'

She could have created a game show to give away her riches. Does a confession show really help people?

'I already give money away. That's easy for the wealthy. I

wanted to help other kinds of people, who have problems that charities don't cover. I'm not the only radio presenter who hosts confession programmes, you know. For instance, Simon Mayo has run a show on and off for more than thirty years.'

Now the female spoke. She was about the same age and blonde and round-faced like Noa, but was much shorter and had a voice that would have better suited her two decades earlier. 'I doubt that Radio 1 show exists for a charitable reason. Also, it's broadcast during drivetime, when people aren't drunk and are less likely to have just committed a crime they want to get off their chest. It's also prepared in advance, with the staff selecting confessions already sent in. Yours airs live, late at night, unweeded, no delay that allows for editing what's said. Don't tell me you're unaware that this format invites the, shall we say, shocking?'

'I'm not. We have a kill switch for censorship and safety, like if someone tries to give an address or real name. My listeners know that a late-hour show is likely to be funny rather than shocking. They like the pranksters more than the genuine callers.'

'Don't forget the third kind. You also get haters. As the Dai Xi case proved.'

'And which was the fault of the police.'

The female detective sat back, a smirk on her face. 'The attack on you ten days ago was the fault of the police? I'd love to hear why.'

And Noa would have loved to explain, except she was eager to get out of here. 'Look, please cut to the point where you tell me why I was arrested. Aiding an offender? This is the fourth time you've tried that one.'

The detective consulted her notes. 'The third for arrest, actually. The first time, back on January 2nd, was a just a voluntary formal interview. My colleagues simply wanted to know if anyone had called the radio station privately, outside of the confessions slot. It happened before.' She consulted her notes again. 'A chap called the show and said he'd been stealing from work. Said he didn't want your listeners to hear his story. You agreed to chat to him off-air.'

'It was a mistake I made and haven't repeated since. The station started to get calls at all hours. I now announce during my show that calls outside of the 12–1 slot won't be answered. That caller didn't call back. I told your colleagues that the first time you wasted everyone's time bringing me in here.'

'Right, right. But that rule of yours didn't last, did it? On January 22nd, you were arrested at the radio station...'

How could Noa forget? During her show on that Saturday night, a woman had called with a shocking story about her father. A friend of hers had seen his car in a red-light area. Annoyed, the daughter had located someone with Hepatitis A, obtained their faecal matter, and put it in her father's food. He had contracted the viral infection and fallen ill. His wife, the caller's mother, had discovered his illness, assumed he'd gotten it from a prostitute, and kicked him out.

The caller had wanted to talk about this event, but had been scared that someone who knew her father might be listening. 'I offered to let her confess further off-air, after the show,' Noa told the detective. 'It was the only way she would talk. So I took that call. The lady just wanted my opinion on whether to admit to her mother what she'd done. Your people wondered if maybe I'd been told about other crimes. Like I said last time, no. She simply asked me what to do. I told her I wasn't sure. I didn't want to cause an argument.'

The detective nodded. 'So, on to tonight's call about a possible abduction–'

'Wait, you want to skip over my second arrest? Dai Xi,

remember? You were eager enough to remind me a minute ago. Why aren't we discussing that further?'

'Just stick to the question, please.'

Noa had instructed her solicitor to remain quiet unless absolutely necessary. He thought this was that time. She told him to relax and faced the female detective again. 'No, we'll talk about Dai Xi. You brought this up. It's unfair to cherry-pick like this. You know the full story of Dai Xi, right?'

———

'It's midnight, February 10th, 2022, I'm Noa, and the phones are already ringing, so let's take the first call.'

'I killed that Chinese student from Manchester Met. You think I'm lying? You're gonna cut me off?'

'Sorry, did you say you murdered someone? A Chinese student?'

'Sure did.' The word 'killed' had set her fingers jabbing at her keyboard. By the time the caller had uttered his last two words, her screen was displaying a story from the Manchester Evening News's *website.*

'Are you talking about Dai Xi?'

'Yes. Although he gave me some lie about his name being Clifford. It's still big news.'

'For my listeners, Dai Xi, aged twenty, was a student at Manchester Metropolitan University. Two Tuesdays ago, on the 25th of Jan, Dai was last seen at a gastropub in the city centre around 11pm. He never returned to his student flat and hasn't been heard from since. Caller, would you like to tell me more?'

'I feel bad. I mean, not because he's dead. The kid was no good, right? Dealt drugs. No one said that in the papers, did they? I just feel bad for his parents. I heard they're trying to come over

from China. Like they think they can just solve this when the coppers don't have a clue after two weeks.'

'Okay, caller, would you like to tell me what happened?'

She put a finger to her lips to silence Larry. Beside her, the station's producer was frantically mouthing questions he wanted her to ask.

'He stuffed me,' the caller said. 'Yeah, I take drugs. Coke. He stuffed me. He said he had some stuff at his accommodation, but when we got to some park close to it, he took my money and tried to run. I slapped him about. He fell, cracked his head. I dumped him in the River Irwell.'

'Caller, can I ask why you chose my show to admit this?'

'I want to give up the body. I've seen the news. The family. I know they're hurting. And now they'll know he's dead, and that's not good. But he was already dead, you get me? They just didn't know.'

'I think I understand.'

'So I'll give the cops the body. But not right now. I just need to go back and check the area. I need to make sure there's no evidence there that can tie me in. Because they'll bag up all the stuff that's around there, won't they? Casts from footprints and all that, too. So I'll be calling back. I'll give you that information.'

'I understand. Nobody is rushing you. What you're doing is the right thing for the family. Goodbye, caller. And to all my listeners, remember, we're also at the end of a private line. For all your local news and gossip, head over to UbyU dot com and on social media.'

———

The female detective said, 'Why did you end the call so abruptly? Even your producer, Mr Faulds, said you should have continued with the call. Raymond Jenkins, the killer, was a man who'd confessed to murder, and you–'

'I made a call to the police right after that phone call,' Noa cut in. 'I gave you the body of Dai Xi.'

The detective looked a little perturbed and had to check her notes again. 'Not quite. You gave us a general area. There was still a massive search. It's only through luck that we arrested the perpetrator.'

'Luck? I told you where he'd be. Was that a lucky guess?'

'I have the details. You said that during the call, you had Dai Xi's Facebook open on your screen–'

'That's right. I saw a post about him meeting a girl outside the Clifford Whitworth Library. The caller had said that Dai Xi gave him the fake name of Clifford. Now, Dai Xi attended Manchester Met, but the Clifford Whitworth Library is part of Salford university. I checked on Google Earth and saw that Salford uni is near a couple of pieces of parkland. Peel Park and The Meadow, both by the River Irwell, where the killer said he disposed of the body. I figured that Xi, to be careful, had taken his eventual killer to Salford university to hide the fact that he attended Manchester Met. So he couldn't be traced. I gave this information to the police right after the call. They staked out those two parks and the very next night they arrested Raymond Jenkins. He had indeed returned to the body to destroy evidence.'

The two detectives looked at each other before the female said, 'And you claim you worked this out during the call with Jenkins, which lasted just a couple of minutes? You did all that internet and Facebook searching while talking with Jenkins? It's intriguing that you ended your call so abruptly and with–'

'With the reminder that callers can call back on a private line, yes. The police assumed I was giving Jenkins a hint that he should call back and chat off-air. I've had this conversation before, detective. One of your people sat right where you're sitting and accused me of talking with Jenkins after the show. Of delaying my call to police until after I'd gotten him to admit where he dumped the body. I offered to show my computer's internet history in defence, but no one cared to look. And the reason I apparently created a story about working it out all by myself? So I could get in the news, get more listeners, become known as the great confession-show detective.'

'And maybe you would have garnered those things, except we held back releasing news of your involvement. I bet you hate that we didn't help your show.'

'You helped me almost get killed though.'

The penny dropped. 'Now I see why you blame us for the attack on you. Because the police didn't mention your detective work, you feel—'

'*That's what happens to people who think it's okay to let a killer go free. That's what the guy who attacked me said to me. You're as bad as those scumbags.*'

Her mind went back, as it often did. To the man who had stepped out of the shadows when she left the radio station ten days ago. She had gotten all the way to her car, had the door open, when he struck. One arm snapped around her neck from behind, the other hand pressing a knife to her flesh. Not a word said.

At an early age, Noa had learned judo and her instincts had kicked in before she even realised it. She had turned in his grip, grabbed him, hip-tossed him to the ground, and dived into her car. She had managed to lock the door before he got to his feet, and then she'd laid on the horn. The attacker had fled for the shadows, but not before yelling out his reason for targeting her.

The police hadn't shown much interest in finding her attacker and had dismissed her claim that hate was the motive. Simple robbery, they'd said: everyone knew she was rich. And the words he'd shouted when fleeing? Misheard. After that night, she'd felt compelled to hire bodyguards, who watched her 24-7.

Now, her mind returned to the present, and the annoying detectives sitting across from her. 'Because the police failed to mention my input in helping to get Dai Xi's killer arrested, many people think that I took a call with him after the show and kept it secret. Any plans to tell the public the truth?'

'Not my case. Anyway, I want to get back to tonight's call.'

'So do I. But I'd like to talk about the man who claimed he'd killed his neighbour's dog and planned to blow up a school. Does your sheet of wisdom there mention that I called the police about it?'

'Not my case. Not why we're here.'

'Of course not. Could be a prank. I was thinking the dead dog could be his own. Maybe the neighbour killed it and the caller is pretending to be him and saying all that stuff about bombing a school and touching kids to get him in trouble. Or it's all true. Needs investigating though.'

'It will be. That's not your concern or ours–'

'But I helped, didn't I? I got the address for you, while hiding it from the public so you don't get there and find him lynched from a lamp post. The problem is that I had to pretend to hang up on the guy. Unless the police admit I helped, it's going to look like a terrorist threatened little kids and I just ignored it. Similar to the thing with Dai Xi. I gave you something when you had nothing and I get no thanks.'

Noa saw the muscles in the detective's cheeks tighten. Checked anger. 'If Raymond Jenkins hadn't been arrested, he would have called your show the next night. You wanted that. The caller about the dog wasn't asked to hand himself in to a police station. You have a track record of not pushing for information. You even state on your show each night that criminal information will be passed to the police so it's advisable not to offer it. Right there you're telling criminals not to give themselves away. You received three hundred complaints to OFCOM about your handling of the Raymond Jenkins call. This so-called detective work of yours – what if you'd been wrong?'

'But I wasn't wrong. I would have pressed for more if I hadn't already worked it out. I solved that damn crime, detective. Now consider this. You had nothing until Jenkins called my show. Sometimes having an anonymous outlet, even in front of thousands, can give people that extra push. They call in and their souls are lightened, and sometimes they make the right decision afterwards. The man stealing from work – I do not know, but maybe he gave that up. The woman who infected her father – she came clean and it saved her parents' relationship. And Dai Xi's killer was found with my help. Even without, he might have called the next night and admitted everything. My point is, you had no clue about Dai Xi's killer until he called my show. And he, like the others, would not have come forward if I broadcast to all that I'll do my best to see them hang. It's not perfect, but that show has done more good than harm. I don't do this, as you all assume, to get more listeners. Unbelievable as it sounds, I'm actually trying to help people.'

The male detective spoke. 'Doesn't hurt the ratings, though. Like that possible kidnapper tonight said. The birth of something big for your show.'

'Finally, we can get to the reason I'm here again. Not the ninety per cent that's just spite because you don't like what I do. No, the ten per cent where you think I had a secret off-air chat with someone who reckons he's kidnapped a woman.'

The detectives looked at each other. The male said, 'Okay. Did you?'

Noa leaned back in her chair. 'No. Talk to my boss. There

was no call. He said he'll call back tonight and one of two things is going to happen. He trusts that I'm just a willing ear and he'll make that call. Or he's seen me enter this station, thinks I'm working with you lot, and we'll never hear from him again.'

The male smirked. 'He wouldn't trust you if we'd let it be known that you helped with the Dai Xi case.'

Noa wanted to be annoyed, but he had a fair point. 'I've answered your questions. Now I'll be exercising my right to silence. So it's charge or release time. Or you could be extra spiteful and keep me the full twenty-four hours. But if he calls back and the show's not on...'

'If this isn't another prank,' the female said. 'What do you think?'

'I think we'll find out.'

'What do you *hope*?' the male said.

'Piss off.'

CHAPTER TWO

12 NOVEMBER 2020

S he could have blamed herself, indeed should have, but she will later curse the pilot.

A low-flying plane leaving the aeropark catches her attention, and she leans forward over the steering wheel to see it carving through the evening sky. With engineers in her family, she has been behind the wheel of many vehicles, but planes have eluded her. One day, hopefully, she will find a chance to take to the skies.

The great machine flashes by, rising high and heading away, and her eyes come back to the road – and slam wide open.

Her foot stamps the brake. As a car aficionado and expert driver, she puzzled her father when she bought a 2002 Nissan Almera. She claimed to like the shape, because she could hardly admit the truth: that she wanted a vehicle without anti-lock brakes, so she and her girlfriend could do doughnuts in car parks. Right now, though, she regrets the decision to buy an old car.

The wheels lock. The car skids. In the Mazda she'd traded in for this piece of shit, she would have pulled up feet from the obstacle – but the Almera skids right over the dog lying in the middle of the road.

This part of the road is usually quiet, except when planes from the nearby aeropark lift off or land, but there's a car parked just past the dog's body, with a guy standing alongside in a hooded top. As her Almera finally stops and she leaps out, he rushes over.

'My, is that your dog?' she says, bends by the back of her car, to look under. She hears his footsteps coming closer.

'No, I just narrowly missed it myself,' he says.

Staring at the dog, even in the gloom under her car, she can clearly see its glazed eyes. They're dead, but not of the recently deceased kind. The dog isn't real: it's a life-sized cuddly toy.

'Wait a damn minute,' she says, 'someone's pratting about here.'

She stands up, ready to tell the man behind her that all is fine, but he grabs her hair with one hand.

'No, wait, it's not a real d–'

His other hand slams a cloth onto her face. She takes a breath, to scream her objection, but the air is rank and burning. She snaps both hands onto the one smothering her face, to try to tear away the cloth, and that's when a storm of dizziness overwhelms her and all power seems to evaporate right out of every muscle.

———

She wakes to the sight of what she thinks is dark water, and the sense of floating some eight feet above it. Her reflection stares back. As grogginess sluices from her, she realises she has the picture upended: she lies below, on a bed, and the water is a ceiling of mirrored panes of glass.

She sits up, which takes more effort than she expects. She

sees a room around her. A single door. Three long windows taking up almost an entire wall, and giving onto a sea view. Not her bedroom. Not any room she recalls. She throws off the quilt to see clothing she also doesn't recognise: plain grey T-shirt, thick grey knickers, and upon her feet flexible slippers, like soft ballet shoes.

This bombardment of the unknown stirs a memory. It's hazy, but she recalls... lying down, naked... being dressed by another's hands... words... something about animals... and his fingers, going below, where they shouldn't...

Then it fades, as if it never was. Maybe it wasn't.

Undeniable, though, is the knowledge that she did not come here by choice. Someone has kidnapped her. She vaguely remembers the man on the road – he used chloroform or something to knock her out.

A boost of panic throws her out of the bed and towards the door, and she actually reaches out for the handle before realising there isn't one. The door is heavy iron, smooth and bare, like a fire exit, impossible to open. Horrified, she sees dried blood on the upper hinge.

She bolts to the windows, but without hope. When she slams her palms onto the glass, the water beyond vibrates. Her groggy mind takes a moment to realise it's an effect. The glass, which feels like thick plastic, has been covered by a full-length sticker to create the impression of an ocean view. The windows are fixed, and the plastic feels too tough to break or cut through. The sticker is on the outside, so she can't peel it away to see the outside world.

When she's calmed her ragged breath, and the panic subsides a little, she's overcome by disgust. The T-shirt, knickers, slippers: the man has stripped away her coat, original T-shirt, bra, knickers, jeans, trainers. While she was unconscious from the drug, he got her naked. Worse, a quick feel alerts her that her tampon is gone. She sits against the wall, knees hugged to her chest, and begins to cry.

Once she's over the disgust, too, she finally takes in the rest of the room. It seems to be some kind of disused office, given the wooden floor and bare plaster walls and ten-feet high ceiling. But the furniture is out of place.

A single bed with a thin mattress and a metal frame, which is bolted to the wooden floor in the dead centre of the room. A small wooden table with a chair. A sink in a corner, with a shelf above that contains bathroom crap like cosmetics and vitamins and toothpaste. A small bookshelf attached to one wall, full of paperbacks. A treadmill in one corner. There's a single wooden shelf across from the bookshelf, and upon it is a porcelain mask ornament on a stand, depicting a gaunt white face with no eye, nose or mouth holes. The man who took her has tried to make this room feel homely, and that might mean he plans to keep her here for a long time.

But where the hell is she? Why has she been taken? How much time has passed? Is her family missing her?

These questions pale next to the most important: what are his plans for her? Her family is not rich, but they're comfortable and big and there are enough cousins and aunties and so forth to scrape together a lot of money. Is this about ransom?

She hopes so. The alternative, that she is now a lunatic's plaything, doesn't bear thinking about.

———

For a long time – how long she has no clue – she stands in the centre of that room and breathes heavily and wonders whether to shout out. For her abductor, not for help – she knows she's not within screaming range of saviours.

Just because this isn't a dingy cellar like in some of the true crime abduction stories her mum reads, it doesn't mean she won't be abandoned here for days at a time without contact from him. Screaming for help is probably the first reaction of any woman who wakens locked in a strange room, so perhaps he's waiting for this to know she's awake. If the drug he gave her is known to sometimes be lethal, he might even need a sign she's alive, and without it he'll forget about her until it's too late.

But shouting for him opens up all new problems. The moment he knows his victim is alive and well, his plans for her activate, and he might have molestation and murder in mind. Calling out will only hasten her demise.

The internal debate rages for a long time. After what seems like hours, she moves back to the bed because her bad hip is hurting. When she sits and lies back, that is when she notices something curious about the mirrored ceiling.

One of the glass panes above the foot of her bed has a circular portion, about the size of a large dinner plate, that sits half an inch higher than the rest. Like a hatch. It dawns on her: a one-way window. The whole ceiling is mirrored glass in order to hide it.

As she gets to her feet and stands beneath the window, she hears soft thumping from above. Footsteps? Someone is in the room above. Has he been watching through that small window?

The window opens away from her. It's a hatch. She steps away, fearful of something being dropped on her. From where she stands, she can see the wooden guts of the floor. Nothing happens, so she bends down to create the angle to see into the room above. She can see light, and the white paint of walls like those in this room.

She moves closer, tilting her head back, until the hole exposes a ceiling, composed of what looks like white mineral fibre tiles, like in her dad's office at work. This building – some kind of office block? If so, is it abandoned?

'Who's there?' she calls out, stepping closer. More of the ceiling is exposed now and she sees strip lighting. But it's turned off, which means the lighting in the room above is natural. Uncovered windows, and a possible way out. But if she's in an office block, which floor is she on?

Her call prompts no reply, so she steps closer. And closer. Nothing happens until she's virtually right beneath the hatch, and then something appears. The shock makes her stagger away, but not before she catches sight of a face: very pale, very gaunt, human-shaped but not quite.

'What do you want with me?'

'There are rules,' a male voice says. 'First, if you read a book, do not replace it. Put it on top of the bookcase. This is very important.'

'What do you want with me?' she repeats.

No answer. But something happens.

Half of the item is exposed before she realises a dress is being lowered through the hole, on fine needle thread attached to a plastic hanger. It swings a little before the hem touches the quilt, which allows the man to carefully lay it flat on the floor.

It's a blue halter dress, and it terrifies her. The bastard wants her to wear this. He's sexually attracted to her. This isn't about ransom: he's snatched her to be his sex toy after all.

She backs against a wall, crying. Her mum's true crime obsession means she's heard many stories of men who enslave young women and subject them to myriad rapes. And off the top of her head, she can recall no instances of these monstrous captors suddenly letting their female victims walk free.

————

'Second rule: you will dress for feasting, always. That includes make-up.'

She doesn't move from the wall. She wishes the room was larger, so she could move further away from that hatch, that man and his bizarre face. Feasting?

'Do you hear me?' he says, louder.

She can hardly find her voice. 'Yes. What – what are you going to do with me? What is feasting? I don't understand.'

'Food. When I say it's time to feast, you will wear this dress. Keep it clean and uncreased. Also apply the make-up.'

'I will. I will. But, please, tell me what you want? Are you going to let me go? I have a family. My name is–'

'I know your name. I know you have a family. Stop talking. Third rule: never ask me about your loved ones, or anything else in the outside world.'

She says nothing more. From somewhere, surely to do with her mother's books and documentaries, she knows one trick is to try to humanise yourself to an abductor. Inform him of your name, tell him about people who love you, your likes; express your discomfort and unhappiness.

But she wonders: has that tactic ever worked to convince a captor to not hurt a victim, to release her even? She is doubtful, but will not abandon it.

'Where is dinner going to be?' she asks. With the most outrageous luck, he plans to take her to a restaurant, and once there she can easily escape him by screaming the place down.

No answer. Instead, he lowers something else through the hatch. It is a small camera. She catches sight of his hands, which are clad in thick orange gloves.

Next, what looks like a balled-up sheet of paper drops to the floor. The man says, 'You will be interviewed. The questions are on the paper. Memorise them, and film yourself answering them. Afterwards, tie the camera to the string. Do that now, please.'

Her heart thumps with terror, but mixed in there is a little ray of hope. There could be abuse, including rape, and there could be days of hell, but it seems she might just get out of here alive. This is kidnap for ransom after all.

It's why the man refuses to show his face. He's worried about being identified, and there would be no such concern if he intended to kill her after getting the ransom. Her father has money, and he will pay, and she will get to go home.

She's so buoyed by this knowledge that she allows herself to think of her mother. So obsessed with true tales of murder and abduction, and now she's going to read about her own daughter in a book! Sales from that alone will recoup the money paid for her release.

'Feasting? I like fish and chips,' she says as she moves towards the camera.

CHAPTER THREE

An hour after the interview, Noa was taken before the custody desk and told she was being released without charge. Her single item was returned to her: a string necklace with a coin for a pendant.

'I never take this off,' she told the custody sergeant. 'I vowed never to, even in the bath, even if I went to space. Of course, you guys ruined that. Three times now.'

When the paperwork was complete, she was escorted to the exit by the female detective, whose attitude had turned now proceedings were over. She surprised Noa by saying, 'I apologise for all of that. I don't really see a problem with what you're doing. And I agree you helped with the Dai Xi case. But orders are orders.'

Small talk? Was she to get inside Noa for more information? Noa decided to be careful. 'Thanks. I really am just trying to help people. I was lucky. I had a privileged upbringing. Many don't. I feel the urge to help. I guess my father's death changed my attitude.'

'I heard.' She pointed at Noa's necklace. 'That's the old 5p coin. They've been out of circulation for decades. Can I ask the significance?'

'It was my dad's. He said my grandparents decided on his name using a coin. He and his partner used this very one to decide the order of their names when they created their law firm in the seventies. Apparently the Wright brothers used one to choose who got the first manned flight. *Navia aut caput*. Heads or tails. My dad kept it ever after and gave it to me on his deathbed.'

'Ever make decisions with it? Ones that change your life?'

Noa looked away. 'Not something I like to talk about. Nice to meet you anyway.'

They'd reached the exit. The detective gave a thumbs up and Noa walked out into the mild April weather. But she stopped briefly to turn and say, 'I know it's your job. So I'm sorry for my attitude. I said this to a detective last time and I'll say it now. If you wanted help from me, you could have asked. Instead of arresting me. That's not how you get cooperation.'

'You got arrested. Frustration is totally the norm. Have a good day.'

The door shut.

Two men were waiting for her in the car park. Close to the station entrance was a car containing a beefy bald guy. The security firm supplied three men to work eight-hour shifts, for a total of twenty-four hours a day – this was her 8am until 4pm guy, who'd been informed of her location by her solicitor. They ignored each other, as per the rules.

Standing by his vehicle in a quiet corner of the car park was a tall, forty-something black man in a suit under a windbreaker. Once he knew she'd seen him, he got in the car. She headed over and climbed in.

'A pain in the arse?' Bokayo said, starting the engine.

'Always. Can't you stop this?'

He pulled out of the car park. In her wing mirror, Noa watched her bodyguard's vehicle follow suit at an inconspicuous distance. 'Not my call,' Bokayo said. 'Maybe when I make Inspector. They'd shift me to another unit if they knew I was shafting someone they're interested in. So what happened in there?'

Noa tutted at his language. She then outlined her day so far and added, 'What's coming next from you guys?'

'Just more keeping an eye on you. I know they're going to talk to your radio station colleagues again. And your boss is going to be asked a favour. That's hush-hush, so I can't tell you and you never heard it from me.'

'Have your boys traced the call from last night? The guy who reckons he's abducted a woman? It was a withheld number, but they can get onto the phone company.'

'I'd say they're likely in the process of doing just that. Might be a burner phone, like the goon claimed. He's still on the crank side of the fence so far, so I doubt there's a rush job. Other than that, I really don't know.'

'Too much might and likely.'

Bokayo swore under his breath at a cyclist. 'Hey, there's no case at the minute. Crank side of the fence. And if there is a case, I'm not on it anyway.'

'Then what good are you to me?' she said with a sly smile.

'I've wasted my time too. Not a single snippet of good information about the murderers who call your show.'

'Ah, both of us are failing at this using-the-other-for-information lark. But at least the sex is good.'

'Speaking of, we could fly by my place.'

Noa shook her head. 'I have research to do. I have to look into young women kidnapped around eighteen months ago, see if I can work out who he's talking about. Girls from all over

Britain. If only I didn't have to spend those two hours doing that...'

'And once you know all that, you're free?'

'Sure, but that's going to take up my two hours. I mean, if I knew all that in the next ten minutes, I'd have an hour fifty spare to burn all my excess energy. Alas.'

They both laughed. Bokayo said, 'It's all public domain stuff, mind you. I haven't looked that deep. This all happened only ten hours ago.'

'It saves me time. Time that you're wasting. Start talking as you drive to your place.'

'We've got two girls from London that—'

'No. Not London. Don't take this as gospel, but I don't think this guy's from London.'

Bokayo gave her what she could only describe as a cop stare. Pure suspicion, all over his face. Before he could respond, she said, 'Calm down. No, he didn't call me after the show. It's a guess.'

He wasn't satisfied. 'Some guess. I heard the goon's voice and there was no accent.'

'Divine Radio station broadcasts on DAB to most of London, but outside of that it's available only on the internet. The goon, as you call him, said he found my show while "surfing".'

Bokayo seemed satisfied with this explanation. 'Your new friend wasn't too certain of exactly when he snatched a woman because he said *about* eighteen months ago. I concentrated on women who went missing in the last half of 2020. I found fifteen good ones and of those—'

'Slow down. Give me all the names before we look at the most likely. All of them.'

'Fair enough,' Bokayo said. He pulled a list from the pocket of his door and handed it over.

'Crank side of the fence, eh?'

'Hey, I knew you'd want this. And in my job we get prepared.'

The scrap of paper contained fifteen names and basic descriptions of young women. Fifteen women who vanished off the face of the earth one day, never to be heard from again, leaving behind grieving families and puzzled communities. Was the 'goon', if he was genuine, holding one of these girls?

Scanning the names tugged at her heart. She couldn't help them all, unfortunately, but she was determined to save one. If that was possible.

———

'Happy now?' Bokayo said.

'No. There's hardly anything here. This is no good.'

'No good? What did you want? You've got the names and details of fifteen missing women. What else do you need? If the goon calls back and you can get him to admit something, like an age or where he took this girl from, then we'll have a clue to go on.'

Noa sighed. 'It's not proof he took her. You said all these details were in the public domain. Some cranks do their homework. I thought you would get me the files.'

Bokayo stopped at a red light. 'Police files? Most of these disappearances belong to other police forces. I have my own boss and my own cases. If I start requesting files from all over the country, it'll flag and people will want to know why. There's plenty more written about these women online, if you want to look.'

'How about if we cut the number down? The man said he took her a year and a half ago, and some of these are too early and too late. Look, if we lose these six, that leaves nine. I reckon our guy is English, so we could ignore the women kidnapped from Scotland and Wales.' Noa made a pen mark by five names as the traffic light hit green and the car started rolling. 'You could get the files on these five, surely. Five won't flag.'

His pause indicated that a positive answer wasn't on the horizon.

'Bokayo, you said your guys get prepared. The police have looked at these girls and surely they have an idea of which ones are most likely.'

Bokayo tapped the sheet in three places. Noa said, 'So, not this girl, Lisa Manton? Or this one, Kai Harlow? Both homeless girls.'

'The three I just pointed out are the names that are generating the most interest. That's what you asked for not two seconds ago.'

'Let's put aside single white female syndrome. I asked which the police thought were most likely that my caller took. Not the ones they give more of a shit about. Are Manton and Harlow off the list because they're homeless?'

Bokayo looked angry. She knew the very accusation she'd just made was one the police dealt with in spades. 'What can I tell you? Liz Holland is fourteen. Of course she's a priority. Isobel Waring has a pretty big family, they're very popular, she's won an award, and she's disabled. Janine Watson is a police officer's daughter. Homeless girls sometimes run away. These three are very much not the sort to. It seems pretty obvious to me, but write to your MP if you're unhappy about it. Meantime, are you going to renege on the deal?'

'Sex? No, but I might be limp.' He didn't laugh, so she touched his arm. 'I'm sorry. I just have a feeling the caller was legit. So I want to help this girl.'

'If there is a girl. We don't know for sure yet. But I know you care for people.' He rubbed his face, as if tired. 'Look, Holland

and Watson, those cases are making progress and the feeling is they're unlikely to be stranger snatchings. So, if it's a single name you're determined to focus on, now you have it.'

Three became one. Noa read the sole remaining name aloud: 'Isobel Waring.'

CHAPTER FOUR

13 NOVEMBER 2020

'My name is Isobel Waring. I am twenty-two and live with my parents and younger brother. I have a girlfriend, Mindy. We plan to get married and bring up dogs. I like cars, bikes, anything with an engine that you can get on and make go fast. I listen to chilled dance music...'

Isobel continues her biography to camera, standing dead straight to the lens with her arms by her sides, as instructed on the sheet of paper. She is shaking inside, for now she knows this is no video designed to be sent to her parents. There is no instruction to state how she is feeling or that her abductor hasn't harmed her. No newspaper to hold up, displaying the date as proof that she is still alive. No plea for her parents to pay the ransom.

When she falters or looks like covering a detail already mentioned, he calls out with a question to prompt her. It is more like a job interview, and it terrifies her that she can't fathom why the man would want it.

When it is done, she ties the camera to the needle thread and steps away, and he hauls it through the hatch, which promptly shuts.

She picks up a box he tossed through the hatch just before she started talking to the camera. She takes it to the sink. The sheet of instructions he gave her warned her not to get hair dye on her T-shirt or knickers, but she isn't about to remove them. Using the gloves provided, she starts the process of altering her hair colour.

Afterwards, she dries her hair and looks to the shelf above the sink. There seems to be everything anyone could want to pretty themselves. Powders, primers, rouge, foundation, concealer, bronzer, the works. Normally when she can't be bothered with a long routine, lipstick is enough, but there is only one here and it's blue.

However, he has given an order, so she applies the lipstick. She then works on her cheeks and eyes, but only enough to make a noticeable difference and constitute obedience. Finally, the dress, which she slips on at record speed after removing her T-shirt.

It is a good fit, but that is unimportant. The whole idea of the dress appals her, but at least it covers her thighs. She wonders if the perfect fit is because he's measured her body while she was unconscious.

She moves to the bed, lies down, and stares up. In the mirrored glass, the blue dress, blue hair and blue lipstick make her look like some kind of cartoon character. Maybe a Manga prostitute. He must have a fixation on the colour.

She gets to her feet again. Now, only one task remains. She moves close to the door and stands facing it, fingers splayed to show that her hands are empty.

She hears locks being disengaged. Feasting time. He is coming for her. Now, finally, she will get a proper look at the man who snatched her, and possibly the last human she ever meets.

———

The man who enters the cell wears a patterned kimono, baggy, wide-bottomed trousers, and those orange gloves she glimpsed earlier. She relaxes upon seeing his face. The one she saw earlier was not real, but a mask. It is a withered face, pearly white sharp angles instead of curves, and it is the same as depicted on the shelf ornament.

The costume reminds her of something Japanese, like in that Tom Cruise movie *The Last Samurai*. But the man isn't Japanese. Above the mask is light-brown hair, below it a pale neck. With no real face to analyse, it's tough to determine his age, but he's not very old and certainly not younger than her.

The elation at knowing he's not a monster, at least in outward appearance, fades quickly. She does not know what effect he is going for, but if it's to appear mad and thus terrify her, well done. He doesn't have a samurai sword, or any weapon that she can see.

Oh, but he does, she soon realises. He shows her his gloves, whose palms and fingers are inlaid with black pads. 'These are stun gloves. Don't try to obstruct me in any way. I'd rather that you never have first-hand knowledge that they are very effective at incapacitating.'

She believes him. A weapon could be deflected, wrestled from him, but power in his very touch makes him invincible, like a supervillain. To escape, she would have to knock him dead cold, and it's just not worth the risk. 'Step forward in a straight line, eyes closed,' he says.

She obeys, but each step is tentative, as if she's approaching a cliff edge. It's hard to keep her eyes shut, or ignore the worry that he will strike her at any moment.

After what feels like a long, long trek, he orders her to stop. She feels a soft blindfold being put over her eyes. She gasps.

He pulls her, and she moves forward. Where the blindfold lifts from her face to cross her nose, there's a gap that allows her to see the floor. She watches her slippered feet step out of the room, and she tilts her head back slightly to create the angle to allow her to see her new location. It's a corridor. There are five coloured lines of chevrons. Yellow, white, green, black, blue. She's seen such a thing at her local hospital and understands they lead to various places.

'You can see out of the chink in the blindfold, yes?'

'Yes. I'm sorry. It must have slipped.'

'Good. Don't be. And no it didn't. Follow the yellow.'

Bizarrely, she thinks of the yellow brick road in *The Wizard of Oz*. But those characters wanted to follow it, while she's terrified of what lies at the end of this journey.

A touch on her shoulder is indication that she should move. No electric shock, so his stun gloves must be turned off. Still, she cannot risk attacking him. She starts to walk along the yellow line. Her slippered feet make no noise, but his boots emit a loud clump right behind her.

'You were too drugged to respond last time,' he says. 'I see no ailment, but I must ask again. There was a packet of strong painkillers in your car. Are you suffering from an illness? Or pain from your old injury?'

He knows about her car crash? The injury still affects her, but it is something she always hides, even from her family. How does he know? Who has he spoken to?

Even if she knew, it would be useless information. He requires an answer. If she admits that she is suffering, he might return her painkillers. The only medicine in her cell is vitamins.

But something in his tone sounds worried. She gets the feeling that he will be upset if she is injured, although she cannot fathom why. It's a gut feeling and it makes her say, 'No, they're not my painkillers. My mother's. I'm fine. Why?'

'Curious. The yellow chevron – follow it. Go.'

She walks, hiding her pain as she moves. He follows. A short way along is another door. She can only see the bottom few inches, but enough to see it's another heavy iron slab. This place no longer seems like an office block, more like a government facility. But not one in use, for she can hear no noises bar his footsteps.

After three more similar doors, she hits a junction. One line of chevrons runs ahead, two turn left, but the yellow ones go right. She follows. A short way along is a curtain of PVC strips, like in a freezer, and she pushes through. The walls end a dozen steps later and the chink in her blindfold shows her a widened floor, but when she tries to tilt her head back to see the whole room, he says, 'No. Look forward at all times.'

The chevrons run on through the open area. A few seconds later, the floor drops away. She stops a half second before he tells her to. She realises she stands at the edge of a swimming pool. It looks about two metres deep.

'Down the steps. Careful.'

'What is this place? What are you going to do to me?'

He doesn't answer. She can't shake the terrible vision of being handcuffed to the floor of that pool as it fills with water.

She climbs down the ladder. Once her feet are on the floor, he says, 'You can remove the blindfold. Put it back on before you climb out to leave. You have thirty minutes for feasting. There will be a bell. You must stop eating as soon as it rings.'

Dinner in a swimming pool in the middle of a government facility, provided by a man in a bizarre Japanese outfit and mask? This is a wacky dream, surely. She will wake soon in her own bedroom, to breakfast delivered by her own mother.

She's still facing the ladder as she takes off the blindfold. He is standing at the edge of the pool, staring down. As he lifts the ladder away, to prevent her from escaping, she turns, to see whatever he has planned for her here.

What she discovers withdraws her breath as precisely as a kick to the solar plexus. She drops to her knees, and draws air back in, and expels it in a ragged moan of despair.

CHAPTER FIVE

I sobel Waring was white, twenty-four, five-foot eight, with short brown hair and a pretty, round face. She lived in Walton Hill in Isley Walton, Leicestershire, just a half mile south of Donnington Park Circuit. Her father was a Motorsport Vision Trackdays manager and from a young age she had been obsessed with motor vehicles. As a kid, she built go-karts and won various competitions flinging them about a track.

As a big speed fan, her father helped Isobel to obtain a Race Interclub Licence. When MSV took over Donnington Park, in 2017, she begged her father for a job. He started her as a cleaner to test her commitment, but she quickly got promoted to recovery driver, her task to collect trapped cars on grass and in gravel pits. Three years into the job, at twenty-one, she became a drift instructor.

She was in that role for just six months before a high-speed crash at Melbourne Hairpin put her out for months. When she returned to work, high technical expertise was beyond her and she was back to recovering stranded vehicles.

She went missing on Thursday 12th November 2020, aged

twenty-two. Her car was found on Hill Top Road, close to East Midlands Aeropark. According to her parents, she had gone out alone to the cinema. Various friends, however, claimed Isobel had gone to see a girlfriend her mum and dad knew nothing about. She never arrived at either location and nobody had heard from her since.

Her disappearance was a big story in Leicestershire and reached the news nationwide. Thirty detectives were on the case at one point, but clues were scant. No belongings other than her car were ever found, inside of which was her mobile phone in a holder on the dashboard. No CCTV shed light. Police were still trying to trace the myriad cars seen around that area around that time, but those already found had been eliminated. There were no prints or DNA found at the scene that couldn't be traced to someone innocent.

There were reported sightings of Isobel, but none confirmed. Although there was a single arrest of a friend of her girlfriend's brother, for sending her lewd messages, he was quickly released and deemed to have no connection to her disappearance. Family life was good and nothing indicated that she might have run away or secretly shacked up with someone. She seemed to have just winked out of existence.

The news website Noa promoted at the end of each show, UbyU, was her go-to place for true crime stories. As referenced in its name, the site was a wiki and often articles were written by those with first-hand accounts, which made it second-to-none for invaluable little details overlooked by the bigger media entities. Noa had searched for information about Isobel Waring's disappearance and had immediately found a story posted by one of the girl's friends. In just over a thousand words, it gave her what would have taken a trawl through months of national newspapers to acquire.

'And this Isobel Waring is your number one?' Noa asked Bokayo. They'd driven in silence while she learned about the missing woman.

The detective yelled at another bad driver before answering. 'Nothing definitively points to her, but she seems the most likely in our opinion. We're keeping our options open about various girls though. So, if this man was Isobel's abductor, it would be cool if you could ask questions about her.'

'Was? Past tense? You think she's dead because of the time frame, don't you?'

'People have been kept longer and returned alive. But people have been to the moon.'

'So why would he claim she's alive and he wants to give her back?'

Bokayo shrugged. 'A game. Boredom. Maybe he liked all the interest her disappearance created and hates that it's all died down. Maybe he's all full of shit. He gave no proof he's abducted anyone.'

'I had no chance to ask. He hung up.'

'We know, we know. No one is blaming you.'

'I want you to keep me informed about what the police think.'

'Not my case, remember? But you'll find out if this guy turns out to be legit, because a whole horde of coppers will descend on your studio.'

'Give me something. You must know. What's the buzz at the minute?'

Bokayo laughed and made a right turn. 'There's no buzz, Noa. At the minute he's just a goon spouting crap to get attention. Keep in mind it's a small radio station. Cranks are ten a penny. A couple of days back some guy called up to say he did the Brighton Trunk Murders as a teenager back in the 1930s. Hell, maybe that was your guy as well.'

———

Noa called the manager of the charity shop where she worked, near Manchester Square in Marylebone. She was apologetic and didn't mention the police. She got there around midday.

The manager had covered Noa's morning shift with a skinny young lad called Peter. She'd never met him, but had been informed that he was as smart as a computer and shared a machine's lack of social grace.

Clearly the manager's gossiping extended to all staff, because the moment she entered the store, Peter looked up from a UFO book he was reading and said, 'Noa the rich girl. So why does a rich girl work here?'

She gave him a smile and pushed through the curtain behind the till area, to dump her bag and grab a tea. When she returned, it was in hope that the kid would have moved on from his query. He hadn't.

'So what gives? Why does a rich girl work here?'

She often gave people a lot of room, but he'd caught her at a bad time. 'That's a blunt question. Quite rude as an opener to a stranger.'

'Just puzzling, that's all. Do you give money to this charity we work for? You could buy everything in this shop right now.'

'I'm here for my shift now, so you can move along.'

He put his book down, but remained in the chair behind the till. 'Thomas Hobbes said that no man gives but with good intention to himself. There's no true altruism in his opinion.'

'He died 350 years ago.'

Peter seemed surprised that she knew who Hobbes was. It seemed to ruin his ploy to impress or surprise her. 'Ah, you are the Butler to my Hobbes. Nietzsche also was a proponent of psychological egoism.'

She had avoided his eyes, but now found them. 'Did you

read up on this because you knew I was coming in? Why does it offend you that I work here?'

'It just puzzles me,' Peter said as he got up and grabbed his coat from under the counter. 'You could give to charity. But maybe that doesn't erase the guilt you feel at having been born into money.'

She held her anger. 'I do give to charity. I also like to do this.'

'Because it's visible, right? Have you read Plato's *Republic*? Or Shaw's *Socialism for Millionaires*?'

'So you think I sit behind that till all day in the hope that people see me, see what good I'm doing, and will think better of me? Let's imagine that was true. Why does it upset you?'

Peter got into his coat. 'It's fake.'

Noa pulled a twenty pound note out of her purse and slapped it onto the desk. 'Let's bet. I say you truly feel slighted by the idea of false altruism, I say your attitude towards me has nothing to do with all the bad luck you were handed by life. I bet twenty quid you're in no way jealous that I was handed money on a plate and never had to go without.'

Peter eyed the money. Then he bit his lip, annoyed, and took the cash, and left. Noa waited until he was out of sight, then her face broke. But she managed to prevent tears from forming in her eyes.

Peter wasn't the first person to accuse her of selfish reasons for helping others. When she'd contacted Divine Radio about a slot on the station to 'help alleviate people's guilt', Larry had called her proposal a cashless form of charity. Even her own boyfriend of three months, Bokayo, had jumped on that bandwagon.

They'd met right here in this charity shop in January, when he'd entered in search of cheap ornaments for his mother. Somehow he'd already known that she had a radio show and a dead father who'd made sure she'd never have to become a nine-to-fiver. Surprised to see one of the elite tending a charity shop till instead of cruising around in a yacht, he'd said, 'Trying to convince God you're sorry, eh?'

His opinion of her had been one shared by many, and entirely understandable. Her father had been so well-known as to almost deserve the title of celebrity, and that had filtered to his sole child. Her father had wanted her to get a career and she'd studied at university, but education paled beside her desire to live life. In her teens and early twenties, she had been one for nightclubbing with expensive champagne, days out with friends in stretch limos, holidays abroad at the drop of a hat, and throwing cash around in all sorts of other ways to have fun. She had been widely known as a spoiled rich kid and had not been surprised by the detective's initial diagnosis of her.

She had been surprised to learn that the day they'd first met... actually wasn't. When she was twenty-one, she had been out with friends, racing their expensive cars at midnight in a large IKEA car park, when a uniformed officer came to investigate. That copper, who had taken names and issued warnings, had been Bokayo. That day in the charity shop, she hadn't recognised him, but he had recalled, with a laugh, her standoffish demeanour and claim that her father could have him demoted to cleaner. She had been so embarrassed that she'd asked him on a date, in order to let him see that his diagnosis of her was obsolete.

It truly was, for she had transformed following her father's death. No more spoiled rich kid. No more flash jewellery, no more partying into the late hours, no more jetting off to sunny shores on a whim. Now she drove old cars, shopped at cheap supermarkets, enjoyed staycations, and dressed to mingle with the masses, just like a regular girl.

She'd also developed a desire to help the needy, and not just by parting with money. Peter, from the shop, had assumed she was trying to pretend her existence was worthwhile. Larry, from the radio station, had pegged her as one attempting to promote a do-good image. And, initially, Bokayo had accused her of trying to atone for being born lucky. The truth was none of these. The truth was something nobody could fathom.

And never would, if she had her way.

———

A quiet afternoon in the charity shop allowed Noa to surf the internet on her phone, and she quickly understood Bokayo's line about her radio station being small. The tidal wave of news stories she'd expected, about an abductor who'd call her show to offer up his victim, turned out to be a trickling stream. There were bits and pieces, but she had to dig to find them and no major news outlets carried the tale. Cranks must be ten a penny, like Bokayo said.

She searched every name on the missing women list Bokayo had supplied. Some of the girls had made the national newspapers, others hadn't, like the two homeless women. The highest profile case was the disappearance of Janine Watson, a policeman's daughter, but abduction wasn't a definite cause. A close second was Isobel Waring, the one highlighted by Bokayo. There were no fresh articles that connected her and Noa's confession show.

Noa did find her name tied to Isobel a handful of times in new comments on online stories from back in 2020, when the young woman's sudden vanishing was fresh, but these were just guesswork from readers who'd listened to the show. These aside, the story of an abductor phoning a confessions show had very little exposure.

That didn't change as the day wore on. No reporters rang her phone. No one accosted her as she went about her daily business, so 4–12 bodyguard got an easy shift. She was well-known at the local gym, but the regulars she was on name-terms with said nothing about her latest show. Even the owner of the local shop, who she knew quite well, made small talk and didn't mention kidnapped women.

By late evening, Noa had half-convinced herself that the abductor was indeed a crank, based partly on a belief that if he truly wanted to confess live on-air, he could have called a larger radio station or provided undeniable details about his captive. But she had so little to form a real opinion on. Time would tell. If the man didn't call the show again, he'd be entirely forgotten by morning. If he returned for more tonight and didn't offer some real meat, he'd be discarded as an attention-seeking wacko.

But if he was genuine, and next time decided to prove it, things would rapidly escalate, and Noa would find herself in the thick of a maelstrom.

———

Sometimes Noa liked to enter the radio station early and have a decaf tea in the producer's office while listening to the 11–12 show *Late Love*, hosted by married couple Zoe and Dale Jones. When she walked in, Larry indicated that he needed a word and she followed him down the corridor and into the small kitchen.

'I hope that end-of-the-world look isn't about me,' she said as she headed for the kettle.

'You won't like this. There's a tap on the phones. Including the private line.'

Noa kept the annoyance out of her face. 'How did they get that?'

Larry also looked frustrated, but it wasn't at the police. 'I let them, Noa. Because we get criminals call up and criminals are people they like to lock up. There's also a policeman coming round soon. He's going to sit in on the show in case that kidnapper calls back. And, yes, he's going to probably tell you what to say to the weirdo.'

She sighed. 'I don't get a say in my own show?'

'Yes, you do. I gave you an hour of my station time and I've never told you what to do or not to do, have I? And I didn't start pre-vetting the calls even when the police asked me to. But that's station stuff, and now this is police stuff. They want to listen in if this guy calls back and how can I say no? I'm sure that comes under some kind of obstruction law. I knew you'd be annoyed, but think of this. If the story comes out that a kidnapper is calling our station, your show will go through the roof.'

That crap again. 'I don't care about fame or millions of listeners. Why don't you understand this by now?'

'What exactly do you care about, Noa? I still don't know why you do this. You say you want to help people, but what help are we giving? Half the people who call your show are liars and the rest just moan about nonsense. Have we helped anyone, really?'

'It's impossible to know what help we've given. That all happens after the show, back in people's homes. But it makes me feel good, even if that's the only result.'

Larry left it there and returned to the studio. For just a single, fleeting moment, Noa was tempted to call him back and tell him what was deep in her heart. But she didn't. That would only invite more questions, perhaps accusations, and probably upset the balance in her life.

The police officer was a young detective constable called Tomas Gillette, who was currently working towards Level 2 of something called the Competency and Values Framework. Was that a course or a guideline? Whatever, it was part of his training towards qualification as a negotiator. As soon as she heard that word, negotiator, her mood darkened.

'I hope you don't plan to be using a microphone tonight,' she told him as he fixed himself a coffee in the kitchen.

'No, no, no,' he said, smiling as if she'd said something silly. 'The caller has a connection to you. You're the one he wants to talk to.'

'A connection? Because he chose a small radio station instead of one of the big players? That could be because he doesn't want massive exposure.'

'You can't claim live on-air to have a kidnap victim and not expect nationwide exposure. Want a coffee?'

'Hasn't happened. I've checked the news. No one cares because shows like this attract all sorts of wild characters. And no thanks.'

Gillette turned to face her and sipped his drink. 'True, but we've had calls about it. Everything starts small and we expect this to gain a lot of traction if he calls again. We'll see if it does. He may not call.'

'You never answered my question about your role here.'

He began to talk, fast, long, as if he had prepared a speech. She heard terms like *crisis state* and *irrational argument* and *precipitating event*.

'Stop,' she said. 'I'm sorry. It's just that this has been thrust on me out of nowhere. Do you understand that this isn't a hostage situation? I mean from my point of view. My job on this show is just to listen. Barely even that. I just let people rant to blow off steam.'

'I'm sorry too,' he said. He sat at the table and bid her to do the same. She did. 'Maybe I was just trying to prove I know my own job. I was warned that you wouldn't be receptive to my presence.'

'Tomas, I'm not doubting your skills and I totally understand that we could have a kidnapped young woman out there. But the way I see it, this isn't a situation where this guy is holed up with no way out and a negotiator is needed to avoid a bloodbath. This could be a man who feels guilty.'

'We don't know that. We don't know his plans or his intention.'

He was staring hard, reading her, and it made her uncomfortable. She fiddled with a drinks coaster. 'No, but he phoned a B-list radio confession show.'

'And what do you think that means?'

She ignored the coaster and met his glare. 'Are you testing me? Like I said, I don't have your skills. Do I think he wants to come clean? I don't know. Maybe he just wants to talk about his state of mind and would prefer to do that anonymously. Not to friends who could give him up. And certainly not to the police.'

'Your show may not have millions of listeners, but compared to a church confessional or a Samaritans phone line, it's a massive audience. The genuinely guilty aren't likely to adopt such a tactic. He has to be aware that someone at the station or a listener would tell the police. That the police themselves could be listening. That his claim would go far and wide.'

'You lot are certainly always listening. So why has he chosen me, my show?'

'We don't know. We don't know if he's for real or not. We don't even have a name for the woman he claims he's kidnapped.'

'Possibly Isobel Waring.'

He squinted at her. 'How did you know that?'

'Try not to overthink. This isn't Tijuana. Kidnappings are rare and big news. She seemed most likely out of the missing girls I found on the internet.'

'Well, remember there's no proof of that yet, so it's not wise to go mentioning that name. Please don't say it on-air. We don't know who this man is or why he's calling a radio station.'

Noa sat back. 'If this was all about simply listening to him, you could do that on a radio in your station. But that doesn't allow you to, shall we say, influence proceedings.'

Tomas withdrew a sheet of paper from a briefcase loaded with them and slid it across to her. 'You're right, we aren't just going to sit back.'

She didn't even scan the sheet. 'Open-ended questions? Show empathy? I should constantly say things like *yes* and *go on* and *I understand*, to show him I'm attentive and sympathetic?'

The detective smiled. 'Look, we're not stupid. Someone called a late-night confession show with a mad claim about having a prisoner for the last year and a half. Hardly breaking news and ninety-nine times out of a hundred it's a load of bull. There's no armed response team ready to kick in doors. The Commissioner isn't waiting by the phone for live updates. I'm here alone, no team with me. Take a look at the sheet. It's just a few tips to help us get some information from the caller. It's nothing. Schoolboy stuff. The weather, for instance. Moan about the rain. If he agrees, we know he's somewhere its wet. Little details like that. All designed to give us an insight into him and see if he's telling the truth.'

Noa looked at the sheet. Sure enough, it was a list of key words and terms designed to elicit simple information. But she knew there was more to this. 'Maybe we don't need the tiptoe approach. I could outright demand proof from him. But if so, then what? There's nothing on this sheet that tells me what to do if we suddenly realise our man is legit. That he's got a young woman imprisoned and he's a dangerous bastard. I'll be lost and out of my depth if that happens.'

Tomas glanced at his briefcase, which was a giveaway. Noa said, 'If that happens, we move on to stage two, right?'

He gave a smile so fake it gave the impression he was at work right here, right now, playing her. 'In that case, I'll read the situation and we'll take it from there.'

'Take over, you mean?'

He paused before deciding to act as if she'd dreamed her last question. 'We have fifteen minutes until your show. Can we go over a few things?'

She was half-tempted to fake an emotional explosion and really test this guy's skills. Instead, she decided to see if a negotiator's course taught how to take a joke: 'Sure. I'm actually glad you turned up, to be honest. I was worried about saying the wrong thing and causing a young woman to get her throat slashed. But now you're here, so that will be your fault instead.'

————

'It's midnight, April 20th, 2022, I'm Noa, and the phones are already ringing, so let's take the first call.'

'I saw you – heard, I mean, heard. Heard your programme last night and... I have to be in bed for work tomorrow, but I just had to stay up for this. It's horrible. Why do you have people on who kidnap women? Why do you make money from these things? It's disgusting.'

12.13am: *'Condoning crime just for kicks. Appalling. You need to get a real job. No wonder you're up so late. You can't sleep at night.'*

12.32am: '*People like that kidnapper, these cranks take up time us real confessioners could use. It's obvious you buy into this crap because it gets the number of listeners up. It's degrading.*'

12.51am: '*I don't get how I'm the first person to complain about this. Why didn't you ask that kidnapper man about the girl he's got locked up? You didn't even ask her name! Nothing! Did you want him to call back, was that why? So people would tune in?*'

The reason this caller had assumed she was the first to mention the kidnapper: none of the others had been broadcast. In order to make sure that the kidnapper didn't get lost in the queue, all calls had been answered off-air by Detective Tomas Gillett and Larry, the producer. It was the first time the show had ever vetted callers.

Genuine confessions were put on hold, ready for their turn on-air, while callers determined to slate Noa and the show got terminated. At first, the method was to apologise and explain why the calls wouldn't be aired, but the volume was high and soon the two men started simply hanging up on haters. Larry even got profane. Noa noted that all eight phone lines were constantly in use, which was a sure sign that interest in the kidnapper had risen over the last twenty-four hours, even if the media hadn't yet reported on it.

Amongst the tide of critics were the standard pranksters, who also boasted of having women locked in cellars, and the do-gooders, who claimed to know the kidnapper or his victim. Unfortunately, these calls couldn't be written off and Detective Gillette, expecting this turn, had his mobile to his ear, down which he was relaying information to another police officer.

While listening to her colleagues deal with abuse, some of it she knew was aimed at her, Noa still had to host her show, for not every caller wanted to talk about kidnap. But it was hard to put all that to the back of her mind and talk to cheating spouses and petty shoplifters. She tried to zone out and ended up employing the tactic reserved for the kidnapper himself, to show attentiveness and sympathy: *yes* and *go on* and *I understand*.

'Noa!' Tomas suddenly hissed. Noa snapped out of a semi-daze and looked round at him, caller forgotten. The young detective was jabbing at his phone, and she knew what that meant. The kidnapper was back, as promised. He was on the line, waiting his turn with her. She immediately killed the current call, without warning, and got ready to patch him through.

———

'Well, we seem to have lost that caller. Let's see if she calls back. We'll move on. Hello, friend. What's bugging you at this late hour?'

'*The fact that you didn't answer my call. A man did. So you have assistance tonight. Perhaps the police.*'

The same semi-robotic and sans-accent tone as before. It was definitely him.

Detective Gillette shook his head: *don't admit I'm here.* Noa didn't want to lie, in case he already knew somehow. But he hadn't asked if the police were there. 'Yes. My producer is checking calls to make sure we found you. You've made my show quite popular.' She cursed herself: wrong choice of words, which would surely return to bite her.

'*Not my intention, but I'm sure you don't mind. Thanks for the honesty.*'

'On the subject of which, I am going to have to ask you questions about what you told us last night. I have no choice. You admitted something quite shocking. Is that okay?'

'*Of course. I can answer or not. I can be slippery and coded,*

50

or not. But first, I want you to ask me another type of question. Bear with me. Ask me a general knowledge question. Just ask. Now. Fire away.'

Detective Gillette looked puzzled. He shrugged, which didn't help. Noa said the first thing that came into her head: 'Which country has the most pyramids?'

The caller ignored the question. *'Okay. Now you may ask whatever you want. Fire away.'*

'Why did you want a general knowledge question?'

'No reason. Move on.'

He sounded more mellow this evening; that, coupled with his agreeing to answer questions, lit a fire in the detective sitting by her side. She already had his keyword sheet before her, but now he started scribbling on a pad. Questions, no doubt. All the answers the policeman had hoped to slowly, slyly extract and could just grab by the handful.

But Noa was also confident. 'Let me start with perhaps the silliest question imaginable to put to a man claiming to be holding a young woman captive. Are you telling the truth?'

'Good point. I'll give the same answer I'd give either way. Yes. I am telling the truth. I'm afraid that is our time up.'

Gillette rolled his hands, urging her to continue, press on, get more, get something. She said, 'I don't mean to doubt you, but you've heard the sorts of stories I get on this show.'

'You think I'm a crank? Be honest.'

Gillette shook his head. Noa decided he worried too much. 'I don't know. I hear the wildest of the wild. It's hard to accept anything without proof.'

'My word isn't good enough?'

The detective grabbed her arm. She glared at it; from Superman, the same look would have scorched flesh and bone. Gillette let her go. Returning to the abductor, she said, 'Did your word work the last time you collected a parcel from the sorting office?'

The caller laughed. *'Are the police there?'*

'Yes. One detective. You're popular.'

'Give me a name. The girl's name. Tell me who you think I have.'

'Many girls go missing. It could be anyone.'

'I'm sure you've done homework. You have an idea. A shortlist, at least, and there will be one that stands out more than the others. Say it.'

Behind her, Gillette hissed *no*. This time they were on the same page. 'If I state a name, it'll sound like the police have information that that girl has been kidnapped. If the family hears that, they'll be very upset if they're trying to believe she just ran away. It will sound like that's the girl the police want to trace the most, and that will upset a whole bunch of other families of missing women. Besides, if there's no woman, you could just say yes to any name I give.'

'Even a crank would have prepared for this call by finding the name of a real missing girl, and not rely on the police to supply one. To not do that is stupid. Am I stupid?'

Gillette tried to interject again, but Noa held up a hand. 'The detective is trying to take over the call. He thinks I don't know how to talk to people even though I host a confession show. I reckon a cheap postal negotiator's course went to his head. Just a sec.' Then, to Gillette, she said, 'Be still and be quiet. This is my show.' And back to the caller: 'Where were we? Oh yes. Do I think you're stupid? Let me be honest. If you're a crank with no name to give me, yes, you're stupid.'

A pause. Then: *'Isobel Waring. Heard that name?'*

Her shoulders slumped. 'I know the name. Are you saying Isobel Waring is the girl you're holding captive?'

'Isobel is the one I'm referring to, yes.'

'And last night you said you wanted to give her up. Was that true? Is it still?'

'*Yes. In fact, I'll give her to you right now. Butterfly. Rucksack. Enable.*'

He hung up. Noa sat in stunned silence, realising that the caller had just given Isobel Waring's location.

CHAPTER SIX

18 NOVEMBER 2020

There is no access to clocks, and no daylight penetrates her room, so the only way to work out how long she has been here is by mealtimes. Three times a day, she is escorted to the swimming pool to eat: breakfast, lunch, dinner.

By her calculations, Isobel figures it's been six days. This is the morning of day six as a prisoner in this room. By day two, fear and panic gave way to a form of... acceptance. With that came an emptiness that pushed her to find ways to pass time. He has provided books, of course, and seems to have covered all tastes by including old classics with romance novels and gung-ho thrillers.

But Isobel is no reader and hasn't touched them, preferring instead to exercise as best she can with her injured hip. Running is out, of course, so she uses the treadmill with her hands. Another time-consuming task she undertakes is to rearrange all the cosmetics and vitamins he's supplied, sometimes alphabetically, sometimes by container size, sometimes by production or use-by date.

For brief moments, she managed to forget that she was a kidnap victim, except the sight of the ornament mask, so similar to his disguise, would yank her back into dreadful reality. On day four, she turned that mask away from her. It helped a little.

Her family must be going spare. For sure they have reported her missing, probably within hours of her not turning up at her girlfriend's house. God, she never got a chance yet to tell her parents that she was dating another girl. Well, they'll know by now because the police will have talked to everyone she knows, and what a bombshell that would have been.

Especially to her dad, who hates same-sex attraction. Sure, that's man-on-man love because she saw his phone once and knows he likes lesbian porn. But it is a different kettle of fish altogether when it's your own daughter who's into girls, even though he once joked about her being gay because of her obsessions with cars and motorbikes. Mum, she would have accepted Isobel's sexual orientation, although she would be upset that there wouldn't be grandchildren.

Who Isobel chooses to date will be of minor concern right now though. Her mum would be worrying the most, because of that damn true crime obsession of hers. Dad was too optimistic about everything. Even six days in, he would probably still think she'd run off to be silly somewhere. But on day one Mum would have assumed a weirdo had snatched Isobel, and by now she would be inconsolable, deadly certain her daughter was buried in a cellar somewhere.

Unless the bastard had already contacted them. For all Isobel knew, he had been taunting them, sending letters and making phone calls and describing the hell she was going through. He might have posted that video he made her create. Heck, the police might have released the video to the public and it is now viral. Isobel's name could be known across the world. Celebrities might have posted on Twitter and Instagram, giving their hopes for her safe return. Maybe even Lewis Hamilton. Wow, imagine if she got so famous that she becomes a star when she's released? How cool it would be if the Formula One Group allowed her to ride an F1 car around Circuit de Monaco!

But she can only wonder, because one of the bastard's rules is: never ask about the outside world. Maybe there's bigger news and no one cares. Maybe nobody outside Leicestershire even knows she's missing. Maybe her parents have already had a funeral and moved on. Maybe deep down her mother actually likes what's happened because she can write her own true crime book. Many mothers of snatched and murdered sons and daughters have done so.

Maybe, if Isobel is here long enough for that book to be finished, Mum will be annoyed at her return, alive and well. Maybe her dad has already filled her job at his firm.

The not knowing is bad, but she welcomes it. She uses it. She has to obsess over something, and it beats thinking about his intentions for her. That worry had bloated and grown as the hours passed on day one as a captive, until its bite became a physical pain in her gut. At the end of that first day, when he'd turned off her light and ordered her to sleep, she had called out to him:

'I need to know. This is killing me. I need to know what you want.'

No response at first. Not until she'd started pacing in the dark, wild as a headless chicken. Then, he'd called down through the ceiling hatch, his voice faint and muffled.

'Calm down, stop.'

She had continued to pace. 'No. I should beat my head in right now if you plan to torture and murder me. I won't give you that satisfaction. Then you'll have to dump my body and it'll be found and my parents will know what happened. At least they'll know.'

'Lie down. This does not help you.'

'You're torturing me now by not telling me. That's part of

the fun for you, isn't it? Yes. You're doing what those people in war do, when they capture enemies. They tell them they're going to be executed, and then they say, oh not today, tomorrow. And it happens all over again. That's what you're doing. Torture.'

Perhaps because he'd feared he was losing control of her that night, he had answered her.

'You will be challenged. I told you that. You're here because you're special. I have been watching you.'

She had stopped pacing, abruptly. When she had raised her hands to rub her face, they'd hit a wall. She had been inches away, half a second away, from slamming right into it head-first. 'Challenges' he'd mentioned earlier that day, although he'd not elaborated, but this was the first time he'd admitted that he'd been watching her or that he considered her special.

'What do you mean? You've been stalking me?'

'That word could apply. I know how special you are. I know you have great skills on the racetrack. I know you were a top athlete at school sports. I know everything. Now ask no more questions. If you don't sleep, you will regret it.'

That could have been a threat, or a tip. She'd settled down afterwards, but only physically. Her mind had been overrun by memories of her life over the past few weeks, but with the scenes edited to include him. At work, at the pub, at her girlfriend's garden party, there he was, lurking behind a tree or sitting in a car. Sleep, that night, had been impossible.

Thoughts of stalking were soon replaced by a new fear: the challenges he refused to elaborate upon. On night two, in the dark, she had called out, 'What do you want from me? What are these challenges? To see how fast I can run? What, away from crocodiles or something?'

He'd laughed, but she hadn't been joking. Madmen weren't normal, and she had genuinely thought he would subject her to bizarre tests, like those in that documentary her mother had told her about. Nazi doctors in World War II prison camps had experimented on prisoners, pumping chemicals into them, transplanting body parts from one person onto – or into – another, testing the effects of intense heat or extreme cold on flesh. And worse.

'Stop laughing,' she'd yelled. 'I'm scared.'

'No challenge will harm you. Only the results will. If you fail.'

She looked up at the ceiling, where she thought the hatch was, even though it was closed. It was too dark to see anything though. 'And if I pass?'

'You leave this room. You're free.'

He'd first mentioned challenges on day one, but it is now day six and she's heard nothing more. Her mind is spinning. On the one hand, she wants no part of what he has planned, because it could be something painful and horrific. On the other, success might give her back her old life, if he's true to his word.

She tries to clear her mind. He is the one in control and will not be swayed by her impatience. She has no choice but to continue the routines he has set for her, and await something different. So, when the hatch opens a few minutes later, she does not call out to demand answers. She does not even look up. This will be the breakfast call, as usual. She will get up, get into the dress, and –

'The first challenge begins after feasting,' he says. She sits up, shocked. His masked face is at the hatch, and she stares at him. She knows better than to ask what the challenge will be. But she wants a clue and thinks of the perfect question:

'Is it wise to eat? I mean, if I have to exert myself, that's probably not best on a full stomach.'

'I provide meals. You eat if you want to. Please dress.'

He closes the hatch. When she rises from the bed, her bad hip emits a stab of pain. Suddenly, she regrets having hidden the extent of her injury from him. If he has set a physical challenge, she is in big trouble. Mortal danger. She considers calling out again, to explain her trouble, because he might redesign the challenge to help her out.

But she stays silent, hit again by that old feeling that he will be upset if he knows she's injured. Maybe it won't be a physical challenge after all. If she's lucky, it's a quiz on the working of a vehicle engine.

She washes her face, brushes her blue hair, slips on the blue dress, applies the blue lipstick, and turns to face the door to await him.

———

18 November, 10.36am

'I really am leaving?'

Isobel doesn't dare to look around at him. After events in the swimming pool, the masked man had escorted her back to her room, walking behind her as always as she followed the yellow chevrons. When he'd opened her door and taken off her blindfold she had walked into her cell without a word. All he'd said during the journey back was that she should clean her room and take a memento. It certainly seemed as if she was leaving this place.

But now, as he is closing the door, she speaks up, not fully trusting him.

His response is, 'You didn't fail the challenge. So yes.'

'For real? I mean, alive?'

'Yes. You will be leaving this place alive. Take a memento. Dress in your original clothing, if you like.'

Now she turns. The mask means there is no face to read,

but there is another way to get a sense of his truthfulness. 'Can you prove it? I mean, can I call my mum?'

'Of course not. A call could be traced here. Now get dressed.'

He shuts the door. Locks it. She stares at her room, still not fully believing she will be released back to her family. But if it's a trick and he plans something terrible, it will happen regardless of whether she's packed and ready to leave. The last thing she wants is a delay if this is indeed her last day as a prisoner, so she reaches under her bed and pulls out the small suitcase that has sat there since the start. According to him, it contains all her belongings, yet she was warned never to touch it. She never did, certain that he wouldn't have left her phone.

And he hasn't. But her clothing is there, folded neatly. If the police traced her mobile, God knows where the trail led them. Not here. It's been six days. She holds up her jeans and there's an uncomfortable flutter in her stomach. She knows why. Putting on these jeans will feel pretty final. It will push her off the fence, into I'm-going-home territory. The fall will be greater if this is all bullshit and she's going nowhere.

But why delay if she's truly homeward bound?

She wonders what those first moments will be like when she gets home. If the story of her disappearance is big news, will strangers in the street stop and stare and point? Will she see her face on newspapers? She's not sure she wants that. In fact, no furore at all would probably be nice. To go home and have nobody bat an eyelid. The neighbours just nod hello. Her parents just say, 'Hi, dear, nice holiday? Fancy some lunch?' And all runs as if the last six days never happened.

Once dressed, she stands in the centre of the room, looking around. He said she could take a memento, but her first thought had been: why the hell would she? To remember him, as if this had been a nice holiday after all? The blue hair is getting shaved right off at the first chance, even before she talks to the police, and she'll happily go bald for a few months.

Now, she reconsiders his offer. Thanks to her mum, she knows all about touch DNA. Everything portable here has been handled by him. If she can give something to the police, and his DNA is in the system...

The door opens. She turns. He's standing there. The sight of him gives her a boost, because his stupid Japanese samurai costume is gone. He still wears the mask, but now he is in jeans and a jacket. In a way the look is even more preposterous.

The outdoor clothes are both a good and a bad sign. Bad, because they remind her that he can hide the monster inside him, and did exactly that in order to snatch her. Good, because outdoor clothes means he's going out. With her. Although not definitive, it's a really good sign that the nightmare is coming to an end.

'It's time for you to leave, Blue.'

'What about...' She stops. On that first day, he gave her a list of 'house rules', one of which was his Golden Rule. The one thing she must never mention.

'What about what?' he prompts. She thinks fast for a fake concern. 'The dress. Should I put it back on the hanger?'

'Don't worry about it. Are you ready?'

Of course she is. She's never been more ready or more eager for anything in her life. She wouldn't delay this for the world.

But there *is* one thing she must do first. 'Can I use the toilet? One last time?'

———

Once outside her room, she turns left to follow the red chevrons, which go to the bathroom. She knows the way by heart.

As always, he waits outside. This iron door is different to the others in that it has a six-inch section missing at the bottom, so he can see what's going on within. By now she's quite adept at spotting a slight shift in the shadows just beyond the door, and knows he's on his knees, watching her feet.

But he can't see her hands. Or the secret pen she holds. Or the piece of toilet paper laid on her thigh. She's already stuffed some pieces of toilet paper down her knickers.

Writing on the paper is hard because she has to be soft and slow, but she completes her note before she finishes urinating. When she stands up and flushes the toilet, that's her chance. He's never still on his knees when she exits.

His shadow shifts as he gets to his feet. In a fluid motion, one hand shoves the pen and the note behind the toilet while her other unlocks the door. When she steps out, he's standing, waiting.

'Is it time to leave?' she asks.

He nods.

CHAPTER SEVEN

T he phone lines were still engaged, but Noa had no energy for seeing out the final minutes of the show. Every radio presenter had toilet tracks, used to cover bathroom breaks, and she needed an extra-long song right now. Her usual was 'Free Bird' by Lynyrd Skynyrd, for nine minutes of time to think.

She paced the studio, thinking. Gillette had taken Larry's office in order to privately talk to his boss. Watching her pace, Larry said, 'What happens now? Do we just continue the show, after that? Is anyone still going to be listening, knowing the police are off trying to find this girl?'

Isobel's disappearance had faded from the public mind after so many months, but tonight's show would change that, no matter what police found at the location the kidnapper had sent them to. Dead or alive, she would be big news again and so would the confessions show.

However, that would be with the coming of the new dawn. Right now only the police and a couple of thousand listeners knew of the latest developments. Knowing this put Noa in a kind of limbo, like a prizefighter waiting backstage prior to going before the crowd and the cameras. She wasn't looking forward to tomorrow and knew she wouldn't sleep tonight.

Not that she wanted to. Right now police were heading to the location given by the caller and before long they'd have an answer. But Noa didn't want to wait, even if the authorities planned to keep her posted.

'I don't think you did anything wrong.'

She stopped pacing and stared at Larry. She remembered the withering look Gillette had tossed her way before bolting into the office. 'Wait, you think he blames me?'

'You were quite blunt with the guy, and he told you not to be.'

'I got the caller to give Isobel up. You heard that.'

'I did. It's just... what if she was fine and now you've annoyed the guy and he's going to kill her?'

'Kill her because of what I said?'

'Yeah. You were quite antagonistic.'

'He wasn't pissed at me. We had a banter going, if anything.'

'Yeah, you'll get crap for that too.'

She looked through the office window, to see Gillette pacing and talking into his mobile – and he did not look happy. 'Larry, if this kidnapper is telling the truth, he's had a woman locked up for a year and a half, and kept her alive all that time for a reason. And now you think a few words from me have made him abandon that plan and kill her in anger? He just gave us a location, so now police cars are racing there. So either this madman is quickly driving there to dump a body, or he's killed her where he's got her and abandoning the place. All highly doubtful. And certainly not because I said a few cheeky things.'

The words felt hollow; she wasn't convinced by her own argument. Not when she was dealing with minds out of control.

Larry shrugged. 'Maybe he doesn't have to do any running about at all. Maybe she's been dead all this time and he's just giving us the body and it's miles and miles from him. I mean, look where it is.'

Noa had considered this, especially because of that location.

Noa and Gillette had heard of What3words, a global address system that breaks the entire world into a grid of squares three by three metres, every single one of the 57 trillion identified by a three-word code. Noa even had the app on her phone. Since it effectively allocated an address to places that had none, be it a bench in a park, a tent in a desert, a dinghy on an ocean, she could be rescued if her car was stranded on a rural road. Britain's emergency services were users and some major car manufacturers had the system installed in vehicles. She had learned of the app through a news article about a woman who'd used the app to give rescuers her location after getting lost near her base camp at Mount Everest.

The moment the kidnapper had said *Butterfly, Rucksack, Enable,* she had loaded the app and performed a search. The location given by the kidnapper was near Morton Lane in Eagle Barnsdale, Lincolnshire. Specifically, it was in Tunman Wood, on the site of an ancient route employed by the Knights Templar.

Woods. That didn't bode well.

But although it was a scary location, there might be nothing to find. The not knowing was killing her.

'Where are you going?' Larry asked as she grabbed her bag and headed for the door. 'You can't just leave.'

'Can and doing so. I need to get home.'

'No way. The police will be coming here in droves. You'll have to give a statement or something. Hey, Noa, just stop.'

Alerted by Larry's raised voice, Gillette looked up, and started towards the office door. It was the last thing she saw before she fled the studio.

———

Noa's 4–12 bodyguard had hung around to chat to his replacement, so both men watched in shock as Noa ran out of the building. She gave a thumbs up and jogged to her car. If Gillette had burst out in pursuit, things could have gotten awkward. Luckily the detective had neglected to chase her and she was able to drive away without incident.

She called Bokayo and was surprised to hear seven rings before he picked up. He answered with a sleepy voice.

'Were you asleep?' she said. 'Weren't you listening to the show?'

'No. I'm at work early tomorrow. What happened?'

She ran through it. His response was, 'Middle of the woods isn't a good sign.'

'No. I need to know what they find.'

He suddenly sounded wide awake. 'Now I get why you called. That's a Lincolnshire Police thing. Not my business.'

'You're all part of the same gang. The kidnapper could be from London. Make some calls.'

'No can do, Noa. I'd have to start asking questions and that could raise suspicions about me and you.'

'Don't be silly. Nobody is going to make that connection.'

'It's too early anyway. Isobel Waring has been missing for a year and a half. If this guy is giving us a body, it's probably buried. Crime scenes have to be preserved. The ground will be checked before any digging starts. Lights and equipment have to be brought in. Cigarettes will have to be smoked. Gossip needs to be shared. Nothing's going to happen quickly. You'll just have to wait for the news tomorrow.'

She hung up, annoyed. But he was right. However, the caller had just told a radio station the location of a missing woman. Thousands had heard, and that would include reporters who didn't have the patience of the police. It would include the morbid sort to throw on a coat and grab a torch. For all she knew, right now a bunch of Eagle Barnsdale residents were boot-stomping their way to Tunman Wood with shovels.

She made another call. This time it was answered quickly. 'My girl Noa Vickerman,' the man said. 'Changed your mind about dinner, have we?'

'You heard my show tonight, right?'

'Always. I hear an engine. You wouldn't be driving up to *Tunman Wood*, would you?'

He had a check-me-out tone, as if she should be in awe that he'd worked out the location given by the kidnapper. 'Don't be silly. Nothing is going to happen quickly. Crime scenes have to be preserved. Lights and equipment have to be brought in. Surprised you're not heading up there right now.'

'Maybe I am. Missing this would be bad. But you're worried, aren't you?'

'Why would I be?'

'Sure you are. That's why you've called me.'

Connor was a reporter who'd written a story about her show last month, in which he'd accused her of playing judge and jury. He had theorised that criminals wracked by guilt and who might have gone to the police had instead found peace by confessing on her show. He had hounded her for a response, but she'd avoided his calls. As she'd expected, he now believed she'd called him for help with damage control.

He was wrong. 'I want to know what the police find. What locals rushing to the woods right now find. You reporters are the Toclafane. You are the children in *The Midwich Cuckoos*. There's a hive mind and you'll soon know what the hacks up there know.'

Connor laughed. 'Actually, we like modern tech like text and email. So, you need my help. And what do I get in return?'

'The interview you so crave. Over dinner you so desire. So call me when you know something. But it better be before I read a single word about this from any other source.'

She hung up and slowed her car, now past the urge to drive all the way through the night to Lincolnshire. She had to avoid worrying about a dead body, a women chained to a tree, a note saying *Fuck You*, or anything else that the kidnapper might have left for the police in Tunman Wood. Supposition would achieve nothing. Only time would tell the tale.

———

By the time she got home, calls and messages had started to blitz her phone. Some were from numbers in her phonebook, some not. Friend or stranger, she ignored them all. An hour after the kidnapper's call, she checked various news outlets, but found little concerning events at Tunman Wood. Social media had posts from Eagle Barnsdale locals about police activity, and some users mentioned Noa's confession show, but nobody knew much yet. Nobody really cared about some bizarre claim by a faceless weirdo on some small radio show. Some had even posted the answer to the question she'd asked the kidnapper: Sudan was the country with the most pyramids. Noa kept looking until around 3am, at which point she fell asleep.

Her phone buzzed her awake. It was just after 5am. It was Connor, the reporter. She answered by demanding to know why he hadn't called her.

'Because there's nothing.'

He told her that Morton Lane was the only road leading to Tunman Woods, so the police had easily blocked access. A colleague had arrived at the cordon to find eight locals standing around. A chat with them informed the colleague that police were admitting nothing, even though word had quickly spread around the village after a resident had heard the show and called friends.

One of the locals at the cordon had suggested they could see better from his house, and he'd allowed Connor's colleague to join them. Sure enough, using binoculars from his bedroom window, the reporter had been able to view a portion of the woods containing police officers. Unfortunately, a hedge at the end of the field beside the woods had blocked his view, and he'd snapped long-range photos of little more than heads. He had, however, taken pictures of a large drone flying overhead, possibly to read the terrain with thermal imaging.

A number of other locals and reporters had tried to get close by coming through the woods, but police had posted men here and there to bar such tactics. A local publican attempted to fly his own drone close enough to capture pictures, but the much larger police device literally rammed it out of the sky. These security measures only fuelled the theory that something major was going on. This was heightened when the Morton Lane cordon was shifted to permit a car driven by a bearded man in jeans and a jacket, who some speculated was too old for a detective and might just be a pathologist.

'I guess we just wait,' Connor said, echoing Bokayo's sentiments. 'Did the kidnapper say anything off-air?'

Good Lord, was everyone going to doubt her? 'No.'

Connor grunted. 'You're hiding something. I thought we had a deal.'

'Interview and dinner, that was the deal. If you deliver. So keep that Borg mind open and keep me informed.'

'How about this? I sit by your side in the studio tonight? It would be great to be there when the guy calls back, maybe ask him—'

'No. Just call me back later.'

She hung up. It was still early and the story might – in fact, would – acquire some horsepower as the day progressed. In just a few hours, she would learn if she had helped save a kidnapped woman. Or given the police her murdered corpse.

CHAPTER EIGHT

18 NOVEMBER 2020

Halfway between her room and the bathroom is a corridor down which the black chevrons turn. She's never been down there, but has always wondered what lies at the end.

'Follow the black chevrons,' he says.

She's wary, but makes the turn, walking slowly. She wants to tilt her head back so she can see the way ahead, still unconvinced that there isn't a bad ending on the horizon. A short way down, her breath catches as she sees something on the floor through the chink in her blindfold.

The floor is smooth enough to reflect the ceiling strip lights, but suddenly there's green amongst the white. She stares in disbelief at an oblong shape with an upside-down four-letter word. A sign reflected from above the door ahead. An exit sign. Can it be real?

He orders her to stop, then walks past her. All the other doors she's seen have handles only on the outside, but no keyholes. This one does, clearly, because she hears him slotting a key home. The door creaks open. Through the chink in her blindfold, she sees stone steps leading down, into darkness. The side walls are no further apart than the door-frame.

Down? Is this a cellar after all? If so, is it her new home?

'Where do these steps go? I don't like this. Can't you just let me go now and I can find my own way out?'

'I have to take you somewhere.'

'Home? You could let me go here. Just let me walk.'

'No. I can't just let you–'

'I knew it.' She moans. 'You're going to kill me.'

'I'm not. I have to take you somewhere far away.'

'No, no, you're lying.'

He orders her to be quiet. Even though there is venom in his voice, he does not raise it. She falls silent. Now she knows she's messed up. She has enraged him, for the first time ever, at precisely the worst time to do so. Now he will change his mind, return her to her cell, and never again let her out of it.

His voice softens again. 'I can't let you go here. Don't you understand why?'

'No. Look, please.'

'This is a large building. There aren't that many around here. It wouldn't take the police an eternity to search them all within a certain radius. I also can't take you home because your face is too well-known. I need to leave you somewhere remote because I need time to get away and I need to make sure you have no clue where I kept you locked up.'

'I won't tell anyone, I promise. Please.'

'Maybe you mean that now. But that's fear. Once you are home safe and the anger sets in, you will want to burn me. I can't risk that. So, I will drive a significant distance to some woods I know–'

'Woods? No! You plan to bury me.'

'I could have done that at any time. You did the challenge. You passed. Now, do you believe me?'

She shakes her head. 'I can't. You kidnapped me. I'm sorry, but I'll believe it when I'm free.'

He pauses. His hand takes her arm, but there's no attempt to force her to move. 'Go down the steps, or turn around and let's go back to your room.'

She's frozen with indecision for a few seconds, before she decides that he will get her where he wants her one way or the other. He is in control. He holds all the cards.

She starts to move, takes the first step. He helps her down the stairs, walking behind her. The air gets colder as they descend. She counts fourteen steps before her feet hit flat concrete. Just two feet beyond the last step, the walls end and the space beyond opens up. It's not just cold here but very gloomy, both of which scare the hell out of her.

She can't help it: she throws her head back, so she can see far ahead. The dim room before her is very wide, and long. She sees a concrete floor, concrete walls, and a concrete roof, and concrete pillars, and... car parking bays.

An underground car park.

She bursts into tears. It's real: he's going to free her.

CHAPTER NINE

'Isobel Waring has been found. Dead a long time.'

Every muscle in her body seemed to turn from relaxed to iron-hard.

Noa was at The Sanctuary, an exclusive health club in Kensington. Amongst the many amenities of the four-storey converted tea house were a restaurant, nightclub, games room, heated alfresco pool, and spa. Each visit cost triple figures and you didn't get that far unless you forked out three thousand pounds a year for a membership. It had a no-photos policy to encourage celebrity guests. It was in the spa that Noa relaxed beneath the smooth hands of a masseur.

As a regular, she knew just about every member by sight and was friendly with all the staff. If anyone attending this morning knew about the current interest in her show, they'd kept it to themselves. Relaxation was impossible given what had happened last night – and what may come – but at least here she was away from prying eyes. It had become too much to keep checking the news for trickles of information, so her plan was to forget the rest of the world for a few hours; hopefully, when she emerged, there would be a mass of new information for her.

But she had been unwilling to leave her phone off and shut the whole world out. When she'd turned it back on just moments earlier, a blizzard of messages and missed calls had popped up. This one was Bokayo's sixth attempt to reach her.

'Noa? You there?'

Still reeling from his announcement, she sat up. Savvy enough to know he was suddenly intruding, the masseur exited the room. Naked except for a bikini, Noa walked to the window to stare out at the plush garden. God. Isobel. Dead.

'Noa! You hear me?' Bokayo said.

She snapped back to the moment. 'I'm here. What do the police know so far?'

'Where are you?'

'What do the police know?'

'They're keeping it quiet for now, so you absolutely have to, too. You didn't get this info from me.'

'I don't need reminding.'

'So where are you? Why has your phone been off?'

'Dead battery,' she lied. 'Just tell me what happened, please.'

He told her that a cadaver dog had led police to the very square designated as *Butterfly, Rucksack, Enable*, where the hound earned another treat. Bokayo had said a body would have to be well buried to remain undetected for a year and a half, but that wasn't the case in a section of the woods that rarely saw human traffic. The female skeleton found by police hadn't been submerged at all, although thorny foliage had kept walkers at an ignorant distance.

'How do they know it's Isobel?' Noa asked.

'They don't, yet. But the hip bone had a clear fracture that tallies with an injury Isobel Waring got in a car crash a few months before she vanished. There's also a missing molar that matches Isobel. This is good enough that her family has been informed, and they've already gone to a hotel to avoid the media once the story breaks. But no formal announcement will come till the DNA is back. Fast-tracked, but still could be a day or so. So, where are you?'

He was quite determined, and she had a sense why. 'I'd rather not say just yet. So they'll have to wait.'

'Who?'

'Don't mess about. You lot. And Leicestershire Police, they'll want a chat with me. It's where Isobel lived. Vanished from. And was found again. Have they got control of the investigation?'

'Yep. They're down here now.'

She'd feared this. While her relationship with the Metropolitan Police was apathetic, it was a world of familiar scenery and known personalities. She didn't like the idea of dealing with new faces. 'There was no call from the kidnapper after we went off-air. Thousands of people heard exactly what I heard. They won't get any information from me that they couldn't get from any of my listeners. Or from Tomas Gillette, the detective who sat staring over my shoulder.'

'I believe you. But it doesn't work like that. You have to talk to them.'

'I will, of course I will. But in my own time. I'm not a suspect. I didn't harm Isobel and I certainly didn't incite the guy to kill, as her status as a skeleton proves. Without me and my show, they wouldn't even have a body.'

'Understood, but—'

'And not up in Leicestershire either. Tell them that. I want to talk to them in a police station down here.'

'Calm down. Already the plan. Now where are you?'

'Just wine and dine them, show them London, and I'll be around later. I need time to decompress. Is my show going ahead tonight or will the police shut it down?'

'We need to discuss this, and that's part of the reason why everyone needs you, now. I'll bring you in. I'll pretend I bumped into you in the street.'

We? He was involved? 'No, I'll go to a police station later. Soon.'

She hung up, turned off her phone, and pressed a button that rang a buzzer somewhere to summon the masseur. She might as well get as much relaxation as possible before the word left her vocabulary forever.

———

She left the health club at 3pm and turned her phone on. More missed calls and texts came through, some from numbers she'd saved under derogatory nicknames – all reporters. She checked to see how big the story of Isobel Waring's unfortunate reappearance was. Many online newspapers carried it, but none of the nationals had it as a front-page scoop. It was trending on the *London Evening Standard* website, but at position four. Otherwise, London itself had more interest in other stories. Best of all, in the handful of articles Noa skimmed through, her name, although mentioned often, was buried deep in the text.

To carry out her promise to Bokayo, she chose Thamesmead Police Station because it was far east from her home, which somehow seemed safer. She parked in the nearby Morrisons car park and her shadow pulled in nearby. He was her 8–4 guy and due to clock off soon, so she approached his car.

'I could be a while,' she said when he buzzed his window down. 'You can get off early. Tell your replacement to watch my house instead. I'll be quite safe in a building full of police. Take this. Get your boy a birthday present from me.'

The guy's eight-year-old son had dyslexia and was being bullied at school. Noa had met him once when her bodyguard had had to bring him to work on a non-school day when his mother was in hospital.

'For real? I mean, wow, thanks,' he said, and took the money she held out. It was £200.

Sometimes those who accused her of selfish reasons for charitable giving weren't entirely wrong. In dour moods, Noa often found comfort from parting with cash.

She entered the police station, where two uniformed officers behind the reception area were laughing and chatting. Neither seemed to recognise her face as she walked up to the glass.

'I'm Noa Vickerman. There might be a BOLO or an APB or whatever out for me. About Isobel Waring.'

The officers looked at each other in confusion. The seated one ran her name into the computer, but nothing came back. Noa waited while he vanished to find out more. Soon after, he returned with a detective who escorted her to one of the family rooms, where grieving relatives or witnesses were interviewed. That was a good sign.

Here she was left to wait alone until 4.26, some forty minutes later, at which point someone offered a hot drink that she accepted. At 4.52, the door opened again and two serious-looking suited women in their forties entered.

They were Leicestershire Police officers, pulled in from wherever in London they'd been waiting. Noa had come here ready for an argument, but the two women smiled and thanked her for her time and asked if she didn't mind answering a few questions. They didn't seem in the slightest put out at being delayed by Noa's time at the health club. She'd expected to be treated as little less than a suspect, but so far so good.

———

When Noa pulled up outside the radio station at 11pm, she noticed Bokayo lurking in the shadows. She got out as he approached.

'What are you doing here?'

'I'm on the case,' he said with a smile. 'I have spare time. Leicestershire Police set up a task force and they need people this end. Did you hear that they confirmed the DNA? The body was Isobel Waring's.'

'I heard. The news is going wild now. Anyway, why you? I thought you were running a couple of these Detective Career Pathway courses?'

'Yes, but that doesn't take up all my time. As for why, well, you have a history with the police and nobody thinks you'll play ball unless you see a friendly face.'

'Yours?' She was shocked. 'They don't know we're sleeping together, do they?'

'Of course not. They'd let me nowhere near this case. But they do know we know each other. We did get spotted at the supermarket that time. Anyway, someone remembered that and it was deemed I could be the perfect interface between you and Leicestershire Police. Better for all parties, right?'

She wasn't sure about that but affirmed anyway. 'So what's happening inside?'

'The two Leicestershire detectives you spoke to earlier are already in the studio. There's a negotiator – properly trained this time, unlike that other guy. We have a university lecturer specialising in sociolinguistics, who will try to work out where the suspect is from.'

'I like radio because I don't want a big audience looking at me. Anyone else? Maybe the Anti Kidnap and Extortion Unit just to round things out?'

'Yes, a lady from the National Crime Agency is here too. But she's effectively on standby since we don't yet know the suspect has a captive. There's a bunch of others working behind the scenes, so you see only a handful of faces. But relax. Nobody is going to take over the call.'

Something about that term – *the call*, instead of *the show* – seemed off. She had a suspicion why. 'And the show will go down as normal?'

He paused for a second, and that was all she needed. 'We're not going live, are we?' she said.

He shook his head. 'Before you object, this isn't my call. But I agree with it. Now that the Isobel story has spread, the confessions show is likely to get a boatload of fools calling up, claiming all sorts. If some guy reckons he's planted bombs at Buckingham Palace, we'd have to make a visible show of checking out that threat. I mean, what if he did it, thousands heard it, and we did nothing?'

'Don't try to trick me, Bokayo. This is about him, not the others. You don't want him giving out ransom demands live on-air.'

'Okay, that's part of it. I imagine most people know we don't give kidnappers and terrorists helicopters and bags of cash. Doesn't mean there won't be an outcry if he asks for that live on-air and we have to say no, or we stall and he kills someone else. Look, I'm giving you a heads-up here. This will all be explained properly upstairs, okay? I'm just lessening the surprise.'

'What if the suspect doesn't call because he sees the show is cancelled?'

'It's not cancelled. Look, let's get inside before we discuss this further. We've got less than an hour to get prepared.'

They started walking towards the building. Noa said, 'All this furore will be for nothing. The kidnapper called a live show for a reason. He'll either not call, or call very pissed off.'

'We'll see what we'll see, young miss.'

'And we'll live to regret it.'

———

When the *Late Love* programme wound down at a minute to midnight, its married hosts announced that the *Confessions* show was suffering technical difficulties; instead of a live airing, an older broadcast would be repeated. Although prepared and forewarned about the police activity in their tiny studio, Zoe and Dale Jones were clearly nervous.

Dale ended *Late Love* with, 'Your confession host, Noa, will still take calls and listen and advise. So please do call in if you planned to. Please call.'

Added to his shaky voice, this request sounded more like a plea. He and his wife always liked to get home right after their show, but tonight their exit from the building was little short of a panicked rush.

As midnight hit, everything was hushed. It was a strange experience for Noa, sitting at the mixing desk in silence, staring at eight phone lines blinking. Behind her, the two Leicestershire detectives and the negotiator were answering calls, seeking the kidnapper's voice. Larry, the station producer, had been allowed to stay as long as he remained in his office with his mouth shut; he just watched in awe through his window.

Bokayo put a hand on Noa's shoulder. 'Stay calm.'

Easier said than done. Noa tried to clear her mind and not try to listen to those working the phones. Time seemed to stand still. When she glanced at the clock on her computer, it said 12.13. Thirteen minutes, dozens of callers brushed aside – and no word from the kidnapper. Perhaps he'd blown his load, had no further desire to taunt the police. Gotten cold feet, fearful that he'd get caught. Leaped off a high building, overwhelmed by guilt. It was still early and previously he'd made contact towards the end of the show, but Noa was convinced they'd heard the last of him. That was when one of the Leicestershire detectives waved her phone.

'I've got a DJ from *Silver Hits* on the line. He says he's got our man on the phone.'

The call was patched through and put on speaker. Bokayo asked the *Silver Hits* DJ to repeat what he'd said.

'Yeah, sure. So, a fella just called my talk show and he says there's a bunch of police down at Divine Radio and I should call you to see if you found what he's left. He says he's killed someone.'

'Okay,' Bokayo told him. 'He's a crank caller, and I want you to ignore what he said. Don't mention it to anyone. Can you put him through on this line?'

'No, he's gone. So who's he killed? What's going on?'

'I'm sending someone to you. Don't say a word about this on your show, okay? Or you'll regret it.'

After that call, Bokayo arranged for a pair of officers to visit *Silver Hits*, which was based in Manchester. The DJ obviously didn't know the unfolding Isobel Waring story, which might help police get to him before he spread the word about the call he'd received. While Bokayo was on his mobile, arranging things, the other Leicestershire detective announced, 'Got him. Line two.'

Everyone froze. The detective had been instructed how to pass a call to Noa's headset and did so now. All eyes were on her. They were not live. There was no reason for Noa to give her standard opening line, so she said, 'It's Noa.'

'I don't do coincidences,' the caller said. Same banal tone. Same guy. *'No live show because of a technical error? That's your lame excuse? Unless the police call-tracing technology is conflicting with your disk jockey set-up. At least you're taking me seriously, which suggests you found what I left for you.'*

'Yes, the police found Isobel's body,' she said. She'd been

instructed to never use the word *we*, so as to not appear aligned with police. She'd also been told to try to *softly* elicit details about the crime that only the killer would know. To aid this, the cause of death hadn't been made public, although Bokayo had told Noa. 'But I don't know much about it because the police are saying little, as you might know from the news.'

She stopped. Suddenly the idea of leading this man slowly towards giving up a vital piece of proof that he killed her seemed silly. She had the feeling he'd be very co-operative. 'They haven't announced the cause of death. Because they want the killer to, to prove he's legit. So why don't you tell me how she died.'

Out of the corner of her eye, she saw that her blunt question didn't sit well with those in the room. But nobody said anything.

'*I gave up the body. Not proof?*'

'Not really. You could be an ordained priest. Maybe one day someone sat in your confessional box and told a shocking story.'

'*And the Sacramental Seal?*'

'No sinner is being betrayed if you claim the crime as your own.'

The caller laughed. '*Ah, but if I sat before a penitent killer, then my giving you the cause of death proves nothing, either. You want the cause of death as corroboration, but I could have been told that she was murdered with a hammer and that one of the blows smashed her left eye.*'

A murmur coursed around the room: the forensic pathologist had indeed determined Isobel's cause of death to be blunt force trauma to the skull, with the damage almost entirely concentrated on the left side.

'*No more testing me,*' the caller said. '*I killed Isobel and I disposed of her body. You know I'm serious now, which makes this the perfect time to mention what I have. Another woman.*'

Muted concern ran around the room. Noa didn't need a prompt to ask: 'Who is she?'

'*If still you think me mad, you will think so no longer when I describe the wise precautions I took for the concealment of the body. The night waned, and I worked hastily, but in silence. First of all I dismembered the corpse. I cut off the head and the arms and the legs.*'

All present knew that no such disassembly of the body had occurred; but if his words caused puzzlement, Noa's next question evoked downright bewilderment: 'Is she okay?'

'*All I will say is that this Polly is a cat, a real samurai. If she can stop eating all my pizza, I may even put her on the phone. I'll also tell you how you can get her back.*'

'Alive this time?'

'*Alive this time.*'

'Okay. What is it you want?'

'*I hate to be so stereotypical, but...*'

'Money? You want money for her release?'

'*And not a shallow amount. I'll be in touch tomorrow. I'm not sure which radio station chat show I'll call. Only that it will be one that's live at midnight. Which Polly won't be, if I continue to face obstacles.*'

He hung up. Noa looked around the room and saw long faces that asked the same question bouncing around her head: could the caller really have another captive girl?

CHAPTER TEN

28 OCTOBER 2020

Within seconds of waking, she calls her dog's name. Usually, the black-and-white Border collie will respond with a bark and leap onto her bed. He's got one white and one black ear and loves to have the white one tickled. When he fails to leap onto her chest, she knows something's amiss, and that's when the memories hit. The night before. The man. The stench of the cloth he put over her face.

She sits bolt upright, but it takes a moment for her to realise she's not at home. Someone else's bedroom. The man's. But it's obvious, even to her groggy brain, that this isn't a standard bedroom. This is for her. A cell. A big iron door is proof of that. She's been abducted like some nerdy teenager. The outrage of it sends her to the door, to pound and yell.

And then to the trio of windows, which she finds are sturdy, fixed, the glass is actually thick plastic. The outside is smothered by what appears to be a large vinyl sticker of a mountain range, as if the madman who snatched her wants her to think she's being held out in the Andes or something.

She stands in the centre of the room, chest heaving with anger. 'Where are you, you sick wanker?' she yells. Her hands are starting to shake, and she doesn't believe that's a symptom of whatever drug he coated his cloth in. It will be adrenaline, which she knows is fuelling her frustration. Once the adrenaline rush is over, panic might just set in. Panic won't help her. She needs to get out of here while she's worked up and has the strength.

She yells for him again, but there's no answer. She wants a weapon in case he comes, and to try to break the windows with. There's a mask ornament on a shelf, which might be heavy enough. A treadmill that might give up a sharp component. The metal bedframe could be dismantled to –

She spots a suitcase under her bed. The item is canvas but has a pair of solid plastic coasters, which might just break the window. She drops before it, hauls it out, then decides to open it: it's a suitcase, after all. Inside, a surprise: her clothing and handbag.

Seeing the clothing, she looks down at herself, and for the first time notices she's wearing a grey T-shirt and grey knickers that don't belong to her. It fires another memory.

A man, or at least his hands. Hands dragging this very T-shirt onto her torso. She remembers refusing to resist because at that point she'd been naked. He'd said something to her, something about *Amur leopards*, although the context is beyond her. Fingers... she remembers him sliding fingers inside her... And liking what he found.

She bites down on another surge of anger, because she needs to stay calm and work on her escape. She looks inside the handbag, because it's where she keeps a collection of sterile syringes to hand to any druggies she spots on her travels. Everything is present except those syringes. And her phone, that's gone too.

But at least she's got her clothing, so that when she leaves here, it isn't in the nasty underwear her attacker put her in. She pulls out the trousers first and is about to strip off the grey knickers when she hears a voice.

'You can't dress. You shouldn't touch the suitcase. Put the clothing away. You wear what I say.'

It came from above, beyond the mirrored ceiling. Immediately, she spots a hole: a circular hatch has opened. The madman must be up there, on the floor above. She grabs one of her shoes and approaches the hatch.

'Who the hell are you, you bastard?' The hatch displays another room above, but all she can see is the white ceiling. She pulls her arm back, ready to throw the shoe when a face appears. It would be sweet to clock him so hard that he falls unconscious into the room with her.

But no face appears. 'Let me see you, wanker. Show yourself.'

'If you read a book, do not replace it. Put it on top of the bookcase.'

'Hey. Show yourself, I said.'

A face does appear. It's wearing a strange mask depicting a gaunt face. Just like the shelf ornament. It could have been a baby's face for all she cares; she launches the shoe.

But there's too much boiling rage behind the throw and the shoe hits the side of the hatch and bounces away.

'Where's my dog? If you've hurt him, I'll damn kill you.'

'He's safe. As long as you behave. Now go sit down so we can talk.'

As long as you behave. The outrage of this lunatic. She goes to the bed, but not to sit. She grabs the other shoe. There's no face in the hatch when she returns, but she launches the footwear anyway. It sails through the hatch and arcs out of sight, landing somewhere in the upstairs room.

'You don't know who you're messing with, arsehole,' she shouts.

'I know everything about you,' he says. 'I knew you would try to cause a problem. Sit on the bed and I will explain how you can leave this room alive. And get your dog back in one piece.'

'I'll show you how, you bastard.'

She returns to the solid door and punches it, hard, while screaming for help. There are five blows before the pain is too much, but she isn't sure which one caused the laceration that spread blood. She turns her focus to the hinges, but that's a far more futile effort.

She grabs the mask ornament off the shelf, meaning to try to put it through a window. But as she stands before the mountain view, she pauses, and momentum is lost.

It's enough to change things. Her breathing slows. She suddenly feels tired. She looks around the room again. The bed, the chair, the iron door, the solid windows: he has put in effort to create this cell, and she's not going to just break out of it. He could have weapons, or more drugs, and there's history of his ability to subdue her. And he's got her dog. She could even literally be out in the mountains.

Calmer, she knows she can't fight him. That means she needs to play ball, to buy time.

She returns to the shelf to replace the mask ornament, although she lays it flat because she doesn't want to be reminded of that face of his. Then she walks to the bed and sits.

'Good,' he says. 'You should wash that blood from your hand.'

At the sink, she notices he's supplied a plethora of cosmetics, vitamins, hairbrush, shampoo, all sorts. Oh, now it's clear why she's here. The sad little bastard thinks he's found himself a nice little living doll he can play with and dress up and fuck.

The outrage of it.

———

'Dress for feasting?' she says. 'Who are you, Henry the Eighth? You just told me not to put my clothing on. Make your mind up.'

Playing ball doesn't include kowtowing to this lunatic. She will keep him forever aware that she's under his control, but only just. Will that inflame him to the point of murder? It's probably his ultimate intention anyway, so annoying the sod might just avoid prolonged torture.

She watches in shock as the man lowers something through the hatch. Shock soon gives way to frustration, especially when he subsequently lobs down a small box. She picks it up.

'You're joking! You think I'm going to dye my hair purple and wear this purple dress? And purple lipstick? For you?'

'You will or you will suffer.'

'That's suffering enough. What's your plan here, a romantic meal? I knew you were insane, but this is another level of wackiness.'

'You will do everything I want. You will dress and dye your hair for meals, or you've already had your last bite to eat. After breakfast, you'll be interviewed on camera with some prepared questions. And in the coming days, you will be set challenges. You will perform your duty, or you will die in this room.'

There's a bang. He might have thrown something. It's the first time he's shown a loss of self-control. It reminds her that he's capable of violence, and she tones it down.

'I'll wear the dress. I don't want to dye my hair or use purple lipstick. You might have noticed my black skin. If you're trying to make me look good, all this purple falls flat. I'll look stupid.'

'Not to me. Don't you like dresses? It might be the last you ever get to wear.'

There's a slightly aristocratic mien to his speech that seems forced, but she's got him so pissed off at times that it's slipped here and there. His veiled threats are another sign that she's overdoing the bad attitude. She reminds herself again: not so heavy, girl.

She picks up the box of hair dye and moves to the sink. 'Where am I eating? Here? Have you got a garden?'

It's worth a punt, but he shuts it down, as expected: 'You eat indoors.'

At least he didn't say we. She doesn't want him sitting with her to eat, although it probably wouldn't be as awkward as her first blind date a couple of years back. This fool certainly has a purple fetish, and maybe he gets off on seeing women eat too. She will allow him that and try not to think about what she'll do if he tries to take his interest in her beyond just watching.

'So where do I eat?'

———

A swimming pool? This guy's brain is more jelly than she first thought.

After being blindfolded and let out of her room, she had been ordered to follow a line of yellow chevrons – he'd left a gap between her nose and the material so she could see the floor – into a large hall boasting an empty competition swimming pool. Once inside the pool, she had been allowed to remove her blindfold. She had to do it one-handed, because her other arm was still a little numb. When he'd entered her room, dressed in some silly pantomime outfit, he'd called her close and grabbed her forearm. The movement had been subtle, yet it had felt as if the Incredible Hulk had gripped her. When he'd let go,' she'd backed away, wracked by throbbing pain and with her forearm's muscles spasming.

'Stun gloves,' he'd said. 'Please do not try to obstruct me.'

'I wouldn't have,' she'd moaned. 'You could have just warned me.'

'I'll bear that in mind.'

Now, she looks in shock at a large dining table in the centre of the pool, with a single wooden chair at one end.

'Go sit,' the man says, standing at the edge of the pool.

She walks across the bone-dry tiles and stops behind the chair. It's attached to brackets bolted to the floor, immovable. Same for the table. There is a single paper plate on the table, a flimsy wooden spoon and fork, and a small plastic water cup. Bang goes her plan to stash a weapon: none of these items will hurt him. She can't even swing the chair.

The cup is already filled with water and there's what looks like egg salad on the plate. There's also a paper bowl with a piece of cake. My God.

She looks round at him. His strange costume and mask; this swimming pool and dining table; his claim that she will face challenges: now, she finally believes she's dealing with a complete lunatic. She's in terrible danger. There's no telling what depravity this guy plans for her. She's now certain he will kill her when he's had his fun.

But still she feels no real fear, only outrage and determination to escape. The anger can't be denied, so she will run with it. Fuck this guy and fuck her plan to pretend to be subservient. Even if it brings about her death quicker, she will pick at and annoy this animal and make him wish he'd picked someone else. He's not going to get happy deathbed memories from his time with her. And when it comes time to die, she will scratch and bite and make sure he suffers too. Her killing isn't going to become jacking-off material.

For that, she'll need energy, so she picks up the crappy fork and jabs it into the salad.

CHAPTER ELEVEN

D own the hall from the studio, past the producer's office and the kitchen, was a small bathroom with a toilet and shower. And a lock on the door. Someone tried the door, found it wouldn't budge, and knocked on it.

'I'm fine,' Noa called out. Then, because whoever was on the other side had tried the door before ascertaining if the bathroom was engaged, she added, 'I eat chia seeds by the spoonful, so I'm having a mammoth shit.'

'It's me,' Bokayo said.

'Shitting all the same. I'll be out soon. Just let me have a minute to let this all sink in.'

She took five. When she returned to the studio, Larry was the only one there. 'Kicked me out of my own office,' he moaned. Through the window, she saw the detectives and the negotiator chatting away. 'This is all a bit mad. You think this guy's for real?'

She nodded. None of the people in the office were looking out the window, so she grabbed her bag from under the mixing desk. Before Larry could protest, she said, 'Can and going to.'

'Up to you, just like last time.'

She stopped at the door. 'I need to decompress. I'm not a cop and can't help. Tell them I'll see them tomorrow if they need me.'

Larry nodded. She left. Outside, the street was empty, which she was thankful for, and surprised about. No reporters. No busybodies. And no bodyguard, since he was still watching her house in case of attack by someone upset with her handling of the whole Isobel Waring fiasco. She kept an eye out for movement in the shadows as she rushed to her car.

Someone called her name as she opened her door, but it was just Bokayo, now aware that she'd fled. By the time he reached her car, she was inside and the doors were locked. After trying one, he threw his arms wide in exasperation. 'What's the game, Noa? You're like a kid running from the dentist.'

If he was trying to be funny, it didn't work. She buzzed the driver's window down a few inches. 'I'm going home. I can't do anything to help, certainly not tonight.'

She started the engine. He rushed around to the passenger door. When she didn't open it, he said, 'We know something. Let me in.'

She unlocked the door. Once seated, he said, 'We think there's a reference to a TV programme. The man said the "cat" he has is a samurai and he mentioned giving her pizza, right? A quick Google search got us an old kids cartoon from the 1990s called the *Samurai Pizza Cats*. There's a character called Polly Esther. He called the girl Polly. Not sure what that means, but for sure he's talking about that programme. It's relevant in some way. Possibly something about the girl's appearance. This Polly from the cartoon has red hair. One girl on my list has red hair.'

'Strange words,' Noa said. It was all she could think of.

'Not the only ones. We're also intrigued by his mention of *wise precautions* and *night waned* and *worked hastily*. It's as if he was claiming to have killed this second girl, yet he also said we could get her back alive.'

'Strange indeed. Are we going live tomorrow?'

'That we need to work on. The public doesn't know he claims he's got another woman. Someone higher paid than me needs to make that decision.'

'He just called another radio station. He gave a threat that he'd do the same if we weren't live.'

'I know.'

'He said if we're not live at midnight tomorrow, neither will Polly be–'

'I know. We're working on a plan.'

'I already have one. I'm going to pay him what he asks for.'

Bokayo wasn't as shocked as she'd expected. 'Not something I can advise.'

'I know. But he wants money and he called my radio show. He must know I'm rich, and that's why he picked me. You once said you thought my charity work was to atone. Well, here we go. Saint Peter will see this and let me through the Pearly Gates.'

Bokayo took her hand. 'You've got a good heart. Your place in heaven is already guaranteed. But this is a bad idea. If you say, live on-air, that you'll pay this bastard, the floodgates will open. Every freak out there will come begging. Kidnappings will go through the roof.'

'We'll work it out somehow. But that's for another day. Now, if you don't mind, I need to go get sleep.'

'Could we get a drink at yours?'

'No, not tonight. I just need that sleep.'

She gave a thumbs up, which was a gesture they often used to say goodbye. But Bokayo made no move to leave the car. He stared at her, then said, 'I told you just one girl on my list has red hair.' She started her engine. He said, 'You never asked which girl from the list has red hair.'

'What? I'm tired and it's all speculation. You think I don't care or something? The birth of something big for my show – that's my concern, right? Okay, let's play. Who is the girl with red hair?'

'It could be Alex Byrne, who was nineteen when she went missing. She's a child genius, sort of semi-famous for YouTube videos. She's from Llanrumney in Cardiff, last seen November 5th, 2020, at work. Left about ten, but never got home. There was speculation that she might have just abandoned everything because she'd argued with her mother that day. The parents deny the possibility and I admit it seems far-fetched.'

'Whoever she is, I hope she's safe.'

'And no, I don't think you're in this for ratings.'

'But you think something's up. Say it.'

'Well, when the guy said that bit about cutting off her head and arms, you asked if she was okay.'

'Did I? I must have been confused or misheard or something.'

Bokayo looked unconvinced. 'Okay, let me outright ask you. Has this guy contacted you outside of the radio show? Like when you ran to the toilet right after he hung up.'

'The fact that you even have to ask is an insult. I'm tired and I want to go, so please get out of my car.'

'Okay. Just remember not to tell anyone about the call. We can't yet let it be known that he has another woman. If he even does.'

'I don't doubt him.'

———

Too wired to sleep, Noa returned to The Sanctuary and entered the nightclub. She turned off her phone, not wanting to be disturbed by police or reporters or anyone else.

Weirdly, the thumping music was soothing. Most of the daytime clientele was her age and above, but the rich kids ruled the night. She felt a little out of place surrounded by so many youngsters, even though it had been only a few years since she'd been the very same kind of party animal. She wondered how many of the dancing teenagers and twentysomethings had made their own money – and what percentage had, like herself, been gifted it by birth from a prosperous parent. How many of the latter had concrete career plans, as opposed to those who, again akin to her situation, felt there was an endless well that would facilitate a life of fun and games.

Because she sat alone on a sofa, a handful of men and one woman tried to come onto her, but she waved them all away. Nobody recognised her, which was good. At 4am the nightclub closed, so she entered the spa, and asked if she could sleep in one of the relaxation rooms. This wasn't permitted, but £100 in notes convinced the staff member to pretend he hadn't noticed her presence.

She tried to relax, but money was on her mind. Her father had left her a million pounds, but even though she'd cast away the flamboyant lifestyle, a vast swathe of that money had been erased over the last three years. It was why she'd taken a lodger. Only Bokayo knew that she had little more than a hundred thousand pounds in the bank. Even though she had adopted a more standard lifestyle, her charitable giving was notable and gave the impression she was mega-rich. Embarrassingly, it was an image she had done little to dampen.

And there lay the problem. If, as she suspected, the kidnapper had picked her show because he felt she would pay him, then what would happen if she couldn't? It was unlikely he'd ask for as little as £50,000, which she figured was the maximum she could dispose of without her way of life suffering. What if he asked for £500,000? A million? If she told him she couldn't afford it, no one would believe her.

There was a chance he planned to use the radio show to demand cash from the girl's family, but it didn't matter. Noa's name was intrinsically attached to this whole debacle, Noa was 'rich', and Noa would be under the spotlight. If there was one thing more damaging than denying an extortionist, it was turning down a grieving family.

Either way, the result would be the same. She would be accused of caring more about her bank balance than an innocent young woman's life.

The problem did have a possible solution. It lay in the hands of a man called Maximus Jones, who had come into her life after her dad's death. If she needed him, she would call. The 'if' part was where her hopes lay, for there was always the chance that the bastard would get caught.

She called Bokayo for an update – had his people had any luck tracing the kidnapper's phone?

'No. That takes time. We've got the phone number, but now we have to contact the service provider and – you need me to explain about cell site analysis?'

'No, I know how it works. It's a priority job, right?'

'Sure. There's a dead girl. Listen, you been following the news?'

She hadn't. She told him her phone had been off until she made this call.

'Well, not going live with the show last night has started tongues wagging. People know the kidnapper was going to call the radio station and they think he did just that, but we kept it off-air.'

'Ah, so, just like the police, the public now thinks I'm having secret phone calls with a murderer? Beautiful. Are effigies of me burning in the streets? Maybe I'll get my own annual ceremony like Guy Fawkes or Ravana. Does this mean we're going live tonight?'

As was often the case, a pause could say as much as words themselves.

'Bokayo, don't tell me we're about to make the same mistake again. You heard his threat. If he kills another girl, that's not going to be on me.'

'Hey, calm down. It wasn't my decision. It got shunted all the way to the top of the pile. But it got made, and not easily. We're damned either way. Now listen, the plan is–'

'Remember that he called another radio station? He could do that again. You can't stop the public finding out.'

'Stop interrupting and listen. Yes, we can't prevent this nobhead from calling someone else. And we remember his threat, okay? So we're going live. But not from your studio. We're going to get a remote set-up arranged at Hammersmith Police Station. We need the extra space, given that the National Crime Agency has now sent down extra kidnap officers.'

She groaned.

'We have to do it this way, Noa. The story is getting big. My money is on a media siege at your building tonight, so we absolutely cannot broadcast from there.'

A fair point, and she admitted so.

'We think we have a way to cover our asses about the lack of a show last night. I'll explain more when I see you.'

'Okay. And look, I'm sorry for snapping at you. Stress.'

'Gotcha. We're all feeling it. Get some sleep and I'll call you when it's proper morning.'

Sleep? She wished she was already asleep, dreaming this whole thing.

———

After wasting more hours at the health club, Noa eventually decided to brave the world around 1pm. She was surprised to see a familiar vehicle in the car park and approached it.

Her 12–8 bodyguard opened his window and said, 'I'm sorry, Ms Vickerman, but I take my job seriously. I watch you, not your house.'

'How did you know where I was?'

'Tried all the usual spots, saw your car. A couple of reporters approached the house last night, I was told. If you're going home, you want me to drive ahead and make sure the coast is clear?'

'No, it's fine. I can't dodge these people forever. Do you know why reporters are interested in me?'

'I heard. I'm not going to ask you about it. If you want to talk to them in your home, don't forget your panic button.'

She showed him she still had the tiny device, which would ping his phone if activated and bring him thundering to her. 'I'm going home now, but first I just want to do a little experiment. It might look strange.'

She walked from the car park, then a short way down the street, to a junction. Across the road was a row of shops. It was a sunny day and the crowds were out. No effigies with her face were being burned in the streets; in fact, as she stood on the pavement, nobody gave her a second glance. Eyes were on partners or kids or shop windows or the ground.

She relaxed. The story of a kidnapper probably wasn't the biggest item in the news, and even if it had been, not everyone cared about what was going on beyond the aura of their lives.

Her 12–8 was waiting a short way back up the road, watching. As she headed back to her car, she called him over.

'Take three or four hours off. I'll be at home. Go shopping or something. I have some friends coming over, so I'll be okay.'

As someone who stayed close to her every day, seven days a week, he probably knew that she rarely saw friends. Her social circle had dwindled since she changed her partying ways following her father's death. But it was not his job to object, and she was the one paying his wage. He told her to text him if she planned to leave the house, and then they parted ways.

At a supermarket till, as Noa was purchasing pasta salad, the woman in front of her looked back, twice. Noa realised she'd been recognised. Then the lady suddenly seemed to have trouble finding her bank card. The checkout girl got impatient, but hid it well.

'I'm sorry,' the shopper told the girl. 'I haven't got my card. To be honest, I don't think I could afford it anyway. My husband lost his job.'

'So you don't want all this?' the checkout girl said. 'That's pretty awkward because we'd have to move it all.'

'Oh, I do, I need it. The kids have barely eaten. It's just I can't pay for it.'

Figuring she might be here a while, Noa pulled out her phone. She became aware of eyes staring and looked up. The shopper said to her, 'Any chance you can help?'

Ah. That explained the performance about a lost card and a jobless husband. 'I'm sorry,' Noa said.

The woman's face turned into a sneer. 'You did before.'

Now Noa recognised her. A few months ago, a woman had genuinely lost her purse and Noa had scanned her own debit card to pay for the lady's groceries. This lady.

'Not today,' Noa said. 'Sorry.'

The shopper addressed the entire queue. 'Millionaire alert, people! This woman's loaded, but she's too good for us, the scum who have to work for a living. Won't even pay forty pounds for my kids to eat. What do we think of that?'

'That's pretty stingy,' someone behind Noa said. Noa didn't look round.

'She doesn't have to pay,' someone else said. 'Besides, can't just pay for everyone. Be here all day.'

A third said, 'Now I know her. She's that confession-show woman. Likes to help criminals, but not us normal people.'

More voices. Noa didn't hang around to find out which way the crowd would swing. She opened her purse and threw all her remaining cash, at least £300, onto the conveyor belt. As it was snatched by various hands, she pushed by shoppers and fled the store.

———

Sitting on the pavement outside her house was a black male about her own age. He had to move so she could drive into her garage, but he did so while staring right at her. Still in the car, she pressed a button to shut the garage door. She couldn't see the man, and when the roller door was half-closed, she relaxed and got out of the car. The door continued to close.

That was when the man rolled through the gap, which was barely big enough to admit him. He quickly jumped to his feet. Noa froze. Why had she dismissed her bodyguard? He was too far away to help if she activated the alarm. The nearest weapon was a steering lock in her car boot.

'I'm sorry, don't panic, I'm not a danger,' the man said, arms up as if she held a gun on him. He sounded Scottish. 'And I'm not a reporter, although a bunch of them have been around.'

She adopted a boxer's stance. Judo was her main martial art, but she'd been taught that a solid jab to the nose could end a fight far quicker. There was no need. Seeing her reaction to him, the man sat down, cross-legged, right there on the floor. He slid his phone towards her feet. 'Call the police if you don't trust me. I just want to talk. I'm not a psycho. I'm Jerome Lytton. Katrina Lytton's twin.'

Noa dropped her hands. She recognised the name. Katrina Lytton had been on Bokayo's list of possible kidnap victims.

CHAPTER TWELVE

28 OCTOBER 2020

'You should sleep,' he says.

Katrina is in the corner furthest from the door, but it's mostly the ceiling hatch she's avoiding. It's closed, but she knows he lurks above it and she suspects it's a one-way mirror. She sits with her knees up to her chest. 'No thank you,' she says with sarcasm.

'Your head is lolling. You're exhausted. It's late. There's a comfy bed right there.'

'No.'

'I can turn off the light, if it helps. Just this one night, to help.'

'So you can sneak in in the dark? Try to rape me?'

'I could do that anytime, if it was the plan. I could have done so while you were out cold.'

'Maybe you did, you damn freak. Just keep away from me. I'll sleep here. God knows what's been going on in that bed.'

He says nothing further, so he's got the message. The bed does look better than a hard floor, though –

– wait a minute. 'Hey. What do you mean, just this one night? How long do you plan to goddamn keep me here?'

'Unfortunately, we're not ready for the challenges yet. Not for... a number of weeks, I'm afraid.'

Katrina jumps to her feet. 'Piss off. You can't keep me here that long.'

'In your camera interview earlier, you said I should hurry up and kill you if I was going to. Now you want to be free as soon as possible? Against the script, by the way.'

'Of course I want out, you dick,' she spits. 'You think I want to stay here? Are you that insane? Death is better than being held here for weeks and weeks. You wanted to know about my thoughts and feelings, so there you go. And you're going to hear a lot more crap like that from me. What did you expect? That I'd like the dress and the food and the books? That I could make this a home? Maybe we'd get married? Lunatic!'

'I hoped we'd soon have a case of the Stockholm syndrome. That I'd open the door for you one day and you wouldn't want to leave.'

She can't tell if he is joking, but it doesn't matter. She is done with talking to him. Done letting him watch her. 'Turn the damn light off so I can sleep.'

The room instantly flicks from white to black. Katrina slowly, silently starts to crawl. She slides under the bed, pushing out her suitcase. That suitcase is a good sign, she reminds herself. It suggests she might be let go. One day. She won't hold her breath.

She lies on her back under the bed. Hopefully he doesn't have infra-red cameras or night-vision goggles. If he comes for her, the bed might block him enough to allow her to fight him off.

In the dark, bravado has no power, and she shivers with fear at the thought of what might happen that night, or over the coming days.

She notes the irony of her situation. She had always been

career-focussed, even before she developed sexual attraction. There had been a few boyfriends at an early age, but sex and love had been discarded by the time she left her parents' home. Consequently, she had never spent an entire night in the house of a man who wasn't related to her. Until now.

———

29 October 2020, 7.55am

Katrina is one for nightmares rather than sweet dreams, which means she enjoys the moment of waking up. That instant when she realises real life is way better than the one inside her head. There had been only a handful of times when she'd woken with disappointment. The last, some months ago, had involved a dream about quad biking on a beach with friends, only to materialise in her empty bedroom, alone.

Today is another such occasion. Last night's dream had been mediocre, involving gardening in the rain, but it's a Shangri-La compared to the truth. As her waking brain registers her purple hair, it immediately reminds her that she's locked in a room, prisoner to a madman. A tear comes to her eye. She would give the world for another chance to garden in the rain.

She's also back in the bed. Did she crawl there half-asleep? Did he manoeuvre her unconscious body?

She stares up at her reflection on the ceiling. The thought of another day stuck in this room sucks at her soul. Again, there's no fear, only resentment and worry. Her concern isn't torture or rape, but captivity. The thought of waking like this, to stare at the same ceiling and spend days in the same room, invites despair. She's got no clue where she is or how to get out of this room, but she does know one thing. She has to escape. Every second that passes is one step closer to madness.

'Dress for feasting,' he says. She glances at the hatch, having missed the sound of it opening.

She sits up. 'I need to know about my family.'

'You only have a brother that you're in regular contact with. And he's fine.'

A deep breath, to tie down the ball of rage that wants to float free. 'Can I find out for myself? A phone call?'

'Not possible.'

'Email? Text? Goddamn smoke signals?'

'I will keep you updated on anything important regarding your family. I promise. But you cannot contact anyone. Don't ask again. Please dress.'

She needs food and the swimming pool is a break from this room, so she walks to the armchair, across the back of which lies the purple halter dress.

Half an hour later, she's sitting in the sole chair at the large dining table in the swimming pool, chewing cereal with her head slightly lowered. The madman stands by the edge of the pool, watching her. He will think she's absently staring into her bowl, but her eyes are roaming, analysing.

She's got a business brain and now tries to adapt it to aiding her escape. First, she puts herself in his shoes. She now runs this prison: how could her prisoner escape? She escorts her captive during the trip from room to pool, so that won't work. She has removed the portable ladder, so her captive can't get out that way.

The pool is two metres deep; if her captive runs to the far side and jumps, they could grab the edge – but could they haul themselves up and out before she gets there? Possibly, but then what? Her captive doesn't know the outlay of the building. It could be massive, maze-like. Even with a head start, her captive will have to rely on blind luck, because a single locked door or dead end will be their downfall.

Katrina grits her teeth. Running from this madman won't work, unless he's not aware it's happening. That means somehow being outside her room without him by her side. The only way to achieve that is to win his trust.

If he believes she's a willing prisoner, he might relax his security. He might not feel the need to escort her to the bathroom. He might allow her to trek alone to the swimming pool to 'feast'. He might even permit her to roam the building unguarded. The downside of this plan is time: winning him over is likely to be calculated in weeks, not days.

But she has no other option. 'Hey,' she calls out. 'You want to pull up a chair and eat with me?'

He shakes his head. She says, 'That costume. I've never seen one like it. What is it?'

'It's from a form of Japanese theatre called Noh. My father was an actor.'

'That's cool. He's Japanese?'

'No. But he was one of very few white Noh actors who made a success in Noh theatre.'

'Was? Did he pass away?'

'Yes. Six years ago.'

'Sorry about that. But this Noh thing sounds interesting. Tell me more.'

Sucking up to him doesn't feel as bad as she expected. She's used to such a tactic in business, and this is a business plan, that's all, except the goal is freedom rather than money.

———

One of the madman's rules is that she must strip off the dress between meals, and when she does so, Katrina doesn't put her T-shirt back on. Walking around topless disgusts her, but she feels there's got to be a sexual reason for snatching a young woman, given that he's already molested her once. If such a move is coming, better that he asks rather than takes by force. So, her plan is to make him think she's game.

The downside is that flashing flesh might speed up his plans, which is bad, or even convince him to take her when he had no plans to, which is worse. But it's worth the risk if she can avoid rape.

Later that day she approaches the bookshelf and pulls out a medical thriller by Robin Cook. Is this novel here because he thinks, as a doctor, she'll be happy with it? She's got no motivation to read. She remembers his order about putting books back on top of the shelf, but little infractions won't annoy him and they'll give her a minute sense of control. So she slots the novel right back where she got it instead.

Later, while she's running on the treadmill, he drops a packed lunch through the ceiling hatch and informs her he won't be around for the rest of the day. Sure enough, she doesn't hear from him. When she feels tired, she calls for the light to be turned off, but he doesn't respond.

Is he still out? Did he go out at all? Maybe that was a lie so he can watch to see if she'll play while the cat's away. She's very tempted to see if that ceiling hatch is flimsy enough to smash open, but if he is indeed still around, all her hard work at earning trust will be wasted. She stays put.

Many hours later, she wakes at the sound of his voice, telling her to dress for feasting. He's at the hatch, as always wearing that damn mask.

'Which meal is it? The light stayed on. I don't know what time it is.'

'Breakfast,' he says. 'And I'd rather you wore your T-shirt when in this room.'

So much for flashing her boobs to earn points. Doesn't mean he's not attracted to her, so she stands really close when he lets her out of her room. While walking ahead of him along the yellow chevrons, she gives her hips a seductive sway. Seated at the dining table, under his glare, she leaves a little more thigh exposed. The meal is salad.

'So, you've mentioned your family,' she says, 'but now I want to know more about you. Wife? Kids? Career?'

She had already managed to learn that not only was his father famous in Japanese theatre, but he was also a rich businessman. When he died, his wife went back to her home country of Japan and the entirety of his estate went to his only child, the madman, who continued to live in the large family home. She had asked if this place was his home, but apparently she's being held at a disused school the madman built with some of his new wealth. (So, a school built by the son of a famous British proponent of Japanese theatre: good information for the police, if she ever gets out of here.) Why it's disused, he won't say, but from what she can see it's not in disrepair. And since he'd made efforts to turn it into a prison, clearly he has no plans to reopen it as a school.

'I don't want to talk about that,' he says. 'Please.'

Please. That's good. He's been polite before, but this sounded more like begging. He's beginning to respect her as a human, which might make all the difference in the long run. But, God, why is he defensive? Because he has a wife and kids? Did he go back to his family yesterday? Does he do the good husband/father thing when he's not here, pretending to be a normal, no-woman-prisoner-for-me kind of guy?

Her plan is to create a bond, and if he won't talk about himself, she'll take the reins. As she eats, she tells him all about her brother, her friends, her GP surgery. Once she thinks she's warmed him up enough, she asks about her dog. She really wants to see her boy, but it's also a good test. Today the dog, perhaps tomorrow some unguarded time outside her cell.

'He will be missing me. He loves me. He wouldn't hurt a fly. This is not fair on him. His name is Jasper.'

'You're right, he's very loyal. He didn't like my taking you.'

She lets loose a biting sentence before she can stop herself: 'It's not fair on him, it's young women you want to punish, not innocent animals.'

'You can't see him, I'm afraid.'

Jasper is prone to extreme boredom and will chew his back legs to relieve it, but Katrina senses a ploy here, if this bastard has seen such activity.

'He's got osteochondritis dissecans in his leg. Arthritis. Only I know how to massage it properly. He'll be in pain.'

'Arthritis? Is that what it is? I thought it was rabies. I had to put him down.'

She snaps the weak wooden fork in her hand, but keeps hold of the pieces to pretend it's undamaged. She needs to hide her wrath.

'I suppose I don't need him if I'm here with you.'

'That is good. And correct.'

She continues eating, but the anger is building as she cannot shake an image of her poor Jasper, dead. That cute, single white ear against a black head, that tail never to wag again. Never mind the police, if she gets out of here. She might just find this bastard herself and pay heavies to break his bones.

The urge to talk is gone, so she finishes her food in silence.

———

Sometimes a good cry can reset emotional stress, so Katrina uses tears to send herself to sleep that night. The task is easy when she thinks about poor Jasper, such an innocent dog. Unfortunately, her dreams are invaded by thoughts of him lying dead, and she wakes periodically through the night. On the third occasion, she vows to demand to see him. If he is dead, she wants to give him a proper burial. If the madman refuses, she'll kick up a stink unlike any he can imagine. Sod the plan to create a bond.

When she wakes in the morning, breakfast is on the table and there's a pair of packed lunches. So, he plans to be away again for a while. She's still got buzzing anger and vents it by exercising until everything hurts. A couple of hours into the day, she's calmed.

The day is long and indeterminable with no clock and unnatural light. When she gets sleepy, she trusts it's night and lies down. She's a little worried now in case something has happened to him and he never returns. The fear of starving to death in this room becomes very real.

Just as she feels herself slipping into sleep, noises above – footsteps – jolt her wide awake. She's glad, which is a feeling she despises. She calls out: 'Are you there?'

The hatch rasps open. She gets up and approaches. The ceiling light in the room above is on, so it must indeed be night-time. She can't see him.

She tells herself to stay calm. Back to the plan. She will not mention her dog. 'Where did you go?'

'I'm sorry for leaving you for so long.'

'All the days are long. Where do you go? When is the challenge? When can I get the hell out of here?' Too much venom in her tone due to sleepiness and frustration. She apologises for swearing.

'Soon. In answer to both questions: soon. A few more days.'

'Can I ask about my brother? My surgery. The rest of my family? I need to know they're all okay.'

'You know the rule about the outside world.'

'Then just talk to me. Tell me something. Just talk.'

She lies on the bed, staring up at her reflection. The light winks off, but the hatch remains open, and he starts to talk. She barely registers the content of his words, but in the dark his voice is quite soothing. It's like a lullaby. She hates that she likes it.

———

Day seven, according to her calculations. November 4th. She's read all three Robin Cook novels in the bookshelf and placed them on top, to try to please him. She's also replaced the mask ornament in a standing position.

As per The Plan, she's engaged him in hours of conversation over the days, but feels that very little progress has been made. He answers every question, even if only to tell her not to ask, but he still sounds unimpressed, as if he, too, has a plan to bond and is simply going through the motions. But he has never granted her request to sit in her room with her, or pull up a chair in the pool at feasting time.

And he hasn't let his security relax one iota. Still the blindfold. Still the escort to the bathroom. Still the locked door. There's no bond yet and maybe there never will be. She'd like to believe that was down to a clash of personalities or his madness, but logic has a theory that won't be denied. He's remaining aloof because he plans to kill her.

Seven days in and she's worn down, and she is considering a new plan – give this madman the abuse he deserves so he'll damn well kill her and end this suffering. When he takes her to breakfast, she decides she'll start her new campaign after she's eaten. But something happens that changes everything.

When she climbs the ladder down into the swimming pool and removes her blindfold, she gasps. The table is there, as always. Her chair is bolted down at one end, as usual. But now, at the other end of the long table, there's another. Another chair. For him.

He plans to sit with her to eat. Finally. The perimeter walls of his emotional defences have been breached. Now she's got access to the inner sanctum. It could still be a long road to travel, but she can see the way ahead at last. As she sits to eat, she's buoyed enough to manage her first smile in a long time.

CHAPTER THIRTEEN

'I'm sorry about your sister,' Noa told Jerome Lytton. He was still sitting on the floor of her garage. 'I heard she disappeared. But I don't know how you think I can help you. I can't. Sorry.'

Jerome got to his feet. He seemed not to have heard Noa's words. 'She's gone because of me. I was supposed to meet her. That day. I didn't. Someone else did though. Not her brother. She didn't go for dinner. Some evil monster took her and instead of dinner she got hell.'

'Follow me,' Noa said. She led him out of the garage and into the downstairs sunroom at the back of the property. It was oak-framed with a tiled floor and wicker furniture, framed photographs of fields, and peppermint plants. A place of relaxation, although she doubted the scenery would achieve much in a man grieving for his lost sister. She sat on the armchair and bid him to take the sofa that faced it across a coffee table.

'I heard about your show,' Jerome said. 'I listened to it. I know that man didn't mention Katrina. And I heard that there was a girl called Waring that was found. Her body, at least.

But there's not much news on that and the police won't answer my questions. Katrina went missing around the same time as her.'

He pulled out a photo and held it up. Noa had already researched Katrina and had seen many pictures, but it would be rude not to look, so she leaned forward and gave the photo a long stare. It showed her posing in a skirt suit in some beer garden somewhere.

'I'm sorry,' Noa said. 'I don't know anything. The woman he has, I don't think it's Katrina. I read about her disappearance.'

As his eyes snapped onto her, Noa realised her error. 'He called last night, didn't he?' Jerome said. 'Just as the papers have speculated. That's why the show was off-air. The police didn't want him saying things live. But he phoned. He phoned and he said he's kidnapped another woman. What did he tell you? I know he told you her name. Is it Katrina?'

'Look, I can't tell you anything. I don't know anything.'

He stood up. 'That's bullshit. And it's my sister. There's another girl and it might be her. Tell me.'

Noa also stood up. 'You need to leave. I'm sorry about your—'

As she spoke, she moved forward and took his elbow, to aid his exit in case he was reluctant. He was very much so. Jerome pulled his arm free and grabbed hers. 'I'm going nowhere until you tell me.'

Noa grabbed his wrist and twisted it, which tweaked his shoulder and made him bend forward. She pushed him and he stumbled into the arm of the sofa, and over. Instead of retaliating, he sat there and started to cry. Noa found it impossible to pursue ejecting him. She just waited.

'Katrina's a doctor,' he said once composed. 'She was working that day she was snatched. October 27th, 2020. She had a surgery near a park...'

Noa knew the story, which, like Isobel's, had been heavily covered at the time.

Katrina Lytton had shown remarkable skills and intelligence in becoming a general practitioner by the age of twenty-nine. This was a girl who'd displayed high business acumen by the age of thirteen, when she began earning two hundred pounds a week selling comics she single-handedly wrote, illustrated, and bound. To finance herself while studying medicine, she'd gotten a bar job at eighteen and had become a manager by twenty. By twenty-five, she had started her own business selling cosmetics door-to-door, although she had employees to do the knocking for her. Katrina had the charm, intelligence and brash to have made herself a millionaire businesswoman, all felt, but she was determined to become a doctor. And what Katrina strived for, she got, always, according to those who knew her.

She had been working at a surgery near MacDonald Park in Arbroath for three months when she went missing. On her lunch break, she'd headed out to walk her dog, which she always left in the enclosed backyard of the surgery. She had not returned for the remainder of her shift. She had been reported missing before day's end, although police hadn't shown serious worry for some twenty-four hours.

Katrina usually parked for work outside a row of lock-up garages across the road from her surgery and next to trees bordering Arbroath High School. At lunchtime she would always drive to the park with her dog. No CCTV covered the exact area and no witnesses had seen Katrina with her car during the lunch hour, so it had been impossible to determine if someone had forced her to drive away.

But drive away she, or someone, had. Police found CCTV of her car heading north on Lochlands Drive, located on the western side of the park, around the time she vanished. If she had been going home, she would have turned right at the end of

Cairnie Road, but her car had swung left. Half a mile later a petrol station camera caught her vehicle taking a left onto the B9127, which headed through open fields.

It was here they found her abandoned car. No Katrina, no dog. With no CCTV out there and myriad tracks and roads leading out of the fields, it was impossible to trace all other vehicles that she might have transferred to. There was no sign she had gone into a field on foot.

As in any major police investigation, there were suspects and suspicions and clues, all followed to dead ends.

Story told, Jerome looked at Noa. 'And I need her back. If this bastard on the phone has her–'

'We don't know he does, Jerome. We don't know if he has another kidnapped woman or not. I'm sorry for your loss. I wish I could help. I just don't know what you want from me.'

He jumped to his feet. 'Ask him. Tell him. If she's alive, you can get her back. He must want something. This isn't a guy who's calling to confess and be forgiven.'

'I agree. But I don't know what he wants. I don't know if he's got your sister or if she's even alive. I hate to say that, but it's true. The police think the girl might have red hair, and Katrina doesn't.'

'Ask him. Beg him. Can you do that?'

She paused. Jerome sat again, head in his hands. Eaten by guilt, she said, 'Jerome, listen to me. He did call. He did say he has another girl–'

'I knew it. Can you–'

'Stop. Please. The woman he said he has. It's not Katrina.'

'You don't know that. Did he give a name?'

'I don't know if he took Katrina. But I do know the woman he's talking about is not her.'

He got to his feet. Noa backed off to give him space as he walked to the door of the sunroom, where he stopped to look back. 'Ask him about rugby. If he likes rugby. Especially Australian rugby. There was a man, a neighbour...'

He stopped. He then extracted a business card – he was a plasterer – and dropped it on the floor. And left without another word.

———

Late in the afternoon, police finally shared what they knew. Isobel Waring. Had died from blows to the head with something heavy and blunt, possibly a hammer. Her killer had called a radio show to admit this, although his confession had not been aired live. There was a chance he would make contact again soon. The Waring family were still secreted away for privacy, but they were planning a press conference later that day. Neither Noa nor her confession radio show were named.

Noa learned this from the wiki news website UbyU while working out in her home gym. Police had tried to be vague, but those following the story would know that she was involved and that the killer was planning to call her show again tonight. The media would want more information, and they'd come after her for it, so she wanted to be elsewhere when her front door started getting hammered.

She quickly showered and dressed and skipped out. Her 4–12 security followed her car to a store three miles from home, where she bought a bunch of pre-paid phones. If she had any doubt that she was now hot property, it faltered when the store clerk gave her a sideways look and said, 'Did I see you on the news? Something about that skeleton found up north? You a detective?'

'I get that a lot. I look like Nancy Drew. Maybe you saw her on TV.'

Back in her car, she transferred her important phonebook

contacts to each device and topped them all up, then transferred all her important contacts to each device. She texted Bokayo from her main phone, to tell him she was on her way to Hammersmith Police Station now. It was much earlier than planned, but the whole of London might soon be a dangerous place once the story of the kidnapper spread.

First, she drove to a hire-car store for an anonymous ride. She parked her own vehicle two streets away so nobody could tie her to the place and find out what she was driving. After that, she sent her bodyguard away, in case his car got recognised and that gave her up. She told him to watch her house for the remainder of his shift and to instruct his midnight replacement to do the same.

Either someone had made a lucky guess, or a copper had talked. Whichever, word was out because she saw a handful of people milling about near the police station, and a news van parked in a roadworks zone outside Hammersmith Library. Nobody clocked that her Kia might be important until she drove to the black gates leading round the back of the police station. People with cameras and microphones ran her way, but she got through the gates before anyone could get a good look at her.

By the time she'd parked in the rear compound, Bokayo was walking across the tarmac towards her. She met him halfway. 'We're getting everything set up,' he said. 'Your mixing desk, computers, everything you need to run your show. Follow me.'

'You've had time to talk things through with the higher-ups. What's been decided?'

They started walking towards the station. Bokayo said, 'We're between a rock and a hard place. Half this country would want us flayed if we refused to give this guy live airtime and he killed again because of it.'

'And the other half would riot if you gave in to his demands and allowed him to have his fifteen minutes of fame on radio.'

'Exactly. But we can't be blamed if some freak called a radio station out of the blue.'

'I think I understand. The police released a statement saying there was a "chance" he'd call again. We're going live with the show so he can, but pretending we weren't expecting it. Like with his first call. I guess that's a safe option.'

Bokayo held the entrance doors open for her. 'Only option we had. If the kidnapper thinks we lied to the public, and he says that live, we just claim we weren't certain he'd call. Partly true anyway, right? Nobody is certain he'll call.'

'I am.'

'Me too. Hopefully he'll just be happy to be on the radio.'

He led her down a corridor and to a female toilet. Puzzled, she went inside and he followed. Half a second after she realised it actually was just a women's restroom, Bokayo turned her around and tried to kiss her. She stepped away.

'What the hell? That's why you brought me here? The worst possible timing.'

'Sorry,' he said. 'Just... stress. I don't know.'

She patted his cheek and left the restroom. He led her onwards. Soon they passed a cafeteria, where she stopped. 'We've got five hours. I'm not spending it all going through more warnings and tips about how to talk to this guy. I could do with some food. What else is there to do here?'

'You sound in a bad mood. Is it me?'

She laughed. 'We can get back on track when this is all over. For now, let me have my nerves and frustration.'

'Okay. The set-up isn't quite ready yet anyway. For now there's a yard to walk in and there's a rec room. TV and pool table. There's books. Apparently there's a top-floor window where you can see into the women's yoga class next door. But that's an evening shift thing.'

'And a dirty old man thing.'

'I should tell you that at seven – so about two hours from now – a couple of Lincolnshire detectives are coming down. I'm afraid you'll have to do another chat.'

She understood: Isobel's disappearance had been the remit of the police in Leicestershire, where she'd lived. But her body had been found in Lincolnshire. 'Which makes police from three forces now involved. These new guys, they don't trust Scotland Yard, you or the Leicestershire ladies to fill them in?'

He shrugged. 'Anyway, they're coming at seven. So what do you want to do for two hours?'

Calmer now, Noa felt bad about the way she'd treated him recently. Her head had spun constantly for days, but none of it was Bokayo's fault. Nobody was around, so she kissed his cheek. 'Great as the yoga window sounds, how about you buy me some food and we'll just try to chat about non-kidnapper things?'

Done. Once they'd eaten, Noa was taken to see the temporary studio on the top floor. It was nothing more than a simple office, with chairs, tables, filing cabinets and whiteboards, most of which had been pushed to one side and blocked off by mobile room dividers. She caught a glimpse of a pinboard with photographs of a mean-looking bastard. Clearly this was an incident room with an ongoing case whose detectives were off-duty or elsewhere for the evening. On a table, police had arranged a mixing desk/computer combo. It was the same model as her own back at Divine Radio.

At seven, the Lincolnshire detectives arrived and interviewed her. This time it was a pair of men. They were professional and polite, but clearly disappointed that she had nothing to offer beyond what they already knew.

After that informal interview, she looked out of the window, onto the rear compound, while Bokayo spoke with the detectives. During her chat with the Lincolnshire boys, she had learned something new. With three police forces and numerous officers involved, the investigation had now adopted a gold-silver-bronze command structure in order to avoid rank conflict. In short, a Gold Commander gave orders to a Silver Commander, who got his or her Bronze Commanders to do the work. An inspector might have to take orders from someone of the same pay grade, or lower.

Also, a handful of additional police personnel would be part of her audience for tonight's 'show'. More National Crime Agency staff, a frontline policing commander, and a detective chief superintendent.

This didn't sit well with her, and she was bristling when Bokayo came to her side to enjoy the window view. 'It seems this room will be packed with police later. What happened to you being my conduit so I don't face people?'

'I'm still the guy you'll deal with. But things have escalated, Noa.'

'I know. I heard about the gold, silver, bronze set-up. Shame the Klu Klux Klan already took the titles of Imperial Wizard, Grand Dragon and Nighthawk. Much catchier.'

Bokayo wasn't amused. 'This investigation is now what we call a critical incident, primarily because it's ongoing and is a public threat.'

'Marvellous. Now a whole roomful will watch me get this girl killed.'

'*Confessions* might be the Noa Vickerman show. This murder investigation isn't.'

Loughborough Town Hall's main hall could sit 500, and there was barely a seat free. The press had the back two rows, while friends and family occupied the remaining seats. The reporters had been asked to make sure images of the filled hall made their publications. The family wanted the country to feel that Isobel was sorely missed. Cameras captured many tear-stained faces.

Some emotional outpourings were overdone, since Isobel's friends and family had had a year and a half to accept that she was gone. The four people behind a table on the stage emit real grief though. Isobel's father, mother, nineteen-year-old brother and an auntie were clearly genuinely distraught. The mother was the least animated and appeared zoned out; at the other end of the table, her brother looked ready to detonate.

The family was introduced to the audience by the detective superintendent leading the murder inquiry, who then handed them the floor.

'The last time I did one of these, I begged my daughter to come home,' Isobel's mother said. 'That's the standard thing. The police also asked me to appeal to anyone who might have taken her, or know where she was. I refused. To do that would have been to admit that Isobel was in danger. I couldn't bring myself to accept that my little girl had been snatched by someone. To me, it wasn't even a possibility. Daughters get abducted and murdered, of course they do, but that's always something for the newspapers. Always someone else's daughter. Not mine. This didn't happen to my daughter. Always someone else's. The foolish mistake I made was to not realise who I was to the rest of the watching world. I was that someone else. That's what everyone thought who was reading about Isobel going missing. This stuff always happens to someone else.'

Here she paused to drink water. Reporters fired questions. Isobel's mother didn't speak again until her water was gone. She spoke as if no one had said a thing.

'Now, I can fool myself no more. Isobel is dead. Killed by a man, a man who seems to be, if not gloating, certainly without remorse. Now, I don't need the police to tell me what to do. I feel

the need to appeal to that man. It is too late for Isobel, but not others.'

She stood up. Some with cameras did the same, or leaned forward. Her eyes scanned the audience, found a particularly large device aimed at her, and stared straight at it. 'So, if you're the man who killed my daughter and you're watching... Please. For the sake of other innocent girls you might have captive. For the sake of those you will hurt in the future. For the sake of their families. Give yourself up. To avoid a costly and heart-wrenching trial, confess to everything–'

Noa had seen this video on major news websites, front page, but it had been edited to remove a portion. The missing segment had been described, but at least the news outlets had had the decency to not show it. Someone on UbyU hadn't developed that mindfulness. Noa watched as Isobel's brother, nineteen-year-old Jack, jumped to his feet and interrupted his mother.

'Confess, like you did on that damn radio show.'

Isobel's father got up to approach his son.

'You're going to hell, you bastard,' Jack continued. 'Forget handing yourself in and bloody top yourself. Jump off a damn building. I'll piss on your splattered body.'

Father bent close to son, but Jack ignored his words and continued to vent. Auntie and mother tried to plead with him, uselessly. Members of the crowd said soothing lines, with no more success.

In the end, his father and the detective superintendent had to grab him and walk him off the stage. As he left, he stared at a camera to give his final statement. 'Confessing won't help. Flirting with that bitch on the radio won't save you. You're dead meat for my sister, you piece of shit.'

The UbyU video ended. Noa sat staring at the paused final frame, which showed pandemonium on stage.

Bitch. That word bounced around her mind. She was

nobody's favourite for the way she was dealing with the killer. And things might only get worse, until perhaps she was as vilified as the killer she sought.

But she could not give up.

———

'It's midnight, April 21st, 2022, I'm Noa, and the phones are already ringing, so let's take the first call.'

Many in the office suspected that tonight's callers wouldn't hit the lines to confess minor sins, but would instead ask questions about the ongoing murder case – or claim kidnappings and killings of their own. The plan was to refuse to talk about Isobel Waring out of respect for her family. It wasn't necessary, because at a minute to midnight one of the three people manning the phone lines gave the signal: they had their guy waiting. The call was patched through.

'Ah, we're back live,' the same, now very familiar voice said. 'Again you take me seriously.'

To fortify the earlier public statement that there was a 'chance' Isobel's killer would contact the confession show again, Noa had been instructed to act as if she hadn't been expecting this call. It felt cheap and base when she said, 'Oh, hello. I wasn't sure we'd ever hear from you again.'

He could make or break the fallacy with his next line. Luckily, he didn't mention last night's secret conversation. 'So, do you still think me mad despite my wise precautions?'

'I will not mistake madness for over-acuteness of the senses.'

The caller laughed. 'You know your classic literature.'

'As I suspect you already knew.'

She glanced around the room, at almost ten people watching her. Some faces were grim, but she felt this was less a dismay about the situation and more a worry that she'd mess things up.

'I want to ask you about Isobel Waring,' she said.

'I'm sure you and the police with you would love information about her. But the living mean more than the dead.'

This was the tricky part. He'd already admitted having another captive, but not to a live audience. Noa had to act as if last night hadn't happened. 'Living? Are you saying you have kidnapped another woman?'

He laughed, obviously aware of the deceit in play. Again, a make-or-break moment. *'Yes, I do. You can have her if you can guess who. Name her and I might give you her. Get it wrong, and she stays with me.'*

The caller had played along, but there was no chance for relief. A blitz of whispers filled the room as people discussed this new angle. Bokayo tried to lean in and give Noa a list of missing women – this a comprehensive printout, not his scrap of paper – but she shrugged him away. She had the names memorised.

'I can't possibly know who you have. If I could blurt names out...'

'Go ahead. You have five seconds.'

A few had been added to the new list, including a woman who'd vanished from here in London yesterday. There were nineteen, all of whom were reported missing in the last twenty-one months. Noa reeled them off, and her throat turned dry halfway through. It was like a school register in opposite, with nobody able to raise a hand and say *Here*. Nineteen young women, gone without a trace and, in this moment, reduced to a pair or trio or words, said and done in one second each.

'Let me help by cutting a bunch away,' the caller said, and reeled off his own list. *'Such a shame. I've read about these missing women. There one day, gone the next. Maybe they'll turn*

up one day. Maybe they all fell down wells and their disappearances have nothing to do with the human monster. I hope their families get closure. Anyway, I've narrowed it down to four. A manageable number. Now you just get one guess. Say the wrong name, and the result won't be to anyone's liking. Except mine.'

'Are you saying you'll hurt her if I pick wrong? I couldn't possibly know. I can't just take a guess like that.'

'I trust you to get it right, Noa. In fact, I have faith that you will not fail.'

The room was full of shaking heads. Nobody wanted her to guess a name. She didn't want to guess.

But she had a feeling she didn't have to. 'I'm very intrigued by this game you want to play. And your certainty I'll pick the right name. I can think of only one way that's possible. So here's the name...'

CHAPTER FOURTEEN

4 NOVEMBER 2020

Instead of joining her at the dining table, he says, 'Do not try to leave the pool. You will be punished. I will be back shortly. When I return, do not make a single noise. Understand?'

She nods. He turns from the edge of the pool and walks away, through the plastic curtain strips at the end of the corridor he brought her down.

Katrina jumps to her feet, hardly able to believe she's in this moment. Outside her room, unguarded: just what she longed for. Her eyes dart to a door marked with CHANGING ROOMS that's open. There's also a fire exit, but that has no handle and a giant padlock securing it.

She steps away from the chair, planning to try the changing rooms, then stops. What is she doing? He could be waiting just out of sight, to see what she does. The changing rooms might not have another exit. If she makes a break for freedom, she will shatter their growing bond. If she fails to escape, there will never be another chance.

The argument boils in her mind for a whole minute before a decision is made. Katrina retakes her seat. She hopes a better escape opportunity presents itself. If not, this moment, this choice, will haunt her until her dying day.

Soon, she hears the clop of his footsteps returning. Her eyes move to the plastic curtain. A shadow appears behind, and then its owner pushes through.

Katrina drops her spoon in utter shock. No, no, no. She rubs her eyes like a disbelieving cartoon character, but the scene remains. The madman is back, but he is not alone. Now she knows why he was missing all day yesterday.

Walking before him is another woman.

———

The new woman is also black, but about ten years younger than Katrina. She, too, is colour-coded: dress, hair and lipstick all in yellow.

Katrina turns her head away and looks into her food bowl. She doesn't want the madman to see the incandescence on her face. This changes everything. Bonding with him will be harder now she knows she is not his only prize. All her work so far was for nothing.

But a second prisoner opens up a new opportunity. His attention will be split, offering chances to plan knowing he's not always watching in secret. Perhaps she and the new girl can work together to escape. If it comes down to such a blunt tactic as overpowering him, that's four arms against two and more weight. Then again, he has those damned stun gloves, from which one touch can end a rebellion instantly. There's also a selfish reason Katrina's earlier anger quickly evaporates. She will not suffer alone.

The woman is led to the edge of the pool and ordered down, where she may remove her blindfold. Now Katrina understands his earlier instruction to make no noise: he wants this new girl to get the shock of her life when she removes that blindfold.

Katrina watches it happen. She's staring right at the girl when her eyes are uncovered, and she sees them widen, the jaw drop, the legs wobble.

'Amongst the house rules, there is a Golden Rule,' the man says, loudly, for both women. 'You do not talk to each other, ever.'

The woman in yellow walks to the spare chair. Katrina expects to see the sort of shell shock that numbed her on her first day, but it's absent from this girl's eyes. In fact, there's an intensity to them. No fear. It's as if she's hardened and experienced, although the eyes belie this. They roam, clearly taking in this room for the first time.

The girl sits at the far end and they face each other across ten feet of wood. To Katrina's surprise, the woman mouths the words *It will be okay*. She feels Katrina is the one needing comfort?

Katrina watches her grab a wooden fork and test the sturdiness of the tines with a finger. Katrina knows why because she did the same thing: to gauge how effective the cutlery might be at plunging into flesh.

'Eat with your eyes down,' the man calls out. He stands by the pool's edge, just watching.

Before the younger woman gets into her food, she gives Katrina one last look over. It's obvious why. The challenges. Katrina knows the madman's plan now: force the two women to compete against each other.

The burning question is not what the winner gets, but the fate of the loser.

———

The man escorts the new girl back to her cell first, leaving Katrina sitting alone. When it's Katrina's turn, she tries to listen at every iron door she passes, hoping to determine which one the new girl is behind. It's hard to see those doors without imagining women behind them all. Or bizarre machinery and games with which he plans to challenge her.

A short while later, she calls out to him, asking to use the toilet. He answers immediately, as if he'd been sitting in the room above. He comes down to collect her.

After peeing, she tugs at the toilet roll and notices something fall out. It's a folded piece of roll. She lifts and opens it. Inside is a small length of pencil lead, which has been used to write on the folded paper. Her hands shake.

Mercy Ford. Hide notes behind toilet. What do you know?

Smart. Knowing he didn't permit talking, Katrina had tried to think of a sneaky way to converse with the new girl. She'd forgotten about the toilet. Obviously there isn't one in Mercy's room either.

There's something cool about this, reminding her of passing notes folded into paper aeroplanes at school. With glances at the door to make sure he doesn't come in, she writes a reply: *Don't know much. Don't know if we're still in Scotland. This is a school. There are challenges planned. We must escape. Name is Katrina Lytton.*

She folds the note, with the lead piece inside, then bends down to make sure he isn't on his knees looking and watching her feet. His shoes are there, but sideways, as if he's leaning against the wall. She stuffs the note behind the toilet bowl. For a panicked moment, she waits for him to kick open the door, but it doesn't happen. He doesn't know. She rises, flushes, takes a breath and steps out.

As always, he moves into the doorway to have a quick look. Nothing stands out, so he closes the door. She's gotten away with it.

———

Katrina waits only an hour before banging on the ceiling by lobbing a heavy book. 'I need the toilet again,' she calls out.

No response. Maybe he's not there – he has two girls to watch now. She waits five minutes before repeating the action. But before she can toss the book a second time, the hatch opens.

'I need the toilet again,' she says.

He sighs. 'You two are to drink less at feasting times.'

You two. Mercy must have been back to the toilet, so there should be a reply to Katrina's note. 'I'm sorry. I will drink less. But I really need to go.'

Two minutes later, he opens the door. Once in the toilet, she reaches behind the bowl, but only her own note sits there. Her heart sinks. Had Mercy been caught?

She dampens that worry. She was too quick, that's all. If she returns here too often, he may get suspicious. She decides she will check again after her next meal. Only after meals, unless she truly needs to go. Besides, at meals she and Mercy can signal each other that a new note is in place.

At lunch a few hours later, she looks up at Mercy as the girl takes her seat. Katrina imitates doodling with her spoon, and Mercy nods. Excellent: a reply is now in place. Lunch is eaten in silence.

Halfway through, Mercy raps the table to get her attention and points. Katrina lifts little paper cake cups of condiments until she gets a nod at the mustard. Mercy then positions her knife and fork a foot apart and stands two fingers between. Katrina understands: a goalie in a goal. She slides the mustard across the table. Mercy's finger goalie blocks the shot and she pumps a fist in the air. Katrina can't help but release an audible giggle.

'No interacting,' the madman calls from the edge of the pool. 'You'll get your fill of that when the challenges start.'

His threat is ominous enough to kill any sense of fun. Both women drop their eyes to their food.

When lunch is over, Mercy is escorted away first. Katrina waits in silence, fiddling with items on the table. She tosses some pepper in her eyes, to see how blinding it would be. That's a mistake and she has to wash her eyes with water. She risks visiting the far end of the table to get Mercy's wooden fork, to see if both pressed together might be sturdy enough to pierce flesh. She even stares at a banana peel and imagines the slapstick scenario of fleeing and tossing strips of it behind her, to foil him.

When he comes for her, she says, 'I need to pee again. Do you mind?'

When she sits on the toilet and feels behind the bowl, she's elated to find paper. Now that she knows the messaging system works, Mercy has composed a much longer note, running to two sheets. Katrina's own note is gone.

You say still in Scotland? I was taken from Betws-y-Coed, Wales. Are we alone? I have seen no other girls. Does he plan to kidnap other girls? What are these challenges he mentions? Like The Hunger Games? What do we have in common that he wants? I...

What follows is Mercy's biography, but while fascinating,

Katrina cannot see a connection between this girl and herself. She'd never thought about why he'd chosen Mercy and herself, but now she's eager to know. Is there a connection between them? Doubtful given that they live in different countries, but who knows? Hoping that Mercy will find a reason why they got picked, Katrina's reply is an overview of her own life.

Mercy had also written:

We need a code for things. Scratch an eyebrow if he rapes us. Pick at an earlobe if we find out he plans to harm the other. We will work on an escape plan.

Katrina wants to unload her existing plan to get into the man's good graces and get his guard down, but it's a risk. If he discovers these notes, it's all over. Plus, she doesn't want to give Mercy the idea of doing the same trick. He could warm to the younger girl and decide to favour her. It feels like a betrayal, but hell, they're not friends. Not really. Just temporary housemates. Maybe Mercy has her own secret freedom campaign. Katrina keeps her mission to herself.

Mercy's note ends with instructions to flush all previous notes, so after reading it again, Katrina uses it to wipe herself.

Her own note ends with an answer to another question Mercy asked: *Does he plan to kidnap other girls?*

Katrina's reply is *I believe so.*

It is two days later that Katrina is escorted to the swimming pool to see a third chair bolted in front of the table.

Eight days later, at lunchtime, Katrina turns her head as she hears the madman's footsteps returning down the corridor. They are slow steps, and she knows exactly what that means.

Sure enough, another girl steps through the curtain ahead of him. This one is white, young, and her colour – dress, hair, lipstick – is blue. This, then, is Isobel.

Katrina silently watches the young woman cross to the pool, climb nervously down the ladder, and turn this way before whipping off her blindfold.

When she sees she's not alone, the girl drops to her knees and screams. Katrina totally understands. It's a serious headmash.

The woman in blue stumbles to the table, numb, zombie-like, and just about collapses into the spare chair. Her eyes first settle on Katrina, who gives a little nod. Then, those wide and terrified eyes move. From Katrina's purple dress and hair and lipstick to Mercy's yellow.

Then the girl's eyes move on, around the table. To green. To red. To pink.

———

Having watched other girls make the walk to the pool and be informed of his Golden Rule, Katrina and Mercy have had time to adapt. Within an hour of waking as a captive, Mercy performed a magic trick by convincing the madman to let her have paper and pencils for sketching. Since then he's supplied such items for all the girls, albeit only thin pieces of pencil lead and the flexible ink tubes from pens so he can't be stabbed. The girls have a system for recruiting new captives and Katrina, closest to Isobel, employs it now.

Her pen is in her right hand, which is under the table. She lifts the new girl's dress high over her thigh and scrapes the nib of the pen across her skin. She draws an image she's practiced many times. Thankfully, the scared young newbie gives no reaction that would alert the madman to wrongdoing. Katrina then nods to the third girl taken, Alex.

After dinner, nineteen-year-old Alex will use the toilet and write a note for the new girl. When the newbie sees the picture on her thigh – a toilet bowl with an arrow pointing behind it – hopefully she'll understand and go find the note. On that folded sheet of A4 will be all their names and a few other details, and what they know so far about the madman and his plans. It won't be much, because he's said little, but that note will contain one special piece of information Katrina got hold of that last night.

Since she became one of many, it's been hard for Katrina to get his time during the day. That leaves the night. She would rather sleep, but lost time can never be made up. So she's been committed to trying to get him to talk. A handful of times now, she's convinced him to sit in the room above hers and have a conversation. He doesn't say much, but last night she scored a major point by getting him to admit something vital.

The light was off, the room jet black, and she lay on her bed, talking up at the hatch. It was open, but the light in that room was also off and he lay or sat somewhere out of sight. After loosening him up by getting him to talk about his favourite movies, she abruptly changed track.

'Hey, answer me something else,' she said into the darkness. 'You were gone all evening. I'm stuck here and know nothing of what's happening in the world. Where did you go? Did you go hunting for another girl?'

He denied it at first, but she carefully pushed, and he broke. 'Okay, yes. I got another girl.'

She had to pretend not be appalled. 'Wow. What's her name?'

'You don't need to know that. She will have a colour. That's how you know each other. I explained that to you. Do you know the others' names?'

He sounded very suspicious, and rightly so. If one girl knew another's name, they'd obviously been talking somehow. Communicating could lead to scheming. But she didn't want to lie. If he already knew the truth, or didn't believe her, a lie would sever their thickening bond.

'Yes,' she said. 'At lunch today, we scribbled them down on napkins. I'm sorry, I know that's against the rules. But we thought, since you didn't object, that this meant it was okay.'

Today napkins had been absent from the dining table, but his concern hadn't stretched to removing art materials from the girls' rooms. More important, he had answered her question, albeit with a stutter, as if he found the words distasteful:

'She is called Isobel.'

Isobel. Poor girl. 'How many more? How many of us do you want in the challenges? I'm eager to get going. Come on, tell me.'

'No more. We will have our six, and we will be ready.'

Bingo. He wanted six women for his challenges. 'Wow. Cool. So the challenges will start? When?'

'Soon.'

Since they had a bond, she decided to press him for a tip, something to help her with the upcoming challenges.

'No,' he replied. 'That is not fair.'

'Not even a little one?'

'No. I can't.'

She'd bypassed his defences before, and was certain it was possible again. She pushed: 'Don't I mean a little more to you than the others?'

His chilling reply was: 'Only the most special of you matters to me, and only the challenges will reveal who that is.'

CHAPTER FIFTEEN

'... Alex Byrne, twenty-one. Mercy Ford, twenty-two. Kai Harlow, thirty-two. Katrina Lytton, thirty-one. There is no wrong name. You have all four of these women, don't you?'

'*Correct,*' the caller said.

Whispered shock ran around the people in the room. Noa ignored it.

'*And you get one,*' the caller continued. '*Just one. A special one. For money. But let's not mention money again until I say.*'

Someone behind her said the word *alive*, but needn't have bothered: she knew to ask. 'All of these young women went missing a year and a half ago. Including Isobel Waring. And she's dead and has been for a long time.'

'*The plan was and is not to kill these girls. Unfortunately, Isobel ruined my plans – oh, don't ask what they are, by the way. So I was forced to dispose of her. But let me reassure you that you can have a girl alive and well. Just name one. She'll take some time to get over her ordeal, but there are experts in the field of psychology. They'll mend her mind, and she'll heal, and with luck she'll go on to live a productive, happy life.*'

'And the other three?'

'When you pick one puppy from the dogs home, you leave behind the others. Forget them. You're here for one puppy.'

People were animated behind her, desperate to tell her not to pick a name. She didn't need such advice and shut everyone out. 'You want me to choose one girl and condemn the others to die? How could anyone do that?'

'If you leave the dogs home with no puppy, they all stay behind in their cages. So you will pick one to save, or none will be saved. You have until my call tomorrow night to decide. When I go live on your show – live, remember – you will give me a name, or you'll condemn them all.'

'This is impossible. What you're asking is... wrong.'

'I don't envy your position. Lives are in your hands. Yours, Noa, not those of the police. You will pick a girl to save, or no one gets saved. Perhaps you could flip a coin. You have a special one around your neck that you make decisions with. That would be perfect to decide a woman's fate, without her knowing a single thing about it.'

He hung up.

CHAPTER SIXTEEN

18 NOVEMBER 2020

When he comes to take Katrina to breakfast, she asks him: is it challenge day?

He stands in the doorway and says, 'Challenges come when they come. You asked me that yesterday. I shouldn't even acknowledge the question. Challenges come when they come.'

It has been six days since Isobel showed up. Six days since he'd claimed the challenges would soon start. Six days of meals, pacing, sleeping, boredom. Six days of his saying no.

Only this time he didn't say no, did he? He deflected the question. And that's as good as an answer, she knows. It's challenge day.

He's one man dealing with a bunch of women, and in no position to challenge their personal routines. As one, the girls have been increasing their toilet requirements; a final pee before bed has been added to the post-meal ones. This allows them to read and post almost live notes to the group. Last night, the subject was what kind of challenges they would face.

Some had had some wild ideas, from eating competitions to pistol duels at dawn. Nothing could be waived off. Their jailer was messed up in the head and who knew what bizarre games he wanted to play. The general consensus, however, was that the tasks would be physical. All his girls were young – Katrina and Kai Harlow, who was white British and in green, were the eldest at thirty. Nobody was overweight. He'd supplied a treadmill. For some days now all six girls had been working out in their rooms to increase strength and stamina.

Everyone had been eyeing their opponents warily. Nobody was scared by nineteen-year-old Alex Byrne. She was some kind of child genius but was a little clumsy and weak. In the middle, the unknowns, were herself, Mercy, Kai, and Isobel. The clear frontrunner for most worrying opponent was twenty-four-year-old Diamond, in red. She was six feet two and a bodybuilder, with solid muscles.

However, there was a dark horse in Katrina's opinion: the newbie, twenty-two-year-old Isobel Waring, who drove race cars and had been a school sports whiz. Diamond might be able to heave Atlas stones like no other, but there was no guarantee the tests would be all about brawn. Isobel moved slowly but gave off a fluid air. Katrina had her bagged as a tiger, able to leap from casual to ninja in a heartbeat. She might just surprise everyone. Time would tell.

Since Katrina had told the group the madman's claim that the challenges were imminent, the atmosphere had changed. It had darkened. The girls had gone from strangers to sisters, and now the air was adversarial. He'd admitted he sought that special one, and one only. Each girl knew that the others were determined to make sure she found out the hard way what fate awaited the losers.

———

The breakfast scene looks the same as always: six girls eating, one masked madman watching from the side of the swimming pool. But something feels different to Katrina. A sense of foreboding rises. She stops eating and removes soggy bread from her mouth. Her heart starts to beat faster and goose pimples appear on her shoulders. It feels like a panic attack is coming. She'll later wonder if it was a sixth sense.

Because right then it happens. The madman hooks the ladder over the edge of the pool and calls out: 'Challenge. Last to leave the pool loses.'

The girls explode into noise and action.

Mercy and Alex sit at the far side of the table, which puts them at a disadvantage. Mercy runs around the table, which lengthens her journey. Alex chooses to scramble over, but her short cut fails as a foot lands in a bowl of cornflakes, which skips out from under her and sends her crashing down with a scream.

Diamond and Kai sit at the ends of the table and can slip straight out, and they take an immediate lead.

Katrina and Isobel sit with their backs to the exit: a shorter journey, but awkward because they have to move around their chairs. They exit towards each other and collide, but Alex, lying on the table, shoots out a hand and grabs the back of Isobel's dress, stopping her dead and allowing Katrina to start running.

Diamond, taller than the others and more powerful, reaches the ladder first. Kai, right behind, slams into her and slips onto her butt. This slows the two leaders enough that the ladder isn't free when Katrina arrives. She grabs one of the side rails to book her place in the queue. Mercy tries to barge her aside, and there's a tussle for who gets to mount the ladder behind Kai. When she looks round, Katrina sees Alex run past Isobel and stick an elbow into her, which causes the newcomer to stumble.

When Katrina reaches the top and throws herself out of the pool, she turns to look back again. Mercy climbs out, followed by Alex. In last place, is Isobel.

Surprisingly, the sports star is still halfway across the pool, struggling to rise to her feet after being knocked down. She starts to hobble.

The madman stands a couple of metres away from the mess of women lying on the floor. He has a pistol aimed at them, obviously concerned that he would be quite vulnerable, even with stun gloves, if his six captives burst out of the pool at the same time.

'Pink, stand aside, over there,' he says, the gun now pointing at Alex. 'The rest of you, lie on your fronts, faces down, hands behind your backs, blindfolds on.' Everyone obeys.

'Why me?' Alex asks as she crawls to one side.

Their blindfolds are around their necks. Katrina pulls hers up and over her eyes. But before all goes black, she sees the madman pointing his gun at Alex.

'Blue, was it the fall?' he says.

Isobel is crying. 'I have an injury, my hip. This isn't fair. I can't run. My hip is knackered. This wasn't fair!'

Alex is just as distraught: 'I didn't lose. Why have you picked me? What's going on. I didn't lose!'

The madman stamps a foot and roars like a bear. Katrina's never seen him this angry and isn't sure what's so upset him. Scared, she waits for the first of six gunshots. Everyone is whimpering.

'Purple, get in the pool.'

Katrina's heart thumps. Has she done something wrong?

———

It seems like hours later that there's finally noise from above – he's crossing the room atop hers. The hatch opens. She remains on her bed. 'What's going to happen to Isobel?' she says.

The madman says, 'Blue's fate isn't your worry. Your own should be.'

143

'This is just wrong,' she says. She's got a plan to stick to, but it's hard to dampen down her emotions. 'You're making us compete against each other. There was no winner. You're looking for losers. To kill. You're going to kill us one by one, aren't you? Last one standing.'

'Yes. Call it a championship, if you like. It's how the best of the best are decided in any field. The winner will be absolutely free and taken care of.'

'And Isobel, what happens to her?'

'She is Blue. You are all–'

'We're not colours,' she cuts in, be damned the plan to work around this bastard. 'We're human beings. Not monsters like you.'

'You're upset, even though you didn't lose?'

'You let me think I was going to die.'

Earlier, when he'd ordered her into the pool, she had been certain that he planned to kill her. That hadn't changed when he'd ordered another girl back in, and another, until everyone was together down there – the pool was the best place to murder people because of the ease with which to sluice away blood. The normal routine for returning to their cells was to be called one by one, but this time Katrina had been certain she was being led to the slaughter.

She had been called third and while walking ahead of him, had asked if Diamond and Mercy, who had already been escorted away, were dead. She had begged for answers, but he'd refused to reply. Even when he'd locked her in her room, the fear hadn't dissipated. Not for a while.

He says, 'There was no reason for you to think that. I told you only the losers would suffer. That was in your own head.'

He knew exactly what he was doing to her. To all of them. Besides, can she really complain? He's her kidnapper, after all.

She should really be thankful for every minute she's still drawing breath. 'So you've killed Isobel because she lost?'

'Blue did not lose. In fact, Blue will be taken out of here.'

Katrina gets to her feet and approaches the hatch. He's out of sight. She imagines he has a chair in that upper room. A nice damn comfy armchair, with a cup of tea on the arm. 'What are you talking about? Did she win?'

'You don't win, you only lose. My special one requires certain characteristics, and one is compassion. That is what I was looking for with that challenge.'

'Wait. You're saying you were testing to see who showed the least compassion. That explains Alex—'

'Pink. You are colours.'

'Pink knocked Iso – Blue. Knocked Blue over. Tried to grab her dress to stop her too. That's why you wanted Pink to stand to one side. Are you saying Pink lost? She's going to die because she showed the least compassion?'

'Pink will not die because of this. She showed the least, but you all exhibited a lack of compassion.'

Katrina wants to laugh and cry at the same time. 'This is a joke. This is evil. You said it was a challenge, last one out of the pool? We're all in fear for our lives, so how can you not expect us all to just want to be first to get out of the pool? It wasn't as if you said we all had to get out in a certain time. It wasn't a team thing.'

'The test is what it is. Nobody helped anyone else. Someone could have taken the risk to—'

'To what, sacrifice ourselves to save the others? You're stupid.'

He says nothing at first. She wonders if she's gone too far. She's insulted his moral code and mental stability, but this is the first time she's insulted his intelligence. She backs away from the hatch, remembering he has a firearm. 'I'm sorry. I didn't mean to call you stupid. You're not.'

'The lack of compassion will only be punished by your own regret. The challenge would have rewarded anyone who showed care for the others. As it is, you all lost that challenge. As punishment, I will take Blue out of this place. She will be leaving you all behind.'

Katrina takes a breath to calm herself. If Isobel is truly to be released, she can summon help. It's likely he's thought of this and will take precautions, such as the knockout drug he used to get everyone here, but Katrina tries to focus on the positive. With a girl free, the chances of rescue increase. If Isobel can save them before it's too late.

'So what happens next for the rest of us?'

'The challenges continue. But from this point on, it's a knockout competition. One will fall each time. Do I need to remind you of the prize for failure?'

No, he doesn't.

CHAPTER SEVENTEEN

'If still you think me mad, you will think so no longer when I describe the wise precautions I took for the concealment of the body. The night waned, and I worked hastily, but in silence. First of all I dismembered the corpse. I cut off the head and the arms and the legs.'

Bokayo just looked at Noa. After the caller had hung up, he had asked Noa to step aside. They were in the corridor, alone, while some of Scotland Yard's top brass no doubt seethed beyond the door. He had demanded an explanation for some very strange dialogue between Noa and the caller at the top of their conversation.

'It's a quote from *The Tell-Tale Heart*, by Edgar Allan Poe,' she said. 'Remember the caller used it last night? I recognised it. When I responded by saying I would not mistake madness for over-acuteness of the senses, I was showing him I understood.'

'You knew this last night and neglected to mention it?'

'I wasn't sure it meant anything. I thought he was just playing games, trying to sound cool. People do that with quotes all the time.'

'So you thought you'd save your response for tonight, live

on-air? You withheld possible evidence. A love of old literature is a characteristic about this guy that we could have done with knowing.'

'I understand. I'm sorry. But do you remember when I said he knew about my love of literature? That's because I mentioned Edgar Allan Poe on my show about two weeks ago. So the caller was listening back then. That's a sign that I'm important to him. I'm the reason he called my show to confess on-air. He must feel a bond in some way. So you can't take me off this.'

Bokayo sighed. 'So that's the only reason you're admitting having some kind of secret code with this guy?'

'It's hardly a code. It's just a shared love of something. Maybe that's why he feels he can talk to me. Look, Bokayo, this is a good thing. You know something new about him, although I'm sorry I didn't say this last night. And you have someone he's willing to confide in. Me. You can't take me off this.'

Bokayo rubbed his face. 'I don't call the shots here. It doesn't look good that you two seemed to be talking in code, like a couple of giggling schoolkids. Not only that, but hiding this from me might look like I can't control you. I might get removed, as well as you.'

'It's a rapport I'm trying to build. Isn't that what the negotiator keeps harping on about striving for? I have it. This guy might never have called if not for me. You wouldn't even know about him. Now we do.'

'And you want praise for that? Sure, but rough with the smooth, okay? Are you willing to accept blame if he kills another girl?'

Noa took a step back, angry. 'I'm not after praise. I'm trying to help. You sound like one of the idiots who calls my show, saying it's my fault. If he kills someone else, that's on him, not me. You dickhead.'

He reached for her shoulder but she stepped back again, out of range. 'I'm sorry, I didn't mean that. I'm just frustrated.'

'Look, Bokayo, I know you people have years of practice at deciding how best to talk to criminals. I know there's playbooks. I know everyone in that room thinks I'm a lowly civilian who's dangerous to this investigation. But I know I'm getting through to this man. Surely you can see that I did some good in there. You need me.'

'Well, hopefully you can get what you want. And we can get what we want.'

She glared at him. 'Just what does that mean? We want different things? You want this guy caught, so that must mean I don't.'

'I didn't mean–'

'So I must be after my own interests, right? I want to raise the profile of my chat show, is that it? Maybe create interest in a book I could write? Or do I see me playing myself in a TV movie about this?'

He said nothing. Sometimes he did that to try to diffuse arguments, but here she read more into it. She saw his silence as effectively pleading the Fifth: refusing to answer because he did indeed suspect a selfish motive.

She walked away. 'You of all bloody people to think that. I'm going home.'

'I wouldn't,' he said. 'Reporters are out there. They'll be crawling all over your house for the next few days. People listening to the show won't be happy with the content of tonight's chat between you two.'

She turned on him. 'I got him to admit he's kidnapped four other girls. I got their names. I asked him about Isobel. I did what you lot asked. He said all he was willing to say. Nobody could have done more.'

'I don't mean that. The Poe thing. You two bantering like that. Trust me when I tell you the public will flay you for it.'

―――――

She was worried about vigilantes, but they came to her rescue. The police station had a nondescript rear exit that was sometimes used to whisk hated suspects off to court without baying crowds out front realising. He sent a guy to check the coast was clear. Since the exit was on another street, it was.

She got away without confrontation, but she couldn't go home. If the reporters were still lurking outside the police station, for sure a mob would be at her home too. Since her bodyguard had found her at The Sanctuary, she doubted even that place would earn its name tonight. She asked Google and found a tacky hotel a couple of miles north in Camden Town. Bokayo had a plain car with plainclothes officers in it follow her in case of trouble. There was none.

It was a different story at her home though. Her 12–8 bodyguard, watching the house, called his boss, who called Noa as she drove to the hotel. He described a confrontation between her bodyguard and a reporter who'd tried to jimmy the front door. Noa told him she would not be home tonight and to leave the bodyguard in place.

Damn reporters were everywhere, like flies round shit. They had seen her car enter the police station, so that was burned. Once settling into her grimy little room, she called another hire company and arranged for a car to be dropped off outside the next morning.

Morning took its time coming, but she eventually got some sleep. She spent most of the following morning stuck in her room, checking the news. She almost wished she hadn't. The story was growing faster than bamboo.

One girl dead and possibly five more alive and in the hands of what one publication called the 'schooled screwball', as if trying to give him a moniker that would stand the test of time. All of the families of the girls claimed as captives of the kidnapper had reached out to the media and the police, demanding to be part of the action. A year and a half after they'd faded from the news, all of the missing women were once again hot property.

Social media had gone wild with stories, theories, and abuse. Scotland Yard took a beating. Noa got the share she'd been expecting and there were calls for her show to be axed. A mid-range celebrity caused uproar on Facebook when he posted a poll asking which of the four girls people would like to see freed, as if the kidnapping case was a piece of soap opera fiction. People voted. Kai Harlow, a homeless woman, got just two per cent of the votes. Mercy Ford took twenty-one per cent, just behind Katrina Lytton's twenty-two. The remaining fifty-five per cent was in part attributed to Alex Byrne because she had a YouTube channel with 443,000 subscribers.

Someone else in the news was a man called Lee Redburn. He was a convicted rapist who had been arrested for Katrina Lytton's abduction in December 2020, a month after she vanished. He was a former rugby player, which made Noa remember Jerome's mention of such a man. Although he'd been quickly released without charge back in December 2020, renewed concern about Katrina sent police back to his door for another chat. This convicted him in some people's eyes, even though he was not rearrested.

After the police came reporters, one of whom stuck a camera in his face when he was walking to the shop:

'Yo, man, you're giving me bad press,' said a gangly man with a dirty T-shirt and more tattoo ink than skin visible on his arms. He had bad teeth and the sunken cheeks of one on more than a nodding acquaintance with drugs. 'I'm sure you had a laugh watching me take the rap for your shit. I know you ain't giving yasen up. Why would ya? But how about you sling the cops some proof it was you, so they get off my bleeding back? That woman DJ, I want to talk to her. She can get him to say stuff, prove it wasn't me.'

A heartfelt plea that for sure would tug at the emotions of anyone sympathetic. Woman DJ was Noa herself, of course. Just about every time a piece of news dealt with Isobel Waring, Noa's name got mentioned. Some accused her of being inadequate for the task, which she accepted. Others said she'd treated the scenario like a joke, which was more hurtful. She had some fans, which was nice. But so did Adolf Hitler.

Worst of all were the keyboard warriors who slammed her for what they called 'flirting' with the kidnapper. One idiot posted a story on UbyU whose opening sentence was *While innocent, tormented girls try to claw their way from his prison, Noa Vickerman tries to clamber into the lunatic's pants.* Bokayo's warning had been spot-on.

Not everybody wanted to pass judgement; some discussed solutions to the problem. Noa found a Facebook discussion about who would cough up the cash, if indeed Isobel's killer wanted money for releasing hostages. Her Majesty's Government vowed never to make ransom payments, so would the families have to open their purses? Most of the readers who'd commented felt Noa should provide the funds.

Rich dad, so it's on her, said one. Another offered, *Her show, her responsibility.* There was *Thinks she's making fans off this, so let her pay* and *Millionaire bitch cut me off the damn show one time so this is payback.* She was annoyed at the tone of these comments. Instead of someone with the ability to help, she was being treated as if she'd already refused to pay.

Another of Bokayo's warnings was starting to develop some

flesh. Her email was bombarded by jokers demanding cash for women they'd either snatched or were planning to. Her social media private inboxes were full of messages from users suggesting other missing women, some from decades earlier, that she could pay to save.

One user had even replied to a Facebook post about Isobel by tagging a friend called Mia Preston; when Noa clicked on the name, it took her to a page dedicated to a missing Scottish girl, Mia, who had winked out of existence in Canada eight years ago. Run by her parents, the page currently hosted a fundraiser so her mother could fly to Calgary and continue her search of Mia's last known whereabouts. This post upset Noa the most because it was heartfelt, genuine. Criticism she could handle, but how would she deal with sobbing mothers begging for help? How would she feel when she had to refuse, for she could not rescue everyone?

———

At eleven the next morning, she watched a hire car park outside the hotel and called down to the guy approaching the door. She was on the first floor, so he was able to toss up the car key to her window. Noa caught it on the second try.

She washed, but was forced to dress in yesterday's clothes. As she was preparing to leave, someone knocked on her door. She expected a police officer, but opened the door to a man who aimed a mobile phone camera at her and said, 'Noa Vickerman, are you hiding out here because you're scared the killer might come for you? Or because disgruntled members of the public might?'

Luckily, she had all her things in her bag, which was over her shoulder. With no reason to stay in the room, she wordlessly pushed past the reporter.

With a flurry of questions and accusations that she ignored, he followed her downstairs and to reception, where the manager had been swapped for a young man. She gave the receptionist the finger as she walked out. She jogged to the hire car and got in, and locked the door just as the reporter tried to open it.

'I can have a bunch of us down here in minutes,' he said. 'Just talk to me. Better if it's just me. Come on. Which girl do you plan to pick to save?'

She started the engine. The reporter ran to a car parked about ten metres behind hers. When she didn't move for a minute, he got out. She started driving and he jumped back in his vehicle. And she stopped again. She used her main device to call her 8–4 bodyguard, who was watching her house.

After the call, the game continued. She sat in place, but moved her vehicle if the reporter tried to walk up to it, which would force him back into his own car. In fifteen minutes, both cars stop-started their way a hundred metres, at which point she got a text. She turned her car in the road and drove back, to park again outside the hotel. She headed in, followed by the reporter. At the door, she passed a guy standing on the step and playing on his phone.

Halfway across the lobby, she turned and walked back out. When the reporter tried to exit, he found the man with the phone blocking his way, and holding a fistful of his shirt.

'Give me two minutes,' she told her bodyguard. He nodded. Leaving the reporter to rant and rave, she got in her car and got the hell away.

She found another budget hotel a couple of miles away. This time she hid her face as best she could when at reception and then hid in her room.

She'd given Bokayo one of her new numbers and he called around 5pm with something she'd been expecting. Police were well aware of the disdain caused by her presence bang in the middle of a murder investigation. Now Isobel's family had added their opinion, and it only heaped to the weight upon Noa. So:

'Higher-up decision. Not my call,' he said to open the conversation.

'The show is cancelled, right?'

'The whole show is a bad idea, giving this lunatic free rein to say what he wants live on-air. But we can't cancel it. We can't risk another life. However, it now has to be a police matter. Wholly.'

'So I'm off my own show, right?'

'Sorry.'

'He's expecting me. It's me he wants to talk to. This is a mistake.'

'I actually agree. Nothing I can do. I fought your corner. We're going to tell him you're ill. We just have to hope that money is more important to him than who's on the end of the phone.'

'Ill? That's weak. He's no fool. I should still be there, in case he wants me.'

'No. They don't want you involved.'

'He wanted a name. One of the girls. What's your plan for that?'

'To delay. Somehow.'

'That could be dangerous. Look, I'll call the show at midnight. I'll be on one of the lines. If he asks for me, you can patch me through to him. Surely that's safe?'

'I'll suggest it to my boss, but don't hold your breath.'

'I've been holding it since this damn thing started.'

———

As midnight rolled around, Noa found Divine Radio on one of her burner phones. She caught the last five minutes of *Late Love* and the hosts were clearly perturbed about what was coming next. Outside her hotel, two cars were parked with music playing and a group of young men chatting loudly. The strange environment. The fact that she was going to listen to her own show from afar. These things gave her body a strange numbness, like a waking dream. Most of the bottle of wine on her bedside table was gone. An empty one sat beside it.

At a minute to midnight, she called the station on her main number. She knew it was stored on the machine, so her name would flash on the display. That would allow her to jump the queue.

What she'd foolishly overlooked, though, was call volume. The radio station's answering machine could answer and put on hold only eight calls, with a further ten acknowledged and placed in a queue. Anyone else who phoned the show got what Noa heard now: a busy line tone.

'Shit.'

Well, they had her number and could call if necessary. She wasn't sure she even wanted that.

After the jingle that preceded her show, a voice spoke. It was the police negotiator. There was no pretence about making a show of it. No intro. He simply came on and said, 'Caller, are you there?'

'Where is Noa Vickerman?'

It was him. Noa imagined thousands like her, sitting in bedrooms and cars and baths, listening. The negotiator's reply was, 'She is ill. I can speak with you.'

'Oh, really,' the kidnapper said. His tone said that, like Noa, he felt this was a lame excuse. She was suddenly worried. *'I told you to make this show live and you heeded that warning. Which was smart. Now you pull this stunt. Which is not. I called to*

make a confession to a confession show hosted by Noa Vickerman. You've changed things...'

She glanced at her main phone. No call flashed up.

'...So I'll change things too. This is on whoever made the decision to remove Noa. I'll call back tomorrow night. Until then, Louder, Piper, Pint.'

CHAPTER EIGHTEEN

18 NOVEMBER 2020

The madman has often been away all day, but he'd always left her meals in her room. Not this time. Katrina hasn't heard from him since breakfast, and she's worried. She has been for hours.

He'd said Isobel was leaving, so she figured he had gone to take her home, or to wherever he planned to release her. Had that gone wrong? Had his car crashed and he now lay dead?

Or has he been arrested? If he had been taking Katrina home, she wouldn't have sat around and hoped he would remain true to his word. She would have escaped him at the first chance, even if it was in the middle of nowhere. Perhaps Isobel had managed to leap out of his van at traffic lights, scream for help, and a mob had grabbed him and called the police.

Isobel would have told the police about the other girls, but she would have no idea where to send them. If this building wasn't connected to him by some paperwork, they'd require the madman to talk, and perhaps he was staying silent. Without the other girls, they could charge him only with a single kidnapping. He might well be willing to let five girls starve to death in order to avoid a meatier prison sentence.

Usually her time alone here involves exercising or pottering about in some way, but now she lies on the bed in dead silence. She's seeking a sound that could mean he's back.

And she is rewarded.

It sounds like the very faint sound of a car engine, somewhere below. A single engine, though, and no sirens. He hasn't been arrested after all. But at least he's back and she can eat.

The fact that the sound is below her is curious. An underground car park? A possible way out, if so.

Ten minutes later, she hears a door slam, and then voices. They're very faint, and no words are distinguishable, but Katrina knows it's the other girls yelling for him. The distances involved tell her this school is big and the cells are spread wide apart.

He's given plenty of warnings about not shouting out, so Katrina says nothing. Perhaps she should have yelled, because it's another hour at least before her ceiling hatch opens. She runs beneath it and a banana bounces off her shoulder. She's quick enough to catch the wrapped sandwich that falls through a second later. She sees only the arm that dropped these items before he's out of sight again – he's wearing some kind of jacket instead of the Japanese top.

'Where have you been?'

'I am sorry for missing feasting.'

She stays on the bed. 'What time is it? Is it late?'

'Not far off midnight. Get some sleep.'

'Did you take Isobel home?'

'She's no longer a prisoner, and that's all I'll say. Now eat and sleep.'

'I need the toilet.'

He sighs. She realises why he took so long to come to her room: the other girls have demanded a bathroom break too. Her desire to go to the toilet, however, isn't just about needing to pee. She wants to see if Isobel has left a parting note.

I hope you bitches rot in here. Especially you, Diamond.

Katrina smirks. The girls have each made a promise that, should one escape or be released, she will do whatever it takes to rescue the others. There's every chance that the madman could find their secret notes, so Isobel has done exactly as planned and pretended to not care about her comrades. The idea is to make the madman think she won't tell the police about them.

A nice touch is the part about Diamond. That's a genuine f-you. The muscle-bound bitch is everyone's enemy and the one most likely to backstab them to curry favour with the madman.

Even better than the presence of that note is the absence of the others. Although they have been flushing new notes away, six special ones had been kept safe. On each, a girl wrote her full name, address, and a letter to her loved ones. Katrina hoped to be the one who would make the journeys to five different homes, but the task is now Isobel's.

The notes will convince the police that the madman has five other captives, and they will bring a modicum of comfort to the families. Surely, the letters will make the case high-profile and this prison will soon be discovered.

Figuring she's the last to see Isobel's note, Katrina flushes it. Now it's a waiting game.

By the middle of the afternoon of the next day – November 19, by her calculations – Katrina's confidence is wearing thin. To avoid pacing and looking suspicious, she runs on the treadmill to ask herself myriad questions.

What are the police doing? Are they mobilising a strike team? Is the prison under surveillance? Are they still questioning Isobel? Are they even aware of the other girls?

Maybe Isobel got cold feet about the notes and dumped them and her plan to help, preferring instead to just wipe the whole sorry episode out of her mind? Maybe the madman searched her, found the notes, realised the plan, and killed Isobel for her insolence.

Later, at dinner, she discovers she's not the only one who's been worrying. Everybody's got a long face. When he escorts Mercy from the swimming pool, young Alex takes a risk and, in a whisper, says, 'Isobel is dead.' Katrina recognises a Welsh accent.

'No talking, bitch,' Diamond hisses. She sounds like a Londoner. 'There could be audio recorders.'

'Or you'll tell him,' Kai says. Katrina is pleased to hear a fellow Scottish accent.

The table falls silent, but Katrina gets a chance to speak when Diamond is next to be returned to her cell. 'Why?'

'Because he's not angry with us,' Alex says.

Two sets of eyes look at her, puzzled.

'Put yourself in his shoes,' she says. 'If I was him, I don't want Isobel giving away any clues to this location or my identity. If I was him and I really did plan to release her, I'd do it naked so her clothing isn't matched to fibres in that van. And to make sure she hasn't stolen something with my DNA on it. If I found those notes, I'd kill her. That's my guess as to what's happened.'

'We don't know that.'

'What's the first thing your parents or your brother will do if they get a note off Isobel?'

'Throw a party,' Katrina says. 'I'm still alive.'

'Not keep it hush-hush?'

'Hell no. The police–'

'Exactly. Police. Media. Missing woman Katrina Lytton, alive and held prisoner. With four more girls. Big news. The world over.'

'Yes. At least, I would hope so.'

'So get in his shoes. A hundred trained detectives are after you. You'll want to know how the police investigation is going, right?'

Understanding hits Katrina like a runaway train. If Isobel had been released, the story would be on everyone's lips. The madman would know about the notes, or at the very least know the girls had been secretly talking. He would be angry. He was not. Because there was a no-talking rule and they had obviously been talking lots, and he would be angry. But he was not.

'Doesn't mean anything,' she says. 'Maybe the police don't want to alert him and they're investigating in secret.'

Alex gives her a look like she's stupid.

The next morning, Katrina gives her own ceiling reflection the *you're stupid* look. Alex was right. There is no secret police investigation. No SAS team is about to kick in the doors. Nobody knows about the secrets in this place. Either Isobel has somehow buried the truth behind a *been-staying-with-a-friend* story, or it's her decomposing corpse that's buried. No one knows the truth. No one is coming.

When the hatch opens and the madman says, 'The next challenge has begun,' Katrina leaps to her feet. She grabs the dress, balls it up, approaches the hatch, and lobs it at him – or at the empty hole. It hits the ceiling and falls.

'What did you do with Isobel? There's no way you would have released her. What did you do? Is she dead?'

From out of sight, he says, 'The challenge has begun. I will be down shortly.'

'Listen to me, you damn—'

The hatch shuts. Only then does Katrina register what he actually said. The next challenge has already begun.

———

Katrina stands facing the door, waiting to go to eat. She is in knickers and T-shirt. She wears no make-up. The purple dress is torn and splayed open by her feet. The floor is littered with pages that composed the three Robin Cook novels that had been sitting on the top of the bookshelf. Amongst this mess are fragments of porcelain, from the gaunt-face mask ornament. She had thrown it at the floor.

She has had it with this madman. When he comes to take her to the swimming pool, she will attack. The stand from the mask ornament is a base with a sharp pole, and she holds it behind her back. She will put it through his eye, or his throat. While he lies dying, she will go open doors, releasing all the captives. If some of the girls want to have a few moments to make him further regret being born, she won't object. Would they get in trouble for killing him after what he did?

But when he comes, it is to the door hatch, which opens downwards and outwards to create a little shelf. His mask is framed within the square hole. The door itself remains shut, locked.

It was the dress, she realises. She should have worn the dress. Shouldn't have trashed the room. Anyone could see she is in rebel mode. He knows her plan and is going to come nowhere near her.

'Bring me the books from on top of the bookshelf. The ones you've read. Trickery equals forfeit.'

'Balls to your books.' She sweeps a hand to indicate the mess of pages around her. 'Here they are. Come get them.'

'Bring them.'

'You want them? Sure thing, bozo.'

She gathers up some pages in two hands, goes to the hatch and tosses them out. He's standing too far back to be hit, but he watches the pages fall. He bends down and lifts a torn cover, and shakes his head.

'Not good. Bring me the mask ornament. No tricks.'

'Piss off. Come get it.'

He doesn't come in. Standing against the far wall of the corridor, well out of reach, he says, 'I have news about your brother. About the world. Have you heard of the Leonid meteor shower? Debris from a comet falls to earth every November. But this year it isn't a normal meteor shower. Debris the size of golf balls has been raining on the country.'

'Well I hope one lands on your head and smashes it open.'

'It's funny you say that. There are thousands dead in that very way, all across the world.'

'Piss off.' That's a snap reaction, but now she thinks about what he's actually said. Can this be true? She's got no way of knowing. 'Show me a damn newspaper.'

'I'll try. Soon.' He shuts the hatch.

'Wait. Get back here.' No response, other than his footsteps clopping away. She kicks the door. 'Hey, you freak, come back.'

The footsteps fade. He's gone. And it looks like she's missing breakfast for her insolence.

Or he's going for his gun.

———

Ten minutes after he left, Katrina's relieved: it means he isn't planning to put a bullet in her. But her joy is all gone within the hour: he's planning to punish her by holding back food.

More hours pass before he returns. He opens the hatch and says, 'The mask. Bring it to me.'

Katrina's walking on the treadmill, putting her anger to good use. There's still a healthy dose when she steps off. She looks around for the biggest broken shard of the mask, which she then tosses at his face through the hatch. Mask hits mask with a clink.

'Step inside here, dickhead, and you can have the rest of your little self-portrait.'

'I couldn't bring a newspaper. Production has ceased because of the fiery rain of meteors. All shops are destroyed. Millions lie dead across the world.'

She'd spent some time wondering if his meteor story was true. If he'd overcooked it like this back then, she would have known he was full of crap. 'Shut up, you fool.'

'I have a tank. I'm heading out soon to find supplies. I'll look for your brother.'

'He's got a sixth sense for cowardly maniacs. I'd be careful.'

He bends down, out of sight. When he stands again, he places onto the hatch the large fragment of mask she threw at him. She notices that he doesn't wear his gloves today, for the first time ever. Obviously, he plans not to open the door. When he shuts the hatch, the fragment falls into her cell.

It's stained with something orangey red. Blood? She cut him through the hatch somehow? She ignores it and kicks the door. 'Still there? Too scared to come in?'

No answer. She knows he's gone. She returns to the treadmill. She's not hungry yet, so the game can continue. She can't win, of course, but he has a plan for the girls and she doubts he'll let her starve. If the game becomes too much, she'll change her tactics.

After another half hour, she steps off the treadmill and goes to the sink for a drink. But the taps do nothing.

He's shut the water off.

'You bastard.' She grabs a small bottle of eyeliner and lobs it hard at the ceiling. The glass cracks a little. 'You up there? Are playing childish games? Think you're getting to me?'

An hour later, Katrina has to admit to herself that he has gotten to her. Of course he has. He is the one in control. Of the food, the water, everything. Her anger foiled logic, but now she's calmer and well aware that she's playing a dangerous game.

She tries the taps again, with the same result. Now she's very thirsty because of all that damn running. Fear starts to settle in, and her resolve suddenly collapses.

'I'm sorry,' she says to the ceiling hatch. No response.

She decides to clean up. When she picks up the dress, it hits her. She didn't dress for eating. He's always very determined about that. This is why he's annoyed and punishing her. It's torn, but if she can fix it and wear it, maybe he'll feed her again.

She clears up the scattered book pages and puts them into piles atop the bookcase. She kicks the broken porcelain mask shards into a pile against one wall. When she picks up the large fragment near the door, she realises it's not stained with blood. A lick confirms it. My God.

When he returns some hours later, at dinnertime, Katrina stands in the middle of the room, one hand holding the dress together at the front, the other cupped and containing all the fragments of busted porcelain.

'Bring me the mask,' he says through the door hatch.

Katrina steps forward, slowly, to show she means no harm, and carefully tips the porcelain shards onto the shelf.

The piece she'd thrown at him was returned stained with tomato soup. She watches him lift a ladle and tip more of the same all over the fragments. The soup immediately starts to run off the sides of the hatch.

'Take it,' he says.

'You fucking bastard,' she snaps at him, and kicks the door.

He slams the hatch. Soaked porcelain rains onto the floor and tomato soup slides down the smooth surface of the door.

Katrina retreats to her bed, tears off the ruined dress, sits, and cries.

———

By breakfast the next morning, the hunger pains have receded, but thirst is wreaking havoc. Her eyes feel sticky and she's got a killer headache and no energy. Her throat is also on fire, but she's pegged the cause as calling for him throughout the night. It started with threats. Then it was apologies. Soon, she was begging for mercy. All unanswered.

Her hazy head has also lost track of time. She's got no idea if her next 'feast' is breakfast or lunch or dinner. Maybe he skipped meals, even days. For all she knows, a week has passed.

When the door hatch opens, she doesn't get off the bed. 'Why are you doing this to me? I'm sorry about the dress and the mask. I'm sorry for everything. I'll be good.'

'Bring me the mask.'

He knows the mask is no longer such a thing. Is he using these words to remind her that she messed up? 'I need water.'

'Bring the mask.'

'I have chronic diarrhoea and I'm supposed to take electrolyte tablets.'

His head shakes. 'None of you is on medication. You're the second to try that trick. Bring me the mask.'

'Dammit, I need water, you bastard.'

'Bring me the mask.'

She left the pieces where they'd fallen yesterday – or last week. She stumbles over and scoops them up with both hands. Her hands are so shaky that when she dumps the pieces onto the hatch, a portion skips off the sides.

'What about water? You're giving food, but no water. Why? What did I do wrong?'

'This is not a punishment. By the way, the meteor storm has brought the world to a standstill and I could get only a few tins of food. There are bloodthirsty gangs roaming. But we will be safe here. I located your brother.'

What? Gangs? The world has come to a standstill? She cuts such wonder, aware that it all means nothing. 'Just tell me what I did wrong? I just need water. Can't you pour water onto the mask bits instead? Just this one time?'

'Your brother is part of one such murderous gang. They rape and kill and destroy villages.'

She laughs with sheer frustration. 'I guess I'm safe here then. Oh thank you for saving me.'

This time when he shuts the hatch, she's able to catch some of the fragments that fall. Holding them in both cupped hands, tight against her chest, she licks the door as trails of soup trickle down. Then she turns her tongue to the floor. When she's gotten all she can, she returns to the bed and lays the porcelain pieces on her thigh. One by one, she sucks at each.

———

Bring me the mask.

Bring me the mask.

Bring me the mask.

How many meals has she had? The number eludes her, but each time he came and she dumped mask pieces on the hatch, her shivering hands clumsily sent a few sailing off onto his side. He never returned them. The number remaining has dwindled. She tried to put the mask back together, but the jigsaw was too complicated. None of the cosmetics in her room was any good as a glue.

But she has a plan. The lack of water is making her brain do funny things, but it's still got reserve power and threw her a memory: he'd said she was the second person to try a lie about medication. She wasn't suffering alone! He was starving all the girls. Hadn't he also said the next challenge had begun? This wasn't a punishment, but a challenge.

The mask is part of it, but so are the books. He had asked for the books she'd read. Thankfully, she'd only destroyed a handful. So, when the hatch opens again, however many hours or days later, she's ready.

The remaining books from the bookshelf are stacked in neat piles before the door. On legs that barely keep her upright, she starts feeding them into the hatch.

'Look, I read all these. It's the books, isn't it?'

Two, three, four at a time the books fall to the floor outside her cell. The madman just watches through the little eye slits in his mask, silent.

'All, read all, this one here, great book, and this, read all, here, have them, sorry, really sorry for what I did, great books.'

He waits until every book is by his feet before saying, 'I said no tricks. Bring me the mask.'

The single book she held back is *Gai-Jin* by James Clavell, a fifteen-hundred-page paperback four inches thick. She places it onto the hatch. Her fingernails are ruined from digging into that book, tearing away at the cover and the pages beneath. Over many hours, she created a hollow an inch deep, a makeshift bowl that she hopes might hold half a tin of tomato soup.

But she's not stupid. It's all about the mask. The broken porcelain pieces sit inside that book. She smiles at him so deeply that her dried lower lip splits and she feels a trickle of blood run down her chin.

'Also read this first, great, you read it, can we chat about it while we eat?'

'No tricks,' he says, and slams the hatch. She's standing so close that the book and the mask fragments are propelled into her neck and chest before falling to the ground. She drops to her knees and picks up a large fragment, and she sucks at it for a couple of seconds before realising it's bone dry. No soup. He gave her no food.

'Wait, soup, I gave the pieces, please.'

Through the door, he says, 'Your brother's cut-throat gang of vagabonds tried to come in and rescue you. I just killed them all. When I slit his throat, your brother made the same whining as your dog.'

Jasper. She forgot about him. She stands and starts to punch and kick the door, but it depletes her energy and ignites a painful spike of dizziness. She turns to the bed, needing to lie down.

She gets halfway before crumpling to the floor.

———

When the hatch is dropped next, the creak makes her eyes open. The world is sideways. She is still on the floor, halfway between bed and door.

'Bring me the mask.'

She's glued to the floor. Her head won't rise, nor her hands. But it's comfortable here. Painless. She just stares at the masked face framed in the hatch. There's no energy to beg him to bring her the food.

The hatch slams. She closes her eyes. Oh well. Next time.

CHAPTER NINETEEN

Louder, Piper, Pint was a What3words address for a wooded area just off rural Habton Road in Kirby Misperton, North Yorkshire. Noa spent the entire night checking social media, UbyU and other news outlets for updates.

Right next to the wooden area was a twenty-four-hour truck stop – the only building out there – that was in full flow and crammed with truckers, but none of the clientele had heard the news. First on the scene, given their proximity, were local reporters and village residents. North Yorkshire police were right behind and ousted people from the woods before they found anything.

A chain-link fence at the edge of the trees separated the woods from the grounds of the truck stop; just inside that fence by the backyard was an area carpeted with rubbish. Beer bottles, plastic pint pots, crisp packets and more, tossed there by truckers through the years. In a ditch in the middle of the littered area was a plastic water barrel lying on its side. It was in the square designated by the three-word address.

Habton Road was the only route here so police blocked it a hundred metres each side of the woods. Officers were posted in the fields to stop gawkers getting too close. The trees made perfect cover for officers to conduct a search in private. But they made a mistake and, after a video was uploaded to Facebook, were forced to start truthfully answering some questions.

That video was taken by the teenaged son of the truck stop's owner, who'd secretly filmed the crime scene from his attic room on his mobile phone. His footage showed detectives and crime-scene technicians in the rubbish-filled area. It showed a man opening the barrel and giving a reaction that said there was more than just air inside.

Reporters and locals who'd reached the scene before them had seen that barrel. One man had refused to let anyone touch it, but now it was obvious what was inside. North Yorkshire police soon admitted the barrel contained a skeletonised body.

Speculation about the identity ran rife, but not for long. Noa drifted to sleep at about 5am and woke again at 7.30; by then dental records had come through.

The skeleton belonged to Katrina Lytton, thirty-one, from Arbroath, missing since late October 2020.

Noa immediately thought of Jerome. She had confidently told him that the woman held captive by Isobel's killer wasn't his sister. She'd never promised that Katrina wasn't already dead by his hand, but Jerome had been heartened by her words.

After the country had woken and digested the news, focus turned away from the victim and onto the Met Police, and not in a good way. They came under fire for going ahead with the live show, as expected, but also for removing Noa, which had upset the killer. A midday edition of a large e-newspaper ran a feature about the main players in the investigation, with emphasis on their career faults. It was in this article that Noa discovered something about her boyfriend of three months.

Bokayo was facing a misconduct disciplinary hearing. Late last year he'd been caught abusing his powers by flashing his warrant to receive free train rides. His hearing had been set to take place at the Empress State Building on April 27, just a few days away, but had been pushed back to June.

By midday, police had issued a statement in defence of their actions regarding removing Noa from her own show. Katrina Lytton had clearly been dead a long time, they said, so their actions had not caused her murder. In fact, the decision to oust Noa had made the killer give up Katrina's body, which he might otherwise not have done. A puzzle had been partly solved and there was a chance the crime scene or the body could deliver evidence. Some nodded in agreement with this, but some shook their heads in disgust. Lose–lose. Noa had an entirely different emotion: frustration. The police had slated her for using the very same logic.

Across the morning, a new angle to the story had been gaining traction. Given that Isobel's body had been found in Lincolnshire and Katrina's in Yorkshire, the sky was the limit and people all over the country were wondering if the next body would turn up in their neck of the woods. And the appearance of a 'next body' was something few doubted.

Belief was rife that the killer of the two girls would announce another location, another body, on the confessions show tonight, and they were getting prepared. An hour after it aired on their 13.30 slot, Noa found a news article from a BBC Look East reporter, who was on location at a housing estate in Norwich. To camera he said, 'Much like in the land rushes of nineteenth century America, people across the country are geared up for action. Instead of high noon, high midnight is when these townsfolk will make a mad dash. But instead of claiming land, they will hope to claim a dead body...'

The camera panned to three people standing by a car. A tall

man was with a woman and a teenager, introduced as the Markham family. The teenager held a shovel. The woman had a flashlight. The man had a roll of tape.

The reporter said that he'd spoken to many people that day who planned to race off in search of the next victim of what he called the Confession Killer. Each of them was kitted out and ready to roll the moment another three-word address was announced. Police were worried about the destruction of evidence by such people, but the Markhams only wanted to help. Care to explain that?

Mr Markham did. He waved the tape he held. 'We're not the morbid types. I've heard people say they want to get selfies with the body. I know one guy who said he wants to find the body so his name will be out there, in the true crime books, you know. But if the next body is around here, I just want to do the right thing. Can't have people walking all over a crime scene. We just plan to tape off the body and stop people getting close.'

'And what's the reason for the shovel?' the reporter asked.

After a pause in which he looked like a deer caught in headlights, Mr Markham said, 'Just to clear away junk and dig a little so the police don't have as much work to do. Just trying to help, that's all.'

Noa's name was everywhere. The public wanted to know where she was, what she was doing, how she felt. Reporters were desperate to talk to her. So were the police. She was determined to avoid all of them for as long as possible.

———

She called Bokayo around 5pm, and he was quite upset. 'Where are you? Why has your phone been off?'

'That number I gave you is dead. I destroyed the phone last

night in case I got death threats. This phone will go the same way. I'm cycling through numbers. I don't want anyone contacting me. I'll do the contacting.'

'You can't just hide like this. We've been trying to get you all day. Where are you? You left the hotel.'

'Another hotel. I'm keeping that secret too. So why are you calling?'

'It wasn't my call to remove you from the show, remember?'

'I'm not annoyed at you, just the police in general. So I'm guessing the higher-ups have had another change of mind?'

'Yes. You know we got another body, right?'

'I heard. Impossible not to. Look, I'll be at the police station at 11 tonight. Your people can brief me then about what trickery they want me to try with the kidnapper next.'

She hung up. She bust the phone because it was now a compromised number.

She finally found the courage, around 8pm, to make another phone call, on a fresh burner phone. The man who answered said, 'Sorry, I'm not taking on new jobs for the next few days.'

'Jerome, it's Noa.'

Katrina's brother was silent for a moment. 'If you'd called this morning, I would have sworn to kill you.'

'You'd have every right.'

'No. Your words kept playing in my head. You said you didn't know if that bastard had kidnapped Katrina. You said the girl he had wasn't her. It was actually right. Because he doesn't have her. He killed and buried her probably right after he took her. She was rotting out there for a year and a half. At least I now know what happened to her.'

'I'm still sorry. For your loss.'

'Don't worry about me. I'm no one. Did you call for something or just to say sorry?'

Noa wiped her eyes. This call was more emotional than she'd expected. 'I just feel bad for you.'

'Don't. I'm okay. Katrina was popular. I have enough people around me giving useless sorrow. No offence. It just doesn't help. But if you want to help me, keep me informed about what the police are doing to catch this bastard. By the time the police come to my door to tell me he's dead or caught, I already want to know that.'

'I will. I promise,' Noa said, but she felt she had already spoken to him for the last time.

———

Unlike last time, there was no media mob outside the police station. A camera saw her car approach the black gates and they opened immediately. Bokayo was waiting in the yard out back of the police station. He was so eager, he yanked the driver's door open before her car had fully pulled up.

'Can you stop running off and hiding like this? My bosses are considering detaining you for your own safety under the Mental Health Act.'

A slight smile said he was joking, but she recognised annoyance in the rest of his body language. 'Is there another crowd in the room like before?'

'Yes, so let's get up there.'

She got out. 'Why's there no reporters outside?'

'We let slip that the show is being hosted from another station. They're all hanging out there.'

He tried to take her arm, but she pulled away. 'Flashed your warrant card to get on any trains for free lately?' she said.

He looked puzzled, or pretended to. He quickly gave it up. 'You heard that crap on the news then. I made a mistake. I have an Oyster card that lets me travel free, but only on the overground trains. I was taking Thameslink trains to see my family. Didn't realise.'

'And now you're facing a disciplinary hearing. Which just got pushed back. Why was that?'

He shrugged. 'I don't question the suits. Why the interest?'

'Why would someone facing a disciplinary suddenly be given this big case? Is it because you know me?'

'I told you before—'

'I don't mean some crap about us being spotted at a supermarket. I mean, do they know you *really* know me?'

'No one knows we're sleeping together.'

He looked nervous, and she knew she had him. 'Bullshit. I think you went to your boss and blurted it out. I think you said, "Hey, I'm shagging this woman and I can work her. She's a little kid to my Pied Piper." I know we've joked about this, but I'm also now seriously wondering if you're only with me because of my show and the criminals that call in. Or it's a bonus, at least.'

He folded his arms defiantly. 'Silly, Noa, silly. You've been doing this show for four months. How many real criminals have called up? A handful at most. The biggest case you got was the murder of Dai Xi, and that was a big deal, granted. But, if you remember correctly, I wasn't involved.'

True. But she still had suspicions. 'Then you were just in a lucky place at the right time. I still think you used our relationship to get on this investigation. Maybe to help with your reprimand. Which worked because it's been put back. Do well on this and maybe it goes away.'

'Listen to yourself. Silly. I was taking the wrong trains, Noa. I wasn't caught taking bribes. Jesus. And no one knows we share a bed. Are you serious?'

A uniformed police officer approached, probably sent by

someone. Bokayo waved him away. 'Then prove it,' Noa said when they were alone again. 'Prove you didn't get on this case because of your connection to me. Prove you're not here just to help yourself. Walk away. Tell the head of this task force that we're banging. If you got on this case on your own merit, then they'll whip you right off if you admit that to them. Do that and we can continue to see each other. Or stay on the case and give me up.'

'Seriously? You're that paranoid? There's a killer out there and I'm a police officer and I want to catch him. No copper would ever claim he didn't like the idea of solving a big case.'

'That's not what I said. I asked you to choose between me and the case. Right now.'

'We're not having this conversation. How about you give up your radio show for me? That fair?'

'Okay. When this is over, I'll give it up. So, are you going to walk?'

He paused. 'So, give up my career or lose you? That's an ultimatum. I don't give in to such things. Look, let's just get inside.'

'Choice made then.'

'No, no, no. You've made a choice, not me.'

Neither of them said anything for a moment. They just stared at each other. Bokayo broke the silence. 'So, I guess that's it between us. Okay. It was nice while it lasted.' He stepped back and straightened his tie. 'Okay, Miss Vickerman. Thank you for coming. Shall we go inside?'

'Yes, Inspector Tomori. Lead the way.'

She searched his eyes, trying to determine if this was part of a jest, and she saw he was doing the same. 'You're serious, right?' he said.

She wasn't certain of that at all. But it felt right, because if he'd gotten on this case by convincing his bosses that he had an edge due to his intimate relationship with her, then that was a massive betrayal. An unforgivable one. So, she nodded.

He turned and walked towards the building. Keeping a couple of metres behind him, she did the same.

———

'It's midnight, April 23rd, 2022, I'm Noa, and the phones are already ringing, so let's take the first call.'

The killer wasn't amongst the bunch vying for first call, so the show had to go ahead as normal. It was the best way to convince the public that he was part of the show, not the other way round. This would also make the killer wait in the queue, to surreptitiously remind him that he didn't call the shots.

Aware that he might not call at all, Noa pushed aside all thoughts of him for now and decided to treat it as a normal night. The only difference was that the callers were vetted, and only those with genuine confessions were patched through. It was a smart move, but the police weren't the only ones with savvy.

A man had told an officer manning the phone that he wanted to admit to stealing garden gnomes. When he was patched through to Noa, she said, 'Hello, friend. What's bugging you at this late hour?'

'My neighbour has these garden gnomes that are really annoying, so I *how do you feel knowing you killed those girls by being a stupid bitch who—*'

He caught her off-guard, so it took a second to thumb the kill switch. Noa got really prepared after that. The second caller was also only interested in the killer, but was polite enough to enquire if he could ask some questions. Noa apologised and cut him off. The third was another crank and Noa got her early. Caller four tried the same trick as number one, and that did it for Noa. She announced a short break and played 'Free Bird'. None of the police officers in the office objected.

All waiting callers were removed. Genuine or not, everyone who phoned while the song played was ejected in order to free the line for the killer. Eight minutes into 'Free Bird', someone vetting the callers gave a signal. The killer was here.

The call was patched through. Noa faded out the song and went live. She had planned to use her standard *hello friend* line, to pretend his call hadn't been expected, but she was on edge and forgot. 'Give me a name to use.'

'*Call me Saturn,*' the same bland voice said. '*Or Ringo, from The Beatles, if you like. Perhaps even something normal like William. Or Poe or Edgar, since we're fans. Let's go with that. I am Poe. Tonight I want to learn more about you, Noa. Married, separated, single?*'

She tried not to glance at Bokayo when she said, 'Single. Can we talk about your prisoner? I need proof she's alive.'

'*Soon. First—*'

'I'm sorry. It's just that you said Isobel was the only girl you were forced to kill. Yet you then gave us Katrina Lytton, and she, too, had been dead a long time. You say you kidnapped five girls. How do I know they're all not dead?'

'*I feel quite bad about things I told Katrina. Lies I told about her brother. She died believing he was dead.*'

'You feel bad for lying to her, but not for killing her?'

'*She doesn't exactly feel upset about that, does she? I'll answer your first question: you don't know the others aren't dead. We'll get to that soon, I said. First, you. Ready?*'

She looked around the room. No one nodded, shook their head, or said anything. They wanted this man to talk and now, finally, at least partly, trusted Noa to make that happen.

'What do you want to know about me?' she said.

'*Your father was a lawyer. Your father's company was*

Vickerman Marriot. His information on the website said he specialised in banking and capital markets work and restructuring, with extensive knowledge of leverage finance and corporate lending. His clients included banks, financial sponsors and corporates.'

She stiffened, wondering when the killer had learned this information. Today, in preparation for this chat? Or had he studied her long before making first contact? 'Yes. It's all a mouthful.'

'That information was in his obituary. He died Feb 2019 from lung cancer. He was a heavy cigar smoker. How did that affect you? Were you close to him?'

'Yes.'

'I wasn't close to my father. He took care of me, but he didn't love me. What about your mother?'

'Yes. I was close to her. She died not long before him. A car hit her bicycle.'

'I also wasn't very close to my mother. My mother, she did love me, but he brainwashed her into not doing so. How did they meet?'

'Another bike crash, bizarrely. My dad had just been to the Almeida Theatre to watch *Scenes from an Execution*. This was in January of 1990. She was riding past when he came out and she hit him. He joked about suing her. They got chatting. His firm had another office up in Scotland so he used to travel up there a lot. Do you like Scotland?'

'Oh, Scotland, suddenly? Where Katrina Lytton was from. Is this where I'm supposed to say something that the police can use to work out if I live in Scotland? Noa, what did I say? We'd get to the girls. So, you were born on Christmas Day 1991. How's it feel having that as a birthday?'

'As a kid, horrible. That was my special day, but it always got overshadowed.'

'Some might say that would make a special birthday. Your life was always a bit special, wasn't it? As part of the beau monde, the jet set, the cream of society. James Allen's Girls' School, the oldest private school in London. Oxford University. Wimbledon membership. Rubbing shoulders with movie stars. Quite the existence.'

Noa snorted. 'I hated school. I didn't want to study at university. It was actually the Wimbledon Racquets and Fitness Club. And my father was the shoulder-rubber, with me as a little girl by his side who knew none of these people.'

'Still, you had chances and opportunities that I never had, even though my father, like yours, had clout in his community.'

That stung. She was angry and only partly managed to hold it back. 'Not everyone wants what they're offered. I wanted to go to a normal school. And as for university, that wasn't exactly a dream come true. I had no desire to study. So I chose the useless. Liberal arts. Fashion design. Literature. I was burning time.'

'But none of those courses are what you studied at Oxford University. He wangled it to get you in there for a Bachelor of Laws.'

'Because he was quite insistent that I follow his footsteps. So I went along with it, for three years.'

'Just going through the motions? You achieved that degree. I'm not sure that's something someone can do on autopilot.'

'Oh, but I did. And afterwards, I felt trapped. My father and I had a raging argument. He wanted to make me a lawyer. I wanted no such thing. It did no good to tell him this though. My only way out? Something loftier. So I took another course I had no desire for. Economics at Imperial College London. Three more years of hell. But I pretended I wanted to help save the world, and he could hardly argue with that.'

'And then he died. And you were free of his control. We do at least share that in common.'

'I spent ten years trying to work to something he wanted. It wasn't just university. I studied in my free time, just to better myself and please him. I took etiquette classes, for Christ's sake. Six months of that crap, just because one day he said I could benefit from it. I didn't want any of it.'

'Minor inconveniences. You lived the high life, reaping the benefits of his wealth and social standing.'

'Yes, I was able to dump all the plans he had for me after he died. But I also dumped the high-flier lifestyle. I grew out of it. Maybe deep down all I was doing while partying was rebelling. Or simply letting my hair down. You say I had chances? I was fortunate? I was forced down a path I didn't want to walk.'

She had raised her voice without realising it. She glanced around the room. Everyone was transfixed, but at what exactly? The killer, or her? She'd never told anyone what she was now unloading to the whole country.

Poe laughed. 'Are we supposed to feel pity? Your father dumped a lavish lifestyle in your lap. Holidays, exclusive club memberships, cars, fancy restaurants, rich friends, cash on tap. And what's changed since he died? You live in high-end London in a house very few could afford and suck from a nipple attached to a bloated will, and behind you there's not a single hard day's work. You were born lucky, Noa Vickerman. And lazy–'

'Lazy?' she snapped. 'You don't know–'

'And ungrateful. Massively so. You act as if you've had a tough life and hated it, but let me ask you right now. Would you swap it for mine?'

'No, because you have a rotten, sick brain.'

The room erupted into panicked whispers. Noa felt her heart sink. Thousands were listening, and millions would learn about this conversation over the coming days. If Poe did something bad, something lethal, the finger of blame would point only one way. Including her own finger.

After a pause, Poe said, *'You need to learn how to speak to me nicely. Maybe this will help. Human. Dozed. Globe.'*

He then hung up.

CHAPTER TWENTY

3 NOVEMBER 2020

Her first thought upon waking is: *He's gone too far this time. I should have told my mum years ago.*

She sits up and takes in the room. Bed, upon which she lies. Sink. Treadmill. Bookshelf. Armchair. These are items one might place into a cell where you expect to keep a captive for an extended period. Not good. Thick iron or steel door, with a hatch and no handle this side, like a police station cell door. A trio of large windows with what at first looks to be a countryside view but upon closer inspection turns out to be an illusion created by a giant picture attached to the glass. The ceiling is large panes of mirrored glass, with a small circular section in the middle that looks like a hatch. Is that how her stepfather will deliver supplies to her?

She realises her shorts and NASA T-shirt, used as pyjamas for two years now, are gone. Replaced with grey knickers and grey –

He touched her in the night, she suddenly remembers. She has a hazy vision of him leaning over her, undressing her. He was saying something – something about global warming, was it? Yes. And habitat destruction. And he touched her down below, and he said it was 'good'. That word she clearly remembers.

She scratches at her forearms, bringing up red marks. It is how she relieves the disgrace and disgust when he touches her. It doesn't seem to work now. Did it ever really do a good job?

Normally he visits her bedroom late at night, but this isn't her bedroom so he's taken a massive step up. But how far will he go? Touching her is one thing, but this is a whole new level. He must know he can't just kidnap her and hide the fact from her mother.

When she was young, simple threats ensured her silence. He would say, *If you tell anyone our secret, you will be taken into care*, or he would go overboard and threaten that the bogeyman would take her to Hell. Those warnings worked when she was a child, but not once she reached her teens. Then, he had resorted to claims like *Tell anyone and I'll kill your mother* or *I'll bury your body and everyone will just think you ran away*. Often she had wondered what his endgame was, when she moved out of the family home or got too old to turn him on. Always she came to the same conclusion: he might kill her rather than risk her opening her mouth somewhere down the line.

Had he reached that point of no return? Was that why he'd snatched her while they were on holiday in the middle of nowhere? Was she here so he could have some final fun before killing her?

This reminds her of her time in the jungle. Back then, she never stopped to wonder if the wild animals might have already eaten. She thought only about avoiding the wild animals in order to survive. Same here. No time should be wasted hoping her stepfather would change his mind, or trying to talk him round. She must just focus on escape. Survival.

The door will be impossible to break open, so she

approaches the windows. They're not the kind that open; the glass is actually heavy-duty plastic, impossible to cut or break or remove; the frames look too sturdy to pry out of the wall. She can't get out that way.

He doesn't want her to see out, either. Why? So he can say she's really in a field or underground or something. Maybe in truth she's somewhere populated and people might hear if she yells for help.

She won't do that yet, because noise will bring him. She needs to look around this room more first.

She cannot get to the window stickers because they're on the outside of the glass, but the ceiling is another matter. Directly above her bed is a pane that's a little different to the others. A close look shows her it's not a mirror but reflective glass. One-way glass.

She's still groggy from whatever drug her stepfather shot into her, but she manages to hoist the armchair onto the bed and climb atop. The structure is wobbly, or she is, but she manages to balance and get her fingers to the pane of glass.

With a nail, she digs at a corner. Yes, she was right! The reflective film has been applied on the exposed side of the glass. She gets hold of the corner in two fingers and pulls, and the film starts to peel away in one piece.

Sure enough, she is right again. Beneath the film is a simple pane of glass. Once a good portion is exposed, she can see a room above. It's plain, bare except for an armchair and a coffee table next to it with a book. But when she peels more, she sees a cup and an ashtray sitting on the glass. The bottom of the cup has a 99p sticker.

Now she understands. The whole ceiling is mirrored in order to hide this pane, which is where he sits or lies in order to stare down at her when she sleeps. How long has she been asleep? Where has he gone?

From this angle, she can see a wooden door in one side of the upper room. It's open. Bizarrely, the room beyond is exactly like the one above: bare except for another armchair in the middle of the floor, a coffee table beside it.

She turns her head to look behind. There's another door in the wall, but this one is closed.

And then it isn't.

It suddenly opens, and a man walks in.

The shock of his appearance almost topples her from the chair. He wears a strange, coloured, baggy outfit. Immediately, he spots her and spins away, to hide his face. But she's already caught a glimpse, and, with horror, determined two things.

One, there is something wrong with his face. Two, it's not the face of her abusive stepfather.

Someone else has abducted her.

———

'My name is Mercy Ford, I am twenty-one and from Prestatyn in Wales. My weaknesses are chocolate and animal cruelty – I mean I like the first and hate the second, that is. I should really add child cruelty, since my stepfather has been sexually abusing me since he met my mum, when I was ten. And now I have another man treating me like–'

'Stop,' the weirdo bellows from the room above. Mercy turns away from the camera and looks up at the ceiling hatch. She can see just his mask and shoulders; in another environment, she might have laughed at the comical, cartoon-like image. 'Skills and weaknesses and future plans, that is all you're required to talk about. But please mention your time in Gabon. Restart.'

She nods and turns back to the camera. After repeating her name and home city, she says, 'On safari in Gabon, I was lost in the jungle for two days at just sixteen years of age. I thought I'd seen the wildest animals earth has to offer, but now I'm trying to survive against a man who–'

'Stop.'

'What's wrong?'

'Look at me.'

She stares up. He stares down. After analysing her for perhaps ten seconds, he says, 'Continue. Please don't mention me or your stepfather in this interview.'

'Cool. Okay, my name is...'

———

The mask, the outfit, the kidnap, the one-way mirror – none of that convinces Mercy that her captor is a weirdo. But she knows it to be true when he drops down through the hatch a yellow dress and yellow hair dye. There's also yellow lipstick. Yellow? Only weirdos like yellow.

As her mum has always told her, she speaks her mind. But she also knows her place. She knows that when he stared at her earlier after she messed up the camera interview twice, he was trying to read her. Trying to work out if she was a troublemaker. But she wasn't. She just wasn't that scared of him. Those two days lost in the jungles of Gabon in Africa had made her into a new animal.

Back then, worry, panic, fear, any one of those emotions could have killed her. Instead, she had focussed on the job in hand, which was survival. It was no different now. The cards had been dealt. Her hand is a cell in an unknown location with a weirdo controlling her, a guy who probably wants what her stepfather always lusts after. Her job is to stay calm and plan her escape, making moves only when the time is right. Rushing headlong through the jungle, screaming for help, would have gotten her mauled to death or lost forever. Same here. The weirdo probably thought she had been giving him attitude, but she was just being herself and dealing with her lot and biding time.

Right now he wants her to go yellow for what he calls 'feasting'. So she will do that. There's deodorant and soap and a hairbrush, and she will use all that stuff too. If she does what he says, he'll overlook her attitude. Days may pass before she can get a chance to bolt from whatever place this is, but that doesn't matter. The longest trek up the toughest mountain is taken one step at a time.

———

When Mercy enters a large hall with an empty swimming pool in the centre and sees another woman sitting at a dining table, she's not shocked. Not yet. This is helpful to escape plans. The man's time will be halved. He won't be concentrating on Mercy as much.

The other woman is also black, a bit older. Her colour scheme is purple, so he's not a yellow fan after all. He must be one of those fools who thinks black people all look the same, so the dresses and hair and lipstick are to tell them apart. Weirdo.

Obviously this woman has been here longer, so she'll have some good information about the guy and this place. Mercy's desperate to get that info, but the weirdo instructs them not to talk to each other.

Up close, Purple Woman looks to have no scars or bruises, so that's good. The weirdo isn't torturing his women. But she looks worn down and that's probably a sign she's been here ages. Or maybe not. She looks the prim and proper type who'd fold after a day locked up by someone. This lass would have been eaten within five minutes in the jungle. When Mercy sits, she silently mouths some words of encouragement to the purple woman.

She needs to find a proper way to communicate with this woman and has an idea. She needed to pee before she came here and expected a bucket, but the weirdo took her to a small bathroom and waited outside. Probably the same score for Purple Woman. So that's a good place to leave a note for Purple Woman. All Mercy needs is to convince the weirdo to let her have some pencils and paper. He reckons he knows all about her, and if that's true he knows she likes to draw, so there will be no suspicion.

Best if she and Purple Woman don't become good friends though. The weirdo said there will be challenges. He didn't elaborate, but now there's another woman so it's obvious they'll be competing against each other. Could be violent stuff. Could be that the loser will be killed. She hated that time when she had to send her gerbil off to be put down by the vet, so it'll feel pretty bad if she has to sacrifice a friend.

———

So, step one, she asks for drawing materials when he's walking her back to her room. He agrees, no questions, and dumps the items through the ceiling hatch a bit later. Fifteen pens and pencils, which she scatters around the room so it's harder for him to track if one's gone missing. An hour later, she hides a pen in her knickers and asks to use the toilet, so she can leave her first secret note for Purple Woman.

Back in her room, she draws a bridge over a river while thinking about escape options.

There are two ways to do it. Short-term or long-term. Long-term involves gaining his confidence until he starts to get a bit lazy with security. She remembers there was an Austrian girl who got locked in a cellar by some guy. Natascha Kampusch? She slowly got her captor to trust her and he began allowing her outdoors, and one day she just ran.

But that took years, and that just won't do. So, the short-term way. That has two sub-options: escape while he's not around, or take him down when he's with her. Back in the swimming pool, he left her alone while he took Purple Woman to her cell. If he repeats that next time, it will give her a good couple of minutes to escape before he realises. But then he would be on the hunt, and she doesn't know the outlay of this place. In the jungle, the key had been hiding, not blindly running. She couldn't hide here for long, yet running could see her trapped in a dead end. Even if she escaped the building, she could be in the middle of open land. Not good if he's got a sniper rifle. Or a motorbike to chase her down.

The only chance she has, then, is to take him out, so she has extra time. She could also rescue Purple Woman. Then they could look for a way out or a phone.

To take him out, she'll need a weapon. The cutlery is crappy thin wood and no good. The pencils he gave her are just the weak lead and the pens just the floppy ink tubes and nibs. None of the books in her room are really heavy enough. The hairbrush is too flimsy. She could break a cosmetic bottle for sharp glass, but she doesn't want to get into a lengthy fight with a man six inches taller and wearing what he claims are stun gloves. She needs something that will incapacitate him with one strike.

She also needs to pick the right moment. He walks behind her when they go places, so that's too risky. The toilet door opens inward, so she can't really rush out or bash it into him.

The swimming pool. Two metres deep. If she can push him in when he's not expecting it and he lands awkwardly, he might break a leg or arm, or at least be stunned enough to give her the edge if she can attack him immediately afterwards. She will have to see the scene a few more times, analyse his movements, get the physics worked out in her head. But she's sure the pool is the place for the takedown.

Mercy clears her mind. Step one of her escape plan complete. Progress made. She hums as she draws, content for now.

————

22 November 2020, 3.26pm

The whoosh jerks her awake. With no ability to do anything in the dark, she'd fallen asleep on the armchair. She realises the whooshing noise is water and she makes her way blindly across the room, to the sink. Water is gushing out of the tap, which she left turned on after he cut the supply – how long ago now, three, four days? Mercy sticks her face under, and drinks heavily.

Since he had cut off the water, she'd had only two half-pint plastic glasses' worth, which had been given to her in exchange for the books he'd taken. He had ordered that any books read be placed on top of the bookshelf, and she'd given him three. A Stephen King novel, one by Whitley Streiber, one by Jane Austen that she'd tackled only because a friend was a fan of the TV show based on it. She had wanted to drink both glasses immediately, but she knew she might not get more for a while so had sipped, making them last two days. She learned that trick in the jungle.

As for food, nought but tomato soup, which he had insisted on pouring into the mask ornament from the shelf in her room. Weirdo. Now the water is back on, hopefully there will be better food.

When she's drunk her fill, she makes her way back to the armchair. And sits in the dark in silence.

Much later, she hears footsteps above and a bright moon

appears as the ceiling hatch opens. His face is backlit and she can see only the edges of his mask.

'Oh, your light failed. I'm sorry.'

The light had faltered not long after he'd brought her most recent portion of soup. Since then, extreme darkness. 'I thought you turned it off.'

'No. I'll get it fixed. You should have told me immediately. It's not part of the challenge to make you sit in the dark.'

She remembers that he'd said the next challenge had already begun. The water was part of it, probably the soup too. But she still has no clue what's going on. She asks him to explain, but he tells her only that the challenge is now over.

'Did I win? Can I go home like Isobel did?'

'I told you. All of you. The challenges cannot be won, only lost.'

'So I didn't lose. But someone did. Who?'

'You will find out at feasting time. Which is soon. Dress for that, please.'

'What's the next challenge?'

'I cannot say. But I can tell you that that, too, has already begun. In fact, it's been active since the last of you arrived, days ago now.'

When he comes to collect her, she's already dressed and wearing new yellow lipstick. He has a new bulb for her ceiling light. He orders her to stand in a corner, facing the wall, while he makes the fix. She wonders if he's being cautious because one of the other girls has tried to attack him.

When the room is bright again, she remains in the corner, waiting for permission to turn. She jumps when he speaks from just inches behind her.

'I hope you do well. You seem genuine.'

She turns. His closeness appals her and she wants to press further into the corner. All men bother her, because of her stepfather, and usually she tells them to keep their distance. But she doesn't want to upset him, so she keeps her place.

'Thank you.'

'You're not as scared as the others. You don't look disgusted by me.'

Oh, she is, but she can act. She has to act around her mother, pretending that her stepfather is just a regular guy and absolutely not the sort who sneaks into the beds of ten-year-old girls at night. 'There's no reason to be disgusted,' she says. 'You're a person, like me.'

'You're nice. Not fake-nice, like Red. She's trying to convince me that she's the only woman I need. That I should just declare her the winner.'

He means the bad-attitude bodybuilder called Diamond. The red woman sneers at the other girls, but around this guy she's all smiles and flashing eyelashes. Mercy gets that it's an act to curry favour, but isn't that desperate herself. Her 'nice' attitude is somewhat real, because she's not in fear for her life. The other girls are, but that's because they can't think the way she does. They don't have her survival skills. They don't understand that fear can only hinder.

'Thank you,' she repeats.

He pauses. 'I shouldn't help you, but...'

He seems a bit nervous, as if he is breaking a rule and is worried about it backfiring. She wonders if there's a higher power, someone he's working for.

'...but I'll just say this. Take care of yourself. As a woman should. Even though you're here. I've supplied things.'

He glances at the sink. She realises he's talking about the

toiletries and cosmetics. *Take care of yourself.* The ongoing challenge – something about her appearance? Her health?

'It's time to go,' he says, and turns, and she follows him to the door. But then she stops. 'Wait a second.'

He watches as she approaches the sink, where she brushes her hair and sprays deodorant. When she turns back to him, he gives a little nod. And a smile.

Bingo. Now she understands the next challenge. Four girls remain and soon it will be three. She won't be the poor lass who doesn't make the cut.

———

When he places the ladder on the edge of the swimming pool, Mercy makes note of how close he stands to her, how often he looks away, and plays in her head how the takedown will occur. He seems to be careful when he clips the ladder into place, by standing sideways on to the pool and facing her. He's ready for any kind of attack, but that doesn't mean he could avoid it. Then again, he'd need only a second or two to activate those sci-fi gloves of his. She will watch a few more times to get his routine minutely memorised.

She's fourth to sit at the table, which is second from last. And he makes no move from his spot by the pool's edge. No journey to fetch Katrina. There is no Katrina.

She must have died of thirst. All the girls look worn out from their ordeal, although the youngster, Alex, seems freshest. He's put warm food out as well as the cold crap today, which is a first, and everyone is eating ravenously. Maybe he knows the girls will need calories after days of nothing but tomato soup. Maybe it's a reward for not dying.

The woman in red, the bodybuilder called Diamond, is helping herself to nothing but chips and sausages. Kai, in green, is guzzling fizzy Coke. But Alex merely nibbles on a carrot and sips water, as if she hasn't suffered much at all. Perhaps not all the girls were part of his starvation challenge. Maybe she had a secret stash of food in her room.

Or she knows something. She's the genius brain, after all.

Mercy waits until Alex looks at her, then she holds up a cold cocktail sausage. The girls have developed a table-code of gestures and Alex uses it to say *no*. Mercy then touches a piece of lettuce. *No*. Mercy touches a chicken drumstick and pulls her finger away quickly, just to show she feels the heat from it. *Yes*.

Now Mercy knows. The junk food isn't a reward or to help get strength back: it's part of the challenge. A test of willpower maybe? For whatever reason, the girls aren't supposed to touch the hot food.

Mercy grabs a handful of cold cocktail sausages and thanks Alex by gesture.

———

Immediately after being escorted back to her room, Mercy requests the toilet so she can write a secret note. She outlines the no-hot-food rule. Kai and Diamond were too busy chowing down to look at her, so she never got a chance to warn them at the dinner table. She sticks the note behind the toilet.

Then removes it again. They're not sisters. Everyone wants to survive, but four girls will become three. This note only increases Mercy's chances of a shallow grave or being fed to pigs or whatever method the weirdo uses to dispose of bodies. Is it really wrong to want to help herself? Isn't this note damaging to her, almost like a form of self-harm? Why would anyone give up information that would help others to survive in her place?

She flushes the note.

Back at her room, she opens the door and walks to the bed

and lies down. She realises she never heard the door close, and looks over to see him standing in the doorway. She sits up, unsure whether this is good or bad. That mask of his makes reading his face impossible. 'Are you okay?'

'You are my favourite.'

From anyone else, anywhere else, that might have brought a tear or a smile. She awkwardly says, 'I understand. Not fake-nice. Does that give me an advantage?'

'Yes. I shouldn't give clues or help... but tonight there's a cooking test. I like spicy.'

'I can do spicy,' she says, giving a grin. This is the second time he's admitted he likes her, and she sees a chance to push it a little. 'How's life outside there, in the world? Any good new movies at the cinema? Any singers been arrested or anything?'

She doesn't really care about celebrity gossip. It's just something nice and simple to start with.

'I can't talk about that. The rule.'

'You can't break that rule just for me? Your favourite?'

'No. I'm sorry.'

'Okay. I'm sorry to ask.'

He shuts the door. Well, it was worth a try. No damage done to their growing bond, it seems. Maybe she'll try again later. If she could just find out how her mother is coping, that would be enough.

A couple of hours later, he's back. She is blindfolded and led away. They go left out of her room, as if towards the toilet, but he makes her turn right a short way down. An unexplored corridor. Her nerves jangle because she knows she's heading somewhere new.

God, she hopes this is part of the cooking challenge. Maybe her rule-break earlier has upset him and he's taking her to be punished. Some way down this new corridor, past a couple of iron doors, they take a left and he orders her to stop. He unlocks a door in front of her.

He orders her through, and partway across a room, to a plastic garden chair. She sits and he releases her arm. She hears his feet move away.

'Blindfold off,' he says. Mercy pulls hers down and is surprised to see two things. First, she's in a large commercial kitchen. Second, the other three girls are here. Diamond, Kai, Alex. They all sit in a wide circle, facing inward. Nobody says a word. Four pairs of eyes turn to the door.

He stands there, and he's got his gun out. It's aimed at the floor, but his finger is on the trigger. Nobody could get to him before he raised that weapon and blasted a hole in them.

'I told you a challenge has been ongoing since you got here. You are here for a new challenge, but it is not part of the tournament. No punishment for the losers. The winner will receive a prize. A good prize. You have one hour. You will cook a meal for me. Best wins.'

'What prize?' Kai, in green, asks. She receives no answer. He leaves. He shuts the door. He locks it.

The girls look puzzled. Kai moves slowly to the door and puts her ear against it. And shakes her head. Meanwhile, Mercy looks around for another exit and sees two shutters on the walls, which probably bar doors. One is as wide as a set of double doors; he claims this is a school so there's probably a dining hall on the other side. There are no windows.

'Can we talk?' Alex says, loud. For him.

No response from the weirdo. 'We're going to have to talk to each other,' she calls out, even louder. Again, no answer.

'I guess that means we can,' Kai says.

'But be careful,' Diamond says. 'You girls just watch your damn mouths and don't eff this up for me.'

'My name is Mercy Ford. I'm twenty-one and from Prestatyn in Wales. Nice to meet you all.'

Alex and Kai give nervous laughs and introduce themselves, even though they did this by note days ago. Alex Byrne, nineteen, born and bred in Llanrumney. Kai Harlow, thirty, born in Glasgow. Hugs are exchanged.

But Diamond does not partake and watches with distaste. Mercy sticks out a hand, but the much taller bodybuilder ignores it. 'We ain't friends, we ain't fam. We're competing against each other. Only one can win.'

'Maybe we'll all get out of here,' Kai says. 'Maybe this time next month we'll all be roommates. Best friends. Nights out. We'll go to each other's birthday parties. Who knows?'

'You're all dickheads. I'll be going to your funerals, that's all.'

Kai steps closer to Diamond and sticks out her hand. 'What can it hurt? He clearly doesn't mind us talking in here. We know you're called Diamond. Nice name. What's your surname? Come on. We're girls having a chat.'

Diamond shakes her head. When Kai's hand remains outstretched, she slaps it away. 'You all want to survive, right? Only one of us can. And you all want to be that one. That means you want me dead. So piss off before I put you down.'

The woman in red moves to a row of wall hooks where aprons hang and puts one on. The other three girls look at each other with understanding. They can chat and laugh, but this is no holiday. Lives hang in the balance. They have a job to do.

'Okay, ladies,' Mercy says. 'It's time to play 1950s housewife to a killer.'

All kitchens need a head chef and Diamond takes that role upon herself. When Kai grabs a knife from a rack and gives it a long look, Diamond says, 'Don't even think about it.'

'About what? Using a knife in a kitchen? Wouldn't dream.'

'About hiding that thing up your stinking fanny and sticking it in him.'

'Maybe I was planning to win this whole thing here and now.'

Diamond lifts up a frying pan. 'Come try and I'll mark you, bitch.' She waves the frying pan at all three other girls. 'All of you. Don't get any bloody plans about escaping. You ain't effing this up for me. Get cooking and I don't want to hear any bad shit about him.'

'You're not in charge here,' Kai says.

'Don't like it, come do something about it. Come on. All of you bitches, none of you better think about hiding a knife or a damn whisk or anything. He'll punish all of us. Anyone with thoughts of slicing him up and escaping better cut that shit.'

No one argues with this. Kai puts the knife down.

While they cook, the girls chat. They avoid the subject of their captor, where he might be holding them, and what plans he ultimately has for whoever wins the challenges. Mercy knows it's not all about making sure he doesn't overhear something he wouldn't like. They've lived with the same thoughts day-in, day-out and need a break. This is a chance to at least pretend there's some joy to be had from their time here.

Mercy is eyeing up everyone's meals. Alex is preparing mashed potato and seems to know what she's doing. Kai appears a little lost in a kitchen and has opted for a jacket potato with cheese and beans. Diamond is creating her dish away from everyone else and won't let anyone see. The odd glance tells Mercy it's some form of quiche. None is spicy, so the weirdo hasn't confided in anyone but her. She's creating chicken madras.

A short while later, Diamond appears at Mercy's side and snatches the salt right out of her hand. Mercy bites her tongue. Right up until the moment Diamond finishes with the condiment and slots it in the pocket of her apron.

'I could do with that back, please.'

Diamond ignores her and continues cooking. Mercy repeats her line. This time Diamond turns to her, grinning. She's wielding a carving fork, although one of its two tines is missing. 'Did I hear a funny noise?'

'That would be my voice saying I need the salt back, please.'

'Come get it.'

Mercy has faced jungle animals far deadlier than this bitch, and she will not back down. But after taking one step towards Diamond, a voice stops her. Alex has been keeping to herself, uttering little, but what she says now quickly diffuses the situation. The cooking and chatting continues.

———

He gave them an hour and he returns on the dot. Time up. Test over. Mercy's meal is still in the oven and she's worried. Kai's jacket potato was finished twenty minutes ago and she's concerned it's too cold.

'That's on me,' he tells both women. 'Do not worry about that. I'll get the name of your dish as I take each of you back to your cell. Please be seated, blindfolds on.'

The girls make hasty goodbyes and hug again – except Diamond. They know it might be the last time they get to talk openly. He takes them one by one and locks the door each time he leaves. Back in her room, Mercy awaits culinary judgement.

He comes as she's working out on the treadmill and sweating heavily.

When he opens the door, she stops running. Before he can speak, she says, 'Can I shower soon?'

She sees the movement of one cheek beyond the edge of his mask, suggesting a smile. He likes her request. She knew he would be impressed by her desire to be clean. 'Of course. You won the food test, by the way. Your chicken madras was lovely. Very spicy.'

'I aim to please. You said there was a prize?'

'Time outside. I have a walled garden. The winner can see the sun.'

Her left eye itches a little, and she blinks it rapidly. It's been doing that for a while now. 'No one will die for losing?'

'No one will be killed for their cooking skills,' he says. There's mirth in his tone, as if the idea of murdering someone because of a bad meal is preposterous. He's killed for less and she's disgusted. 'We'll do the time out tomorrow morning. Right now I need something from you. I'd like to take your blood pressure and perform a couple of other tests. Do you mind?'

'No. Come on in.'

He's got a canvas bag of equipment. She sits on the bed and he plonks his foul ass right next to her. She hides her revulsion and decides this is her best chance to try something she's been thinking about. So she puts her hand on his arm. He pauses.

So far, so good. She moves her hand to his thigh. He does not object. She leans close and her other hand reaches for his mask, to lift it, so she can kiss him.

'Stop, Mercy.'

She pulls back, blinking her itchy eye. 'Is this not what you want? Am I not your favourite? Your special one?'

'Women are pieces of art. That's why you wear the dress. But I have no interest in you sexually.'

She hasn't forgotten that he put his fingers inside her vagina not long after she was abducted. 'But you called me Mercy. You've never done that before. That must mean you like me. I'm willing. It would be consensual. I'm special, you said.'

'You are indeed, Mercy. You might be *the* special one. It was a mistake to use your real name, but perhaps you deserve to have it returned to you. But the truth is I don't want you in that way. I don't want any woman in that way.'

He really sounds serious and it throws her. 'Then why am I here? All of us? Why did you snatch us? Why young women?'

He leans towards her. For a moment she thinks he's changed his mind and, weirdly, wants to kiss her while wearing his mask, but then he says, 'What's wrong with your eye?'

She rubs at it. 'Just dry. Dehydration maybe. It started up just today.'

He leans closer still, until the nose of his mask almost touches hers. The little slit in the lips of his mask concentrates his warm breath into a fine jet that she feels on her chin. Nasty. She can see his big brown eyes, inches from her own. It's a struggle not to pull away.

Finally he sits back. 'You have a very dry eye, like you say. I shouldn't, but I can get you an ointment for that.'

'Please.'

He stands. Holds out his hand for hers. 'Come with me, Yellow.'

She stands. Takes his gloved hand. She smiles. She's not yet convinced this man isn't sexually interested in her. 'Of course, darling.'

CHAPTER TWENTY-ONE

Noa sank back in her seat, suddenly incapacitated by a spiking pain in her head. Behind her, everyone scrambled to type the What3words address into their mobile phones. She heard someone whisper that she was a damn idiot. She was thinking the same thing.

'Anger management,' Bokayo said a few moments later, thrusting his phone at her. She looked in disbelief. The What3words map showed... not woods or open land, but an urban jungle street. A building on a junction, marked as BETTERYOU. 'An anger management joint in Soho.'

It took her a few seconds to understand... or did she?

'He's back, line four,' someone said, waving one of the studio's phones. Still numb, Noa accepted the call.

'*Scare you?*' Poe said, laughing.

'I wanted the high life,' Noa said, leaning forward so she couldn't see anyone in her peripheral vision. 'I was born into money. I wanted that money–'

'*Just a second,*' he cut in. '*We should calm the frenzy. Right now dozens of morbid souls are winging their way to that location, hoping to find a body. Listen up, people. It was a joke.*'

Calm down. Don't be digging up any floors. Save your energy. Go ahead, Noa. Continue.'

'My father wanted to make sure I didn't waste my life, but all I wanted was to enjoy myself. There were others like me. Spoiled rich kids. I don't doubt I qualified for that title. We'd hire bouncy castles instead of waiting for the fairs to come around. We'd buy electric go-karts instead of building wooden ones. We got to use the VIP entrances at nightclubs instead of queueing. If my phone screen cracked, I'd lob it and get another within hours. I admit it all. And, like you said, now my father's dead, I live in a big, no-mortgage house and spend my inheritance and I've never used a clocking-in card in my life. I might have outgrown the party animal in me, but I still do whatever I want. The only difference is that now I don't have to pretend I'm trying to make something of my life.'

'I, too, was born into a good, well-off and respected family, but that's not always a recipe for happiness. Your father loved you, but not every father automatically loves his offspring by default. Do you accept that to be true?'

Noa paused. 'Yes. I was born lucky and continue to be.'

'Luck is a powerful thing. Lives can be ruined, the world reshaped, at the toss of a coin, don't you agree?'

Noa took a deep breath and fiddled with her coin necklace. 'Yes. I've made certain decisions based on a coin throw, as I've mentioned before on this show. My father decided many things with a coin, including his future as a lawyer. He had a chance to move to his firm's Glasgow office. He was unsure, and he decided it by throwing an old 5p that I still have. His colleagues called him Harvey Dent, or sometimes Two-Face.'

'And if the coin had picked Scotland, his child could have had such a different life, right?'

Noa closed her eyes, took a breath. 'Yes.'

'So Noa Vickerman got a lucky break and lived life to the full,

not a thought for those less fortunate. But now you're making amends. This radio show. A selfless act?'

'I started this to help people.'

'The guilt eats at you. You wish you'd helped years ago, don't you?'

'Yes. Now I'm trying my best.'

'And now you have a chance. In case you think I forgot that I wanted a name from you, well, I didn't.'

She felt the room tense. After last night's call, and the discovery of a new body, focus had shifted from his demand for Noa to give a single name and condemn three other women to death. Now the nightmare was back.

'I cannot name one,' Noa said. 'Just like last time, it's impossible. I can't willingly let three...' She thumped her own thigh, having forgotten that the number they were discussing had changed since last night. 'Two. I can't let two innocent girls die.'

'Not all are as innocent as you think. One has been virtually begging me to kill the others.'

'Regardless, I cannot pick. We want all the girls back alive. Is there no way?'

'Not possible. You get one. Just one. A girl who will forever know she was born lucky because of this. I'll count down from ten, and you will give me a name by zero or lose them all. Such a shame, because one is a real sweetie. Ten... nine...'

———

Noa muted her end of the call. 'I have an idea,' she said.

No one seemed to hear. The room was hurriedly discussing what to do. Bokayo was on a radio call to his Bronze Commander. Another man, a chief superintendent, lurched forward and grabbed a cable. Noa knew his intention, for it had already been discussed and decided. There would be no captive girl voted for, because it would create a new Great Fire of London as an angry public targeted every police station with Molotov cocktails. Instead, the plan was to pull the plug on the call and the live broadcast. If the Gold Commander authorised it. They could not allow Poe to announce a kill to the country.

Noa grabbed the superintendent's hand to prevent him from yanking the cable. He hadn't yet, she knew, because he needed a nod from Bokayo.

Poe's voice said, '... six... five... four...'

'Shit, come on,' Bokayo hissed to no one. Bronze needed a nod from Silver.

'I have an idea,' Noa said, louder.

'four... three... two...'

'Shut it down,' Bokayo said eventually.

Noa dug her nails into the superintendent's hand, and he let go of the kill cable with a yelp. At the same time, she released the mute on her headset and said, 'Polly! I pick Polly. The samurai. The cat. I choose her.'

The room froze. After a moment, Poe said, *'Ah, Polly, gone, with her many sides. Can't wait to see all the media speculation about who she could be. You have a deal. I'll tell you how much money I want on our next call. Here's a number. 2-8-3... 9-8... 1-5... 9-6-0-7.'*

And with that he hung up.

———

Like probably thousands of radio listeners across the country, the police tried to call the number. It was eleven digits, like a mobile number, but didn't start with the standard 0. So, a code of some kind? Noa left the occupants of the room discussing it and headed to the toilet. When she stepped out of the bathroom a few minutes later, Bokayo was waiting in the hallway.

'I had to pick someone,' she said. 'This way it was anonymous.'

Bokayo held up his hands. 'Hey, I'm not judging. From the start of this whole thing we've all been damned if we do and damned if we don't. This guy, Poe, said in an earlier call that he wants to give us the girl he calls Polly. So he had one in mind. Possibly the only one left alive. If there's any.'

She'd made the same consideration. Twice now Poe had gotten annoyed and divulged a body: it was hard to doubt he had others out there, waiting their turn to be found. 'Are the suits back there on the same page?'

'We have dead women, so this can't ever have a happy ending. Blame will be shared amongst a bunch of us. Human nature to try to deflect it.'

'I understand. Look, I just want to get out of here now.'

'Sure. Look, for peace of mind it's best if you don't go home again. But don't mess around with a crappy hotel either. I can get you placed at a safe house.'

Noa sighed and leaned against the wall. 'I can't believe how things turned to shit so quickly.'

Bokayo took the other wall, directly across from her. 'So what do you make of that number he gave us?'

'No idea. Not a phone number. I tried. A code of some kind. Another location? A play on coordinates maybe.'

'No idea at all?'

He was giving her a stare she didn't like. 'How would I know?'

'You knew about that Edgar Allan Poe thing. There was some very vague and strange dialogue between you two back there. It almost sounded like you both skirted around something you knew.'

'Ah, of course. Banter. Flirting, as some have said. More fodder for the media. If I knew something, don't you think I'd say?'

He stared some more, as if he couldn't work out if he trusted her or not. Then his shoulders relaxed. 'So I guess we just work the code and wait to see if he calls again. Let's get you to that safe house.'

Half an hour later, Noa was in an unmarked police car, headed to a secret location in Uxbridge in West London. On the way, she checked various news outlets and social media sites and learned what she'd expected. Boiled down, Noa Vickerman had made no new friends tonight.

But she wasn't the main focus of media scrutiny. Poe had been right: the whole country was eager to find out who the mysterious Polly was.

CHAPTER TWENTY-TWO

5 NOVEMBER 2020

I f there is one silly thing she always does, it's leaving her car way over in the dark corner of the car park. At the start of her shift, when it's daytime, it allows a nice stroll to the building. At night, though, the dark corner is scary.

And finally, tonight someone takes advantage. As she pulls open her car door, fireworks burst in the sky, and her attention is elsewhere until it's too late: she catches only a glimpse of a shape emerging from the bushes. It's upon her before she can react.

'Get in,' he hisses, and pushes her inside the vehicle. He forces her roughly across the centre console, into the passenger seat. She complies completely, locked down in fear because the passenger door won't open as she's parked right by a junction box. Another idiotic mistake.

Once he's in and all doors are shut, he forces her to swap places with him, which involves close contact that's repulsive. She performs with her eyes screwed shut in terror. Once she's in the driver's seat, he snaps a handcuff over her left wrist and attaches it to his right.

'Start driving. I'll tell you where.'

She tries to get past her terror and think straight. She's smart, smarter than most, and surely can work her way out of this. But all she's got is the knowledge that screaming won't help, not given their empty location and the pounding of fireworks.

'What if you have to run because we crash or something? You're cuffed to me.'

'Then don't crash. Don't have that idea. I'll kill you, hide the handcuffs, and claim I was a hitchhiker you picked up. I'll get sympathy and I might even go to the funeral and comfort your parents. Drive.'

She takes deep breaths. She dare not open her eyes, but has to: he wants her to drive. She'll also need to see him in order to give the police a description.

When she looks, it's just a glance. He's low in the passenger footwell. Obviously he plans for nobody to see him as the car moves around. In his free hand is a large knife. He's wearing jeans and a red hoodie with that hood pulled around his head so tightly that she can see only sunglasses and a portion of a surgical facemask. She takes all this in in one second; in the next, her gaze is out the windscreen, at trees and bushes flashing red and green and blue in the light from explosions in the sky.

'Get driving,' he says.

His intention is not to steal her vehicle, for there is no better place for the theft than right here, where nobody can see. It's her he wants. 'I'm only fifteen,' she moans. 'They kill child molesters in prison.'

'You're nineteen. I know all about you. That's why I'm here.'

Alex Byrne starts to cry.

———

He directs her to a road between dark fields and tells her to pull up at a certain spot. There's a gap in the bushes for a dirt track into the field and she sees a dark van parked there. Her fear worsens, but her body is numb, unable to find the will to fight, or scream, or run as he leads her to that vehicle and forces her into the back.

He climbs in with her and shuts the door. A weak yellow light barely illuminates them. High above, another round of fireworks thump the air. He removes the handcuff from his wrist and attaches it to a bar welded to the metal floor. All thoughts of escape flee her mind. She waited too long. Now there's no way out.

'Pull your trousers down.'

Rape. She expects this, but it's not her primary concern. It's what comes afterwards. Will he let her go, or kill her, or does he have longer-term plans?

'Trousers. Knickers. Now.' She obeys and he says, 'I apologise about what I have to do now. I planned to do this after I knocked you out with a drug, but I left my bottle here. I need to make sure you really are the special one.'

His fingers delve inside her. She grits her teeth. He removes himself just seconds later.

'Good. Very good. Pull your trousers up.'

She's so surprised that for a few seconds she doesn't respond. While she hauls up her trousers with her free hand, he exits the van and shuts the door. He's back within twenty seconds and in his hand are a cloth and a small bottle. His thumb hides most of the largest word on the label, but she can see SEV.

'That can damage my liver. Please don't. I won't resist. You don't have to knock me out. Please.'

He tips liquid from the bottle onto the cloth. She covers her head with her arm, but he yanks her hair to expose her face, and she can't prevent the soaked cloth from attaching to her nose and mouth.

As her head begins to swim, she wishes he had planned only rape and murder. Instead, she knows, he plans to keep her and do God knows what with her. Her parents always told her she was one in a million. Being special got her money and adoration. Now it's made her a psycho's toy.

———

6 November 2020, 7.14am

Alex's eyes flick between the pink dress on the floor and the pink hair dye box in her hand. Then she looks up at the ceiling hatch. 'I'm not the only girl you have, am I?'

He doesn't show himself, but from out of sight says, 'What makes you say that?'

Sleep seemed impossible last night, but she forced herself because the alternative was to lie awake and fret. He'd told her he'd see her in the morning, and the quicker that came so she could find out why she was here, the better. As the hours passed and she grew less panicked, she got round to thinking about what he might want, why he wanted it from her, and what she could do to try to get out of here. She needed more information from him and hoped that, as his special one, he would not harm her for asking questions.

'There's nothing pink in your van. None of your clothing is pink. Nothing suggests you like that colour. Pink seems to be a colour one would pick after others had been employed.' She points at the reinforced windows. 'There aren't even pink stars or planets in your space picture.'

'Very good. You seem to be every bit as intelligent as they say.'

'Is that why I'm here? You said you know me. I see the

thermometer on the wall. You say you know I have a special brain. But I am no savant. I'm not famous. I just created some YouTube videos. There are more genius people in the world.'

'You placed fifth in the World Memory Championship at just fourteen years of age. You can solve a 7X7 Rubik's cube in three minutes. Those videos are full of masterful displays of super IQ.'

'Some of that was faked by my mother.'

He laughs. 'You know you are blessed, but it seems you're a little reluctant to use your genius to your advantage. I know your mother was the one who pushed you. You would prefer to shun the spotlight, which is what you did after school. Why would someone with your mind take a lowly job at a leisure centre?'

Alex says nothing. He really has done his homework.

'I like the humility,' he adds. 'But don't be shy or modest. Now, please dress for feasting.'

'You didn't answer my question.'

'Ah. Yes, I admit you are not the only girl I have in this building. There are two others so far.'

'Then that explains your claim that I will be challenged. You plan to pit me against these other women. In memory? Or are we to work together, perhaps codebreaking? Is this a secret government installation? Challenges for what reason? Two girls so far, you say? How many do you require?'

He laughs again. 'So many questions. I cannot imagine what your brain is like. The challenges will be varied. I will say no more, so please don't ask. Now dress for feasting.'

The hatch closes. Frustrated, she lobs the box of hair dye at it. 'Wait. Please!'

The hatch reopens. Alex says, 'My mother. We had a falling out before I went to work. I said I hoped never to see her again.

She will think I ran away. I need to contact her. She will be blaming herself. I can't live with that.'

There is a long pause before he says, 'Actually, untrue. Your mother is being quite vocal even though it's been only half a day. You have already been reported missing. You're in the news.'

'Really?' She was always too smart to be accepted into her peers' circles, too young to hang out with people closer to her level. There has long been a chasm in her social life. Knowing that people beyond her parents care about her, even if it is just a police force doing its job, gives her a warm feeling.

But the emotion is short-lived, for she cannot forget where she is. 'Mothers do that. They never think their kids will run away. But I told people at work I was annoyed at her. I even said I wanted to move out. The police will talk to them and think I ran away. The police won't believe my mum. They won't search for me.'

His tone is suddenly more serious. 'What do you suggest, I make a call and set the police right? Tell them you have been kidnapped and they should intensify their efforts to find you?'

She can take apart complex electronics, calculate Pi to a thousand decimal places, do jigsaws blindfolded, but sometimes everyday logic confuses her – 'no street smarts', as her dad likes to say. Usually these snippets of foolishness are nice self-reminders she's normal. But the psycho seems upset by her foible, as if now unsure that she's so special. She's suddenly desperate to prove she's smart, which is an alien sensation.

'No, of course not, that would be stupid. I meant, can you at least let them know I'm okay? My mother worries so much about me. Mothers do that.'

'Mothers do a lot. Including holding out hope about their kids. Unless she sees your dead body, she'll believe you're okay.'

Another term her dad uses to describe her is 'a sponge', because of her ability to retain information. It annoys him whenever she's in the room while he's watching game shows, because she gets almost every answer correct. For someone who retains almost every piece of information that goes into her brain, being uninformed rattles her.

When he's in an annoying mood, he'll ask her something niche. Like the other day, when he wanted to know the name of the main temple of worship in Kharak Khurd. She knew the village was in the Indian state of Haryana, but still she was displeased and had to immediately hit Google.

When the psycho comes to collect her, she paces with eagerness. She wants to see his face, figuring he won't need to hide it now they're off the streets. It's a major disappointment when he arrives wearing a mask and a costume. Bizarrely, she worries that the police will ask her about his features and she'll be embarrassed to have no answers.

Like with her father, the next best thing is to prove, if only to herself, that she isn't totally ignorant. As he stands in the open doorway, she points at him. 'A Noh outfit, apart from those gloves.'

He shows her the gloves. 'These are–'

'RareDefender taser gloves,' she interrupts. 'They don't affect the heart, but the shock can numb and incapacitate. I won't try to fight you. I promise.'

'Thank you. I don't want to use them. I'm impressed that you're aware of Noh.'

'Yes. It's Japanese dance-drama that has been performed in theatres since the fourteenth century.'

He nods. 'Very good. Are you a fan?'

'Your mask is the yaseotoko form of Onryō. It depicts The Emaciated Man. The Vengeful Ghost. Who returned to Earth from Hell to seek retribution.' She pauses to digest her own words. 'Are you seeking retribution against someone? Do I depict someone you know? Do the other girls play a role in the story?'

He laughs. 'I guess the ultimate thinkers often overthink. Don't. This is just a disguise. I can't have any of you describing me to the police when you get out of here.'

She never thought of that. And doesn't buy it. 'Even before I saw that outfit, I had in mind *Battle Royale*, a Japanese dystopian novel by Koushun Takami. Now you wear a Japanese costume. Do you plan to make us fight to the death?'

His head slowly shakes. 'I won't deny that would make spectacular viewing. But my plan is not sport. Now, come with me. It's time to meet the other girls.'

She doesn't move. 'But you plan to kill some of us, don't you? Those who fail your challenges? People *will* die.'

'Let's just say it's in your best interests not to fail.'

She doubts that. Failure might result in murder, but she's certain this psycho won't just release the winner. Why determine a special one only to give her up? He has plans for the last woman standing, and Alex is worried that she might come to regret her success.

———

20 November 2020, 6.57am

Alex is washing her face when the water shuts off. She's been here just over two weeks and that's never happened. It's a sign of something, she just knows it.

Her worry is confirmed when, some thirty minutes later, he appears at the ceiling hatch and says, 'The next challenge has begun. I will be down shortly.'

'I didn't sleep well. The temperature was twenty-one.'

'I apologise. I will make sure it's sorted for later.'

'But I didn't sleep well. I need sleep for my mind. I don't think I'm at my best for challenges.'

'I can only apologise. I'll be down shortly.'

'The water has gone off.'

He shuts the hatch. So, the water has relevance to whatever challenge she faces. Something that's already begun, apparently. She also suspects there's going to be no breakfast, because for the first time he didn't order her to dress. She doesn't like this. The temperature will have had a negative effect on her mind, and a lack of food and water will only exacerbate that.

When he comes for her, he only opens the hatch in the door. That confirms everything. 'Bring me the books from on top of the bookcase. No tricks. Just the ones you've read, remember.'

She remembers. As one always seeking fresh knowledge, Alex never rereads the same book twice. Her tastes are specific and she doesn't waste time with useless fiction; however, the majority of the supplied reading material is of this kind and she was forced to reacquaint herself with classics she already knew well. There are eight books on top of the bookcase: *Frankenstein*, *Anna Karenina*, *Moby Dick*, *The Grapes of Wrath*, *Great Expectations*, *Middlemarch*, *Lord of the Flies*. These she'd read three times during her stay here. There was also a *Star Wars* novel she'd flicked through just for a change.

The psycho takes each book as she lays it on the hatch. Each gets carefully placed on the floor by his feet, except for the *Star Wars* novel, which he throws aside.

'Seven,' he says. 'That's three-and-a-half pints.'

One by one, he places seven half-pint plastic cups on the hatch. One by one, she places each under her bed so they won't get knocked over. Back at the hatch, she says, 'You've rewarded me for reading books you deem worthy. I'm betting some of the other girls haven't read the correct books, is that right?'

'Don't think about the others.'

'I bet some have no water at all, right?' Like the brash, red-haired bodybuilder, Diamond, who looks like the sort who'd only use books to level a wobbly table.

He ignores her question. 'Bring me the mask ornament.'

When she hands it over, he lays it face down on the hatch and fills the hollow back with tomato soup from a ladle. Alex walks it slowly back to the shelf. The hatch shuts before she can return to ask more questions, so she starts to eat by sipping at the edge of the mask.

She's pleased by her decision to take care of the ornament. When she had realised it matched the mask he wore, she knew its presence had significance. She had been reminded of world leaders like Joseph Stalin and Mao Zedong and the Kim family, in whose dictatorships it was law to hang and maintain their portraits. In North Korea, for instance, the citizenry were obliged to adorn the most prominent walls of homes with pictures of their leader. It was law to keep them clean and safe. Random checks were performed by state officials, and those found in violation could be jailed in labour camps.

She had suspected that the psycho wanted the mask ornament treated with the same reverence, although he'd never said this. She had kept it clean by dusting it daily, even letting him see this on one occasion. She wasn't certain all the other girls would have shown such care.

Katrina, for one, had said in a toilet note that she would like to smash the mask against his actual mask. Anyone who had broken the ornament is probably regretting it right about now.

---

23 NOVEMBER 2020

Sure enough, Katrina is missing at dinnertime in the

swimming pool. Alex notes, with a little glee, that everyone else looks pretty rough. It's confirmation that nobody has read as much as she did, or they had made a poor choice of books.

He's laid out hot food for the first time, and a plethora of it. It's like a reward. Everyone is tucking in like queens at a royal banquet, but Alex pauses. She suspects a trick. He's already told everyone the next challenge has begun, and for sure this extravagant feast plays a role.

But how? Are they supposed to avoid certain foods? The hot food is new, but it can't be that because the tomato soup was warm and about a week ago he supplied oxtail soup. Not the meat because they've had pasta containing chicken. Alex crunches on a carrot as she scans the table, trying to work the puzzle.

And then she's got it. Everything new is what could be considered junk food, where before they were offered only healthy meals. He allows the girls to shower. He sometimes checks the distance counter on the treadmill. In her room are vitamins and rejuvenating face creams. He likes the girls to take care of themselves, yet suddenly he's laid the table with this crap. The next challenge has already begun, and the grub is part of it!

When she looks at Mercy, the fellow Welsh girl holds up a chicken drumstick and raises her eyebrows: the secret gesture for a question. She wants to know if she should avoid it, perhaps because it's meat. Alex realises that Mercy is also suspicious of the food.

Alex darts her eyes left and right: no. Mercy then touches lettuce, probably to confirm she should stick to vegetarian foods. Alex shakes her eyes again. Mercy next silently employs a finger gesture to ask if she should avoid hot food.

There's plenty of cold foods that aren't healthy. So Alex nods her eyes. Mercy winks – thanks – and grabs a chocolate cake. Alex drops her eyes, suddenly guilty. To atone, she'll give to charity when she gets out of here.

But then she thinks, fuck that. They're competing against each other, and any one of the girls would sell out the others to win. So they can all go to hell. It's their own fault for being stupid.

—————

From the secret toilet notes, Alex knows that all the girls have asked the psycho to explain his challenges, but so far he's kept his cards close to his chest. That afternoon, she finds proof of a change.

After breakfast, the four remaining women requested the toilet and wrote their thoughts. The rule is that the last to read the notes flushes them, and Alex always goes last for this reason. She sees that Mercy has played good Samaritan and mentioned the 'no hot food' rule she was tricked into believing. More intriguing, Mercy claims the psycho has confided in her that there will be a cooking test later.

Kai has responded with a bunch of questions. Diamond has replied with: *You slags need to stop secret notes. He's good to us.*

Diamond always writes such praise about him. Alex suspects the woman in red wants to look good should he find the notes. Alex has often wondered if he knows about their secret communications, but lets it continue so he can get into their thoughts. For that reason, she never mentions her desire to escape and certainly not her plan to kill or hurt him. But that is a very real plan, and today's cooking test might provide a good opportunity to carry it out.

—————

'Seems we're all forgetting about Isobel and the swimming pool challenge.'

Everyone stops and looks at Alex. The kitchen falls silent for a few seconds, until Diamond says, 'What? Are you talking shit to me?'

When Diamond and Kai almost got into a fight with a knife and a frying pan, Alex didn't care and concentrated on her cooking. Now, Diamond has stolen salt from Mercy, and it looks like another argument is about to rage, and this time Alex feels compelled to interject. If the psycho gets wind of an argument amongst the girls, he might terminate the cooking challenge. She can't risk that.

'Isobel. Swimming pool,' Alex says. 'Remember when he came to our cells after and told us Isobel would be leaving? Because we showed no compassion? Every woman for herself? He was no fan of that motto.'

'I think what Alex is getting at,' Kai says, 'is that if we mess with each other in here, if we sabotage someone else's food, he might see that as a lack of compassion. Like before.'

Diamond shakes her head, and she calls all the girls bitches, but she also slams the salt down onto the worktop. Mercy takes it.

The cooking continues. Perhaps in an attempt to make amends, Kai asks Diamond what she thinks is going on in the outside world, and the bigger woman seems to try to curb her bitterness for a change. Mercy approaches Alex. 'Thanks for that.'

'No worries. But watch your back. That carving fork Diamond had. I used that just a few minutes ago and one of the tines wasn't missing. Now it is.'

'You think she snapped it off? She's planning to stab me?'

'Or him. I guess we'll see.'

Mercy watches Alex work. 'Hydrogen peroxide? Where the hell did you get that?'

'From under the sink, over there.'

'What's it for? You're not going to bleach out your pink, are you?'

Alex laughs. 'Lots of kitchens have it. Soaking vegetables in hydrogen peroxide can help kill the bacteria that discolour them.'

'Aren't you the smart one?' Mercy moves to the sink and opens the cupboard below. She roots through all manner of chemicals and cleaners, and pulls out a small black plastic box and gives a cheeky smile. 'Wow. Rat poison. Maybe we should use this.'

'That works by coagulopathy. Internal bleeding. You'd need a lot to kill someone and the pellets in that contain brodifacoum, which is blue so it's noticeable in food.'

'Ah, like those plasters over there. See, I know some things too.'

'Also, rat poison would take too long. He'd go to the hospital after he started bleeding and they'd save him. Besides, the idea here is to create a nice meal, not a dangerous one.'

'Oh, I know, I know,' Mercy says. 'I was just kidding. I mean, he's probably listening anyway. It was just a joke.'

Now a little nervous about what she'd said, Mercy moves away to continue her cooking. Alex smiles to herself, as always happy to know something someone else doesn't. Mercy is unaware that hydrogen peroxide mixed with a certain household ingredient creates peracetic acid. She has no clue that the acid could be mixed into mashed potato with another ingredient and wouldn't alter the taste or smell of the meal.

She is blindly ignorant of the fact that 150 milligrams of the acid will kill the psycho within an hour.

————

When he comes to her room later, Alex is terrified and has to hide her emotions behind a fake smile. Nobody got to see the psycho eat the meals they'd prepared. So she has no idea if he's even touched her lethal mashed potato. But he is clearly not dead.

She knows she messed up. To hide 150 milligrams of peracetic acid, she had had to create a massive portion of mash, probably too much for him to eat in one go. Even so, a tenth of the acid she'd put in should have caused discomfort in mere minutes. As he stands in the doorway, she sees no laboured breathing from inhalation of steam from the dangerous concoction. He's suffering no abdominal discomfort as far as she can tell.

But that doesn't mean he didn't feel something untoward as he ate. And if he did, he might suspect poisoning. This could become very bad for her very soon.

'How was my meal?' she asks, and hears the tremor in her voice.

'I didn't eat. It was for show really. One bite, with the eye, and I'm pleased to say you won.'

She puts her hands over her face and laughs – it's as much relief as happiness. 'I can go outside? That's what you said.'

'Yes. Tomorrow. It's nearly bedtime.'

'My room is too hot again. I need eighteen, remember.'

A little quirk of hers. The World Health Organisation suggests eighteen degrees Celsius for best sleep and healthy thinking. Alex always wants to be at the top of her game.

'I will look into that, Pink.'

'Thank you.' She pauses. He's made no move to leave. She tenses, again worried about her mashed potato. 'Is something wrong?'

'I'd like your help with something. How are you with rats?'

'Rats? Why?'

'I hate them. But there are rats downstairs in the storage room. I need a bag moving from the storage room and into my car. Get the bag for me, and I'll reward you. But you can say no if you don't like rats. I would hate to be forced, so I won't force anyone.'

Is this a trick? She's not sure, which annoys her. She can't read his face behind a mask. But he holds all the cards, so why would he need subterfuge to get her to a certain place? Plus, helping out will please him, and she'll get more knowledge of the outlay of this building, which could be of use if she decides to mount an escape. There could even be such an opportunity during the task.

'Okay,' she says.

CHAPTER TWENTY-THREE

When Noa woke the next morning, she looked out the window of her latest temporary bedroom. The safe house was a detached property on a bland residential street, at the edge of an estate next to fields. Her window offered a stunning view. It made her want to go on holiday. When this whole thing was history, she'd do just that. Get the hell out of London and chill in the countryside for a week, or six months, or maybe the rest of her life.

About a mile away, she saw a road running between two fields that led to a little area containing a post office/convenience store and a quaint pub. She decided to visit the shop. Today would be one for easing the mind, she decided. Hopefully no one in that little commune would know her face.

She was told she couldn't leave the house.

This happened in the kitchen. There were three other people in the house, two males and a woman, and she found the men playing cards at the kitchen table.

'What do you mean, I can't leave?'

Both men were pretty nondescript, one around forty and the other about ten years his junior. Last night, her roommates had been introduced as National Crime Agency Officers, but Noa hadn't really thought about that last night. She'd gone straight to her room after uttering just a weak greeting. Now it worried her a little.

'I meant not yet,' the elder man said. While he was staring at Noa, his colleague sneaked a look at his cards. 'Do you know how this works?'

'Have I been arrested or something?'

'Course not.' He quickly explained: police couldn't just whisk people off to safe houses, so Inspector Bokayo Tomori had had to go through the UK Protected People Service. Now her safety was NCA managed, and they took it very seriously.

'I'm hardly a Mafia witness. Get to the bit that explains why I can't go to the shop for sweets.'

'You can, of course you can. You're not a prisoner. But if you walk out of here and get injured or something, even by accident or your own fault, I get in trouble. Just being blunt. But I can absolve myself by getting permission for you to leave.'

'So do that, please.'

She folded her arms, clearly saying she'd wait. The officer lost his smile and pulled out his phone. She expected a phone call, a quick explanation, and a wave at the back door. Instead, the guy sent a text and put his phone away. 'Now I have to wait for the answer. Best if you just go back to your room or go watch TV. Sorry about that.'

She could argue. She could threaten. She could just dart for the door. It didn't seem worth the hassle.

So she went upstairs to get her phone. It wasn't on the bedside table. Nor was a piece of scrap paper she'd written on last night.

The two males slept downstairs, but the female, Simone, had the bedroom across from Noa's. Both women almost collided as they exited their rooms. The woman was about

Noa's age, tall, with short red hair and a face few would call pretty. She was dressed but her hair was damp.

'My phone is missing,' Noa said. 'And a poem I wrote.'

'Er, yes. We had to take the phone. I had to show Detective Bokayo the poem.'

'You're joking. So I can't go out and now you're saying I can't have my phone?'

'Ah, so that's been explained to you. I really do apologise. It's a security thing. Phones can give away locations, did you know?'

'I need to know what's going on. You know about the missing girls, right?'

'I don't have any updates for you. Inspector Bokayo will contact you about all that.'

Really. Intriguing. 'Call him for me and find out what's going on. And get my poem back. Please.'

Simone pulled her phone, but went downstairs to make the call. Noa fidgeted in her room until she heard footsteps returning. She met the woman in the hallway again.

'He will call you soon,' the officer said. 'Just wait, I guess.' She held up the scrap of paper containing Noa's poem. 'So what does that mean? It's obviously about the murder investigation.'

'He seems to like old literature, so I thought he might be a fan of poems. I guess I wanted to try to appeal to his heart.'

'If he has one,' Simone said, and left.

Noa considered sneaking out, because it was out of order for these people to keep her locked up, even if it was for her own good. But perhaps they had good reason. Maybe there had been a direct threat against her. Still, she should have been told.

So she decided against running out. She watched TV, ate, read, burned time. The day dragged. She also lurked around and listened in to conversations between the three officers, but they didn't discuss her or the Poe case. She learned that the elder officer had an uncle facing jail time. The younger man wanted to dump his long-time girlfriend because she'd gone off sex. Simone was unimpressed by results from a GoFundMe account she'd set up to raise money so her disabled brother could go to Disneyland.

Noa's anger at Bokayo came and went like a tide, depending on how bored she was, and luckily for him he called during a mellow period. She was brought a phone by one of her handlers as she soaked in the bath.

'Hi,' she said. 'So what's new? Any luck tracing who Poe might have kidnapped?'

'Are you okay?'

He sounded a little worried, probably because he had to know by now that she suspected he'd tricked her into what was effectively witness protection. 'Sure. Just chilling in this safe house. Tell me. What's new?'

'No luck with the code numbers. No luck with any forensics on the bodies either. But we have one development. You're out again, I'm afraid.'

'Let me just faint in shock.'

He laughed, misreading sarcasm for humour. 'A negotiator will talk to Poe tonight. This thing has become a public spectacle. Last night, the trick Poe pulled with the anger management class location? Police went there anyway, just to check, and some members of the public had already arrived. Idiots. There was a mob digging up the front lawn of the establishment. Like a treasure hunting party. We can't have that again. And that countdown he gave? I mean, live on-air!'

'I understand, although we can't be sure how Poe will take that.'

'Well, that's the way of it. Whether he likes it or not. But you'll be used if needed. I'll be there later to explain in detail.'

'I'll be here. Of course I will, since I'm not allowed out. Care to explain that?'

He paused. 'For your own good, Noa. We've had threats against you. You've seen how unimpressed some people are with your role in this.'

'You could have suggested the safe house. Instead of tricking me. And how long do you think I'm going to be cooped up here?'

'Not long, I promise you that. Let's see what tonight's call brings.'

She'd tried to hold in her frustration, but she failed. She hung up on him.

———

Bokayo arrived at the safe house at ten that evening, and ten minutes later Noa had been informed of the updated plan, as designed by white collars. The negotiator would answer the call from Poe. He would be the only caller, because there was no confessions show. Bokayo would stay right here, connected to the negotiator on another phone. The people in charge wanted to see if they could develop communication with the killer; if not, Noa would be allowed to speak to him.

'You hope he won't talk to us, don't you?' Bokayo said.

'I don't care either way,' Noa lied.

Tension in the house rose at midnight, but Poe didn't call until 12.15. The NCA officers were elsewhere, not permitted to overhear. Bokayo and Noa sat on the living-room sofa, close, the phone held between them, each listening through a bud from a pair of earphones.

However, when the negotiator greeted Poe, and used that name, the man on the other end said nothing.

The negotiator gave his name and role and said, 'Noa

Vickerman is no longer part of this. And, as you might be hearing, there is no confession show tonight. I cannot go into detail. Are you willing to talk to me?'

No response. The negotiator tried again, with the same result.

'I think that's a resounding fail,' Noa told Bokayo.

Again the negotiator tried to engage Poe in conversation. Another fail.

'I guess I'm suddenly important again,' Noa said. 'Do you need to get royal assent to hand me that phone?'

Bokayo pressed a button on the mobile. 'Dan, we're going to switch to Noa.'

There was no argument. Bokayo gave her the phone. Into the phone, Noa said, 'I'm here, Poe. But I'm thirsty. I need milk. I really need some milk. There's none here.'

She looked at Bokayo, whose eyes narrowed. Suspicion.

'Hello, Noa,' Poe said.

'I wrote a poem. Would–'

'*Stop. I won't speak unless this show is live, hosted by you. I will call again tomorrow, and if we're not live, it will be the last call I make. I will hear your poem then. Understand?*'

'Yes. Have you–'

'*None of this is your fault, Noa. Remember that. We'll speak tomorrow. Goodbye – oh, one more thing.*'

'Tell me.'

'*Caged. Dwarves. Unhappily.*'

CHAPTER TWENTY-FOUR

23 NOVEMBER 2020

After a journey that terminates with a trip down some stone steps and through a third iron door, the psycho tells Alex to stop. She can feel a chill and a sense of space, but it's too quiet to be the world outdoors.

He removes her blindfold. She's surprised to find herself in an underground car park. A grey square with a low roof, it has six bays each side of a central aisle that runs ahead of her and terminates at a metal shutter. She sees three vehicles, all the same small van in a trio of dark colours. She recognises the one he brought her here in.

'In there,' he says, points behind her and to the right. She doesn't look at first, instead staring at that metal shutter. The way out. A single sheet of metal between her and freedom.

He's pointing at a door beside the one that delivered her here. Unlike that one, this is wooden and has a window. The glass is wired for safety, which gives her a somewhat useless piece of help about her location. Not the USA, which banned such panes fourteen years ago because the infusion of wire makes the glass weaker. Canada is also making efforts to discourage –

'The bag is in that room,' he says, cutting into her thoughts.

Because of the way he hangs back, Alex is in no rush to approach that door. She steps up slowly, cautiously, to look through the window. The only illumination is from the car park ceiling lights, but it's enough to show her shadowy boxes and gloomy tools and other junk.

And something that makes her knees almost buckle.

Near the back wall is a body. The face is turned away, but she doesn't need to see it for identification. The skin is black and the torso is clad in yellow.

Mercy Ford. She survived crocodiles, but not a human monster.

———

Alex turns from the window. The psycho stands five feet from her, which is enough room to run past him. She desperately wants to flee – but where could she go?

'She ran from me,' he says. 'She ran into that room. There's rats in there. I never go in. I should have kept it locked. I need you to get her body.'

'You're saying she died in there? That you didn't kill her? That rats killed her?'

'That's not your business.'

Alex tries to get her thoughts in order. Mercy is dead and nothing will change that. She needs to think about herself. 'If I get the body out, then what?'

'We drive. We get rid of it. I need someone special, remember. Someone who isn't afraid of dead bodies and rats scores extra points.'

'If you want my help, please be honest. You brought her down here to kill her, didn't you?'

'She was eliminated because... she was not in good health.'

The vitamins. The treadmill. The blood pressure test. The junk food. Alex turns back to the door, and lays her forehead on the glass. She shuts her eyes, so she cannot see the body in the room. 'I caused this, didn't I? I could have told her to avoid the bad foods. I...'

'No. I saw something. A worm moved across her eye. She was in Africa a couple of years ago.'

Alex turns to face him again. She watches him press on a blue pad on the back of each glove, and figures they've entered stun mode. Why the sudden concern for his safety? Because he expects retaliation for Mercy?

'You're talking about Loiasis,' she says. 'Loa loa. African eye worm. Symptoms can show up months after infection. You killed her for that? That seems trivial. How do I know you won't kill me?'

'You don't. I don't need to tell you any of this. But you have a chance to become my special one. There are three of you left, and I need two.'

'Two? You said one.'

'I wanted to avoid teamwork. So, impress me enough to beat one more girl and you are in the, shall we say, final.'

He was so quick to admit why he'd killed Mercy, she hopes to get more. 'Why did you kill Katrina? Was she imperfect? Did she destroy the Noh mask on the shelf in her room and read the incorrect books, and so die of malnutrition?'

The slight movement of his mask gives away a smile behind it. He's impressed by her acumen. 'See how special you are?'

Mercy and Katrina. But she's desperate to know about Isobel, who nobody believes was let free despite his claim. Katrina vanished without trace. Only his musophobia unearthed the truth about Mercy. So she asks.

His reply is, 'Don't ruin your chances so late into the game.'

'I worry I already have. That this is a trick. That I did

something wrong without even knowing it. Why wouldn't you ask Diamond to help you with the body? I'm smaller than her, not nearly as strong, and she's going out of her way to impress you.'

'I just picked you. I don't even know why.'

'I do. Isobel's dead, I know it. And she died because she didn't have physical impressiveness. She had that old hip injury. You spotted it during the race in the swimming pool. If not for that highlighting her, you would have picked me. In fact, you did. When you told me to stand aside. It was a test of compassion, and I failed. I knocked Isobel out of my way. I tried to grab her when we started running. I was destined for the chopping block. If not for Isobel's disability, I would have been killed. And now you want to do it.'

'Yes, I was looking to lose one without compassion for others. But that challenge is over. Blue took your place. You will not be punished for that, I promise. Call it luck, if you like, but now you have a chance to win.'

'Win what?' She almost spits. 'You want a woman who's special, yes, but also someone fit for you. Fit to be here with you, as your soulmate. The winner isn't getting out of here, is she? She's condemned to a life with you.'

He pauses for a long time before answering. 'There's a chance for the winner to return to a normal life, and that should be all you're geared towards. Time is pressing and I need an answer. Will you now help, or... not?'

Since that first day, which now seems aeons ago, Alex has never pleaded with this man to do her a special favour, fearful of his wrath. Here, now, he has opened up more than ever before and she cannot waste this opportunity, even at the risk of angering him with more delays.

'My mother. If I do this for you, can you contact her? Just an anonymous phone call? Just to let her know I am okay? Just to let her know that I love her and I'm not angry about our argument. It hurts me to think the last time we were together, I shouted at her. My last words to her were hurtful. She needs that peace. Can you do that? And think of this. The police will know I am alive. It will be a missing persons case, not a murder investigation. Far less time and far fewer resources in play. You will have a much greater chance of avoiding capture if everyone knows I am alive. Please?'

His answer is immediate: 'If you do this for me, then yes, I will contact your family.'

Awash with relief, Alex's response is also instant. She turns back to the door, beyond which lies Mercy's corpse, and opens it.

CHAPTER TWENTY-FIVE

The three-word address was in a field at a narrow point between the B6160 and the River Wharfe, in the Yorkshire Dales National Park. There were no buildings or streetlights close, so the area was pitch black. The only feature in the field was a boundary stone wall, which had crumbled and collapsed in two places. The precise three-by-three-metre location was a portion of the field and wall halfway between the two stone mounds, but there was nothing there. No box or bag or barrel or anything else that could contain human remains, and no disturbance to the grass that might indicate the ground had been dug up at some point.

So police turned their torches to the collapsed sections of wall, and a cadaver dog went straight for the one to the west of the designated spot.

Noa had been sent to her room, like a naughty kid, but Bokayo made the mistake of going into the backyard to take the latter part of a long phone call. She sat under her open window, listening as he spoke to what she assumed was an officer at the scene. She heard him say, 'What kind of shoe? Does it have...'

He tailed off. What Noa couldn't hear was the voice at the

other end of the line, which said, 'There's a foot in it. Jesus. Skeletal. But a damn foot. We've got another one. That bastard.'

———

Half an hour later, she crept downstairs and through the kitchen. Bokayo was still out back, sitting at a garden table and smoking. He'd given up that habit a month ago. He saw her and waved her over. She sat across from him. His phone was on the table.

'I called the big guns in,' he told her. 'Body under some rocks, part of a collapsed wall. Middle of nowhere. Just a skeleton. They'd uncovered the legs and hips so far. Still getting it out, but I've fast-tracked a bloodstained shoe for DNA. Hopefully it's his. But he's left us none so far.'

'So he's got two girls left. And we'll know who when the DNA comes back.'

Bokayo shook his head and tossed his cigarette butt. 'I think we can assume now that we don't have anyone alive. This wanker has killed them all. He's played a game from the start. This serial killer is serialising the discoveries. I think we get two more bodies, maybe one each night, and then he vanishes. To start killing again, maybe.'

'We don't know that. But I do agree there might be another body. However, I'm pretty certain he has a girl alive. He's just keeping her name secret, and that's part of his game.'

'If so, he's had her a year and a half. She knows a lot. She can tell us a lot. He won't risk that.'

'He killed the others pretty soon after snatching them. This one he's kept. He could have a bond and can't bring himself to kill her.'

'So he'll just free her? No.'

Noa had to admit Bokayo had a point. 'But he asked for money.'

'That one time. He's said nothing more about that. I reckon it was to just keep us guessing. But we'll soon see. Maybe this goon plans to give us a body a day for weeks. There's no telling how many he's killed.'

Noa started to reply, but his phone rang. He snatched it up.

'What we got?'

She heard a faint voice reply, 'Jesus. You wondered why that three-word thing wasn't on the pile of stones? It was between both piles, and now we know why. Someone just checked the other rocks. A goddamn skull is staring at him.'

Bokayo sat up straight. He stared at Noa, and made no move to take this call out of earshot. 'Wait, the body was decapitated?'

'Hell no. I can see shoulders and we've got a torso back at the other pile. It's another one. A second body.'

CHAPTER TWENTY-SIX

23 NOVEMBER 2020

As before, so long ago now, Alex rides in the back of the van, handcuffed to the welded bar on the floor. The back windows are translucent and, this added to the darkness, it's hard to make anything out. But she will always look that way.

The vehicle passes balls of light that belong to streetlamps, and rounded shapes that might be trees, and blocky forms she assumes are buildings. She hears the grumble of other vehicular engines, and the cacophony of roadworks.

At one point the vehicle stops at what she thinks is a set of traffic lights, and just feet behind the van is a roaring black shape that she believes is a motorcycle. She can make out the dark dome of the rider's helmet. A second shape approaches and she hears male voices even over the numerous engines.

The urge to scream is high. Or she could kick at the walls. Both. If the rider or his pal hears, there's a chance at freedom. If not, the only odds increase will belong to her chance of a violent death. It bears thinking about, but sometimes she can get lost in internal debate. Before she realises it, the van starts moving. The biker's fuzzy form recedes, and turns off down some side street. Chance lost. Next time, she won't delay. Or will she?

Soon, external noises diminish. There are fewer balls of light and blocks of stone. The grey blur of road stretching out behind the van loses vehicles. Either side of that road is flatness. The world is darker. She's out in the country.

There's nothing to see, but she keeps her eyes locked on the rear windows. Anything beats looking behind her, where Mercy's body, wrapped in bin liners, lies against the cab wall. Unavoidable is its rancid stench of voided excrement.

When the van stops, she expects him to open the rear doors, but it's a good ten minutes before he exits the van to do so. She notes that he's wearing different clothing. Jeans, hoodie, surgical mask, just like the outfit of so many weeks ago, when he altered her life. And those gloves, as always. He must have changed in the van.

She barely looks though: more captivating is the world beyond him. The van is in a lay-by near a wall with a field on the other side, and trees in the distance. Sure enough, they're in the middle of the countryside, late at night, far from wherever he kept her captive. Far from home.

He tosses her the handcuff key, perhaps unwilling to put himself at risk by climbing into the van. She doesn't pick up the key.

'We don't have all night,' he says.

'Say my name.'

'What?'

'I am Alex Byrne. I know why you use these colour nicknames. Prove to me that I mean something to you. Use my name.'

He shakes his head. 'I have rules to follow. You know that. You *are* a special one, with a chance to become *the* special one. There are three of you left. Just beat one and you win. Isn't that why you fought for so long?'

'I'm not going to be the winner. You kidnapped us, ripped

us right out of our lives, and what is the point of finding that special one if she constantly plots against you?'

'Plot against me? Surely you wouldn't do such a thing.'

'You know. Don't trick me. You already know.'

'Know what?'

'Don't play. Your special one must not only be strong and healthy and compassionate and respectful of you, but also able to cook for you? I don't think so. You left us alone in that kitchen, together, because you were testing our commitment. To you.'

He sits on the edge of the back of the van. 'If someone put in great effort with her meal, that would indicate something, yes.'

'And if someone put in another kind of effort?'

He stands up again. 'I watched and listened on a secret camera in that kitchen.'

'And you saw what I did.' He nods. She starts shivering. 'And now you plan to kill me. After I help you dispose of Mercy's body.'

'I don't have a choice.'

'Please. I beg you. My family. They will be distraught. I know what I did was foolish. But I was worried back then that I would die. If I win and I'm the special one, I wouldn't have that fear and I would become the woman you want. Please.'

He extracts a knife from a pocket. The gun from another. 'If you help me bury Yellow's body I will kill you fast. Not one ounce of suffering. Millions don't get that choice. You're lucky.'

'Wait! Diamond! She's planning to kill you. I saw her in the kitchen. There was a carving fork with only one tine. She took the other one. To stab you. See, why would I tell you this if I wasn't sorry and willing to change? You don't have to kill me.'

'You crave extra time here on this earth. I understand. Well, you have a chance. It could take up to an hour to bury Yellow. You could have one more hour. And you'll die outside. When I put a bullet into the back of your head, I'll let you stare at the stars twinkling in the sky, or watch the moonlight glinting off the river. Painless, at peace–'

'Please, no, I–'

'Or you can go now, in the back of this grimy old van, slashed and torn by a knife. Go on your terms, not mine. Millions don't get that option. Please make a choice.'

Alex cries. He waits.

CHAPTER TWENTY-SEVEN

Noa wanted updates as quickly as Bokayo got them, but he wouldn't stay the night at the safe house. He promised to call her as soon as he knew the identities of the two dead girls, but when she woke at eight the next morning, after very little sleep, still there had been no word.

She rushed downstairs and found the older male handler asleep on the living-room sofa. The other guy was nowhere to be seen. Simone was reading. The TV was off, unplugged.

'Call Bokayo for me,' Noa said.

Simone did so and handed her phone over. Noa moved into the kitchen to take the call. She noticed that a radio that usually sat on top of the microwave oven was gone.

'You didn't call me,' she said when Bokayo answered. 'What the hell?'

'Okay, calm down. Got side-tracked. And I need sleep, too.'

'Who are the girls?'

'We got dental records for both. We've got Mercy Ford and Alex Byrne.'

Noa dropped into a chair at the kitchen table, hands shaking. She knew of both women.

Twenty-one-year-old Welsh girl Mercy Ford, from Prestatyn, had gone missing on November 3rd, 2020. She had been holidaying with her mother and stepfather at Pili Pala Luxury Cottages in Capel Garmon in Wales. On that Tuesday morning, her mother entered Mercy's ground-floor bedroom to find the window wide open and Mercy missing. Her shoes, clothes, phone and handbag were present. There was no sign of a struggle, but her mother knew something was off.

Police weren't so certain at first, because her disappearance mirrored an event that occurred when Mercy was sixteen. She and her mother and stepfather had visited Gabon in Africa.

A safari trip had always been Mercy's dream, and a grandfather's will had paid the £30,000 for the three of them to spend exploring Loango National Park. Over eleven days, they would trek along rivers, play on beaches, wade through jungles, drive across savannahs. The trip, however, was cut short on night six, while they were camped on a beach. Mercy had been wowed by the lowland gorillas and wanted to see one asleep in its nest, and she had sneaked out of the camp. She was found by a search and rescue team some forty hours later, on another beach three miles away, unharmed, hungry. According to her, she had trekked miles inland, faced-off against a hippo and a crocodile, fed an elephant, played with monkeys. There were doubts.

Police initially wondered if Mercy had sneaked out of her bedroom to explore the countryside, since there had been no sign of a struggle. The search intensified on day two. Police found no CCTV of any use or any witnesses who reported seeing Mercy or suspicious cars or men. They never had anything to go on, as if she'd evaporated in the night.

Nineteen-year-old Alex Byrne, also Welsh, vanished from a Llanrumney, Cardiff, leisure centre where she worked on November 5th. She left work as normal at 10pm and none of her colleagues reported anything amiss with her. Police tracked her car on CCTV heading two miles east, but on the A48 they lost and never regained it. Also on the A48, her phone dropped off the network, never to reappear. No sight or sound or digital footprint of Alex had surfaced ever since.

Alex was a child prodigy whose life reminded Noa of her own. Seeing the possibilities that Alex's high intelligence could bring, her mother pushed her to exploit it. She entered her daughter in competitions left and right, including the BBC's *Mastermind* and the World Memory Championship. She set up a YouTube channel for Alex to show off her mental skills. She made the young girl study languages, complex mathematics, and computer programming. Worst of all for Alex, mummy dearest forbade her from seeing her lifelong friends and tried to bring in ones deemed 'on her level'. Alex rebelled when she turned eighteen by getting the job at the leisure centre, new friends, and abandoning academia.

Police initially wondered if she had run away to pursue a more standard life, perhaps with a boyfriend, for her mother had outlawed those too. One newspaper covering her disappearance had referred to her as a female 'Good Will Hunting'.

'Noa? Still there?' Bokayo said down the phone. 'You know what this means?'

'I do. He's got just one girl left.'

'Kai Harlow. Last woman standing. She's our Polly, the samurai, the cat. If he's to be believed, she's still alive and he wants to give her to us.'

CHAPTER TWENTY-EIGHT

10 NOVEMBER 2020

Although it's his dress and his hair dye and make-up and he probably has a perverted sexual reason for them, Kai actually feels better. Life on the streets always meant dirty clothing and sideways glances of disgust. But right now she feels worth at least a little something, even if it's only in the eyes of a maniac.

From his hiding spot beyond the ceiling hatch, he says, 'I must ask. You were tossing and turning in your sleep and sweating. I never saw you take drugs. But are you addicted to something?'

'Maybe bananas,' she replies. There's not much to remember of what happened, but she recalls the banana. She had been waiting in a cemetery behind a church, having learned that grieving relatives were less likely to refuse a begging homeless person. A man in a hoodie and jeans and a surgical mask had approached her, with a bag of shopping from the nearby Tesco. Words had been exchanged and he'd offered her a banana and a soft drink. Of course, she had taken them.

After that, things had gotten hazy. A few translucent memories had surfaced. His hands messing with the button on her trousers. Fingers delving into her private spot. Words: 'Excellent. All is normal down there. Shall we do this?'

It had sounded like a choice, but she had had no choice. She had remembered being carried in his arms like a baby. He had said something like, 'Endangered: threatened with extinction.'

There had been a van, but her memory had painted a picture of her own face on the side, and that couldn't have been real. Nor the fact that the van had seemed to vertically take off, like a jump jet. After that, her next memory had been a moment of joy and childish wonder as she woke on a bed for the first time in a long time. She had wondered, had she met a rich saviour?

There had been heavy confusion and she hadn't known what memories or feelings to trust, except one. The banana. A drugged piece of fruit, which explained the hallucinations. Sitting up in that bed, she had realised she had been abducted.

When she had woken enough to fully understand her predicament, she had called out to the empty room: 'Are you going to kill me?'

A hatch had opened in the ceiling, and a voice had replied: 'Let me be honest. You will be challenged during your stay here. Failure won't be beneficial. I have no intent to kill you. I don't plan to get kicks from sexual abuse. Rest assured about that. Do not ask any more questions.'

She had remained silent as he explained a few rules, gave her the dress and the hair dye and a camera.

Now, though, her banana crack has made him laugh and she snatches a chance to get more answers.

'What are these challenges? How long will they take and what happens to me afterwards?'

'No more questions. You will learn in due course. But first, your interview to camera. Open the sheet of paper I gave you.'

'I'm hungry. Can I eat? Not bananas.'

She meant that as a joke, to ease him. She is starving and maybe that, not the side effects of the drug, is the cause of her upset stomach.

'After interview. Then you can go feast with the others.'

She sucks in a sharp breath. 'Others? What others?'

CHAPTER TWENTY-NINE

Police activity in a remote section of the Yorkshire Dales in the dead of night should have gone unnoticed, and it had. So Noa was surprised to find that they'd not only publicly announced their grisly discovery of two bodies, but released the names Mercy Ford and Alex Byrne.

Having also done the maths, the media knew Kai Harlow was the sole remaining captive of the man who had gripped the country for the last few days. That morning, Kai's picture and biography were splashed across the front pages.

Born on Christmas Eve 1991, she had been reported missing in November 2020 by a newsagent who ran a store on Handsworth Road in Sheffield, South Yorkshire. Kai had been homeless and often slept in his backyard, which he allowed because she acted as security against burglars and vandals. Each morning, as thanks, he'd give her a sandwich and a few pounds, and she'd be off for the day. Most nights, she'd return late and bed down. He had found her to be pleasant, well-spoken, but very defensive about her history whenever he'd asked.

The newsagent had gone to the police on the third night that she'd failed to reappear in his backyard. Although she was homeless and could relocate at any point, he'd doubted she would have done so without a goodbye.

He felt she'd come to harm, but police didn't share his concern and performed only a superficial search for the missing woman. Like most homeless people, she had very little by way of a digital base. She did have a Facebook account, but she never posted, only read, and always signed in from various phones belonging to homeless friends. None of these had a clue where she might have gone, for apart from the newsagent's, there were no known haunts. But, when pushed to guess, they all said the same thing the police thought: Kai had been born in Scotland, so perhaps she'd opted to go back.

Kai had been born not knowing her father...

CHAPTER THIRTY

10 NOVEMBER 2020

'... I heard about him though. My mum would talk about him a lot. But not in a good way. She blamed him. She always reckoned she had a good life until he came along. They met in Glasgow in February 1991. She was working as a cloakroom attendant and he came to watch some concert. They slept together that night. He had a wife, though, and she was also pregnant around the same time, and so he couldn't be with my mum. That was it: he left her as a single mother and it ruined her life, that's what she said. That's all I really know.'

Kai stops here. One of the instructions on the sheet of paper is TALK ABOUT FAMILY. Job done. But the maniac isn't content.

'Continue. Tell me about life afterwards.'

She returns her stare to the camera, wondering who aside from him will see this video. There's no family, no friends. She wonders if the recording will one day end up viral. Shown by police as part of their investigation into her murder. Part of some serial killer documentary years from now.

'Continue, please,' he pushes.

'My mum got into drugs, got into the wrong crowds, and she

died when I was five and I went into care. I left care by choice at sixteen and later joined the armed forces–'

'No, you're skipping. Life until she died. Life in care. More details.'

He seems very eager and she doesn't want to disappoint him, but she also hates talking about her life. Being homeless, it was easy to avoid since nobody in her group of street-living friends enjoyed reminiscing about when life meant something.

'We lived in a shithole bedsit and my mother became a cuckooing victim. Know what that is? I bet you don't. It means all the scumbags from the estate treated it like their base. Because she needed drugs, she'd let them do what they wanted there. They had parties, sold drugs, hid wanted criminals, the works. Mum was happy as long as they shot her full of drugs. And I just crawled around all day, on needles and rubbish and God knows what. They never let me outside because I was such a mess and had no clothes.

'Until she died of an overdose one day. September 9th, 1996. So I was five. They all damn scarpered after that. Didn't tell a soul, though, and it was two days before the police came knocking. No food in the house, doors and windows locked. They found me sleeping on top of her body, is what I heard. I was weak from malnutrition at that point. I was too young to remember this. But she was bald, I later found out. Apparently, I'd cut off and eaten her hair.'

Kai turns away and wipes a tear. It is not his eyes above the hatch that she wishes to avoid, but that camera. Hopefully, if she's destined for a shallow grave, he will dump the video footage right there next to her corpse.

'Continue,' he says, sternly. 'Face the camera. Tell me about life in care. Tell me about the army. And afterwards. All of it.'

She doesn't want him upset, so she turns back to the camera.

But she looks past it, at the wall beyond, and tries to forget it's there.

'The care home was Reclaimed Souls. I liked it, but I ended my care order at sixteen because I wanted to see the world. The best way, I thought, was in the army. In 2008 women were still excluded from close combat roles. The Ministry of Defence deemed that women in ground combat positions would ruin unit cohesion – that was the term they used. But that was what I wanted. I ground on, waiting. The Royal Armoured Corps was the first to permit women. I joined. In 2018, the rest of the army followed suit and I attended the Potential Royal Marine Course. Barely a handful of women did that.

'But I got injured. I was off the course, and after that I didn't care to carry on. I quit not long after. I lived with a former services friend for a few months, but when that was over, I found myself on the streets. There's help for former soldiers because a lot have no homes when they leave, but I refused any assistance. I don't even know why. I had no friends or family, and Glasgow had nothing but bad memories, so I hitched a ride out of the city and settled where I was dropped off. That was Sheffield. There's a term – the world is my oyster. Sheffield was mine. I had a choice of all the streets and alleys and dirty holes in that whole city to call home.'

The joke gives her confidence a little boost. She looks away from the wall to the ceiling hatch. 'Until a maniac kidnapped me. Haven't I just had the most blessed life?'

CHAPTER THIRTY-ONE

Bokayo called again around midday with a surprise. One of her handlers offered a phone and she took the call in her bedroom for privacy.

'The show will go ahead as normal tonight. Live. With you hosting.'

That knocked her for six. 'Why the sudden change? You said it was too risky to give this guy airtime.'

'He's down to his last girl. She's alive or dead. If he gives us a body, he has nothing left and it's over. We don't think he will. He'll either give her up, or he'll delay. The public knows we're talking to him every night, especially after we just went and found two bodies. Transparency.'

'You want the country to hear everything so there's no doubts? Even though he could make another threat or demand? That goes against the attitude the police have had from the start.'

'Well, it's the plan. I'm just a messenger. So, stay at the safe house. Read some books, eat, play with yourself, and I'll collect you tonight and take you to the police station. We're using a new one.'

'And the plan for me during the show? What I'm supposed to say?'

'You know him by now. He respects you. Just talk to him and find out what you can. Chat later.' He hung up.

His demeanour played with her mind over the next hour as she made and ate lunch alone in her room. The police were going to allow her to 'just talk to him'? Something seemed wrong. She remembered Bokayo's suspicion when she'd uttered that strange 'I need milk' line to Poe. For some reason, he hadn't questioned her about it. Why?

A little later, Noa heard the front door open and close. She ran into another bedroom and looked out of the window, to see the two male officers walking down the garden path. They got into a car and vanished.

Noa went downstairs and found Simone in the kitchen, cleaning the cooker. 'You know a lot about me, don't you? How much I'm worth?'

Simone looked up. 'Yes. Why?'

'Give me your phone and cancel your GoFundMe campaign.'

Simone stood up. 'I can't give you a phone. Not yet. How do you know about the GoFundMe thing?'

'I overheard. I know you want £10,000 to get your brother a trip. I'll give it to you, all of it. Ten grand. I just want to see the news. Bokayo is being evasive.'

The lack of immediate puzzlement on Simone's face was answer enough. Noa said, 'That explains it. I won't call anyone. I just want to see the news.'

Simone's face changed, and it told the story. The busted TV and the missing radio. They wanted to make sure the news was something Noa didn't get hold of today.

'I'll tell Bokayo I heard two people outside talking about it.

Let me have your phone, and then you can have it back to tell your brother he's going to Disneyland.'

Simone thought, and there was a real struggle given the frown on her face. But then she reached into her pocket.

Shortly afterwards, Noa knew the truth. Many newspapers, including national, had her big secret displayed for all to see. This code had been harder to break than *The Tell-Tale Heart* one, but the internet made everyone smart these days. On UbyU she found a story that encompassed everything:

Many familiar with the recent telephone calls between Noa Vickerman, a late-night confession show host, and a killer calling himself Poe, might remember him stating that they were both fans of Edgar Allan Poe. He even quoted a line from *The Tell-Tale Heart* when describing what he might or might not have done to a victim.

Poe was a regular contributor to *Alexander's Weekly Messenger* and it was in this publication in December 1839 that he sought to test himself by challenging readers to submit to him substitution ciphers. He helped popularise such things.

In 1843, *The Dollar Newspaper* published *The Gold-Bug*, a short story by Edgar Allan Poe. In that story, William Legrand and two comrades head off to Sullivan's Island on a treasure hunt after finding and decoding a secret message.

The Gold-Bug displays Poe's intense love of cryptography. In it there is a substitution code, which we have listed below.

In one of his phone calls, the confession show killer said, 'Call me Saturn. Or Ringo, from The Beatles, if you like. Perhaps even something normal like William. Or Poe or Edgar, since we're fans. Let's go with that. I am Poe.'

Many Poe fans on social media have talked about this. 'Saturn' could be a sideways reference to Jupiter, a character in *The Gold-Bug*. The mention of The 'Beatles' could relate to *The Gold 'BUG'*.

'William' could relate to legrand, from the story, or William Kidd, a 17th Century pirate who buried the treasure mentioned in *The Gold-Bug*. William Friedman, a cryptologist who helped break Japanese codes in World War II, got his interest in codes after reading *The Gold-Bug*.

The killer was heard on the show to say, 'Ah, Polly, gone, with her many sides. Can't wait to see all the media speculation about who she could be. You have a deal. I'll tell you how much money I want on our next call. Here's a number. 2-8-3... 9-8... 1-5... 9-6-0-7.'

One of Poe's codes in the *Weekly Messenger* was 'Poor Mary's dead! why is she a many-sided figure?' The answer: Polygon. Could this have been the killer's way of trying to get Vickerman to speak in code?

Using Poe's famous substitution cipher code key, we ran the so-called phone number the killer gave and got the code BEG ME FA MILK...

Noa groaned. Now she knew why Bokayo hadn't questioned her about the 'milk' line. The code had been broken, finally. The police knew Poe had asked her to beg for milk, to prove she understood their secret language. Now it made sense why they were allowing her to talk with Poe tonight. They wanted to see if she and the killer would speak again; if Poe would say something that would lead them to his doorstep.

She would be buried for this betrayal, but that was the least of her worries. Now, she would never get a secret message to Poe. Her plan, weak as it had been, was dead.

———

Noa got Simone to call Bokayo and tell him that Noa had gotten hold of her phone and read the news. He was at the safe house an hour later. Noa took him to her bedroom for the confrontation.

'You tricked me. You knew all along.'

His response: 'I'm not sure you're the one who should be annoyed here. You went against the police. You were trying to secretly communicate with Britain's most wanted criminal. I had to talk my bosses out of having you arrested.'

'But instead the plan was to listen carefully and see what we spoke about?'

'You could have confided in us and worked together. Poe was up for coded talk. That could have been helpful to us. Instead, you decided to play a dangerous game. But now you know that we know, let's get down to it. What was your plan?'

'To pay him. To work out a way. I was scared that the police would try to trap him, and he'd get away and hurt his prisoners. I was just trying to help.'

'Anything else?'

Noa watched him carefully, and knew he knew the truth. 'Okay, look. Let me show you. I wrote a poem.'

Bokayo showed her his phone. A text. It was a copy of her poem, doubtless sent by one of her handlers. 'Is this just something you hoped would appeal to the killer's heart?'

There was no point lying. 'No. It's another code. But you knew that.'

So many girls, a hell of a lot.
1, 3, 5, 7, how many does he have?
1, 2, 3, gone like the wind.
But 999 can't do a thing.
It is zany, this world of ours.
Life axed in a split second.
If only 1 could survive.

This man Poe, we think him a monster.
But he is a mortal, with compassion.

He said, 'We easily worked it out once we knew you were using Edgar Allan Poe ciphers.'

'Yes. It's based on a short story called *An Enigma*. Line one, you take the first letter. Line two, the second, and so on. A very simple code.'

'S33 9ZX 1 pm,' Bokayo said, too fast to have worked it out. He already knew the postcode. 'So you were planning to try to meet him in secret. But was it really just to pay him?'

'Yes. I promise. And it can still happen. So you can't take me off this.'

'That decision has already–'

'Then get it changed,' she snapped. 'You need me. If we go ahead with this code, Poe will think he's in the clear. And I know he'll meet me.'

'The postcode is for a pub in Bradwell, a village in Derbyshire. Why that place?'

'Based on where he's been snatching women and dumping them, Derbyshire seems right in the middle, so I'm assuming it's close to where he is holding Kai.'

Bokayo moved to her window, to stare out at the backyard or the countryside beyond. 'So you really thought he'd do this? Take your money and then release Kai?'

'Yes. I also knew the police wouldn't allow a killer to just walk, so you'd try some trick and it might make things worse. I can still do this. You can put us under surveillance. He won't meet anyone else. Besides, he's expecting me live tonight. We can't risk him killing the last girl. He could do that and go underground if I'm taken away from him.'

Bokayo was silent for a time. She watched the back of his head and waited.

Eventually he turned to her. 'I'll have to get this authorised. I need to go see some people. Let's say I let you know in a couple of hours.'

He tried to leave, but she blocked him. 'Wait. Let's not try to pretend you're doing me a favour. You wanted Poe to speak to me in code, and you still do. I'm helping you, not the other way round. Now you know everything I was up to, and there's no reason to keep me locked up here.'

'That was mostly for your own safety.'

'I'll keep my face hidden. I want out. Have people follow me if that makes you feel better. But I'm going. So arrange it to happen via the front door, or I'll jump out the window.'

CHAPTER THIRTY-TWO

12 NOVEMBER 2020

K ai's body clock tells her it's lunchtime, and she's dressed and waiting when the maniac comes for her. But he opens only the hatch in the door, through which he drops a banana and a wrapped sandwich. She catches sight of his hand, sans glove. It's pale, smooth, and the fingernails are painted black.

'I don't get to eat with the others?' she asks. 'Did I do something wrong?'

'Everybody eats in their rooms. I have to go out.'

This worries her. 'Where are you going?'

'I can't say. I will hopefully be back for feasting. If not, save the banana for then.'

'What if you get hurt and can't come back?'

'That now makes all of you. All my girls have displayed the same concern.'

'And a legitimate one. You fall down dead somewhere, we all starve to death.'

'I'll be fine. You'll be fine.'

'No one goes out planning to die in a car crash. You won't get your special girl. All your work will have been for nothing.'

He stares in silence for a few seconds, thinking. It's a common habit of his, and it gives his gaunt-face mask a more ominous look. 'You really are worried about that. The keys to this place will be in my pocket. They have the address. They'll be passed from hospital staff to police, who will come to break the news to any family I might have. They will search this place and you will be rescued.'

Sometimes she cracks offensive jokes and he seems not to mind, but it might be a step too far to say, *Oh, well, let's hope you die then.* She decides to head in the opposite direction: 'Please drive carefully.'

Another long, silent stare. 'I like you. I will tell you that I am going to collect the final component.'

'Component?'

'The shortlist contains six competitors.'

Kai realises what he means. 'You're going out to kidnap another girl?'

'The final one. Isn't that good? We'll be ready finally. We can start the challenges.'

She pictures an innocent young woman, snatched by force. Drugged into oblivion. Terrified as she wakes in a strange room. Shocked at discovering she's one of many captives. Distraught upon realising she's not going home, at least not for a long, long time.

'No, you can't. You have five of us. Five is enough. Don't take anyone else.'

'I have to. I chose the number six. I know that tonight she is visiting and I have the perfect spot lined up.'

Wait – how does he know this? 'You mean this isn't random? You know who you're going to kidnap?'

'Of course. I said you were all my special girls, didn't I? The girl who will become Blue is twenty-two. You will meet her soon. And then our challenges can begin.'

He starts to shut the hatch, but stops when she says, 'You're insane.' Even though he's on the other side of the door, she takes a step back, aware that her uncontrollable outburst has offended him.

'Everyone has broken the rule about not asking about the outside world,' he says. 'But none so much as you, Green. You've been here a week and so far you've asked far more often than girls who've been here longer. The others, they want to know about their families and friends. You seem more interested in the public reaction to your disappearance.'

It's true that she's sought such information. It would give her a little hope to know that she hasn't been forgotten, ignored. But he's refused to say a word on the subject. 'Remind yourself that I have no family or friends, then see if it's really that surprising. Look, I know it's the rule, but does it hurt? Just to tell us a little bit of news? It doesn't even have to be about us. We all want to know what's going on out there.'

'It doesn't hurt, no, and that's why I've reassessed my rule. You know, I actually considered a running joke at one point. I thought about telling you all there had been a nuclear war and the world was a burning ruin. Just to see your faces.'

Kai bites her lip to avoid saying something she might regret.

He continues: 'Strange, though, that the one who enquires the most about the outside world, about the police investigation into her own disappearance, is the homeless one. The one with the fewest people to miss her.'

'It's to keep me calm, not because I think I'm some queen who will dominate the news headlines. This place, this damn cell, might as well be on an alien planet. I just need to stay grounded, for my own sanity. We all do. We just need something to make us, I don't know, smile inside once in a while. Why can't you understand that?'

He lowers his head slightly and the effect upon his mask's

lips is to make them seem to turn downwards in sadness. 'I'm afraid there's no outcry, Green. Your disappearance hasn't made the national news. There's far more media interest in the other girls.'

Kai drops her eyes, unable to look at him. 'Okay.'

'Even in Sheffield it's minimal,' he continues. 'No reward money. No billboards bearing your face. What little I could find tells me the police think you might have run off back to Scotland.'

She turns away. 'Okay, I get it, just stop.'

'In fact, they haven't even declared you, at least publicly, a missing person. You're a homeless adult, and no one cares. No one is talking about you. No one is searching. All my hard preparation and planning for you was wasted, for I could have snatched you from a shopping centre on Black Friday without worry.'

She whirls on him, eyes full of tears. 'I get it, point made, I'm a worthless scumbag nobody will miss. Please stop.'

He puts his face closer to the hatch. 'They're wrong, Green. You *are* important. To me you are very special, and soon we'll know if you're the most special girl in the world. Isn't that something to make you smile inside?'

CHAPTER THIRTY-THREE

S ince her hire car had gone back, Noa got a taxi to Mayfair.
She exited on Mount Street, the road next to hers. She'd
borrowed a hoodie off one of the safe-house handlers to hide her
face. The taxi driver hadn't recognised her and nor did anyone
on the street as she walked towards her house.

Adam's Row, where she lived, was usually active because it
provided rear entry to The Biltmore Mayfair. But not everyone
was coming and going: two men were lurking near her front
door. Parked a short way up the road was a news van. Between
vehicle and users, her 4–12 bodyguard's car. Or rather, his
wife's smaller Ford.

She chose to sneak in the back way. Nobody was watching
the rear of her house.

She was in the shower when the phone rang. It was Bokayo.
'Authorised,' he said.

He outlined the plan. The confession show would go ahead
as normal. If Poe called, Noa would recite her poem. She would
be allowed to drive to the rendezvous, wired up for sound and
video recording. Google Earth maps showed that the pub's rear

yard had just a single way in or out, which could be blocked by a vehicle. The building was on a single road that ran through the village of Bradwell, which could easily be blocked at both ends if required. Officers from the Metropolitan Police's Specialist Firearms Command would have the area in their crosshairs in case Poe tried to harm Noa.

'Sounds like you like my plan now,' she said.

'Like isn't the word. We'd rather not put you right next to this guy. He might still have a prisoner, and we want her. I doubt he'll bring her. But we can't allow you to get in a car with him. If he wants to take you to her, you have to make sure you drive separately. And we'll pull you out if he tries to go somewhere we don't think we have a good chance of protecting you. Someone will go through all of this with you later. How long till you can get to the station? Earlier the better. I could send a car.'

'No car. I'll make my way there in an hour or two.'

'Call me if you have problems. Like traffic. I'll send a helicopter if I have to.'

After the call, she finished her shower and put on a tracksuit. She chose one with elastic trouser cuffs. She also put up her hair and stuffed it beneath one of her roommate's baseball caps.

She phoned her bodyguard. After the call, he got out of the car and approached her house. He used the code she'd just given him to open the garage. From a high window, she saw the two reporters watching intently, but they kept their distance. She figured that was because they'd already had a run-in with the big guy.

When she heard the garage door rumbling down again, she headed downstairs to meet her bodyguard. Five minutes later, the garage door rumbled up again, and her Fiat 500 slipped out. Her bodyguard looked packed into it.

From the top window, Noa watched the Fiat drive away. The two reporters ran for their van. The plan had worked: they thought her bodyguard was bringing her car to her. Once they were gone, she slipped out and got in her bodyguard's vehicle.

———

The man called Maximus Jones answered the phone in his usual professional tone and gave his name and location.

'It's Noa Vickerman. I need to see you.'

'Good afternoon, Ms Vickerman. I sense urgency in your tone. I'm available now, if you'd like.'

'I'll be there soon.'

His polite manner continued once she was in his office. They shook hands and sat at his desk. He said, 'I've seen the news, Ms Vickerman. I think I can hazard a guess as to why you're here.'

'Yes. Money. As much as you can give me. And I need it tonight.'

Ever the professional, Maximus hadn't stopped smiling like a politician since he met her at the front door. 'For a ransom, I would guess. Let me say upfront that I don't think I'm going to be able to do that.'

'Well, Mr Jones, let me also be upfront and tell you I don't think you have a choice.'

———

A thirty-three-year-old former schoolteacher called Beth Hinds hosted *Cooldown Hits* between 5pm and 8 on weekdays. Her show was halfway done when Noa entered the building. As always, Larry, her producer, was in his office.

'What are you doing here?' he said as she walked in.

'The kidnapper is going to call my show.'

'Here? I thought it was going down from a police station?'

'No. Here.'

After her chat with Larry, she used the restroom then headed out to call Bokayo. He was angry and demanded to know where she was.

'At the radio station. I want to do it here. Get your technology and people and whatever you need.'

'What? What are you playing at, Noa?'

'Playing at wanting to be somewhere comfortable. Just get down here. Quick. I'll send a helicopter if you get traffic problems.'

Two hours later, people started to arrive. Bokayo was first. Now that he had Noa in his presence, he was relaxed. They stepped outside to talk while his people entered and set up their equipment in Larry's office. Shifting her radio show to a police station had convinced reporters to abandon staking out Divine Radio's headquarters and the street was empty of people. They stood just metres from the corner of the building, close to the Ford she'd driven here. He didn't recognise it and asked where her car was.

'Home. I came in a taxi.'

———

'It's midnight, April 26th, 2022, I'm Noa, and the phones are already ringing, so let's take the first call.'

Callers had gotten booted immediately to clear the lines and find Poe quickly. Noa wanted him to be the first and only caller, but someone in the higher echelons of the police had had a different idea. He'd decided to have one of their own call the show and state what a good job the police were doing. Noa though it was a bad idea, because it might make Poe think there was progress in the hunt for him. She was overruled.

'I...'

That was all the undercover officer got out before Noa hit the kill switch and went to the next caller. Poe was up. Like the last time he'd called, it wasn't a withheld number, but it didn't matter. Like all the others he'd used, the call origin would be traced to a city in the east of England, or a town in the north of Wales, or a village in the west of Scotland, and wouldn't help one iota. As before, they'd learn that the phone was bought for cash with over a dozen others more than a year ago, from a shop that didn't have CCTV, run by a guy who couldn't remember a customer from so long ago.

'Hello, friend,' she said. 'What's bugging you at this late hour?'

'You have what I want?'

Noa alone knew that her show was dead. Once this Poe lark was done and dusted, she was getting out of the radio-show business. Because this might be her last ever broadcast, she had decided to use many of her standard lines. But there was no reason to continue to pretend that this monster's call wasn't expected. She didn't bother with fake surprise. 'Two bodies were found. Both long dead. Alex Byrne and Mercy Ford. That leaves one, Kai Harlow. This might be a pointless question, since you can say anything, but is she alive? We're expecting another trip to a remote location to find a body.'

'I expected as much. I'd think the same way. I understand you feel I can't be trusted. So here.'

There was a click, then a faded voice accompanied by the crackle of static. It was a recording. A female voice said, *'My name is Kai Harlow. The country with the most pyramids is Sudan.'*

'Fuck,' Noa wheezed, right into the microphone, and across

the world. Behind her, ten people started chattering. All remembered the question she'd asked Poe a few days ago. Kai Harlow, last woman standing, was alive.

Not everyone was as confident. She heard someone whisper that Kai could have been killed since. She muted her end of the connection and turned to the man.

'Shut your face. He's kept her alive all this time, and planned this bit of proof, and suddenly he's murdered her at the last moment? She's alive, you dickhead.'

Whoever he was, that got him even more upset. She ignored him and unmuted herself. 'Poe, no one doubts you now. It's clear you have plans for Kai, and if they involve swapping her for a whole lot of money, it's going to happen.'

Poe said, *'She is alive. She is my last. But she sits in a bunker whose air I have to replenish daily. I can't do that from a cell, or a grave. I won't do that if I feel betrayed. So I don't advise having police nearby when I collect my money.'*

'I understand.'

'Vague. Out of your control, right?'

She would not lie. 'You understand. How much money do you want for Kai?'

'How much do you think you owe?'

Owe? He felt *owed* money? 'A million. I will pay one million pounds,' Noa said without missing a beat.

'I like that number.'

'I also wrote you a poem. Would you like to hear it?'

'You've mentioned it twice. It would be rude not to.'

Noa had the slip of paper containing the poem, but she also had it memorised. She read it out.

'That's very nice–'

'Shit.' She jumped out of her chair. 'I just hit the kill switch.'

There was a stir in the room. Bokayo said, 'He'll know it was an accident. Let's see if he calls back. Calm down.'

But she wasn't calm. She kicked the chair. 'Jesus. Jesus.'

He came to her side, but she pushed past him. 'I need the toilet. Tell him to wait if he calls.'

Against protestations, Noa scuttled from the room, down the corridor, and locked herself in the bathroom. Bokayo had followed her and started banging on the door. 'Noa, get out of there. Come on back.'

'Just give me a minute.'

She stuck a pen into her throat, to induce vomiting. It was loud. 'Noa, you okay?' Bokayo asked, trying the door.

She flushed the toilet. While it roared, she typed Poe's number into one of her burners, praying that he hadn't already destroyed his phone.

He hadn't. The call was answered, but Poe was silent. Quietly, she said, 'Take this number down. Call me back in a couple of hours?'

Poe hung up without a word spoken.

Noa put the burner back in her sock, under her elastic joggers' cuff, and left the bathroom. Bokayo asked again if she was okay. Ignoring him, she rushed back to the studio. Watched by shocked faces, ignoring their questions, she retook her seat at the mixing desk.

And they waited.

———

After half an hour, it was clear Poe wasn't going to phone back. Noa had played four different toilet tracks to cover the time, then came a decision to end live broadcast. No more confession show. She was ordered to call his number, but the line was dead.

They waited. People made calls, discussed what had happened, what to do, and gave Noa fiery glares. Momentum faded, and by 1am, it was all over. People started to saunter out of the room slowly, numb, unsure what was going to happen next. Larry took his place at the mixing desk, to start his own show.

Outside, watching cars drive away into the night, Bokayo said to her, 'Need a lift?'

'I'll call a taxi.'

'Still annoyed at me, eh? I hoped we could make up. Maybe make out to make up.'

'No. At least, not tonight. Sorry. And don't wait with me. I want some alone time. Let me call you tomorrow morning.'

They spoke some more, and then Bokayo, too, was gone, leaving her alone in the street. She got into her bodyguard's Ford and drove to a hotel in Southwark. It was next door to a twenty-four-hour gymnasium where she'd acquired a locker. Inside that locker were two bags. One contained toiletries and a change of clothes.

In her room on the first floor, she sat in silence, staring at her phone. Only one person on earth, her aside, had that number.

Exactly two hours after she'd given it to him, Poe rang her.

———

'You got away from the police. Or so it seems. I'll trust you, because this Polly isn't someone you'd like me to kill because you tricked me. You have the money?'

'Yes. Is she okay? And you will release her if I pay you?'

'She's a gem and she's fine. And you can have her. I'm going to give another three-word address then hang up. Make sure your phone is charged when you get there. I'll phone you at 8am, on another brand-new number, of course, so get some sleep. I need to find out if you're secretly working with the police.'

'I'm not. But I'll do what you say. And then I want to have my say.'

'Sounds like a plan. The other girls, as you know, were already dead, so you failed no one. But Polly is alive, well, eager to go home, and relying on you to do the right thing. Any sign of trickery, you'll ruin that, and her gruesome death will be squarely on your shoulders. Here's the location...'

CHAPTER THIRTY-FOUR

24 NOVEMBER 2020

'I have my final two.'

Kai looks up from the book she's reading. The madman's face is at the door hatch. 'What?'

'I have my winners. You and Red.'

Red: Diamond. 'What about Pink and Yellow?'

'Failed. Don't ask. It is not something that should concern you.'

She realises he's a little unhappy that she hasn't shown more elation at being announced as a winner. She gets off the bed and drops to her knees, and puts her face in her hands. It's not entirely an act. 'Really? Me? I've won?'

'Yes. You and Red are my special girls.'

'But you said you wanted just one.'

'Don't sound so suspicious. I said that to avoid collusion and conspiracy. This is real. It is time for you to leave this room. Collect whatever you want. Take books, if you so desire. Take a memento. Reapply your make-up, if you like. Knock on the door when you are ready for the next stage of your life. You will feast for breakfast in your new place.'

'Do I have to wear the make-up?'

He looks puzzled. 'You don't want to?'

'Can I be honest? No, not really.'

'Do you like the dress?'

She shakes her head. He says, 'I might have made an error. I tried to supply things that would help a woman feel womanly.'

'It's about circumstance, environment, mental well-being. There's times and places for such things as short dresses and coloured hair. But, if I can be honest, a cell isn't the right place.'

'I don't have much experience of women.'

'I'm not judging you. I was in a care home, and the army, and then homeless, so I can't say I am an authority on the workings of the male brain.'

He gives a slow, single nod, like an accepting servant. 'I do like the dress, but you may wear what you want. Knock on the door when you are ready.'

He shuts the hatch.

Is this real? The maniac told Isobel she was leaving, and Kai is certain the English girl is dead. He's been full of tricks and lies and this claim that she's won could be more of the same.

However, it doesn't matter what she believes; he has ordered her to prepare to leave this room, and that she must do. If he has a secret challenge prepared, she can't make it go away by demanding to stay here.

She pulls out her suitcase. Her original clothing is months old and worn down, and she's not exactly eager to put it back on. He likes the dress, so perhaps retaining it is the best option. Also, he might have offered her a memento in order to read something into it, so she knows exactly what to take. The mask ornament.

There is only one other choice to make. She sits on the bed, and her fingers touch a tiny hole in the mattress under her pillow. She pushes down on the mattress to expose the metal end of the carving fork tine she stole from the kitchen.

Five minutes later, she knocks on the door.

———

When he opens the door to see her standing in the dress, wearing the green lipstick and carrying the ornament, he gives a happy nod. 'You like the mask?'

'Yes. And the dress. Because you like it.'

He beckons her out with a gloved finger. 'Strip. Fully.'

That's a surprise, but she obliges without pause. She puts down the ornament and shrugs the dress down her body and legs, and steps out of it. She folds it neatly and places it atop the ornament so it doesn't touch the floor.

Then she drops her knickers.

He barely looks at her naked form. He takes the knickers and looks at them, then the dress, his orange fingers checking every inch of the garments. Afterwards, he picks up the ornament and turns it this way and that, before putting it down.

'Turn around.'

When she does, his fingers dip into her hair, searching. He's after contraband, she knows. A weapon. Thankfully, at the last second, she chose not to bring the fork tine, too worried about exactly this kind of search.

'Excellent. You didn't bring the weapon. Where is it?'

If at any point she isn't instantly and completely subservient, it will scream disloyalty. So, without pause, she says, 'In the mattress, a little hole by the pillow.'

'Why did you not bring it?'

'I am a winner. There is no need to hurt some bitch.'

He stumbles over his next words before collecting himself. 'You planned to hurt another girl?'

'Not for definite. The only chance would have been at feasting. And you always watch.'

'You... you weren't planning to kill me?'

With her back to him, she can more easily fake horror. 'What? Kill you? No, no. I want to win.'

Again, one of his investigative pauses. She stiffens, awaiting a strike. Soon, the tension hurts her muscles and they relax a little, and she starts to shiver in anticipation. She stares at the wall and he lurks in silence behind her for what seems like whole minutes. Too long for analysis of her words: is he waiting for her body language to betray her?

'Please dress,' he eventually says.

———

After almost two weeks, Kai knows the routes to the bathroom and the swimming pool by heart, so, even blindfolded, she fathoms the change in path immediately and stops. The chevrons on the floor of this new corridor are grey, so this isn't the way back to the kitchen either. Somewhere brand new.

'Something wrong?' he asks.

Show no worry, she reminds herself. Mistrust shows disloyalty. 'No.'

The chevrons lead her to a set of stairs. At the top, she walks straight a short while, then left, right, and through an iron door. And into a brand-new world.

Through the gap where the blindfold lifts away from her nose, she can see clean carpet and blue papered walls. This is supposed to be a disused school, but this section looks more like a hotel. Or part of the school that he's turned homely. Which means she might be in his private residence. For sure it doesn't seem like the sort of place where he would want to spill blood. That should be a good sign, but she's too worried about what lies in store.

Ten feet down this hallway, he stops her at a door in the left wall. The door has a heavy hasp and padlock, but it's wooden. Definitely a good sign.

'Here is where you'll stay the night,' he says from behind her. 'Eat and drink what you like. Watch TV. Have fun. Tomorrow morning, I will show you the rest of my building, your new home. You will have free rein of all areas. And I will tell you why you are here. Until then, I hope you both have a good day.'

Both?

He steps past her to open the door, then removes her blindfold. Inside the room stands Diamond.

If this had been a hotel, the room would have garnered five stars. It's spacious, with a bathroom and separate toilet and an alcove for a small kitchen. The floor is polished wood. On the right side is a single bed, bedside cabinet, bookcase, drinks fridge, and an old TV connected to a DVD player. Everything is clean and looks new.

That's her half of the room. Because the other half is identical, like a reflection. On the left is where Diamond has already made herself at home, with a drink and crisps on the bedside cabinet, the bedcovers messed, a movie playing on the TV. The only difference is the object that surely drew Diamond to that half of the room: a window.

The moment he shuts the door behind her, Kai races to that window. The view is amazing. Countryside stretches for miles. There's a field, a river, woods, walking trails, and a village off to the right a few miles away. Best of all, every single molecule is real. 'Better than a fake desert,' she says to no one.

Diamond replies with, 'That's what you had in your room? My picture was endless snow and ice.'

Kai glances at her, but Diamond had spoken without looking away from her TV.

As real as the view are the heavy bars on the outside of the window. Her mind can escape, but her body is staying put.

They're on the first floor. When she looks down, there's concrete. Painted lines form a basketball court. There's also a hopscotch area and a climbing frame. Off to the left some forty metres away is a single storey annex with a pair of shuttered double doors above which is the word RECEPTION.

A school after all, out in the middle of nowhere. But why is it empty? It looks new and fresh, and strikes her as a highly unlikely place to be abandoned.

Kai soaks in the view until she almost forgets where she is, and is brought back to reality by Diamond:

'Don't think about trying to escape. You try to mess this up for me, I'll mess you up.'

Like Kai, she chose to keep her dress. She lies back on her bed, almost all of her muscled legs exposed. Kai realises Diamond has cut off a portion of the dress so it rides higher. She also wears red lipstick and has prettied up her eyes. Clearly she's trying to please the maniac.

'I don't plan to escape,' Kai answers, just in case he's listening. Given that the door is only wood and the window glass could be easily smashed to allow someone to scream for help, there's no way he's not watching them carefully. She's already spotted a small hole in a corner near the ceiling that could house a tiny camera, and audio recording equipment could be hidden anywhere. 'Do you know what's in store for us?'

Diamond sips her drink, which looks alcoholic. She watches the TV. Some action movie from decades ago. He's obviously supplied an old device so there's no smart features with which to access the internet and send an SOS.

'We'll find out,' Diamond says. 'But this room is nice. I have no problem here.'

Her words carry a sincerity that goes beyond playing a role. 'Why are you so eager to stay? I'll go along with whatever he wants, but you actually seem happy. Like you'd ask to stay if he let us go.'

Diamond glares at her. 'Maybe I don't have much of a life outside.'

It's risky to talk this way if he's listening, but Diamond's attitude is thoroughly confusing. 'And this is better? Why?'

'I don't want to talk about it. It's my secret.'

Kai says nothing further. She sits on her bed and looks through the books and DVDs. There's nothing she wants to watch or read, but it prevents her from pacing and worrying.

'What surprises me most is why you don't feel blessed to be here,' Diamond says. 'What the hell kind of life did you have out there, eating from dustbins and sleeping in rags?'

'I guess you're right.'

Of course she isn't. But the maniac isn't the only threat: Diamond is a bomb waiting to explode at the slightest knock, and she's probably upset that she has to share this space. Arguing with her wouldn't be wise.

———

Diamond commandeers the kitchen first, so Kai waits her turn to eat. There are some ready meals she can prepare in the microwave, but that's it for hot food. There's salad items and various other cold foods, but she doesn't have the ability to really cook because there are no pans, no kitchen utensils or cutlery beyond a few flimsy plastic or wooden items.

Everything that could be used as a worthy weapon is absent from this kitchen. Even the glass plate from the microwave is missing. The fridge has no freezer compartment, as if he's paranoid one of his captives will freeze a cucumber to swat him with.

Kai makes cereal. As she eats on her bed, watching a DVD copy of *The French Connection*, Diamond strips off her dress and, wearing just her grey knickers and bra, starts exercising. Push-ups. Sit-ups with her feet lodged under the bed. Shadow boxing with a paperback book in each hand.

Kai tries to ignore her, but her bed suddenly jerks. Diamond is at the foot, having hoisted the end from the floor. Muscles are standing out across her chest and arms and neck. When she lowers the bed again, Kai jumps off. It's obvious that if she attempts to keep a low profile, Diamond will look for an excuse to cause trouble.

'What the hell are you doing? Doesn't it seem clear he's split the room so we have half each? Stay your side.'

'I need the extra weight,' Diamond says. 'Get back on.'

'No. Piss off. Maybe he wants us to be friendly to each other. Ever think of that?'

Diamond lifts the bed and again, lowers it, and repeats. 'Ever think about him not wanting two girls after all?'

'He says he wants two. You think this is another test?'

'Or one is coming. He wants a wife, and two of us can't–'

'What?' Kai almost laughs. 'How do you know he wants a wife?'

'Look at what you're wearing. Is a man who doesn't like sexy women likely to put you in that? Did he stick his fingers in your pussy?'

Kai has no desire to talk to this woman, but she has a point. Kai nods.

'Me, too. And he said something about all being nice and fine down there. He wants pussy, baby. He wants a wife, or if not that then a woman slave.'

'Be quiet. He's listening.'

'He won't mind. And she's got to be special. This isn't just about loyalty and all that. Look at who we are. You were in the army. I've beaten the hell out of people. That weedy Alex had brains. Mercy survived jungle animals. Katrina ran companies. Isobel was a whiz with cars and sports. Now he's left with the two toughest girls, and what hasn't he tested us on yet?'

Kai wishes Diamond hadn't said a word. Because what she's talking about... it's something Kai has given long, hard, repeated thought. 'You mean strength? Power?'

'Mano a mano. Every day I've been expecting to have to pound someone.' Diamond lifts the bed. Drops it hard. Lifts it again. 'Sorry, babe, but only one of us can win. At least, being homeless, there's no one to cry if you never make it back.'

CHAPTER THIRTY-FIVE

Noa got an hour's sleep and woke at 4am. She headed out of the hotel and to the gym next door, where she used a key to open her locker. She locked it again after removing the bag with toiletries and clothing. In a cubicle, she changed out of her old gear and dumped it in a bin, although she kept the baseball cap.

When that task was over, she returned to the locker for the second bag, a rucksack that was quite heavy.

Noa's father had spent years cultivating the right relationships and giving advice and other aid to people with power and wealth. Neither Noa nor his lawyer partners had ever fully realised the full extent of his wealth or how he got it. But yet it had. Upon his death, Noa had been visited by a suave man called Maximus Jones.

Noa had been given £1,000,000 and the Mayfair house in her father's will, but he had also left her a hidden little something extra. On the day he visited, Maximus Jones had explained that he had been her father's schoolfriend, university tennis doubles partner, and later his personal banker at Hyatt's, one of the world's most exclusive private banks. It had offices all over the world, including right here in London.

Opening an account at Hyatt's was not easy. Besides certain non-financial requirements, including ties to the aviation industry and certain Chinese power families, clients needed minimum investable assets of £10,000,000.

Her father, it turned out, had been worth over £60,000,000, with £16,000,000 of that in hard cash right there in the bank's vault. She knew that this would allow her to sell the house, worth about ten million, when she turned forty, but she hadn't been aware of a special clause regarding his bank account. When she turned fifty, the rest of his estate would become hers. Maximus's news that day had required a lie down and a stiff drink.

Perhaps because of the wild spending of her youth, and a worry that she'd go broke before she inherited the estate, her father had written a twist into the clause. If Noa required funds beyond what lay in her own bank, she could plead her case to Maximus. Despite having no contact with Noa since that visit of three years ago, the banker had not been surprised to get a phone call from her yesterday.

Her argument had been simple. She required money she didn't have. Convincing him had involved unloading a truth that she had kept hidden from the world for three years – or so she thought. Little had she known that Maximus was already party to her innermost secret. It seemed he and her father really had been the best of friends for years. In fact, he had been waiting for this day. Suffice to say, he immediately got to work.

Hyatt's' clients were afforded the ultimate in secrecy, no signatures, no restrictions, no report to HM Revenue and Customs. And there was no messing around to get the rich their riches. Two hours after her phone call with Maximus yesterday, she entered the building on Strand in Westminster with an empty large rucksack. Twenty minutes later, she walked out alone – having refused the offer of an armed escort – with that same bag now bloated.

Inside: £1,000,000 in £50 notes. Now, Noa slung the fortune over her shoulder and walked out of the gym.

———

Perhaps inspired by Noa's rendezvous location, Poe had also picked a pub car park. It was in a village called Ringinglow in Sheffield, and was only eight miles from where Noa had suggested they meet. Given that this was roughly where she'd figured he was centred, it gave her confidence that Poe intended to honour the plan.

Before leaving the hotel room, Noa had completed a couple of tasks. First, she visited the website of Inpost, a parcel locker service. Second, she wrote some details on a note that she left behind the wall clock.

It took her just under three hours to reach Ringinglow, which included a stop a little way northwest at a supermarket, where she lightened herself of a million pounds.

She entered Ringinglow from the east. The main road sliced the village in half and it was here she found the pub. Its car park was dark and walled and overlooked by the upper rear windows of a row of houses. That gave her some comfort, even though at this early hour those windows were curtained and dark: surely Poe wouldn't attack her in view of so many.

No cars were present. She parked in the middle of the area, so she would have time to see anyone approach either through the entrance or over the wall. She cut her lights and engine and locked the doors. Just over an hour to go. It dragged. She was very nervous. She was about to meet a man who had killed women just like her.

At eight, her phone rang. Unknown number. She had no doubt it was him. The black of night was dissolving, but there were still gloomy shadows in the corners, which she scanned for movement or the light of a phone. Nothing. It didn't mean he wasn't watching.

She answered the call with, 'I drove here. I proved I'm not with the police. I just want Kai and I don't care about money. If you know Ringinglow, you know about the Shire River?'

For a second there was no response, and she had the sudden fear she'd messed up: Bokayo had somehow gotten this number and now she'd just told him where she was.

Then Poe said, '*I do.*'

'Good. Then here's my plan...'

Three quarters of a mile northwest of where she was, not far from Wyming Brook Nature Reserve, was a Tesco superstore with its car park against the river. Directly across the water was the car park of a dentist's surgery. '...I will be at the end of the dentist's car park. You will be on the other side of the water, parked on the Tesco grounds...'

By the side wall of the Tesco was a row of metal Inpost lockers. Inside one Noa had already placed the rucksack containing one million pounds. A courier was due to collect it – but senders were allowed a grace period of three hours to change their minds. Poe would let Kai go into the water, to swim across to her. '...As soon as she is out of your reach, safe, I'll give you the PIN number for the locker.'

'*This is not what I envisioned, Noa. Sounds like trickery.*'

'No. The way we do this is, you tie Kai's ankles. I will toss my car keys into the river. That way, if you let Kai go and I don't give you the PIN number, there's no escape. Even if she could swim to the other side before you got her, she can't run with tied ankles. We will have no car to escape in. You could come across and kill us both. The water is also my safety if you turn up expecting money but without Kai. I will be safe in Tesco before you could get across.'

'*You'll see Polly, don't you worry. Now I have conditions of my own. There's a garage at the west end of the village. Take a good look as you drive past. Then carry on, out of the village and along Ringinglow Road. It goes through the countryside. There are woods on the left and fields on the right. About 250 metres along, there's a single tree on the right. Stop there. There's a grass verge, so park on it.*'

'We need to do this quick. The PIN number for the Inpost locker expires in two hours. After that, we can't get it and it will be posted.'

He hung up without a response to her warning. Noa started her engine. She was aware that he hadn't asked if she'd arrived at the location. Did he already know because he was watching her?

———

She turned right out of the car park. There was no other traffic. As she passed the garage Poe had mentioned, at the edge of the village, she obeyed his instructions and took a good look. If she was meant to see something important, she didn't know what. Firelighters half price? MOTs available?

She drove past, out into open land. A wood was on her left, a large yellow field on the right, just as promised. Way ahead on the right side she could see the lone tree. As she closed on it rapidly, she had just seconds to scan the land for a person or another car. There was nothing.

The tree stood alone. She pulled up alongside. Still nothing around. She looked out of her passenger window, at the woods. If he was here, hiding, then unless he was lying in the oilseed rape like a sniper, the trees were the only viable place. Her phone rang. A new unknown number.

'Look left,' Poe said. She already was. 'Go into the trees directly across from where you are. Twenty metres in, you'll see a ditch. And a garden fork inside. Start digging.'

'What? Digging for what? Kai better not be–'

'I promised you you'd get to see Polly,' he cut in, and killed the call.

She sat for a couple of minutes, trying to discern the slightest movement in the trees. There was nothing, but that meant just as much. There was nobody in the fields. No traffic on the road. She couldn't just sit here, couldn't just toss away everything she had worked for. She had a choice and Kai Harlow didn't, and that meant Noa didn't either.

She got out of her car and crossed the road, and entered the woods.

The trees were thick but widely spaced, and she saw the ditch ahead of her. It was shallow, barely worthy of being called a hole. Twenty steps later, she could see a garden fork lying inside, atop a lake of dead leaves.

She stepped up to the ditch and plucked the fork from its bed. It felt good to have a weapon, although needing it would mean everything had turned to shit. She used the fork and her foot to sweep aside leaves, until the ground was exposed. She stamped the fork into the hard earth. She put her weight against the shaft to loosen the soil, and a clumped mass came away. Her hands grabbed and lobbed it, before again ramming the tines deep.

Ten minutes later, with sweat soaking her back and mud covering her palms, she had a hole fifteen inches deep in the bottom of the ditch. Her next stab into the ground found a different kind of resistance. When she yanked the fork free, it came accompanied by a tearing noise.

She bent close, staring. She'd punctured a membrane of some kind. A dark-coloured cloth, it appeared to be. A bag? Her fork had torn a flap in it, which had fallen back into place. She bent down and pulled the flap – and staggered backwards with a yelp, falling onto her ass in the leaves. Her heart thudded. Even over her fear, she cursed her damn stupidity.

A bag buried by a serial killer. She should have expected its contents long before she laid eyes on fleshless bones.

CHAPTER THIRTY-SIX

---

24 NOVEMBER 2020

D iamond had refused to talk about herself, but she had been eager to hear all about Kai's life. So Green had talked, Red had listened, and as the hours passed the two women had formed a bond. Diamond had made her new friend a fruit smoothie, mushing up the ingredients with nothing but a plastic egg slicer, and Kai had massaged the bodybuilder's shoulders, so tense from daily workouts. As it got dark outside, they had both stood at the window, taking in the sights of the world before it faded away. After that, they had sat on their own beds and chatted some more, and even found the ability to laugh. It was impossible to forget where she was, but Kai had found she could put it to one side for brief moments.

Well after dark, neither woman is sleepy, but the order comes through. This room, too, has a ceiling hatch and he opens it to say, 'Lights out in five minutes. Big day tomorrow, ladies.'

Kai is sitting at the end of her bed, close to the hatch, and she can see darkness beyond. Real darkness, not the gloom of a room. The night sky. The maniac is on the roof.

After he shuts the hatch, Kai waits a minute. Then she

stands on the end of her bed, reaches up, and raps the hatch with a knuckle.

'What time is it, please?'

She doesn't care about the time: it's to test if he's still there and to ascertain the sturdiness of the hatch. The maniac has to sleep sometime and he won't do it up there. In a few hours it might be safe to try to bust that hatch cover, which seems fairly flimsy and is wide enough to permit her body. She could leap from the roof of this building and onto the roof of the annex, and escape across the dark countryside.

Her question receives no answer. He's gone. When Kai sits on her bed again, she sees Diamond looking at her. 'Can you fit through that hatch?' Kai whispers.

'I wouldn't even try.'

'You really do want to stay, don't you? This is why you were so against any of us taking a weapon from his kitchen that other day.'

'Yes. And if you escape, he might blame me.'

They both look towards a rumbling sound. A shutter on the outside is coming down, to block the window. Unnecessary, given the bars. Once it clicks into place and silence reigns again, Kai says, 'Would you stop me?'

'You should wait and see what tomorrow brings.'

'Would you stop me?'

Diamond thinks for a few seconds. 'I can't control you while I sleep.'

It sounds like a compromise.

The light suddenly flicks off. So does Diamond's TV. And the digital readout on the microwave. Kai tries to turn her own TV on, without success.

'He's cut the power,' Diamond says.

'Why would he do that?'

'Everything connected to the light, maybe? And maybe to make sure we don't watch TV all night.'

Kai can't see a thing. She wonders if she can crawl to the kitchenette, find a good tool to bust the hatch cover. She would have to wait for Diamond to fall asleep, which she'd probably only determine in the dark by snoring.

'He's got money,' Diamond says. 'I think a wife deserves to spend a lot of that.'

She giggles at her own joke. Kai can't find a sliver of humour in their predicament. Even if the maniac whisked her to a castle on the French Riviera and bought her jewels and waited on her hand and foot, she would still be his slave. She would still have memories of kidnap, sexual assault, starvation, threats of death, the deaths of comrades. No way. She's getting out of here. The next time she sees that bastard, twenty armed police will be by her side.

She lies back on the bed, to wait. With nothing to do, hopefully Diamond will be asleep soon. She is not sure how much time passes, but her eyelids start to get heavy.

Then they slam open at a scraping noise.

The darkness isn't absolute, for above there's a portion a little less black. A circle. The sky, she realises: he's opened the hatch.

'Speak now,' the maniac says. 'Are we awake?'

'Yes,' both girls say at the same time.

'At eight in the morning, I will open the door. My special girl will step out.'

Kai wonders if she's dreaming when an arrow of light stabs downwards through the hatch, piercing the darkness and illuminating a small portion of the wooden floor between the ends of the beds. There's a flash of movement within the beam, and a thud.

Kai sits up, realising he's just dropped something into the room. Seeing that object, she sucks in a sharp breath.

In the centre of that small puddle of light, like a trophy or monument, is a large steak knife, standing up with its sharp point buried in the wood.

'And only my special girl will leave this room alive.'

He slams the hatch. Total darkness reigns and, for a second, silence.

Until Kai recognises another sound: Diamond leaping off her bed.

CHAPTER THIRTY-SEVEN

Her phone rang.

She sat on the leaf-strewn ground, feet just inches from the buried bag, from the dead body inside. Her body was locked in place, unable to do what her mind demanded of it and get the hell away. Her hands shook so hard that she had trouble hauling the phone from her pocket, and when she put it to her ear, the shivering beat a rhythm with it against her temple.

Poe. And he was giggling. *'It's not Polly, so calm down.'*

She got control of her muscles and got up, stumbled out of the ditch backwards, eyes locked on the portion of bag – a sleeping bag, she thought – exposed in the hole.

'Who?'

'Just some societal scum no one misses. Don't worry about it.'

He was still giggling. How had he known she'd found the body? Was he staring right at her? She looked around, but she was alone. Or appeared to be. 'Why have you done this to me?'

'Because driving down here through the night is no proof that the police aren't involved.'

'So what are you saying?'

'That's a murder victim right there. There's a chance for the police to find evidence in that ditch. DNA from the bones. Fingerprints I left behind. Who knows what? But not if you burn it. If you burn that bag, that ditch, those bones, the police will get nothing. That's what you're going to do. If you want Polly. Can you do that?'

'Yes.'

The immediacy of her answer shocked her, but briefly. Whoever had once loved and laughed as she carried that skeleton within warm flesh, she was long dead. The worst Noa could do, by destroying evidence, was deny a grieving family answers. The best: save someone who was still alive.

'Then do it,' Poe said, and hung up.

Now she knew why he'd mentioned the garage back in the village. It was where he wanted her to go, to buy fuel. To bring it back here, and light up a dead woman's remains. She walked back to her car in a daze, not even looking around for a watcher. But once inside the vehicle, she got her wits back.

One hand turned the key in the ignition, while the other placed her phone on her lap and called a number. She put it on speaker so she could use two hands on the wheel as she drove. She would need both, so shaky was she, but that wasn't the reason. It was in case Poe was watching.

The call was answered with, 'Where the hell are you? What's with all these new phone numbers? Why'd you dump your security detail?'

Bokayo must have contacted the security firm when he realised she'd skipped town. 'I don't want the families and friends of the dead girls contacting me,' she lied. 'My security guy was giving me grief about the show. And I can't tell you where I am.'

'Jesus, I knew it. You sneaked off to go meet that bastard.

Noa, I need to know. This is criminal activity. What the hell are you planning?'

'I think he wants me to prove there's no police watching me, because there's no way they'd allow me to do what I'm about to.'

'What? Noa, this is—'

'There's another body,' she cut in. 'I don't know who she is. He says it's not Polly, but he only told us about five girls, not six. Polly is still alive, he says, and I'm going to save her. But that means this body is someone we don't know. Someone he never told us about.'

'Another body? Where? Have you seen it? Did he tell you that? Another dead woman? For certain? Noa, you need to come back here, right now.'

He sounded panicked, but suddenly she was calm. 'I can't tell you where. Not yet. But the fire will draw people. Bokayo, I have to do this. I have to do what he says to get her back. Please understand that I have to, even if you don't know why.'

'I do know why, Noa,' Bokayo snapped, frustrated or angry, at Poe or at her — she couldn't tell. 'We got contacted by someone from Reclaimed Souls, the children's home Kai Harlow attended. This woman was one of the staff and she remembers Kai. She even remembers Kai being a very big fan of a TV programme, and dressing up as one of the characters. Kai discovered some VHS tapes in the home. It was episodes of *The Samurai Pizza Cats*. She liked to dress as Polly Esther.'

'We sort of already knew that, Bokayo.' Still calm, but a feeling of dread began to rise.

'Stop with the charade, Noa. The staff member also remembered Kai telling her about her mother. That her mother had told Kai about her father, who abandoned her before her birth. Her mother had pointed out a picture of him in a newspaper. Kai's father was a rich lawyer from London, her mother had said. Do you see where I'm going with this, Noa?'

'No,' was her wheezed answer, and it was a lie.

'Yes, Noa, yes. I'm saying that rich lawyer from London is the same one who gave you that coin around your neck. I'm saying Kai Harlow is your sister.'

CHAPTER THIRTY-EIGHT

25 NOVEMBER 2020

The first indication it's morning is when the shutter over the window opens. As a thin, horizontal line of light widens and climbs over her, it exposes a slashed foot sitting in a puddle of blood. A sliced shin. A bruised knee. A torn dress. Then her bloodied hands, one of which still holds the knife.

When the light, now a rectangle, climbs to her face and stings her eyes, she raises the knife and holds it sideways to block the glare.

She grips the knife hard when the door opens. The man stands on the threshold, as always in that mask and outfit. He's carrying a first aid kit. His eyes scan the room, which is peppered with bloody blotches and streaks and pools, and alight on feet sticking out from under a bed. Only then does she remember pushing the other girl's body out of sight in a black world.

He claps and says, 'I'm sorry for such a lie. But the final challenge is over. You stand alone. You are my special one. I promise there are no more challenges. Please go clean yourself and I will fix you up, and then we will leave this room.'

She moves the knife so she can peruse her reflection in the blade. Blood is all over her face and neck. Some is hers; most isn't. She sees a busted nose and bloodshot eyes beneath red hair...

CHAPTER THIRTY-NINE

'I am no good,' Noa moaned, clutching at her coin necklace.

'You knew from the start, didn't you?' Bokayo said. 'Even before I showed you her name on a sheet of paper.'

Her car entered the village and she slowed to turn into the garage. 'The police did nothing to help her, Bokayo. When she went missing, she was just a homeless runaway in their eyes. They gave up in no time. And even if they suspected she'd been snatched, so what? There was no sorry family on their backs, demanding answers. No media eager to tell the tale. The police had a quick look into her disappearance and then, bang, cold case, time to move on to people who matter. I followed that case, what the hell little there was of it. I knew no one else would do anything to find Kai, so I had to be the one.'

'That was a year and a half ago, Noa. What did you do? Are you saying... this whole thing with the confession show?'

'A wild stab in the dark. But it worked.'

'I can't believe this. You're saying you created a confession show in the hope that her kidnapper would feel guilty and contact you?'

'And it bloody worked, Bokayo. It bloody worked. I got him.'

She clearly heard him expel a deep breath. 'You know your sister. That means when the killer mentioned "Polly", and "samurai", you realised he was talking about Kai. You've known that for days. Does Poe know?'

'No, of course not. No one knows. I tried to paint myself as sympathetic in that radio show, and I damn well made sure everyone knew I was rich. I wanted Kai's killer to contact me. I wanted him to think I might be on his side, that I might give him money. It worked a dream. My hope was to just get answers about her death, but never in my wildest dreams did I expect this. That she's still alive. But she is, Bokayo, she is. And I'm going to get her back.'

He didn't share her joy. 'So why didn't you tell anyone? The police? Me, for Christ's sake? Why all this trickery?'

Noa parked by a pump and grabbed the phone in both hands. 'I didn't give a shit about Kai when she was alive, but I do now. I'll do whatever it takes, and that includes proving to him that I'm serious by not involving the police. I'm not going to risk something going wrong. He wants money to release Kai and that's what he's going to get, no tricks. So don't ask where I am, Bokayo, and if you trace this call, I'll be long gone. The next time you see me, I'll have my sister by my side. You can bet on that.'

'This is madness, Noa. You can't do this alone. It's too risky.'

'I'll call you back.'

She hung up and got out of the car. She filled a petrol can she had in the boot and entered the shop to pay. There was a guy looking at magazines near the till, but he didn't notice her and didn't seem suspicious, so he wasn't Poe. She did look suspicious, though, with her muddy hands and clothing and wild eyes. The attendant avoided asking the obvious.

She paid for the petrol and a lighter. If that combination stoked the attendant's suspicion, she wasn't around to see it. Back in her car, she called Bokayo again.

'You never told a soul about Kai. Why did you hide the fact that you had a sister your whole life?' He'd dispensed with pleas for her to abandon foolhardy plans. She was pretty certain that meant he'd set in motion a phone trace, and South Yorkshire Police would soon be buzzing their way right here.

'I kept Kai a secret because I was selfish,' she said as she pulled out of the garage. 'And I didn't hide it my whole life, Bokayo. Not even close.'

'What happened?'

Noa again clutched the coin around her neck, and told him.

————

Noa's father had built up a network of rich and powerful friends, one of whom was a lampshade magnate with a collection of holiday cottages in Sussex. When Bellamy Vickerman's health took a sharp plunge in January 2017, the businessman literally gifted him one in Itchingfield, Horsham, complete with a full-time nurse/carer. It was where Bellamy chose to see out his final days.

Noa's car at that time was a sleek black Jaguar F-type worth £60,000, which she loved to race around the country roads when visiting him. It put her in a high enough mood that her sadness wouldn't be on show when she was with him. After his lung cancer diagnosis and a six-month countdown, they had spoken at length about her future, swapping the house into her name, and his funeral, and with all preparations made and complete, he never again wanted to talk about his passing or his illness. So at weekends, when she travelled down, they would play games and chat nonsense. But on that Sunday evening, after a weekend of fun and as she was nearing the time to leave for home, he said, 'There's one more piece of business, Noa.'

They were in the backyard, wrapped up against the cold winter wind. She felt a deeper chill at a sudden terrible feeling that she wasn't going to like what happened in the next few minutes.

He gave her a coin on a necklace. It was an old 5p, long out of circulation, and she knew it was the one he often made decisions with.

'That changed your life, Noa,' he told her. She waited. He said, 'My Glasgow office. I nearly relocated there. I chose London with that coin.'

'I know. You're saying I could now have a Scottish accent if this coin had flipped tails instead of heads?' It was a joke, but she still felt tense. Where was this going?

He fixed his eyes on her. 'No. If it had flipped differently, you would never have known your father.'

Her mouth moved, but she couldn't make a sound. Her father sipped his tea and stared into it.

He spoke fast, to get the story out as quickly as possible, as if to hit her with a single sledgehammer blow rather than a series of punches. 'I met a woman, back in '91 in Scotland. Feb 2nd at the SECC, as it was called back then. Bob Dylan's Never Ending Tour. *She worked the cloakroom. I got talking because I left my coat behind and she brought it to my hotel room later. I got her pregnant. She and your mother, carrying my daughters at the same time. You were born just a day apart, amazingly. You have a sister your age, up in Scotland, and I've kept that secret.'*

Noa got up and ran into the house. Her father didn't have the stamina to chase her, and she knew this. So she drank a double shot of vodka, took deep breaths, and returned to him. She took her seat again as if she'd only popped to the restroom. It seemed much darker out now.

Her voice was cracked. She couldn't look at him. 'If the coin had fallen the other side, you would have moved to Scotland.'

'Yes.'

'The other woman would be your wife. The other girl... my sister... you would have brought her up.'

'Yes. You were both just foetuses, Noa. There was no real love yet. You weren't you.'

Was that supposed to make her feel better? She didn't. 'And have you told this other girl the same?' She couldn't bring herself to refer to her as sister.

'No. I don't know if her mother has told her. Her mother knew, obviously, because–'

'Because you had to tell her to piss off.'

'Basically. Truth be told, I informed her of why, and I hate to say this, but I also told her how.'

'The coin? You told her you'd chosen to abandon her and your daughter because of a coin flip?'

Bellamy tensed, as if at a wave of pain, then relaxed. 'Shameful, I know. Your mother didn't need to know, because nothing changed. You didn't need to know.'

'But now, today, suddenly, you think I need to?'

'I'm dying, and I want to give up my secret. This hurts, but it's only fair. Or maybe deep down I think I might need this unburdening to get through the Pearly Gates. I really don't know. I just know it feels correct to tell you.'

The coin necklace was still in her hands. She wasn't sure if it was a bad item or not. It had made no choice: a person had. But holding it felt like wielding a gun that another had used to commit murder. 'And why are you giving me this? Why would I possibly want this? In case I need to choose which one of two drowning babies to save?'

'I don't have a good answer. That coin was always used to make decisions. I always felt it was lucky. It's terrible to make such a choice with it, but that choice had to be made somehow. I guess I feel that coin was lucky for you. It gave you a good life.'

She got up, unsure how to feel about his last sentence. 'I still love you, Dad. None of this changes how you treated me or Mum, so I can't hold a grudge. But I need time alone. I need to leave. Let's get you inside.'

She wheeled his chair indoors, where he took over. She walked past, down the hall, towards her bedroom. She would get her bag, drive home, and see how her emotions were come the new day.

She stopped when he called her name. 'Do you want to know about her?'

Noa paused, but didn't look back. 'No,' she said, and walked on.

———

Noa yanked the coin from around her neck, snapping the string. 'This damn coin. Lucky? With how I feel now, was that worth it?'

The phone was still on her lap. Bokayo's voice said, 'But you eventually found out about Kai.'

'Yes. She was never brought up again, by my wishes. But after his death, I collected all his stuff together to clean it out of the Mayfair house, and that was when I found an old chequebook. A counterfoil showed a payment of £10,000 to a woman called Glenda Harlow in February 1991. I think it was probably his idea of severance pay. With that name and a location of Glasgow, finding out about Kai Harlow was easy.'

'So you found out you had a sister three years ago. Why did you never mention Kai to anyone? Or contact her?'

'Because she was homeless and her mother was dead,' Noa snapped. She was admonishing herself as much as she was answering Bokayo's question. 'I was rich and happy and had no one to depend on me, no one to suck away at all that money. But Kai would have. She would have wanted to become part of my life. I was carefree and didn't want the baggage. If she didn't know about me, then she wasn't losing out. That was my stupid, selfish, evil theory.

'But I had to know about her. I hired a private detective to delve into her life and to watch her. He found her old care-home records, army records, even spoke to her homeless friends. I found out everything about her, as much as I could have by sitting down with her for long chats. But I stayed distant. I knew she was homeless, unhappy, but still I kept away, hidden. I did nothing to help. I just watched from my ivory tower and my silk sheets as she slept in the dirt and ate scraps.'

Bokayo paused before saying, 'So when she went missing, you knew straight away.' He had not phrased it as a question.

'I knew. And that was when the guilt really knocked me sideways. I could – should – have prevented that. But I swore to myself afterwards that I would repay her. If she was ever found, I would give her half of everything. And I would bring her into my life with open arms.'

'The police couldn't find her. They didn't try too hard. So you chose to do it yourself with this radio show.'

'I got my private detective to pay homeless people to hound the police, make them get off their arses. He worked full-time on that search for seven months, but got nothing. If the police or the media knew a PI was looking for a homeless woman, they didn't care to mention it. The confession show was just a silly idea I had after reading about something called the Apology Project. In New York in 1980, a man set up a phone line for people to call and apologise for their sins. The confession show was a whim, a mad experiment, but I had nothing else to go on and nothing to lose. But it worked. I'm going to get Kai back.'

'Noa, this is madness. What are you planning? You don't have a million pounds in cash. Please tell me you're not going to try to trick this bastard. That's dangerous.'

She laughed. 'I never told you this, but my father left me £60,000,000.'

'What?'

Noa got serious again. 'I thought my father had died believing I'd never contact Kai, but he'd made arrangements in case I did. He instructed his bank manager to release £5,000,000 for her if I asked. I only found that out yesterday. She's homeless, and all the while she had five million sitting in a bank. So this one million here is Kai's anyway, and it's a bargain if that's all Poe wants.'

'Wait, one million *here*? Please tell me you're not sitting there with a bloody bag of money?'

Bloody bag conjured up an image very different to the one Bokayo had in mind. 'I am. And I am going to give it to him. And I don't care if he escapes justice after that. I just want her back. This lucky coin gave me a good life, and now it's going to be lucky for Kai because a sister she didn't know about is going to save her life.'

'Don't do this,' Bokayo said, and she heard the worry and stress in his voice. 'You're sitting there with a fortune and you're about to meet a killer who wants it. It's mad and dangerous.'

'You're not paying attention. Kai has a fortune sitting in a bank. I kept it from her by being a selfish bitch. This is all my fault. So I don't have a choice. Think of it as my giving Kai her own money, which she'll use to buy her freedom.'

She cut off his next words. 'Be quiet and listen. You can't stop me, but you can do something if this all goes wrong. There's a crappy hotel called The Swan in Southwark. Room 14, behind the clock on the wall, I've left you a note. Download the app it tells you to, use the password and username, and you can track a device I've put in the bag with the money. You shouldn't need it though. By the time you find that note, I'll be driving home with my sister.'

'Or her corpse.'

CHAPTER FORTY

25 NOVEMBER 2020

H e orders her again: go clean up. She gets to her feet, which is tough because one thigh is hurting and her heel has been deeply gouged by the knife, before she got hold of it. She drops the weapon, knowing she's too injured and weak to successfully use it against him. Then she limps into the bathroom.

'Well done,' he says. 'My money wasn't on you from the start. But you did it. You are the ultimate woman. A true warrior. The perfect specimen. Highly deserved.'

As she stares at her reflection in the bathroom mirror, his appears over her shoulder. He watches as she strips off her blood-soaked dress, and steps into the shower.

He says, 'When you are done, I will show you something magnificent.'

He continues to watch. She lets the water course over her body first, until there's no more red to sluice away. A fresh deluge appears when she puts her head under the spray, as blood is jettisoned from her hair. There is a small mirror in the cubicle and she watches until all the other woman's life fluid is gone. And her hair is once more the colour he made her dye it.

He calls her by that colour, but then slaps his forehead, somewhat cartoon-like. 'That is wrong of me. Five of my girls were disposable. My reason for the colours as names was... I suppose the criminal psychologists would call it *dehumanising*. But now only you remain, and you are my special one. So, you are now Kai, and I apologise with all my heart. Now, please dry yourself, Kai, then we'll get you patched up, ready for your new start. A new dawn in your life. Your rebirth.'

CHAPTER FORTY-ONE

She had arrived back at the lone tree by the side of the country road.

Noa exited the car and crossed the road, carrying her filled petrol can. It was 8.32, but still the road was bare, the fields desolate. She entered the gloomy woods and approached the ditch, and without missing a beat started pouring petrol all over the leaves and the rotten sleeping bag and the bones within. When the can was empty, she tossed it aside, far out of reach of any fire. Poe wanted evidence destroyed, but, if everything went to hell here, police would find her fingerprints on that plastic container. She then pulled out her lighter.

Her phone rang. The timing seemed planned, and her eyes roamed the woods. No one around. She answered the call with, 'Who the hell is she?'

'*Nobody who's missed, like I told you,*' Poe said. '*Her name was Diamond Faye. She was the fourth girl I took, right before Kai. She was a drug dealer and general ne'er-do-well from Bishop's in Lambeth. Her gang liked to roam around Brockwell Park, robbing people. Nasty individual. In March of 2020 she stabbed someone and went on the run to Coventry.*'

'And you found her?'

'*I watched her go. I'd been watching her for weeks. The police couldn't get her, but I did. Nobody missed her when she ran and they don't now she's dead. Now light the fire.*'

'Why were you watching her? Did she offend or hurt you? Did all the girls? Why did you take them?'

'*None of them offended or hurt me. They impressed me. I watched them all for a long time. I watched dozens and dozens. Katrina, Mercy, Alex, Diamond, Isobel, and Kai, those were the ones I selected out of many. They were the best of the best.*'

'Why did you want them? Why did you kill them? Why did you let Kai live?'

'*I only need one. The others were, in the end, disposable. Kai was the special one. And I didn't kill Diamond, Kai did. Now burn the body.*'

He hung up. With no other choice, Noa set a flame to the fuel-soaked ditch. Fire abruptly blossomed, forcing her to step back. The crackle of burning dried leaves was loud, too loud, and she realised it could hide the sound of –

– she was suddenly grabbed from behind, and a wet cloth snapped over her mouth. Her self-defence skills immediately kicked in, but too late. An arm that was raised to grab the head behind hers fell away, all strength gone. Her eyes swam. Her legs gave out.

The man holding her, as he lowered her to the ground, spoke from right by her ear.

'Endangered: threatened with extinction. Amur leopards are on the IUCN's Red List of endangered species, and so are Javan rhinos and South China tigers. Critically low numbers. Global warming and habitat destruction are the main causes, but there's an endangered animal unaffected by hot air and felled trees. And there's three billion of them, so it's a country mile from facing extinction too...'

She felt herself slipping away, her body on power shutdown, but her eyes snapped open again as she was lifted. By arms. He was carrying her. A face was above her, obscured by a hood pulled tight around the features and a surgical mask. He spoke again.

'Endangered: threatened with danger. Amur leopards are not hunted in the mountains of Nepal, Javan rhinos are not slaughtered in the frozen wastes of the Antarctic, and South China tigers are not stalked in the streets of London. But there's an animal that is. It is hunted in every city, barrio and deforested wasteland across the boiling planet. Three billion of them means it's under no threat of extinction, but it is far and away the most endangered animal in the world, because the planet's most powerful hunter wants to kill it for fun.'

She felt herself slipping deeper, going to sleep. Her last thought, before oblivion reigned, was a repeat of his earlier words. Past tense, he'd used:

Kai *was* the special one.

She was already dead.

CHAPTER FORTY-TWO

---

25 NOVEMBER 2020

When he fixes her wounds with plasters and bandages, he talks soothingly, and she starts to believe he might just free her soon after all.

And then, when she's patched up, he snaps a handcuff on her wrist. From doctor back to gaoler. She's ashamed that she fooled herself. For a moment, just a flash in her head, she's envious of Diamond, dead under a bed.

'Why are you laughing?' he asks.

Because I'm an idiot, she wants to say. She opts for a shrug that he doesn't question.

He gives her a sleep mask, not a tacky blindfold this time. It's a tight fit, no chance of spying through a gap. Holding the loose cuff, he leads her from the room. In another moment of confusion, she almost tells him she's forgotten to bring the mask ornament.

They walk the hallway. He tugs when she falls below his speed. They make turns until they reach a door, which he opens.

From the sounds, this door is iron.

He pulls her inside, across a carpeted floor, to a bed against a wall. He makes her sit and attaches the loose cuff to something on the wall. A bracket, she will later see. He moves a safe distance away before instructing her to 'Remove your blindfold.'

She does. The room is bigger than the last and more elegantly furnished. Later she will see a bath, a sofa, a massage chair, framed paintings, and a host of other items absent from the previous room. But for now her attention zeroes in and locks upon a single item, which transforms her breathing into ragged gasps.

A baby's crib.

———

'You're insane,' she yells. 'You want me to have a goddamn baby?'

He slowly, almost matronly, shakes his head. 'No, no, not goddamn. Don't swear. It is to be a special baby. From a special woman. You're strong, resilient, fearless, you will fight rather than falter. This birth will be also be your rebirth.'

'No damn way, you freak. You just stay the hell away from me.'

'Intelligent, smart, savvy. But I knew all those things about you already. It was the rest I was eager to learn.'

'If you come near me, I'll bite your throat out, you bastard.'

He removes what looks like a pencil case from a hidden pocket, and from that withdraws a syringe.

'What's that?' she moans.

'You've had it before. I'm sorry, but I need to put you asleep. I can't allow you to resist.'

'No,' she screams, and begins to fight against her handcuffs. It is no use. He takes her arm. His grip is stronger than she expects. He jabs in the needle, and she watches the plunger sink, the barrel emptying into her.

'Compassionate, caring, selfless. That's why you will make a great mother, and why you'll be able to put your own wants aside and bring up a baby here, in this room. I know you can educate him. Make him wholesome. Love him.'

Done, he lets go of her arm and steps back. She tries to fight the handcuffs again, but the strength is leaving her.

'You picked the mask ornament as a memento. You tried hard with the meal you cooked. And although you failed by selecting a weapon from the kitchen, you gave it up when you had the chance to use it. That's why I know you'll come to respect, obey, perhaps even eventually love me. As his father.'

Haziness is coming in like a fog from the sea, filling her head. 'I'll kill it,' she yells. 'I'll smash my belly until it's dead. I'll starve us both to death.'

'No, Kai, you won't.'

'I will. You think I want to have a maniac's baby? I'll eat glass, rat poison, anything. I'll stab my belly. I'll trap its throat with my muscles when it's being born and strangle it.'

He slaps her. It's the first time he's been physical since he snatched her, so long ago. It shocks the dissent out of her.

'I always feared the days until birth. Until you could see our baby. You might not feel a bond to an unborn child, but what about your sister, Kai? You told me enough about her in your interview that I was able to find her. I knew I might need her. I know where she lives. I can get to her. If you try to harm my child, I will kill her. Both of you. I will kidnap her and bring her here and gut her right in front of you. Or perhaps I'll watch you both fight to the death. In fact, since the game has been so much fun, I might even just bury you and start over with a new batch of players.'

Her whole body is numb now, and the world is turning grey. The last thing she sees, before everything goes black, is hands she can't feel, spreading her legs.

_____

26 November 2020, 1.54pm

'It's too early to know if I'm pregnant.'

Yesterday, she'd woken from his drug in the early evening, some seven or eight hours after he'd administered it. Since then, he'd brought her dinner, supper, and breakfast the next morning. On each occasion, he had dumped the meal and left without a word.

But when he brings her lunch, he sits on the armchair in the corner to watch her eat and in his hands is the pencil case. He plans to knock her out again, and take her while unconscious.

'I'm sorry?' he says.

'It's too early to know if I'm pregnant. I think we need to wait a couple of weeks.'

'We can't waste so much time. Please eat before your meal gets cold.'

Gets cold? She will gladly eat freezing pie if it delays his vile schedule. But she cannot postpone forever, and perhaps getting it over with is the best option. At least he'll go away instead of staring at her, waiting. Until next time.

So she eats, fast. He seems to like this. When her plate is half empty, she abruptly can't stand the idea of any more and might just jettison what's already in her stomach. Seeing she's done, he stands.

She wants that delay after all. That needle scares her. The black oblivion it brings. The headaches afterwards. 'You said _he_. You kept referring to the baby as _he_. It could be a girl.'

'Male. No girl.'

She manages a laugh at what she thinks is stupidity. 'What's the rule again? We do it at a full moon while reciting the days of the month backwards to make sure it's a boy?'

If he gets that's she's being sarcastic, he doesn't show it.

319

Serious as he's ever been, he shakes his head. 'No girl.'

Now she understands. She feels her anger rising. 'At least you've got practice in murdering innocent young girls. That will make it easier.'

He extracts a syringe from the pencil case. She lies back, opens her legs. 'You don't need that.'

When he had brought her first meal since waking from the drug yesterday, he had given up his stupid Japanese outfit. Now he wears baggy tracksuit bottoms and T-shirt. And no mask. Her initial shock at the sight of his face is long gone and she registers only his surprise at her words.

He stumbles over his own. 'You – you don't mind? You now... you're willing – you want a baby with me?'

'Strip and get over here.'

He approaches, but wary, eyes here and there, seeking a weapon. She shows her empty hands, pulls up her dress, smiles at him.

Convinced of her willingness, or at least certain she won't attack, he strips and climbs atop her. She grits her teeth when he buries his face in her shoulder.

'I knew you'd finally accept me,' he says, and slides into her.

She *has* accepted, but not him. Only the futility of escaping this place without serious leverage. She can see only one way out. Threats against an unseen embryo or foetus are useless, and she's disposable. But once she has a real, live, visible baby in her arms, everything transforms.

So, the moment it is born, the instant the maniac's eyes light up with joy, she will hold that baby vice-tight and put something sharp to its eye. And so become invincible. The father of that tiny thing he so craves will take her out of here, or he will watch the severing of his bloodline.

It will be a long nine months of hell, but she can deal with it. She's special, after all.

CHAPTER FORTY-THREE

Noa woke on an armchair. Sitting with her head down, her arms were the first thing her groggy eyes saw: bare flesh on the arms of the chair, both wrists locked by old iron manacles bolted to the wood. Then her legs, also bare except for thick grey pants. No socks, no shoes. On her torso was a blank black T-shirt she didn't recognise. And below the chair, all around her, was carpet.

She wanted to let her brain wake before she looked up, because she was terrified to learn where she might be. She knew she'd been kidnapped by Poe – but where was he holding her? Her location, and whatever was here, would tell the story of what he had planned for her.

When she did look up, she got a surprise. She had feared seeing a dingy cellar, despite the carpet. A heavy iron door. A bucket to use as a toilet. Other things that would suggest he planned to keep her locked up for a long, long time. Kai had been his prisoner for a year and a half.

But the room was unlike anything she could have imagined. It seemed to be a small study, and it was clean and stocked. Flowery wallpaper. A TV in a corner. A bookshelf. Ornaments on small wall shelves. A single, simple internal door. One two-pane casement window, no heavy locks, although the glass had been painted white so nobody could see in or out. The room could have passed for one in a house like her own, or a building like Divine Radio's. It told her nothing.

What floor was she on? Could she leap from the window? The panes were big enough to get through even if the window was locked. Using the door was a no-go because there was no telling what labyrinthic hell lay beyond.

The armchair wasn't the only seat. Another just like it sat before her, just five feet away, facing her. Its placement would seem absurd in a standard family home, but Noa knew exactly why the two seats faced each other. Poe would sit there, to talk to her. He would come, soon.

She tried to calm her breathing. She knew she had no choice but to wait. Escape was a fantasy because the manacles were heavy, sturdy, immoveable. Poe had been in charge since the start, she his slave despite having the run of London, the country, the world. He had manipulated her every move, each play designed to bring her right here. She was caught, his, and soon she would learn his plans for her. If there was a chance to get out of this predicament, it lay with the tracker she'd put in the bag of money. It lay with Bokayo.

Thinking of him put a stupid and bizarre image in her head: Bokayo being brought into the room, also bound, a prisoner just like her. He would have told no one about the note behind a cheap hotel room clock. The tracker would never be found. The world would never know where she was.

Her thoughts were interrupted by a scraping noise from beyond the door. It drew her eyes, and caught her breath. She watched that door open.

———

The man who entered was tall, but other than that she could discern no details because he wore a mask and a costume. He was white, though, and shiny brown hair above the mask hinted that he wasn't far older or younger than her.

She instantly recognised the costume as that worn in Noh, an old Japanese art form. It was sometimes known as 'mask drama' because performers usually wore them. The one Poe had chosen was called Onryō and portrayed the dead. Poe's mask was the 'emaciated man', a vengeful ghost who had returned from hell to seek justice for suffering in mortal life. She wondered if his choice had legit reasoning – he had mentioned a fractured relationship with his father. Or was it simply something designed to unnerve her?

Into the doorway behind him stepped a small Border collie with a black head and a single white ear. It came no closer, wary of her. Poe, however, had no reservations. He approached the armchair that faced her, and stood beside it.

Now that he was here, close, she wasn't as scared as she'd expected. She needed to be strong to get through this. She tried to find his eyes behind the mask, but the light didn't allow it. 'I can help you,' she said. 'You were wronged by your father. You said you were not close to him. Just tell me how I can help you.'

Now he sat. 'Woman,' he said. She recognised the voice as the same one from so many phone calls. He had no reason here to hide an accent, and didn't. She pegged him as Yorkshire-bred – was she still in Sheffield? 'Woman is the answer. The world's most endangered species. The young, pretty human female, like yourself.'

'You are angry at me,' she said, still staring at his fake face, unwilling to show weakness by averting her gaze. 'I was privileged, and you were not. But I can help you. The money. The money will have been posted by now, but it's going to my house. You can still have it, and more. I didn't bring the police. That proves I'm trustworthy. Is Kai alive?'

'You were dealt a dangerous hand way back in the womb. Man is dealt lethal intent. It's the only way to control overpopulation in the animal that sits atop the food chain.'

He had some kind of profound and bullshit speech to get out, perhaps to justify his actions, and she was white noise until it was done. So she said nothing. They stared at each other.

After a few seconds analysing her, he spoke again. 'That would be called doing a deal, and for any cash agreement over £10,000, I'd have to register as a high value dealer or face money laundering charges.'

'Take the money. It was for Kai. Even if you don't let me go, let her go free. It's what you wanted.'

'I never wanted money,' he said, and her heart almost stopped. If he didn't take the money, the bag, then the tracker was useless. When Bokayo and his people found it, they'd be at her home, or an Inpost storage facility, or some other place. But not here.

With that plan dead, she needed another. She was here for a reason. He had taken women for a reason. 'What do you want from me? I will do what you say. Anything.'

He gave a slight nod, as if happy with this answer. Or because he'd expected no other. 'You are right about my father. Like yours, he was successful. As well as a businessman, he was an actor, one of the few white English men to succeed in Noh theatre. He performed all over the world. Perhaps having a Japanese wife, who he married over there, helped. Like your father, he was highly respected in the community. Like yours, he had a child that he had big dreams for. His son would do great things, and he would be loved by all, and he would carry the family name with pride into the future.'

Here Poe touched his mask. He paused with his fingers on

the bottom of it. Then he yanked it off, fast. Noa held her gasp of shock.

His forehead was lumpen, the chin, too. The left ear was nothing but a lumpy crease and the left eye, left corner of the mouth and left side of the nose – indeed that whole side of the head – were stretched towards the ear, as if his head was made of rubber and had been pulled from behind.

'Hemifacial microsomia,' Noa said. 'I'm sorry.'

When Poe spoke, the words were neat, but the mouth moved in the wrong way, giving the impression of bad dubbing in a foreign movie. 'Congenital. Nobody's fault. Certainly not mine.'

'But your parents were unhappy about it?'

'Only daddy dearest. All his big dreams for me, cut down in a flash. I was not the perfect child he sought. I was an embarrassment. If I was going to follow him into theatre, it would only be as the opera ghost.'

She knew he meant *The Phantom of the Opera*. Because of the mask worn by the Phantom. 'He didn't like you to show yourself?'

'I was Baron Meinster, Bertha Mason, I belonged in Matheson's *Born of Man and Woman*. My playground was home. To those outside who knew of me, I was the kid obsessed with Spiderman. A convenient costume that I never went anywhere without. By order. Rain or shine, there I was in that costume, dressed as a superhero, except for the odd doctor's appointment.'

'School?'

'Home-schooled. I hoped the mask might allow me outside, to play with the other children, but no. My father couldn't risk that they'd remove the mask. So, I just watched them from a window. Your father forced you to learn and better yourself so you could achieve greatness. My academic prowess was the result of his stifling me, for what else could I do but learn, alone, when friends were forbidden?'

'So you don't enjoy Noh like your father did? The costume is just a way to hide yourself?'

'Even here, when I was surrounded by women in my control, who I didn't need to impress, going maskless would have been like going naked. This outfit, by the way, is not my father's. He did not play the spirits of the dead. I chose it because as well as camouflage, I needed something to keep the girls in order. A man who dresses like this must be a wacko, right? Wackos you don't mess with.'

'I know the Onryō mask depicts a vengeful spirit. I wondered if you wanted to get revenge because he hated you.'

Poe's head slowly shook. 'He loved me, in his own way. I was taken care of. Never missed a meal. Never got beaten. Was always pushed to do my homework. But I was his embarrassing secret. Like a birthmark shaped like a penis. Such things are locked away from others who might judge us because of them.'

'Is this your home? Where you were brought up? Do you still feel like you have to shy away from the world?'

Poe spoke through gritted teeth; she knew she'd hit a nerve. 'I don't have a problem. Everyone else has the problem. My father died and my mother fled back to Japan. She gave me the house – sound familiar? I was eighteen, suddenly free, able to live the party life as you did. But could I? Did I have the social circle you had? No. The village shunned me. I was still the freak. Was I free? Hell if I was.

'I tried to show kindness in order to be accepted. The single school in our village wasn't up to par, so I built this one. I did so in secret, miles from civilisation, because I wanted to unveil it like a present. I spent the money left to me by my father on helping others. You spent yours on fancy trips and showing off. But when I flung the doors open, no one cared. No children came. They didn't want my school. Because I was the freak all the parents warned their kids about. At least I had saved enough to turn this place into a prison.'

So she was in a school outfitted as a prison? Noa said, 'No, that's not it. You need permission. There are rules. You have to propose something like a school. Paperwork. You have to prove it could work, be financially viable, all sorts of things. It takes time. You can't just open one and–'

'No. They said as much, but that isn't it. I was the freak. Nobody liked me or cared about me. My father was gone, so my family name no longer mattered.'

She had hoped to find in his ramblings something to help her survive his madness. Now, she felt that would not happen. She didn't want to hear any more. 'I'm sorry for all of that. But I don't know why I'm here. Why you kidnapped all those girls. Where is Kai? Is she alive?'

'Kai was the special one. That's why I took her.'

That made twice: two times he'd referred to Kai in the past tense. 'Is she dead? Tell me!'

'She's alive, don't worry. Just no longer special. Do you want to meet her finally? After three years watching her from afar, you must be eager.'

Her mind was still hazy from whatever he'd drugged her with, but her memory was sharp. And it recalled a number of things Poe had said over the days.

Your father loved you, but not every father automatically loves his offspring by default...

Perhaps you could flip a coin. You have a special one around your neck that you make decisions with. That would be perfect to decide a woman's fate, without her knowing a single thing about it...

And if the coin had picked Scotland, his child could have had such a different life, right?...

327

The guilt eats at you. You wish you'd helped years ago, don't you?...

A girl who will forever know she was born lucky because of this...

Realisation dropped like a hammer blow. Noa couldn't find the words at first. 'You know who Kai is to me, don't you?'

He nodded. Noh masks were designed so wearers could emit emotion with slight movements; the lips seemed to smile when his head lifted, and frown when it dropped. 'Sisters. That's why you were chosen.'

'Does... does she know?'

The smiles and frowns again. 'How else would I have known about you? She watched you, as you watched her. A private detective you hired. Apparently he was followed to your home, and that gave you to her. Kai told me about you and the first thing I did was type your name into the internet. I found your confession show. That show, it was no coincidence, was it? You were hoping to find out about Kai. Hoping whoever took her would call to confess.'

Noa was still awed by the fact that Kai had long known all about her, yet had done nothing about it. But she had to get past that, and get out of here. 'The police didn't give a shit about Kai. I do. I'll do anything to get her back. The money proves that. Just tell me what you want.'

'That confession show became my only opportunity after my failed abduction attempt.'

He waited to see her reaction to this, and if he desired absolute shock, then Merry Christmas. Noa would have launched herself at him if able. 'That was you? You tried to attack me two weeks ago?'

'Yes. My parting line to you, do you remember it? *That's what happens to people who think it's okay to let a killer go free?*'

'So I wouldn't connect the dots later down the line when you called my show?'

He nodded. 'I called your show afterwards because following that failed abduction attempt, you had bodyguards. But I wouldn't have tried again anyway. You'd already shown strength and resilience. I knew you were smart. All I needed to know after that was if you could be loyal. And you were. The codes, the secrecy, and slipping away from everyone in the country to meet me alone. Those proved it.'

'But why kidnap me? Why all the girls? Why do you need someone special?'

He stood up. 'It's time the sisters finally met. Kai can explain everything.'

He left the room. The dog followed him. He shut the door, but a minute later it opened again. Noa gasped. She didn't trust it, but there the woman stood.

Kai. Healthy-looking, hair neat, face clean, white dress creaseless. She didn't look injured or worn down. She was not bound.

Not a prisoner.

———

Noa had thought often about the day, if it came, when she'd finally meet Kai. She'd wondered, when standing before her, what would her first words be? General chit-chat of the kind long-lost siblings might utter? An explanation, as given by her father? A claim of ignorance until just before that reunion, and burial of the truth of having watched Kai suffer on the streets, cold and poor?

Noa had had no idea. Seeing Kai stand just feet away, she still didn't.

So she was frozen, unable to utter a word. But Kai waited.

Finally, Noa opted for the apology, since Kai knew everything. Three words: I am sorry.

Kai nodded. She believed it. Or knew it would come. She remained in the doorway.

'Are you okay?' Noa said. 'Is he going to let us go? Is he listening?'

Kai slowly nodded, but said nothing, and Noa figured she was answering the final question. Or was it all three? Kai's eyes now registered as milky, and she was a little unsteady on her feet. That explained the lack of restraints: clearly she was drugged.

'Why did he take you, Kai? And me. And the others?'

That worked. Kai entered the room, sat across from her. She didn't even look at the window, so escape wasn't on her mind. The door remained open – was he just out of sight and that was the reason for Kai's reluctance to at least see if the window could offer a chance at freedom? Was something else causing her to pause?

'Bloodline,' Kai said. Her voice was strong, perhaps a sign there was no sedative in her system. In fact, up close, her eyes no longer looked tired. Had Noa read them wrong?

'Bloodline? Explain that. What does he want? Tell me.'

'A child. A son.'

Noa gripped the wooden armrests, horrified. She hid it. There was more to it than that. Even with his deformed face, Poe could have found a woman to bear him a child. 'Go on.'

'The bloodline is weak,' Kai said. 'He wants a strong woman, a warrior woman. Only the very best of the species can bypass his inferior genes and deliver a superhuman.'

Her last sentence had sounded like something from Poe's mouth. 'He wants a woman who can give him a special baby? That's why he wants a special woman?'

Kai nodded. Noa believed it. It made sense. All of the

women Poe had taken had been expert or experienced in some way. Isobel had been a racing driver, with fast reactions, and had survived a car crash. Katrina had been a doctor and businesswoman. Mercy Ford had been a survivalist, fighting for her life, alone and against the odds. Alex Byrne had been a child prodigy. Diamond Faye had been a gang leader. And Kai had been trained by the army and had survived life on the streets.

It explained why Poe had been watching dozens of women and had picked these six. The cream of the crop were better placed to give him a healthy, strong child to repair his damaged lineage. It was freakish, but she had not a doubt that a rotten mind could develop such a project.

'Why did he kill the others, Kai? Why did he pick you over them? How did he choose? He said you killed a woman called Diamond?'

'Tests. Competition. It was me and Diamond at the end. I won. I was to have his child. But that is a long process. A mother needs comfort and help, not restraints. A mother could harm her child, or threaten to, or do any of a number of things to abort that baby.'

She paused. Noa wanted to scream at her to continue. 'Why am I here? To make you do it?'

'He said, "A sister held captive would persuade a mother to obey". We'll be released afterwards.'

Noa had her doubts, but that wasn't her primary concern. The madman planned to hold her captive, as leverage, for months, until Kai gave him a baby? No way would she accept that. She –

Something hit her. 'Wait. Kai, you were kidnapped eighteen months ago.'

Kai didn't respond.

'Did the tests take eighteen months?'

No response.

'Are you pregnant now?'

Silence.

'Kai, have you already had the baby?'

'There is no child. Yet.'

Eighteen months, and no baby. Kai *was* the special one. Noa, right then, realised she'd made a massive mistake. About why Poe had used past tense.

CHAPTER FORTY-FOUR

4 APRIL 2022

For the first time in all the dozens and dozens, he decides to leave the room to check the results of the pregnancy test. It's a bad sign, she knows. Worse even than last time, when he threw the test device against a wall. Sure enough, when he returns, it's with an angry look. And his gun.

Which he aims at her. She starts to slip off the dress. 'Let's try again. Please.'

The gun stays aimed at her. 'I should have kept all six girls. I feel foolish for not checking in some way. I only made sure everything was in order externally.'

Kai stops undressing and clasps her hands, as if praying. Head bowed, she says, 'One more chance, please. I'll get pregnant.'

The words feel useless. She knows he's long lost belief. And interest in her sexually. Two Christmases ago, he'd lavished her with gifts, including a hoverboard she could use to zoom about the room. But she'd gotten nothing at the end of 2021. The hot pizzas he used to bring had ceased. He'd stopped letting her shower months ago. She can't remember when he last brought her newspapers so she could follow the progress of the outside world. Her video recorder had broken at least half a year ago and he hadn't replaced it. These days he hardly looks at her, as if they're a couple whose marriage is on the rocks.

She has expected this day for a long time, and here it is.

'No more chances,' he says. 'You cannot get pregnant. So much time and effort wasted. I should have checked in some way. A working womb is the minimum criteria I required. When she was eighteen, Yellow – remember her?' She did: Mercy Ford. 'She aborted her stepfather's child, so her body works as designed. And she was my favourite at one point. I should have kept her instead of you. You're not special at all, Green.'

He steps closer, and squints down the barrel of his gun, and she knows he's about to finally carry out a threat she's seen in his eyes over the last few weeks. And he's reverted to calling her by that designated colour.

'Wait! My sister, Noa.'

He looks up from the barrel, but he continues to aim at her heart. 'What about her? Kill her instead? Explain.'

'No, you take her. *She* can have your baby.'

He pauses. The gun arm isn't so firm now. 'Why would I?'

'Genes. Isn't that why you want a special woman, a warrior, the best of the best? You picked me because I'm special. I won your challenges.'

'Those were a bit silly. I should have stuck to real warrior tests.'

'My point is I won, I'm special, but my father picked her over me, and why was that?'

The gun stays put, but he's intrigued. She pushes on. 'Because he saw something in her. He thought she was better than me. And she is. I'm homeless scum, but she's rich and successful, and smarter. She's highly educated. She has my special genes, but better in every way. She's me, but 2.0. Next level. The upgraded version. None of my faults, including infertility. Just imagine the perfect superhuman son she will give you. And if you let me go, I can get her for you.'

He lowers the gun. A little.

Kai sits forward, as far as the handcuff attached to the wall will allow. She senses that she's almost got him. Just a little further pushing... 'And think of this. If she accepts you, she brings you into her life. She's popular, with a wide circle of important friends. None of them will care about your face. Once she has your baby and she's in love with you and you're together, you'll also get to be part of that life. Part of all her money.'

He lowers the gun completely. And puts it away. 'She does not care about you. Not enough to do that. I would have to snatch her. Even then she could fight me in some way.'

Good. But she, Kai, is still disposable. She thinks quickly. 'She does care about me. I told you she's been watching me. That means I'm the perfect leverage against her. If my life is threatened, she will take care of herself, not try to escape, and have your baby. I know it. I know her.'

'You would stay? By choice?'

'Yes! As soon as she's in love with you and has given birth to a very special baby, you can let me go. I will help you until then. I will be part of this with you. I like the idea of being an auntie. I'm sorry I couldn't have a child of my own. Why would I want to leave? My sister and nephew by my side? Sounds great. I can't wait.'

He gives her a wary look. 'In your interview, you said you wished your sister was dead. I read you. You hate her success.'

Kai shakes her head and forces the kind of smile that says,

Don't be silly. 'That was just the drug you gave me, making me frustrated with everything, even her. I don't hate her. How can I? We're sisters! We love each other, deep down.'

'Yet you just betrayed her.'

'She betrayed me,' Kai snaps before she can stop herself.

REBIRTH

'You've betrayed me,' Noa said.

Kai seemed very alert now, sitting upright in her chair. 'You've shown you don't care about your own sister. My mother told me about our father. It was simple to research him when I grew up and find out about you. I knew you knew about me. You sent people to spy on me for you. I was on the streets after I left the army, and you did nothing but stare. And gloat.'

'I'm sorry. I do care. That's why I started the confessions show, Kai. I'm trying to make amends now. Really. I just...'

'If you're going to explain why you left me to rot, don't. I know why. Who would want to bring a homeless sister into their comfortable life? But why do nothing? Even an anonymous money package would have said you cared. Even just a thousand pounds, a drop from your well, would have helped. But there was nothing.'

Noa couldn't look at her. She forgot about this prison wrapped around her, and the freak murderer beyond the door. 'I am ashamed, truly. But I will help now. You can be a millionaire.'

Only when she took it from her throat did Noa realise that Kai had been wearing a necklace. Not just any, but her own coin on string. Kai held it aloft like a trophy. 'Maybe I should decide with this. This damn thing that caused me to have a life right out of hell. Care homes, and then the streets, and now this place, and all because it was tails instead of heads or whatever.'

'We can help each other, Kai,' Noa said, no care for if Poe overheard. 'And we can argue about this later. A madman has us locked up, and he's planning to keep us.'

'Ah, at last you see the truth. You can stop acting as if we're free and spending your money already.'

'So let's help each other get out of here somehow.'

'We are. We're doing it right now. He doesn't need me, but he needs you. So he needs me because of you. He will keep me alive as long as you're carrying his baby.'

There it was. Confirmation of the horror. 'And you think he'll let us go afterwards? Don't be stupid.'

'I guess, deep down, I know that. To risky. But a drowning woman will clutch at straws. I don't want to die today. If I can live another nine months, I'll take it. So, Noa, sweetie, you will do what he wants. You'll do that and maybe he'll let me get my life back. That's what you owe me: a life.'

Noa shook her head. 'No. We have to fight somehow. Listen to me, Kai–'

'This is the start of your new life. Get used to it. You will have his baby, you will be a good mother, and by doing that you will help me get out of here. I mean, of course you will do that. We're sisters.'

And with that, Kai rose and headed for the door, and she ignored Noa's yells to stop, to come back, to help.

Kai stopped in the doorway and faced her. She removed the coin from the string and held it up. 'You said your name was picked with this very coin. He likes James and Karl as names for his son. Choose one.'

She tossed the coin. It hit the floor in front of Noa and bounced and twirled. It was still spinning when Kai slammed the door.

THE END

ACKNOWLEDGEMENTS

Many people deserve thanks for helping to put this book in order. I used What3Words in this story, so I figured I'd give it a shot here, too. A full list of the people requiring thanks can be found at Salsa.Panic.Native.

If anyone with the app fancies two minutes of trivia-hunting, here's some others.

The first nightclub where I threw up, then got thrown out: **Shins.Rang.Opens.**

Scene of my first bicycle crash, which may or may not have contributed to my bizarre imagination: **Useful.Clock.Speech.**

Where I screamed in relief after surviving my first plane ride: **Depended.Nail.Bashful.**

Where I lost a purse containing £1,000: **Joking.I.Am.**

And, finally, the location of my stolen garden gnome: (please fill this in if you know.)

A NOTE FROM THE PUBLISHER

Thank you for reading this book. If you enjoyed it please do consider leaving a review on Amazon to help others find it too.

We hate typos. All of our books have been rigorously edited and proofread, but sometimes mistakes do slip through. If you have spotted a typo, please do let us know and we can get it amended within hours.

info@bloodhoundbooks.com

Printed in Great Britain
by Amazon

21259680R00202